City of Silence

City of Mystery, Book 3

By Kim Wright

To my friend and editor, Kabee Kokenes, and to my friend and publicist, Sandy Culver Plemmons, who each provide so much support

Prologue

June 13, 1889

The Winter Palace

St. Petersburg, Russia

3:02 AM

The room is dark as she enters, but this does not alarm her. Katya Gorbunkova has gone down this marble staircase many times, while wearing feathered masks, great looping headscarves, costumes of every imaginable shape and size. From memory, she knows that the staircase leading from the performers' level onto the stage of the Grand Ballroom has precisely thirty-four steps. She knows that the walls are robin blue, and the ceiling above her is dome shaped, with the pearlized sheen of an eggshell. The Russians love eggs - those symbols of rebirth, fertility, and spring. In the city of St. Petersburg, these humble oval shapes of the barnyard find their way into even the grandest architectural designs. The tsar's private theater is no exception.

The staircase could be notoriously difficult to navigate, even under the best of circumstances, for this theater, just as every other room in the Winter Palace, was designed more for the delight of the imperial family than for the convenience of their household staff. And each night when the curtain fell, even a prima ballerina became no more than a servant. Katya owed her livelihood and her life to the continuing good will of the tsar, a man who, despite a hulking frame which had earned him the nickname "the bear," was in many ways a benevolent patron of the arts. Her life here in the palace might not be perfect, but it was an emphatic improvement over her first eighteen years on earth and she was not inclined to jeopardize that position.

In fact, the only thing which would entice her to take this present risk was the chance to be alone with Yulian.

It was ridiculous, really, that they should have to meet like this. She had her room, and he had his, both in the same wing of this monstrous 900-room palace, each tucked at the ends of halls so long that staring down then sometimes afflicted newcomers with vertigo. But her dance master was an unsympathetic sort, preoccupied with rehearsals for his upcoming ballet, and unlikely to be charmed with the news that the girl he had cast as Juliet had slipped from her room in the middle of the night to meet the boy he had cast as Romeo.

The ballet would be presented in honor of Tchaikovsky himself, soon to return to St. Petersburg after a triumphant tour of the capitals of Europe. Did the tsar truly admire music or dance? It was impossible to say. He had been caught snoring in the middle of more than one performance. But he was undeniably pleased by the thought that a Russian composer had been feted in Paris and Vienna and Rome, and so a grand ball was being planned for the occasion, despite the fact it would fall in the wretchedly unfashionable month of June and would thus require the nobility to delay their sojourn to their summer homes in the countryside. The ball would feature highlights from all of Tchaikovsky's major works, including a brief passage from his "Romeo and Juliet," played by the St. Petersburg symphony and danced, at least in part, by Katya and Yulian.

Of course they had fallen in love. Of course. At this very minute, across the great span of the globe, in cities large and small, Juliets are busily falling in love with Romeos. The dance master should not have been so surprised, should not have been caught so ludicrously unaware. But when he'd learned the truth he had thundered that he was running a ballet school, not a brothel, and had ordered that Katya – still a virgin - should be kept separate from the equally unfallen Yulian. They were escorted from their cell-like rooms to rehearsals in this grand theater and then escorted back. Even to plan this nighttime meeting had required not only daring on both their parts, but the assistance of any number of their fellow students and the minor ranks of teachers. She was eighteen, he a year younger. They had come from far-flung provinces where a roasted chicken and a sack of potatoes was cause for celebration. How could they not lose themselves in the moment? How could they not believe that Shakespeare's story had been written precisely for them?

And such are the circumstances which have brought Katya Gorbunkov now to this marble staircase in the middle of an egg-shaped room in the grandest palace of the world, at just past three in morning. She knows the time because the bell in the tower of the tsar's private chapel has just struck. The chimes reverberate through the night air and everyone within the palace stirs, from emperor to scullery maid.

Katya's foot, delicate and highly arched, leaves the thirty-third step and dangles for a moment above the thirty-fourth. The room, she has realized in the course of her descent, is not as absolutely unlit as she first assumed. Her eyes have now started to adjust, her pupils expanding to take in a nebulous sort of light. The capital of St. Petersburg is high. It sits on the Baltic Sea, more Scandinavian that Russian, and in the summer there is a persistent soft glow, a sense of a sun that never sets, a sky that never fully darkens. Even at this hour, a faint rose-gray floats through the windows, and as the light grows, she sees him. Her lover, her Yulian and her Romeo.

He is lying on the floor. He has taken up the pose of the final scene.

For in their choreographed death, the lovers are to sink into the shape of a heart. Their feet come together in the bottommost point, their bodies arch out to form the curves, their hands strain down towards each other to make the final indention at the top. The perfect symmetry of the shape is not visible to anyone watching from the level of the floor. Only those in the balcony, looking down, can catch the full effect of the pose. Much of dance is like that, Katya thinks, pausing as she at last reaches the bottom of the staircase, waiting there to allow her eyes a few more moments to adapt. Even the waltzes require bizarre and tortured shapes from the women – leaning away from their partners, arching their backs and raising their chins. The very unnaturalness of the position is designed so that they might show their faces to the royalty sitting above them on the balconies. It is not enough to be pretty. One must be pretty when one is looked down upon, when one is under the consideration of her superiors, those gazing upon her from an exalted height. The idea of the lovers dying in the shape of a heart is contrived, overly sentimental, but Katya's dance master claims that the Romanovs like such things. They do not require realism. In fact, they disdain it. They are not in the least troubled by the fact that even the most devoted lovers do not customarily die in the shape of a heart.

And it is here, on the last step of the grand staircase, that Katya sees the man.

Not her lover. Yulian lies before her, curved on the floor. He is but a boy, after all, and his youth is clearest when he is immobile, his chin unshaven and his ribs as insubstantial as those of a pheasant on a plate.

No, she sees the other man. The bad one, the dark one, the man that all girls know somewhere exists.

As the truth of the situation sinks into her, a British girl might scream, or a French one, an American or German, even a princess of the far east. They might struggle, bite, or kick, but Ekaterina Gorbunkoya, known as Katya to her family and friends, possesses a fatalism so profound that it does not occur to her to fight. She looks around her and considers her limited options. This theater, she knows, has been designed to contain sound, not release it. They are in the performance wing of the palace, which is deserted at night. There is likely no one with a hundred rooms of this place. An egg is much like a coffin, she reflects, a container that can transport one between life and death and back again. There is nothing surprising in any of this. A forbidden affair has come to a predictable end. Yulian has only briefly preceded her to the place where we all must someday go.

And without Yulian in it, the world suddenly seems much easier to leave.

The man who is coming towards her, his hands gloved, his face swathed in cloth, has placed Yulian at the exact point on the broad stage where the lovers are supposed to die. He knows the show, Katya realizes. He is part of the company and she twists in his arms to see his face. It is not a desire to outrun death that prompts her to turn against him like this, but more a curiosity. A reflexive and futile effort in these final moments to know her assailant.

He has a knife. Of course. The weapon of peasants, the weapon of kings. It comes fast. And then she is on the floor too, placed carefully, her blood smearing the black and white tile as she is dragged into position. There is a sense of something burning in her chest but, beyond that, surprisingly little pain. Just a great numbness, the impression that one is dissolving, fading mist-like into the beginning of a summer morning. She stretches her hand. Touches Yulian's cool fingertip with her own. The man with the knife is one of us, she thinks. He knows the story. Juliet dies last.

Chapter One

London - The Lawns of Windsor Palace

June 13, 1889

2:29 PM

The Queen was not pleased.

Her Most Royal Highness Victoria of the House of Hanover, monarch of the United Kingdom and Empress of India, might have been regent to the largest, richest, and most powerful empire of the civilized world – but she was also a grandmother. The impulse to protect beat strong in her chest, especially when it came to Alix, who, of the Queen's thirty-four grandchildren, had always been her favorite.

And it seemed that Alix was determined to go to Russia.

The problem was that Alix's request appeared so reasonable on the surface. Her older sister Ella had lived in Russia ever since she married the Grand Duke Serge four years earlier. In her letters Ella claimed that life in St. Petersburg was quite delightful - full of balls, hunts, and a continual enjoyment of the fine arts. She was even making noises about converting to Russian Orthodoxy, a threat that the Queen could only assume to be some sort of bizarre joke. Ella was the sort who would always pretend that everything was fine, no matter what the actual truth of a situation might be. A whistler in the dark, adaptable and confident, a girl who knew how to muddle through even in the midst of the most appalling cultural barriers. But Alix was only sixteen and different in every way from her sister. Besides, even if she were not, Victoria would have opposed Ella's plan to bring Alix to St. Petersburg for the summer.

The real problem, of course, was Nicky.

Ella might say she was merely inviting her little sister to enjoy a grand ball at the Winter Palace, some celebration in honor of a Russian composer, a man with one of those long, ridiculously unpronounceable Russian names. Ella might say that she only wanted to play hostess in her lavish suite of rooms, to enchant Alix with the endless light of St. Petersburg in June. But the Queen was no fool. She saw behind the charmingly-stated request of Ella's effusive letter, which had begun with "Darling Granny" and ended with "Your Most Devoted Ella," each phrase written in Ella's large swooping handwriting, a penmanship so distinctive that the Queen had known the author of the missive before she had broken the seal on the envelope. No, it was quite clear that Ella did not merely want to show off a Russian composer or the vastness of the Winter Palace – this visit was all part of her plan to bring Alix into the intricately webbed world of the Romanov royal family, to align the girl with Nicholas II, the young tsesarevich, a man who would someday rule a kingdom far larger than Victoria's.

Even if that kingdom did exist almost exclusively of frozen tundra, vodka, and illiterate peasants.

An alliance between the Romanovs and the Hanovers was not without precedent. Alix and Nicky had, after all, first met at the very wedding of Ella and Serge, her sister and his uncle. At the time he had been sixteen and she, merely twelve. Why a boy of his age would have noticed a girl of hers was beyond the Queen's capacity to imagine, but notice her he most certainly had, and the two children had since engaged in an unlikely but apparently quite persistent correspondence. Alix had confided to her grandmother that she felt warmly for Nicky; for a girl of Alix's calm and careful temperament this was the equivalent of someone like Ella leading a parade.

The Queen's first impulse had been to recoil at the news. She had already lost one granddaughter to those barbarous lands of the east and did not intend to offer up another. One can only, after all, throw so many pearls before swine, can only watch so many English roses be trampled under Cossack boots. But another part of Victoria, the part who answered to "darling Granny," had been more alarmed than angered by Alix's shy declaration of love.

Victoria was propped in her padded chair on the rolling lawns of Windsor with her large, deep eyes focused on Alix, who sat some distance away, reading a book whose title the Queen could not quite decipher. This was no surprise. Alix was always reading. At first, appropriate books of the Queen's own choosing, but as of lately, who could tell? Alix was fluent in four languages, as were most of the royal grandchildren, but there were times when Victoria regretted that she had been quite so rigorous in her instructions regarding their education, especially the girls. This modern necessity of speaking multiple tongues may have been exaggerated; upon deeper reflection it had occurred to the Queen that any words which could not be said in English were perhaps best not spoken at all. The Queen's own French was spotty, her German half-forgotten, her Russian non-existent. Therefore, she could never be quite sure what any of the children were reading in her presence. She might possibly have bred a nest of vipers within her own family.

Ella and Alix had been among the seven children born to Victoria's daughter Alice, who had been married to the Grand Duke of Hesse, a tranquil but admittedly rural and somewhat backward section of Germany. From the start, Alice's family had seemed marked for tragedy. When Alix, the fifth in line, was merely a year old, her older brother Frittie had tumbled from a window onto the stone patio below. He appeared to come through miraculously well, with only the predictable lumps and scratches, but shortly afterward had died from internal bleeding, a relentless seepage of his life force that the German doctors had been helpless to stem. It was a profoundly unfortunate event which had given rise to even more profoundly unfortunate speculation: That the royal family of England might carry the dreaded disease of hemophilia, a curse most often passed from mother to son, with the women being carriers but rarely victims.

So poor little Frittie had bled to death, slowly and in agony, and Alice had never been the same. Although she had gone on to bear another child, a daughter named May, the loss of her son left Alice anxious and diminished. When a wave of cholera swept through her family five years later, carrying away little May with it, Alice had no fight left in her. She eventually succumbed to the disease as well, leaving her grief-stricken husband and royal mother in charge of her five surviving children.

Victoria took a vigorous interest in the lives of all of her grandchildren, but had always had a special soft spot for Alice's motherless brood. Ella, Alix, their sisters Irene and Vickie and brother Ernest had spent all their summers at Windsor with the Queen and she had grown exceptionally fond of Alix, whose nickname of "Sunny" was deeply ironic. For ever since her mother's death, Alix had been a somber, serious child, lost in her books. Unlikely to be talked into or out of anything.

The Queen was of split mind about what to do next, an unusual state for her and one she found unpleasant. On one hand, a correspondence between two youngsters, even one which had endured over four years of separation, was hardly the basis of a royal engagement. Most likely they were more in love with the idea of each other than anything else. But on the other hand, the Queen knew her granddaughter's temperament – gentle on the surface but with a ribbon of steel underneath. To simply forbid the girl to continue to write the boy would only turn him into an even more highly desired prize. Darling Granny would have to be far more cunning than that. She would have to devise some way that would make it seem as if the severance of the bond was the girl's idea. Or perhaps the boy's. Certainly not the result of squabbling between their two families. The Queen most emphatically did not wish to cast Alix and Nicky into an imperial version of Romeo and Juliet. No matter where or how it was staged, that story never seemed to end well.

A servant offered her tea, but Victoria turned her chin away in refusal. Her ladies in waiting were doing just that, waiting in various pleasant situations about the lush green lawn, some of them reading or holding needlework, others sipping tea, a few more on their feet and wandering about, presumably in search of flowers to press into volumes. Victoria had been queen for the entirety of her adult life, since she was barely older than Alix, and one of the distinct but rarely mentioned advantages of her position was that a queen was never required to look busy. She need not poke needles with bright threads through cloth or pretend to read books that did not interest her or make a great fuss of drinking tea that she does not crave. The utter absence of distraction, the endless opportunity to bob within the pool of her own thoughts, had throughout the years turned Victoria into a bit of a mystic.

For if one was granted the privilege and the patience to simply sit for hour after hour, interesting images begin to arise. The Queen's gaze moved down the bright lawn and settled again on the still form of Alix, perched in the grass beneath a tree and possibly the only one of all the ladies present who was actually reading the book she held in her hands. The Queen felt a discomfort inside, a slight lurching of the heart, at the sight of the child's sweet face. The continuing stability of her monarchy – indeed all of Europe – demanded that Victoria give up her daughters and granddaughters into marriage with foreign husbands, but these were decisions she always made reluctantly. Sacrificial lambs, the girls were, brokered into unions that were rarely of their own choosing, packed off and shipped about the continent as if they were bolts of cloth. Although they wore diamonds around their necks and slept in high soft beds, it seemed to Victoria that the women of royal families were little more in control of their destinies than the serfs of Russia.

The depth of the Queen's skepticism toward marriage would have shocked the vast majority of her subjects, for her own union with Prince Albert had been a resoundingly successful one. But Victoria knew that she had been lucky, perhaps singularly so; love matches between royals were rare and happy families even rarer. Marriage was a lottery, a gamble that rarely paid off for either gender, but while a bad match could damage a man, it would destroy a woman altogether. The Queen had never attended a wedding without a pit of dread in her stomach, the sense that the spinning wheel of fate could come to rest on disaster just as easily as providence.

Alix had now leaned back against the trunk of the tree which shaded her, had turned a page of her book, and was frowning intently at its successor. How abstracted she is, the Queen thought. She not only reads, she reads too much. She has the character of a nun, if indeed Lutherans had nuns, and it would be especially intolerable to see this delicate girl cast willy-nilly into the dark pit of marriage, most specifically marriage to a Russian, potentially the deepest pit of all. Ella's letters were contrived to be amusing, but the Queen had seen the truth behind her droll descriptions of life at court. The imperial family did not fully accept her. Serge was proving cool and distant, not as careful to steer his wife socially through these strange new surroundings as he should have been. The Russians were self-impressed. The very word "tsar" was derived from "Caesar" and they considered themselves descendents of gods, placing their crowns on their own heads at their coronations, since they claimed to accept no human authority over their reigns, not even that of a priest or a bishop.

Arrogant they were, arrogant and barbarous, a bad combination in a race of people. If they had cherished Ella, that would have been one thing, but she had written that the tsar had greeted her as "a minor princess from a minor German principality," a phrase that made Victoria's skin prickle. If Alexander III did not deem Ella a fit consort for his brother, it was highly doubtful he would consider Alix good enough for his son. Victoria's head reeled at the thought that there was somewhere on earth a man presumptuous enough to mock the lineage of the British throne, a man who honestly believed his boys were too fine to marry her girls, a country where even the highest English princess would be expected to curtsy to the lowest Russian empress.

Of course Ella wanted her sister at her side, an ally and a friend. And it was easy enough to understand Alix's attachment to Nicky. Any sixteen year old boy could manage to dazzle any twelve year old girl, and besides, even the Queen had to admit that Nicky was a remarkably handsome young man. Everyone agreed that he was furthermore kind and gentle, with the Princess of Wales, his maternal aunt, going so far as to confide to the Queen that the young tsesarevich was "sweet."

Sweet. A strange term for a man who would shortly rule one-sixth of the globe.

So the boy was handsome and sweet and wealthy beyond imaging and he and Alix had now indulged their special friendship for nearly a quarter of their lives. This would not be an easy courtship to disrupt. But the Queen knew she had a powerful ally, for the tsar did not want this match any more than she did. And while the nickname "Sunny" no longer suited Alix, the tsar's nickname of "the bear" most certainly captured the essence of Alexander III. The man was a clumsy beast, but Victoria was certain that if the Queen of England and the Tsar of Russia aligned forces they could manage to thwart a half-imagined romance between two over-sheltered children. Someone had to save Alix and Nicky from themselves.

Alix had now closed her book and pushed to her feet. She was slowly walking up the lawn in the direction where her grandmother waited and Victoria beckoned to the girl to approach.

"We shall go to St. Petersburg," she told her.

A wave of pure joy washed across the Alix's face, lighting her large grey-blue eyes and instantly transforming her from pretty to beautiful. So complete was the girl's delight that for a moment she failed to notice the killing pronoun. Then she blinked and said "We?"

"Yes," said the Queen. "I too crave the chance to visit our Ella."

Alix continued to slowly blink, two emotions in clear conflict on her face as she fought to reconcile the welcome news that she would finally see Nicky again with the far less welcome news that she would be accompanied on this romantic journey by the greatest bloodhound in all of Europe.

"Write Ella and tell her we shall arrive by ship," the Queen said, before adding, with an indulgent smile, "and perhaps you should write anyone else you think might wish to know this news as well."

"Granny," Alix whispered. "Dearest Granny." She bent to kiss the Queen's cheek, which was slack with the years and crusted with a heavy dusting of violet powder. "I'll sign it 'Alexandra,'" she added, pulling back with a mischievous tilt of the head. "He always calls me by my Russian name, you know." And then she sprinted up the lawn toward the palace like a gleeful young fawn.

Victoria waited a minute to make sure the girl was out of earshot before signaling to one of her guards, a man standing unobtrusively to the side.

"Send an order to Scotland Yard," she said. "We wish an audience with a detective there. Trevor Welles." The man nodded and disappeared up the same hill, as swiftly although perhaps not as enthusiastically as Alix.

Victoria did not particularly care for travel, but it seemed there was little else to be done. If Alix must go to Russia, then the Queen must go with her - but Victoria had no intention of sailing through the Baltic unprotected. Nor to take up residence in that ghastly city of St. Petersburg where it seemed that the Russians served up murders at approximately the same intervals that the British served tea. Trevor was a discreet and practical man. He would come with them. He knew his duty.

The Queen sat back in her chair with a sigh and closed her eyes. Alexandra indeed.

They would certainly see about that.

Chapter Two

London – Geraldine Bainbridge's Home in Mayfair

11:22 PM

"I'm not entirely sure what the term 'criminal profiling' even means," Emma said, spooning the last bite of pear tart into her mouth.

"No one is entirely sure," Trevor said with a rueful laugh. "But I've been assured that the technique will play a pivotal role in the future of forensics." He had finished his own pear tart a full half hour earlier and now found Emma's slow savoring of the dessert to be a type of torment - partly because Trevor Welles liked confections, but largely because Trevor liked the girl. The combination of Emma's mouth, the spoon, and the rounded golden arc of the pears had proven so visually distracting that Trevor was having trouble concentrating on this latest meeting of the Thursday Night Murder Games Club. Which was a definite problem, considering that he was the one in charge.

Despite the name, the group did not always manage to meet on a Thursday, and the choice of the word "games" was intended ironically, at least in light of the appalling particulars surrounding much of their work. But the club did always congregate around this particular table, a long walnut affair in the fashionable home of Trevor's friend and patron, Geraldine Bainbridge.

Geraldine's endless supply of good food and wine was only one of the advantages of taking their games outside the confines of Scotland Yard. While three members of the club were police officers and official members of the Yard's fledgling forensics team, the other three were not. There was Trevor himself, then Rayley Abrams, also a detective and recently returned from a sabbatical spent studying with the Parisian police. The trip had been both an unofficial admission that the French were ahead of the British in terms of forensics and was also intended as a bit of a consolation price; the previous November, it had been Trevor, not Rayley, who had been named Chief Detective in the case of Jack the Ripper. Trevor's rise and Rayley's fall had been painfully arbitrary. The Ripper had at one point ranted against the Jews and Rayley was Jewish, a coincidence which had made their superiors uneasy. Ergo, Trevor had been awarded the plum post and Rayley had been packed off to Paris, where he had managed to get himself involved in a case which ultimately proved as complex as that of the Ripper.

At least in Paris they had gotten their man. Armand Delacroix had been convicted and executed with a sort of emotionless efficiency one rarely associated with the French. But Rayley had nearly lost both his life and his sanity in the course of the investigation, and he still bore evidence of the strain. His hands revealed the slightest of tremors as he adjusted his spectacles and looked down at the papers in his lap. Initially

Trevor had wondered if having two full detectives on the forensics team would lead to conflict or an unclear chain of command, but now Trevor was beginning to think his worries had flowed in the wrong direction. Rayley had been uncharacteristically deferential and unsure of himself since his return, proving that the events in Paris had shaken him to the very core.

    The third official member of the team was bobby Davy Mabrey, who had also first come to Trevor's attention during the Ripper case. It had been Davy's great misfortune - or fortune, depending upon how one looked at it –to discover both bodies on the night of the infamous double murders. But there wasn't much of an art to merely finding bodies, especially when they happened to be lying in the middle of the street. What had truly impressed Trevor had been Davy's ability, even when surrounded by a hysterical East End mob, to keep the crime scene pristine. Only a handful of Scotland Yard detectives and inspectors truly grasped the significance of forensics, so discovering a bobby with a natural instinct to preserve physical evidence had been a great gift. Trevor had immediately made Davy his assistant and the lad had been at his side ever since. Davy had further solidified Trevor's estimation with his ability to draw remarkable levels of detail from witnesses and victims alike. That class of Londoners who might have been intimidated by the likes of Trevor and Rayley had no problem telling their tales to a working class bobby, who stood no higher than a schoolboy and whose wide eyes and rosy cheeks made him appear far younger than his twenty-one years.

"Shall we open another bottle of wine?" Tom asked.

"Of course," said Trevor, wryly noting that the corkscrew had already been in Tom's hand when he paused to ask.

If Scotland Yard provided half of the members of the Thursday Night Club, then this elegant home in Mayfair provided the other half. The unofficial members of the team included Geraldine's grand-nephew Tom, who was within a year of finishing his medical training. This fact always made Trevor wince a bit, since Tom had likewise been within a year of finishing on the day they'd met, and Trevor knew he was largely to blame for this extended hiatus. Trevor's ultimate hope was that Tom would join them on a permanent basis as the forensic unit's designated coroner, but even acting in his present volunteer capacity took so much of Tom's time that it was uncertain when, if ever, he would return to the ivied walls of Cambridge. The truth of the matter was that they needed him. Tom was energetic and practical and free thinking, while the brotherhood of coroners at the Yard suffered from many of the same limitations as the officers. They seemed to find only what they expected to find. In public Trevor was constantly encouraging them to consider things from a different angle. In private he considered them antiquated, arrogant, and slow.

And that was on a good day.

The final two chairs at the table were occupied by women: their hostess, socialite Geraldine Bainbridge and Emma

Kelly, who was Geraldine's paid companion and sister to the Ripper's last known victim. Emma's original position on the team was as a translator, since her father had been a schoolteacher and Emma was fluent in three languages. But as fate would have it, she had also proven fluent in the language of crime scenes. The girl was about the same age as Tom and Davy and hardly looked like anyone's notion of a detective. Petite and pale, with red hair and blue eyes which confirmed the Irish roots her surname implied, Emma had illustrated her worth beyond question during their week in Paris. Her standing in the group was rising, although probably not quickly enough to suit her.

Finally, Geraldine. Trevor supposed it was stretching the truth to consider the elderly heiress part of the team at all, but Geraldine had managed to somehow insinuate herself into the heart of the action. Part of it was that they met at Geraldine's house, so her presence at this table each Thursday was a given. They could scarcely shoo her from her own parlor when the games began.

And then there was also the fact that Geraldine had, in her own words, "great piles of money" and she never hesitated to offer financial support to organizations which interested her, no matter how far-fetched or unsuitably liberal her social set might deem these causes to be. Luckily for Trevor, her present interest appeared to be the elevation of the forensics unit in the eyes of Scotland Yard. It was likewise beyond dispute that Geraldine's vast social network and instinctive ear for gossip had proven valuable in the past and likely would again. Gerry seemed to know everyone in London and half the souls on the continent as well, and detection, Trevor was beginning to understand, was often as dependent upon whom one knew as it was on what one knew. Besides, beneath Gerry's garishly colored gowns and feather-plumed hats, existed the cunning of a jackal and the heart of a lion. Although she had left her seventieth birthday behind her some years back and her waistline announced her fondness for pastries and creams, Gerry was in many ways the most formidable of them all.

They were a bizarre group in every measurable way, as Trevor was quick to concede. Around this table sat male and female, young and old, Jew and Catholic, aristocrat and working class, professional detective and amateur sleuth. But he would not have traded their collective talents for those of any unit at the Yard.

The Thursday Night Murder Games had started out as a lark. They would all meet at Geraldine's house where her butler and cook, a hulking but tenderhearted man named Gage, would prepare an invariably delightful meal which they washed down with vast quantities of wines from Geraldine's cellar. After dinner, Trevor would present them with a puzzle. Generally there would be a simulated crime scene with actual physical clues which Trevor had painstakingly reproduced from the files of real cases. Blood splatter, footprints, weapon identification, the lingering traces of poison, fingerprints…. through the last six months their merry little band had tested and discussed them all.

Tonight, however, the challenge at hand was of a different kind. After Gage had carted away the remains of their capons, cheese soufflés, and carrot soup and the carafe of claret was nearly empty, they had all settled back in their chairs and waited for Trevor to begin. But when he had announced their subject du jour to be criminal profiling, quizzical frowns had gone up all around.

"The idea is just this," Trevor explained. "It is quite possible that evidence left behind at a crime scene can tell us not merely physical things about the perpetrator, but things about his character as well. There are two forms of profiling - psychological and geographic. The first will shed light on the personality of the particular criminal we seek and the second will give us clues as to the circumstances of his life. How well he is educated, for example, whether he lives alone or is married, little habituated behaviors such as what he eats for breakfast or the route he takes to work."

The frowns remained.

"As a tool, profiling helps in several ways," Rayley added, so smoothly that Trevor wondered if he had sneaked a peek at Trevor's notes in anticipation of the meeting. "In an individual case, yes, just as Trevor says, it might give us additional information about the specific criminal we are seeking. But the psychologists who are pursuing this particular avenue of forensics also speculate that if they interview multiple men who have all committed the same type of crimes they will find similarities in their personalities or the early events of their lives. Thus the use of the word 'profile.' If we know what sort of man is most likely to commit what sort of crime, this information can help us focus our search at the beginning of an investigation."

"But who needs such – and I use the word loosely - science when you have common sense?" Tom asked drily, leaning back in his seat and crossing his legs. With his well-tailored jacket and artfully-mussed blond hair he looked the perfect prototype of what he was – the indulged youngest son from a family of means. "Let's see," he added, "what sort of man is most likely to steal something? Might it be a poor man?"

"Rich men steal too," Emma said, even more drily. "Perhaps they don't pocket an apple from the greengrocer on the corner but they might embezzle from their employer or finagle an inheritance at the expense of a sibling. We all have known people who have remained honest even in the face of the most appalling need and others who have felt entitled to more even while they sat in the lap of luxury. The difference isn't measureable in a person's level of wealth. It has to be psychological."

"Well stated, Emma. And some of you will remember that we employed a version of this technique with the Ripper," Trevor said, "although our approach was less detailed and specific than what the latest papers on profiling have suggested. We concluded he was educated, that he had medical training, and that he was able to function well enough in society that no one would deem him a threat."

There was the same small painful beat that there always seemed to be whenever the Ripper was mentioned, but Emma remained motionless and after a split second, Trevor continued. "If we had interviewed a dozen men who had also assaulted women, especially men who targeted prostitutes, we might have been able to draw our portrait with more detail."

"I must say I find that the most fascinating part of the whole business," said Rayley. "Not the crime scene work, but the notion that certain character types are more likely to commit certain crimes."

"I hate to eternally play the devil's advocate…" Tom said.

"Oh go ahead," said Emma. "You're so good at it."

Tom ignored her and continued. "Has it occurred to any of these criminal psychologists that men who've been jailed for heinous crimes hardly make most reliable of interview subjects? They lie. Change their stories. The Ripper bragged about his exploits and I would imagine many criminals do. You know, build themselves up to seem more ferocious and dangerous than they actually are."

"They could prevaricate their way through one round of questioning perhaps," Rayley conceded. "But repeated interviews, which were conducted by skilled psychologists? And if they were under hypnosis…"

"Ah," Tom said. "So Dr. Freud has found his way to Scotland Yard at last."

"Perhaps the applications of the tool will become clearer if we move on to an example," Trevor said mildly. As usual, the group seemed to be split, with Emma and Rayley embracing the theoretical while Tom remained skeptical of any methodology that expanded beyond hard science. Judging by the look on his face, Davy was more inclined to agree with Tom and it was impossible to tell with Geraldine, who had merely attacked her second piece of tart. Trevor was not sure where he himself stood on the matter. As methods went, criminal profiling appeared to be the proverbial double edged sword, as capable as sending detectives down the wrong path as the right one.

"Yes please, give us the particulars," said Emma and there was a synchronized turning of chairs.

"The case originates from Scotland," Trevor said. "Three separate rapes, committed over a four month span of time all taking place near a railway depot in a small rural town. The assaults occurred in the afternoon, each within a hour of the time when the train is scheduled to pass through – twice just after and the last just before."

"What sort of train?" Rayley asked. "A commuter train which makes many stops or a direct route train, which does not?"

"Please explain for us all why you are asking that question," Trevor gently reminded him. The goal of the

Thursday Night games was for the thought processes of each member to become utterly transparent to the others, and then use the subsequent analysis to illustrate to the volunteers how the mind of a trained detective might work.

"When you said that the rapes were occurring near a depot," Rayley said, "my first thought was that the attacker was either arriving or departing by train, or both. That he wasn't a recognizable local citizen, in other words, but rather using the railway to assault women who would be unable to identify him to the district police."

"Perhaps someone who rides the trains on a regular basis," Davy added. "It is a pity that trains do not keep registers of their passengers as ships do."

"Indeed," said Trevor. The ability to correlate suspects with the dates of their channel crossings had been an enormous benefit in the Parisian case they had just concluded. But trains kept no such records.

"We could begin with eyewitness accounts," said Davy. "Conductors or regular commuters might recall who traveled that route on a consistent basis, perhaps even on the dates in question. Did we ascertain if the train was a local or an express?"

"Ascertain" was rapidly becoming one of Davy's favorite words, Trevor noted with amused approval, and he had finally learned to put the emphasis on the last syllable.

"No, we did not," Trevor said. "But our conversation has run off the rails rather early this time, if you'll all pardon the pun, and the full ramifications of Rayley's question have thus remained unexplored." He squinted down at his papers. "This train was a local, the route running between Aberdeen to Edinburgh with seven stops, three of them very close to the small town where the attacks occurred."

"So the man could have boarded the train at any point along the route," Rayley said. "And gotten off at any of the stops as well."

"I find it most interesting that he must have for some reason changed his methodology," Emma said. "You said the first two times the rapes occurred shortly after the train had passed through the depot. This seems to me quite the logical sequence. A man disembarks from a train in a small town and commits a crime. But then the last time the rape occurs just before the train is scheduled to leave, which implies that he was already in the town. In this final instance he was more concerned with using the train as a means of departure rather than arrival and timed his attack accordingly."

"How often do trains pass through?" Tom asked.

"And would you explain to us exactly why you raise that question?" Trevor asked in turn. He disliked his role as the stern schoolmaster of the group but if the games were to maximize their usefulness, he could not indulge great vaulting leaps of speculation in any of his team members, no matter how apt they might be. They must march together, step by step, through the entire bloody process if they were to emerge as a fully functioning unit.

"Because Emma's statement is quite right," said Tom. "The change in modality seems a major clue to something or another, although right now I can't think what. The first two times, yes, he steps from the train, finds his victim, and does the deed. But then what? He must wait around the town avoiding detection, until the next train arrives? It hardly seems a sensible plan, especially in light of the fact he is a rapist, not a murderer. His victim is presumably left quite capable of running about shrieking out her story, alerting both the police and any nearby brothers or husbands with a pitchfork. How long would he have to wait?"

Trevor smiled slightly. The debates of Thursday night were rapidly becoming his favorite day of the week. "Quite good, Tom and Emma, for this is precisely the first part of the puzzle the Scotland police latched upon. The trains run an hour apart in the mornings and early evenings when workers are commuting to and fro from Aberdeen, but makes only two stop at this particular small depot in the afternoon. One of them is scheduled at 1:25, the other at 2:40. From there, the next train does not pass until 5:15."

"And that is most likely the reason he changed his methodology," said Emma.

"Were the women who were attacked from the train too, Sir?" Davy asked. "Or did they live in the town where the crimes occurred?"

"A reasonable question, Davy," Trevor said. "But a bit premature. I shall give you particulars about the victims in a minute, but for now let's stick to the question of how our criminal was using the trains."

"Here's my notion," said Emma. "The first two times he gets off the train in the afternoon, finding a deserted depot and a town full of women, most of the men either having long since commuted to work in the factories or else they're laboring out in the fields. He finds his victim, rapes her, and is left, just as Tom suggests, with a sizable wait before the next train. I am happy to say that I don't know how long it takes for an assault of this nature to be instigated and concluded, but I can't imagine it would fill a block of time between 1:25 and 2:40." She glanced around the circle, but the four men provided no further illumination, so she shrugged and continued. "Once the act is finished, our man must hide and somehow find a way to safely avoid detection until he can catch the next train. But this is risky in the extreme. They say that most women who are so attacked do not confess it, but if either of the first two women he raped had happened to tell, then Tom is quite right. He would have the whole village around his ears within minutes. People swarming about in pursuit of him and most obviously looking around the depot, the train being the only swift and anonymous way a stranger would have of getting out of town."

"Bravo," Rayley said, taking off his glasses and blowing forcefully on the lenses. He had been in Paris when Emma had joined the group and initially he had been skeptical about the contributions a schoolmaster's daughter could bring to the world of crime. But Emma had continued to impress him, one Thursday night after the next.

"Just so," said Tom. "He has some sort of close call after the second rape perhaps, so he changes his methodology. This time he gets off of the train at some earlier time and hides before the rape, rather than after. He bides his time until he knows a train is due, then commits the rape and swiftly boards the train. He's on his way well before his victim has time to alert her townspeople, if indeed she is inclined to do so."

"But his mere presence would be alarming," Rayley said. "He's already raped two women, who certainly know his face. Might he not encounter one of them, as he's strolling about the limited streets of this tiny burg? A strange man in a city of women in the middle of the afternoon would be bound to draw attention."

"Good point," Tom conceded.

"So why would he keep returning to the same place?" Davy asked. "Detective Welles said the train made seven stops. After the first rape or at least the second, it seems the man would try a different town."

"You aren't telling us everything," Emma said, looking at Trevor with narrowed eyes. "You're cutting the information into very small pieces, as if we're babies who might choke on too large a bite."

"No," said Rayley, as bemused as she was irritated. "He is actually doling out the facts in small increments because that is how you learn things on a genuine police case. You aren't handed a file of twenty pages of information, all neatly sequenced and categorized. You start with these very small bites of information and you progress."

"Please, kind sir, do give us a little more," said Tom, reaching over to pour a splash of wine into his glass and then, without asking, into Trevor's. "Your smile has become unbearably smug."

"Fair enough," Trevor said. "But first let's follow this bit about the train schedule to its logical end, for there's one point that hasn't yet been raised. When our man takes the train into town during the day, whether it is midday or early afternoon, he would be disembarking at a time and place where most passengers are embarking. That in itself might draw the eye, might it not?"

"Is this town a rest stop?" Davy asked. "One of the places along the route where the train pauses longer to give the passengers time to find food or use the facilities?"

"Precisely," said Trevor. "That's what I was hoping someone would ask. The town in question is Montrose, almost the midway point of the route between Aberdeen and Edinburgh. So I'm inclined to think that our man gets off with the throng of passengers and then simply does not get back on. Bides his time and finds his victim, just as Tom says, waiting until close to the time the next train comes through to strike."

"All right, so far you've avoided saying anything at all about the women," Rayley said, stroking his wispy mustache as he gave Trevor a sidelong glance. "Were they passengers on the train or women from the town?"

"Townswomen, all three."

"Assaulted near the depot?"

"Relatively close."

"And what were local women who had no intention of riding a train doing so close to a depot?"

"Selling things."

"Such as?"

"Hot cross buns in one case," Trevor said. "Fruit from a cart in another. And the first one attacked was offering amenities of an entirely different nature."

"So apparently the fact that a commuter train makes a rest stop there provides a large part of the livelihood of the town," Tom mused. "A few businesses spring up around the depot or perhaps the merchants bring their wares down when the train is due. A wheelbarrow of fruit, a tray of pastries, even an enterprising prostitute looking for some midday trade. A flurry of people disembark, transact this minimal business, and then they reboard a few minutes later. So our criminal does not merely use the train to come and go but also as a means of drawing his victims – women who come down to the depot and who, when the train leaves, are abruptly alone."

"The first woman he raped was a prostitute?" Davy confirmed.

Trevor nodded. "Are you wondering why a man would bother to rape a prostitute when a few coins might get him what he wanted?"

Davy quickly shook his head, actually rather offended, although he took pains not to show it. "You've told us often enough, Sir, that we should view rape as a crime of violence and not just of sex. But I was thinking that perhaps he chose his first victim just because she'd be unlikely to tell the story. If a woman is known about town for conducting that sort of business, how serious would the local police treat her claim that she'd been raped? So she'd likely keep mum about what happened, wouldn't she?"

"She would indeed," Trevor said. "The first victim did not come forward with her story at all until the second and third woman had made claims. Very apt of you, Davy."

"So he aims at an easy target with his first shot," Tom said, not noticing that his analogy made both Trevor and Davy wince. "But then he gains a bit of confidence and expands his pool of potentials to include two tradeswomen, victims who we can only assume the town viewed more sympathetically. I would imagine rape to be a rather noisy sort of crime. Apt to draw attention if the woman puts up a struggle. Where did the assaults actually take place?"

"The first in an edge of the woods, the second in a public woman's washroom, the one used by the train passengers," Trevor said. "For the third, the baker, he presumably followed the woman back to her place of business for she was attacked in her own kitchen."

"Did he use a weapon to subdue the women?" Rayley asked.

Trevor hesitated. "He had a scarf."

"A scarf?"

"Indeed."

Rayley frowned. "To choke or to gag them?"

"Neither. He used it as a blindfold."

This last statement brought silence to the table. Trevor noted that Geraldine had not yet spoken at all. Although loquacious by nature, she often held back at the beginning of the Thursday Night Murder Games only to spring forth at the end with a barrage of comments which were either profoundly insightful or astoundingly bizarre. To date, the ratio was about 20/80. But tonight she merely continued to sit thoughtfully, her evening cup of chamomile resting on the broad ledge of her bosom, her eyes fixed on the table before her.

"Shall we summarize?" Trevor asked. Past experience had taught him that when the conversation lagged, a revisiting of the particular points was a good way to get it going again. "We have a man who most likely arrives in a town by way of a midday train. He disembarks and finds a bevy of women working in the area around the depot. After the train is gone and the crowd has scattered, he follows his selected victim and to a private place and assaults her, then catches a later train to leave the town. What would a forensic psychologist conclude about such a man? If we were to apply the basics of criminal profiling, what would they suggest?"

"He's organized," Rayley said promptly. "At least enough to use the train schedule to his advantage and to select his victims along certain criteria."

"And in the same vein, he possesses at least some self-control," Emma said. "He isn't raping in a manic frenzy. He plans his crimes."

"Looks normal or at least fits in well enough to avoid attracting attention on a train," Davy added.

"Seems to select strangers," Emma said. "This isn't a crime of any personal vengeance or due to an obsession with a particular woman." She looked up at Trevor, her eyes seeming darker in the candlelight, deepening from blue to navy. "Did the women have any similarities in terms of age or coloring or some physical characteristic? Were they acquainted or intertwined in any way?"

He shook his head. "Quite the contrary. The only thing they seemed to have in common was proximity to the depot. The two tradeswomen knew each other, but only slightly."

"So it would appear at first reckoning that our fellow is an entirely logical sort of criminal," Rayley said. "But then we come to the business with the blindfold. It keeps the women from being able to identify him of course, and thus makes a type of sense, but it also strikes me as a rather grand sort of gesture. Theatrical, almost. Could any of the victims describe anything about the man?"

Trevor shook his head, then reconsidered. "Well, that isn't entirely true. One of them did say the blindfold he used felt like silk. Noteworthy it would seem in a rural town where most men wear scarves made of wool if they wear them at all."

"If that's all the description three victims managed to collectively produce, then it would seem that blinding the women, even momentarily, served his purpose," Tom said. "And, I'm sorry Rayley, but I don't read anything symbolic or grand into the gesture at all. If you don't intend to kill your victim, and there's no evidence suggesting that this particular rapist is warming up to murder, then your most pressing task is to make sure she doesn't see your face."

"But I quite know where Rayley is going," Geraldine said, suddenly jerking to attention in the manner of a mechanical soothsayer at a traveling fair. "There are certain acts of dominance, are there not, which are designed to break the spirit? The binding of the hands is one, and taking away someone's sight or hearing is another. I've seen it with the suffragettes."

"The suffragettes?" Trevor asked cautiously. It was a bizarre non sequitur even for Geraldine.

She nodded and leaned forward to place her teacup on the table. "Do you all recall that dark day when I was arrested at the protest about allowing women to row on the Thames? You surely remember, Trevor, for that's the very afternoon the two of us first met. And Emma, you and Gage had to come down and give them money so they would let us all out."

"They posted your bail," Trevor corrected her. "You always make it sound like a bribe or some other sort of impropriety when you say it that way, Geraldine. You simply must try to remember the proper wording."

"Indeed," said Geraldine. "Posted bail. Anyway, Emma and Trevor remember, but for the rest of you, there is this most ridiculous law that states women cannot take a boat out on the Thames and my committee for the expansion of women's rights went down to the waterfront to protest, only they sent out the coppers to arrest us and thus dear Trevor and I became intimates."

"I've always wondered at how the two of you initiated your friendship," Rayley said. "Welles usually isn't the type to mix in high society."

Behind Geraldine's shoulder, Trevor made a rude gesture at him, to the great amusement of Davy.

"As always, I admire your pluck, Auntie," Tom said. "Women should most certainly have the opportunity to capsize into the Thames right along with the men. But what on earth do suffragettes have to do with blindfolds?"

"We had chained ourselves to a tree," Geraldine said, "and when the coppers put us in the wagon they left us bound up. One of them in particular was a most rude young man and he said something along the lines of if we wanted the chains, then by God we should have them. And then he said he didn't want the ladies to be cold so he pulled down our hats and raised our mufflers so that we couldn't see and could barely hear."

"Gerry," Trevor said in genuine surprise. "You've never told me this part."

"What was the name of that man?" Rayley said. "Do you recall, Miss Bainbridge?"

Gerry impatiently shook her head. "It was nearly two years ago, darlings, and that's not the point of my story. When we got down to the station and Trevor came in to take our statements, he was so respectful and such a gentleman, that it was like the rain suddenly stopped and the sun broke through the clouds. And then of course Emma arrived and gave him the money to let us all out. But I raise this memory for one reason alone. During the time we were chained and rendered unable to fully see or hear…it was no more than a few minutes, a wagon ride across town, but the man's cruel mission was accomplished. We were all of us lessened by his actions. Cowed. Humiliated. I went into his wagon one sort of women and came out quite another."

Emma was given pause. If a personality as powerful as Geraldine's could undergo a psychological shift in a matter of minutes, it did indeed seem likely that a blindfold might have a dual purpose — not merely to obscure a woman's vision but to also render her passive.

"Such conclusions fall right in line with those issued by the forensic psychologist" said Trevor, with a nod to Gerry. "His remarks agree with our collective analysis of the Railway Rapist as organized, self-controlled, and able to convincingly pass as a normal, well-functioning man when in society. But the psychologist also feels our criminal has a strong desire to control or shame his victim. Not just by raping her, but by dehumanizing her."

"And I presume this is the prototype for all rapists?" Tom asked. His skepticism about the entire line of reasoning had not completely waned, as evidenced by the slight twist of his mouth as he said the word "prototype." There were times when Trevor wondered if Tom lived perpetually on the verge of a sneer, if having been born into a moneyed family had left the boy constitutionally unfit for the realities of police work. But then, just when Trevor's exasperation had built to the point of calling him out on the matter, Tom always managed to do something so bold, say something so kind, or perform a task so useful that he would immediately redeem himself in spades. Trevor was beginning to accept that Tom would always leave him slightly on edge. On the surface it might seem that their friendship was limited by the nearly oceanic differences between them – differences of birth, education, age, and temperament. But in truth their vague antagonism was a result of the singular thing they held in common: their affection for Emma Kelly.

"They're working on the full prototype now," Trevor said. "But the preliminary report is full of surprises. For example, I'd venture to say most people might guess that most rapists are bachelors, men denied the normal opportunities for sexual congress and thus driven to rape by sheer biological impulse."

"A ludicrous assumption," Rayley said. "The four men at this table are each bachelors, with all the frustrations that depressing little title implies, but I'd venture to say that none of us have ever entertained the idea of rape as a way out of our dilemma."

"True," Trevor said. "But what I mean is that the general public sees rape as a crime of sexual desperation so they would be surprised to learn that the majority of rapists are married and thus presumably have access to intercourse by more conventional means."

"Such as begging," said Tom.

"Oh dear," said Emma. "Shall Gerry and I retire for the evening and let you boys break out the billiards and cigars? We seem to have wandered into some sort of men's hunting club or perhaps a fraternity at Cambridge."

"Dreadfully sorry," Trevor said, although he wasn't. If Emma really wanted to sit at the table with the boys she would have to get used to the occasional bout of tasteless humor.

"And do they have anything else?" Rayley prompted.

"Not yet," Trevor said. "Further studies will cover such issues as method and manner. How does the rapist choose his victim, for example, or how long he goes between attacks. If there is a body, how does he dispose of it, and if the victim is left alive, how does he escape? Does he engage with the police, as the Ripper did, or keep souvenirs? So far the Railway Rapist isn't showing any such tendencies, which indicates a different type of mentality. Even the selection of a weapon can be telling. You can threaten someone with a gun from a great distance but an attack with a knife is closer, more personal."

"It's absolutely enthralling," Rayley said. "Just as a fingerprint or footprint tells us what sort of body our perpetrator has, so criminal profiling can give us insight into his mind."

"And if we know how he thinks, we can better predict what he'll do next," Davy said, seeming to come round at last. "Maybe figure how to trap him."

Trevor nodded. "They're studying the same sort of thing with murderers by the way, drawing conclusions about how well the perpetrator might have known his victim by the methodology of the attack. You can poison someone without being in the room, so it's a more distant, calculating sort of crime. But if you smother or choke them, in contrast, that implies a personal rage. You want to be there in the moment of the death, to actually see them suffer."

"I'm sorry to likewise muffle your collective enthusiasm," Tom said, leaning even farther back and putting his boots on the table, "or mock this shiny new forensics toy that you are all so eager to play with. But I must say that in comparison to medicine or chemistry, criminal profiling doesn't seem like much of a science at all."

"I doubt any science seems like much of a science when it begins," Trevor said amicably. "Apples falling from trees, kites and keys in thunderstorms and all that sort of rot. Admittedly, we are dealing with an unformed arena of study, but I expect it shall evolve in time, as they all do. And I should be delighted to think the people at this table might in some small way aid that evolution."

"What if the scarf isn't to hide his face?" Emma abruptly asked.

"I don't follow," Trevor said.

"We've assumed that he covers her face so that she cannot see him," Emma said. "But what if just the opposite is true, that he covers her face so that he cannot see her? Then she becomes a generalized victim, an everywoman, perhaps even a substitute for someone else."

They sat for a moment, pondering this. "You said the weapon of choice was an indication of the level of rage," Emma eventually added, her comments addressed mostly toward Trevor. "And by that logic, rape would indicate a very specific type of anger, would it not? The weapon of choice being the most intimate of all?"

She was looking right at him, but Trevor found he could not sustain eye contact for long. He dropped his gaze back to his glass of claret, aware of the cowardice in the action.

"You're suggesting he obliterates her face to sustain a particular type of fantasy," Rayley said slowly, also looking into his own wine glass, but in his case the gesture was merely meditative. "There's a woman he wants to punish but he can't – because she's unreachable, gone away somewhere, or is perhaps even dead. So his anger is directed toward some random woman who stands in her stead."

"That's madness," said Tom.

Rayley raised an eyebrow. "We're talking about violent criminals. Of course it's madness."

"But what we must remember is that they do not see it as such," Trevor said. The clock behind Tom trembled in anticipation, and then began to strike twelve. Trevor waited for each gong to sound. They had overstayed, as they so often did, had drunk more than they should, had eaten past the point of satiety and into excess, had teetered once again on the edge of discord. The ponderous sequence of the twelve bells of midnight gave Trevor time to compose his thoughts. He knew he might not see these people again for weeks, perhaps the better part of a month, and he did not wish to leave them like this, to conclude their last meeting in such an inconclusive way.

"Criminals most often do not see themselves as criminals," he continued, when the final gong had sounded, leaving a subtle reverberation in the air. "I doubt very many men, or women as the case may be, awaken in the morning and think to themselves 'Today I shall go out and perform a criminal act.' They instead feel justified in their actions, and this is what we must remember. That they consider themselves to be righting some great wrong, as avenging either their own suffering or that of someone they love, as merely setting the tipped scales of justice on balance once again. It is easy for us to sit here with our brandy and declare them animals, but I suspect that in most cases there is an interior logic to their motives, a logic we must understand if we hope to thwart the actions which result from it. Otherwise, we will spend our lives solving crimes instead of preventing them. The science of forensics will become nothing more than mopping up bloodstains."

Davy quickly nodded. Emma bit her lip. Rayley murmured "Here, here" and Geraldine, who had dozed off some minutes before, gave a little snort as her chin bobbed lower toward her chest. Tom, his feet still propped on the table, his chair tilted precariously back, pulled a cigarette from the silver case in his pocket and slowly smiled.

"Quite a speech, Welles," he said. "I'm surprised the clock doesn't chime again, just for emphasis."

Chapter Three

The Winter Palace, St. Petersburg - The Private Rooms of the Orlovs

June 14, 1889

9:20 AM

"There was a disturbance in the theater last night," Filip said, without looking up from his plate.

Her pulse quickened, just has he had undoubtedly intended for it to do.

"What sort of disturbance?" Tatiana said, her voice carefully pitched to sound calm, even slightly disinterested. She had trained herself how to do this throughout the twenty-seven months she had been married to Filip Orlov. Anxiety made the voice rise, especially on the final syllable of the last spoken word. It had the effect of turning any statement into an implied question, of indicating uncertainty, even in the most everyday of matters. Tatiana now automatically lowered her voice as she finished each sentence and the irony was that this soft growl, which had begun as a survival technique, was largely cited among her acquaintances as evidence of a flirtatious nature.

Tatiana and Filip were sitting at their breakfast table just as they had for each morning of their married life. Which would make it – let's see, what was twenty-seven times thirty? Dear God, over 800 consecutive mornings that the two of them had spent precisely as this one: Filip already in uniform, already wearing his boots. She in her peignoir, imported at considerable expense and bother from one of the better ladies' boutiques of Paris, idly grazing over a bowl of fruit and grain, all the while sipping her favorite morning concoction. It was pink froth in a wine glass, a mixture of pomegranate juice and flat champagne, whatever dregs happened to remain from the night before. Filip ate eggs, but exclusively the yolks, an idiosyncrasy that resulted each morning in a plate of abandoned egg whites, lying lacy and flat on his blue plate like the dried foam which was left behind on the beaches of the Crimean Sea. Tatiana and Filip summered there and would be departing for their villa soon, just after the Tchaikovsky ball. Half their trunks were already packed.

Tatiana did not anticipate the trip.

Filip did not answer her at once. Perhaps this hesitation was a type of calculated torture, perhaps merely the result of his preoccupation with his breakfast. He pierced another yolk and yellow spilled across his plate. He requested them barely done, these eggs, liked them as runny as possible, and if he was not in the tsar's own guard, Tatiana had little doubt that her husband would truly prefer to swill the yolks raw from a glass. The social nuances of the imperial court were a perpetual mystery to Filip. He enjoyed the benefits of being within the circle of the tsar's most trusted staff – Tatiana herself was one of those benefits –

but was still ill-at-ease with the constant ceremonies of life within the Winter Palace.

"Two dancers killed themselves," he finally said. "They were to play Romeo and Juliet in the ballet next week. Original, yes?" He grinned at her, showing the square white teeth which always seemed just a bit too small for his beefy face, clearly amused by his little joke.

"Who were they?"

"I told you. Ballet dancers. "

"Yes, but what were their names?"

He shrugged. "Do ballet dancers have names?"

Tatiana hesitated. "They're sure that it was a double suicide? And not something else?"

"What else would it be?"

"Murder might be posed to look like suicide."

"Who would want them dead?" He pierced another yolk, then dragged a crust of bread through the gelatinous puddle. "They were nobodies."

As soon as Filip was out of the apartment, Tatiana dressed. She did not call for her maid, who was probably somewhere having her own breakfast or gossiping with a gaggle of servants. Tatiana was a lounger and often returned to her bed after breakfast, most generally not ringing for assistance in dressing until noon. So she struggled unattended into a smocked dress designed to be worn over her swim costume at the coast and thus reasonably easy to don in a rush. Once she was suitably covered, she pulled on her shoes and exited the front door, looking both left and right as she stepped into the hall, craning her neck like a character in some absurd comic play.

She could not say why she was skittish, so unwilling to be seen. Tatiana had lived within the Winter Palace for the entirety of the time she had been married to Filip and had as much right to come and go through these halls as anyone. The size and location of their private quarters was the result of a single day, years ago, when Filip had taken a bullet in the side during some street fracas and thus immediately risen in the tsar's estimation. It took a man like Filip, bold and broad and very nearly fearless, to earn a full apartment in a wing not far from the imperial family's, to earn his wife a position, even a lesser one, in the tsarina's court of ladies.

Her feet followed the familiar path, turning corners and navigating the great rooms at the end of each hall without thought, moving up and down staircases without the effort of the movement striking her consciousness. The Winter Palace was grand only in appearance, pleasing to the eye with little regard for the rest of the senses. In fact, as homes went, it was not even comfortable. It contained antiquated plumbing, unpredictable lighting, primitive heating, and utterly ineffective ventilation, resulting in the sort of daily inconveniences that would have been unthinkable in a European palace and making it the least popular of the tsar's three residences.

The significance of the place lay largely in the fact that its sheer size allowed it to function as a contained city. In one direction, the Palace took up a huge expanse of shoreline along the Neva River, with several pavilions leading down to individual docks, and on the other side it stretched the equivalent of three city blocks. In the high season, somewhere between six and seven thousand people lived within its walls, more than the entire population of the town where Tatiana had been born. This was not the high season. As its name so obligingly indicated, the Winter Palace was the tsar's primary residence in the winter and the majority of the aristocracy, along with their staffs, spent summers in their country homes or villas by the sea. In this particular summer the season was being delayed until the conclusion of the Tchaikovsky ball.

The Winter Palace was not only the size of a city but was laid out like one as well, much in the manner of the old fortress towns - or an egg, should one pause to think of it - with layers of protection radiating out from a vital hub. The yoke of this particular egg was the lavish chambers occupied by the tsar, tsarina, and their five children. Tatiana had never personally visited these quarters, but if rumor was correct, the rooms there were awe-inspiring upon first glance but in reality just as unsatisfactory when it came to matters of lighting and plumbing as the rest. The next layer contained the extended family members of Alexander and his Danish-born wife - the minor royals, one might say. Then came the halls where Tatiana and Filip lived. They belonged to the segment of the staff that was considered elite, those who resided in the nether world between privilege and service. Governesses, doctors, dancing masters, portrait artists, jewelers and dressmakers, musical directors, the members of the private guard. Beyond them, in the more farther-flung wings, were the true servants. The sort who washed and cleaned and cooked and carried.

Even after more than two years within its walls, Tatiana could not claim to understand how the palace worked. For example, she and Filip both were servants and had servants, a concept which she still found a bit hard to grasp. This morning her porridge and his eggs had come as they always did, on a high-domed tray which presumably had been prepared in some kitchen somewhere, another place she would most likely never see. Their clothing was carried away dirty and carried back clean. Things appeared. Flowers on a table, apples in a bowl. Fires were laid in the winter and damped down in the spring.

The first morning, shortly after her marriage, that Tatiana had awakened in the Winter Palace had been very telling. She had risen and, through the most instinctive of habits, made her bed. The maid had entered minutes later, inquiring what she might like for breakfast. When the woman – twice the age of Tatiana, who had been no more than twenty at the time – spied the neatened bed, her mouth had closed into a hard, tight line and Tatiana understood that her error had been grave indeed. The maid had bustled forward and most resolutely mussed the bed, throwing pillows to the floor and crumpling the coverlet in her hands. And then she had made it again.

Tatiana had simply curled up on her chaise and watched. The woman's gestures could have been interpreted as a slap in the face or were perhaps kindly meant, a silent illustration of how life in the royal palace was intended to work. Tatiana had never made that mistake again. In fact, understanding this new reality in ways she could not have begun to articulate, she often made a point of leaving a bit of a deliberate mess: a napkin dropped to the floor, a bar of soap sent skidding into a corner, a dress with a button dangling, an overturned glass. To create no work for her staff would have been rude, even cruel. It might have cost someone their position and thus left them with no roof over their head or no way to feed their children. Over time Tatiana had slowly but steadily acquired the sort of exaggerated helplessness that always seemed to come with privilege. When she approached a closed door she would simply stand still and wait for someone to open it.

As she now walked through the Palace, navigating from the private wings into the public, the effort gradually calmed her and forced her thoughts into more linear patterns. The dancers who had allegedly killed themselves... Filip had said they were in the ballet, and the ballet troupe was a different entity entirely from the cadre of royal dance masters. Konstantin was in no danger. It was unlikely he had been anywhere near the scene at all. There was no need for her to visit the theater on her own, especially at this hour when there was no logical explanation she might give for why she was there. And yet she walked, hall after hall, room after room, staircase after staircase, passing mirrors and portraits and statues without number, striding beneath grand chandeliers from Italy and across deep carpets from China. Retracing the familiar route as if she were lost in a sort of dream.

At last she reached the theater and slipped through the double doors which led to the performers' level, where the dressing and rehearsal rooms were located. She found the stage below her flooded with light, each bulb glowing as if the room had been lit for a grand performance. She walked to the top of the staircase and scanned the floor below - the box where the royal family gathered, furs tossed around their feet and legs, the entrance doors, the pulleys with the platforms which raised and lowered props, the stage itself.

No Konstantin.

At the bottom of the staircase lay the lovers, as yet unmoved, although any number of men were buzzing about their bodies, presumably members of the palace police, a separate division from that of her husband. The brains, not the muscle, of the large force which existed solely to protect the imperial family.

"Who are they?" she called.

The theater was acoustically perfect. Although she had barely raised her voice, each man below her turned and stood. She doubted that any among them recognized her face, but something in her clothing, or perhaps her bearing, seemed to convey well enough from which part of the palace she'd come. Thus they were prepared to humor her questions, at least for a few minutes.

"Dancers," one of the men answered. "Do not come any closer, please. Not until we've finished."

Tatiana gazed down at the bodies. Both slim and fair, the dancers could have passed for siblings as easily as tragic lovers, and they lay in the pose which concluded their scene in the performance. This final bit of juvenile theatricality made their deaths all the sadder, although not for the reasons they'd likely intended.

"I can see that they're dancers," she said. "What I'm asking is their names."

The request, while simple, gave pause to the men beneath her, who clearly did not think of the bodies in such specific terms. If she had ever doubted Konstantin's claim that the dancers in the royal troupe were all anonymous, interchangeable, as replaceable as flowers in a vase, the reactions of these men were surely proving him right. Even in death these children were not to be granted the dignity of a name.

"Don't worry," one of them called back up, a man who had removed his hat to reveal a bald head and heavy-boned face. "We shall all be out of the way far before your rehearsal time. This incident shall not affect the imperial waltz."

Good god, he thinks I have come here because I'm worried about the waltz scene, Tatiana thought and her eyes swept the room again, more slowly and carefully this time. Konstantin still did not appear. But then again, he did not sleep with a member of the tsar's private guard. Perhaps he did not yet know that this "incident" had even occurred.

"I believe she asked you for their names," came a voice behind her. Cold, self-assured. Tatiana turned to see Grand Duchess Elizabeth Feodorovna, sister-in-law to the tsar, and known as Ella to the court, also making her way down the staircase. Tatiana sank into a curtsy and Ella nodded distractedly. Her focus was on the scene below them.

Everyone claimed that Ella had been the prettiest princess of Europe, courted by royals from every corner of the continent, but Tatiana had never considered the Grand Duchess especially beautiful. Or perhaps it would be better to say that her beauty was not the sort of dainty femininity that Russians men generally admired. There was a stony quality to Ella's features, which were prominent and even a bit masculine. This severity was echoed in the face of her attendant, another Englishwoman, this one sent by the Queen, presumably to quell her granddaughter's loneliness in this land so far from her birth. Despite the fact that Ella's acknowledgment of her curtsy had been perfunctory, Tatiana remained in her pose of supplication, looking up through her eyelashes. The woman above her was born to royalty, married to royalty, and stood far above the wife of a bodyguard by every standard society could apply, and yet there is a meritocracy of nature too, is there not? And in this ranking, Tatiana knew she reigned supreme. There was no denying the doll-like symmetry of her face, the roundness of her breasts, the ringlets which formed, without coaxing, in her hair. Taken in this manner, Tatiana's deep curtsy might even be seen as ironic.

When the men on the stage remained silent, Ella answered her own question. "Their names are Katya Gorbunkova and Yulian Krupin," she said, the comments presumably directed toward Tatiana, although her eyes had never left the stage below them. "Both of the tsar's imperial ballet," Ella continued. "Chosen as leads at an age when their peers are still vying for an invitation to the troupe. Their deaths are a waste of talent as well as youth."

"We have not formally met," Tatiana said, rising at last. "But I am Tatiana Orlov and will also dance in the imperial waltz."

"I may have seen you in the rehearsals," Ella said, flicking her eyes in Tatiana's direction then calling out to the men below, a bit more loudly than was necessary, "Are you quite sure it is a suicide?"

"What else should it be?" answered the bald man. "They are peasants by birth, you know. Such violence is common in the youth of their class." By the brusque tone of his voice it was clear he had not recognized Ella, which was surprising, but perhaps the police, unlike the guard, did not often come in contact with the imperial family. The quality of the women's clothes had earned them a sliver of civility – had they been dressed as servants it's unlikely they would have been allowed to remain in the room at all. But the policeman's tolerance evidently did not stretch so far as to include extended conversation with civilians, especially female ones.

"It's odd that the knife is in the girl's hand," Tatiana ventured quietly.

"I agree," said Ella. "Cynthia, please retrieve my camera."

A quick nod from the other woman, who had remained further back but who now turned to do her mistress's bidding. The British had a queer term for such attendants, something like "the women who stand there" although Tatiana could not think of the precise phrase in the tension of the moment. When this particular woman had first arrived from London there had been some speculation she might have been sent by Queen Victoria for purposes of political reconnaissance. Such was the depth of the paranoia in the court of Tsar Alexander III, that a middle-aged British widow with those odd sort of spectacles that split the eye in half, making the bottom look much larger than the top, could be rumored a spy. This reflexive suspicion of outsiders had always struck Tatiana as foolish, but she supposed the overblown fears of the court was why her husband held his present post. Why she slept on feather mattresses instead of straw mats.

"I take photographs," Ella said to Tatiana, a bit unnecessarily and even a bit defensively. "A camera is a fine way to document the details of one's own life, is it not? But please, continue with your thoughts. Why do you find it odd that the knife is in the girl's hand?"

"If it were a suicide pact between lovers," Tatiana said, "you would think she would die first, and then him, that he would not leave her to…"

"Quite," said Ella. "And will you come stand beside me?"

She knows the acoustics of this room as well as I do, Tatiana thought, as she swiftly moved closer to Ella. She knows that even a softly spoken conversation between two women on the stairs has the potential to echo through the entire theater. She's one of the aristocracy who most sincerely support the arts, which is probably why she also knew the name of the dancers.

"I believe your husband is a member of the royal guard?" Ella asked.

"Yes, Your Imperial Highness."

"And does he ever discuss his work with you?"

The notion was so ludicrous that Tatiana almost laughed. She and Filip did not have discussions of any sort. Their marriage did not take that particular form. Furthermore, even had he been so inclined, there was probably nothing about his work which merited discussion. The grand duchess seemed to be under the impression that Tatiana was married to an inspector or detective, a man with cases which required deduction and analysis. She did not understand that Filip's primary function was to absorb stray projectiles, nothing more.

"No, Your Imperial Highness."

"So he is discreet," Ella said, still misunderstanding. "Which is a good thing, I suppose. But it is obvious that much strikes you as odd about the scene before us."

"The position…" Tatiana said, tentatively. No one had shown the slightest interest in her opinion about anything since she had moved to the palace and it felt odd to be speaking openly now, especially to a woman of rank.

"The final pose of the ballet," said Ella, with a nod. "Intended as some sort of message to the survivors, no doubt."

"I have been trying to envision the sequence of events that would lead them there," Tatiana said.

"And how might you imagine it? Speak freely."

Tatiana narrowed her eyes. "They assumed their pose on the floor and then…he cut his throat and then she…took the knife from his hand and cut her own? Something in it all seems terribly wrong, unnecessarily cruel. For if two young lovers were determined to die by the blade of a single knife wouldn't he do the deed for her and then follow behind himself? And another thing," she added, gaining confidence as she spoke. "Romeo and Juliet fell on their daggers, which would have been a much easier way to die than the arrangement before us. Faster, more definitive, and one could not change one's mind half way though, which is an advantage in a method of suicide. But these youngsters must have cut their own throats and inflicting those sort of deep gashes which would have taken nerves of steel. A feat it is hard to picture a young girl performing, even if she was looking into the eyes of her dead lover."

Ella nodded slowly, but did not add any observations of her own. "And can you tell me, Tatiana Orlov, why it does not disturb you to look so directly upon blood and death?"

"My father is a butcher."

It was a confession Tatiana rarely made, but it was true. From earliest childhood she had been trained to look upon flesh as a type of currency. The guard below them who had dismissed the dancers as peasants hadn't known he was speaking to a peasant himself, a woman only twenty-seven months out of poverty, a woman whose pretty face was a type of currency too. Tatiana had never, not for a single day, forgotten it.

"And so you believe," Ella asked, in a flat tone which did not make the question a question at all, "that they were likely murdered?"

Tatiana nodded. One did not merely nod at a grand duchess, even Filip would have known better than that, but she seemed to have momentarily lost her ability to speak. Ella nodded too and turned toward the sound of her attendant who was marching steadily down the steps with a box in her hands, as well as some sort of device which looked like a collection of canes tucked under her armpit. She is a lady-in-waiting, Tatiana suddenly remembered. That was what the British called them. A foolish phrase. What were all those ladies waiting for?

"Very well," said Ella. "Let us set it up near the railing." The woman handed Ella the box, which Tatiana supposed was the camera. She had never seen one, only finished photographs, and it seemed nearly unbelievable that this square black case, no larger than a hatbox, should hold within the power to freeze history, to doom human faces to remain forever suspended in time. The attendant snapped the group of canes and they fell into a sort of stand upon which Ella placed the camera. She stooped to look through an aperture in the box. Whatever she saw must have displeased her, for she stood and moved the camera and its stand to another part of the railing and then looked again.

"Pardon me," Ella said, rising up and calling down to the men on the floor. "I must request that you all stand back."

"Stand back?" The bald man now looked up at the three women with open annoyance. It was one thing for the ladies of the court to come here out of curiosity, rising early from their beds to gape and stare. One thing for them to wish to witness the scene, for death is exciting, even a bit sexual, and sometimes the most unlikely of people are drawn to stand witness to its power. God knows, he had felt the pull himself. But it was entirely a different matter for one of these women, no matter how well dressed, to order him to stand back.

"I intend to take a photograph," she said.

"For what?"

"For my own edification," she said icily and then, just before he gave way to a sputter she added, "and of course my husband the Grand Duke Serge also takes an interest in my photography."

At the words "my husband the Grand Duke Serge," the entire scene before them changed. The officers on the floor stood, looked up, took a beat to absorb the identity of the woman above them with her camera, and then, to a man, leapt back. The two bodies on the floor suddenly lay in the center of an empty circle, looking small and pitifully alone.

Ella lowered her head and looked through the lens. "It would be better if I had my cloth," she murmured, "but this will do," and then there was the loud pop of a shutter closing, followed by another. With a satisfied sigh, Ella carefully lifted the camera from the triangular stand.

"Thank you," she said to the men below. "You may carry on now."

She is the kind of woman, Tatiana thought, who says phrases like "Pardon me" or "thank you" in a tone of voice that makes even words of supplication sound like an order. The men below seemed somehow shamed by her surface politeness. They moved back around the body but silently, almost furtively. What would it be like, Tatiana thought, to have that sort of power? To be able to not only change people's behavior but to change how they feel about themselves, to level the proud and correct the arrogant, all with a few casually spoken words?

The grand duchess and her lady in waiting proceeded up the staircase, Ella carrying the camera and the woman carrying the stand. As she reached the step where Tatiana waited, Ella paused.

"Our discussion has captured my interest, Tatiana Orlov," she said. "I believe we shall meet again, very soon."

Tatiana curtsied and the two women swept past her, Ella holding the camera out in front of her as if it were a crown, the lady in waiting clumsily banging each step with the wooden stand as they ascended. Tatiana waited until she was sure they were gone to slip the rest of the way down the stairs to the railing.

"Will there be an investigation?" she called to the bald man.

With Ella gone from the room, his attitude had reverted back to its previous level of charm. "An investigation of what?" he asked roughly.

No one will ask about these dancers, Tatiana thought sadly. No one will wonder why the knife lies in the girl's hand and not the boy's, or why they would kill themselves when the ballet will be over by the end of next week and presumably they could renew their courtship then. No one will ponder if they knew each other before they came here, to the Winter Palace, or what their futures might have held. The tsar's guard and the palace police, for all their differences, exist to protect the imperial family. If a crime is not directed toward them, it is not a crime at all.

The stretchers were moved in. The girl was lifted to one, the boy to the other. Carried away, Tatiana supposed, to some cool place, most likely a part of the kitchen, to await the arrival of their families, come in grief from a great distance to claim their children's bodies. And then what? She did not suppose Katya and Yulian qualified for burial in the Winter Palace cemetery, even the section reserved for loyal servants, those who had dedicated their lives to the court within. More likely Katya and Yulian would be carted away, each to their separate village, moldering more with each slow, rutted mile, until even the most devoted of parents would begin to question the wisdom of such a journey.

And meanwhile, Tatiana had troubles of her own. Konstantin had not come and they were running out of time. On how many more occasions might they tryst – two or three? No summer could be held back forever. Soon she and Filip would on their way to the coast and she would likely not see Konstantin again until autumn. During the last two summers, her annual exile had proven a burden, leaving her with entirely too much time on her hands and entirely too much proximity to her husband, but she suspected that this year it would prove especially tedious. For there is nothing like a glimpse of joy to make the previously tolerable intolerable. Over time, she had learned how to forgive Filip for being Filip. She had not yet learned how to forgive him for not being Konstantin.

Tatiana once again studied each of the three main doors leading into the theater but her lover was standing in none of them. Even the guard had departed – the men bearing the stretchers, the bald and arrogant one in the lead. She was left in this brightly lit and enormous room totally alone.

She closed her eyes and said a quick prayer for the dead. Her lips moved automatically through the Russian Orthodox blessing, leaving her mind free to wonder again if and why and how someone might have killed them. Innocents. Ballet dancers. A fabricated Romeo, a substitute Juliet. Tatiana opened her eyes and shivered slightly. A smear of blood remained on the stage beneath her, still in the shape of a heart.

Chapter Four

London – Scotland Yard

June 14, 1889

10:10 AM

Trevor waited until the two men were alone in his makeshift office to break the news. As he suspected, Rayley was not at all pleased to hear that Trevor would be accompanying the Queen and her granddaughter on an overseas trip and thereby leaving him in charge of the forensics unit for an unspecified span of time.

"Do you honestly feel I'm up to the task?" Rayley asked, and then, as if to illustrate his personal doubt of the issue, he blew his nose loudly into a handkerchief. Trevor patiently waited through the extended sniveling and wiping process that followed, making it sound as if a flock of geese had descended on Scotland Yard. On many levels Rayley seemed fully recovered from his period of captivity in Paris – the sharpness of his mind, at least, had returned to normal and he even was regaining his sardonic sense of humor. But the man seemed to have suffered from one small ailment after another since leaving Paris, the latest being a summer cold which resulted in an impressive variety of coughs, sniffles, and sneezes. The big solemn eyes behind his spectacles were rimmed in red and

Trevor wondered if Rayley were sleeping properly. Exhaustion seemed to hover around him like mist. Granted, it was probably not the sort that could be dispensed with a single night of rest, but one had to start somewhere, and it had always been Trevor's opinion that there were few problems in life which could not be greatly mitigated by a generous slab of beef and a good night's sleep.

"Of course you're up to the task," Trevor said heartily, thinking that the heightened responsibility might be precisely what Rayley needed. As long as Trevor was overseeing the unit, Rayley could float in this warm sea of ennui indefinitely, but if he was in charge he would have no choice but to rally. "Besides," Trevor added, more to the point. "No matter how either of us feels about it, I must go. Her Majesty commands it, and our unit dangles in her hands like a toy. We can't depend totally on the funds we raise from periodically arresting Gerry."

Rayley chuckled them almost immediately grew somber. "That story of Miss Bainbridge and her friends being mistreated during their transit to the station…Do you think her version of events was accurate?"

"Certainly. Gerry may be dramatic, but I've never known her to be dishonest."

"That's what I thought. And do you have any guess as to who the officer in question might be?"

"Hard to say," Trevor answered. "It could have been any man on the force, even one you'd never suspect of such crudity. The suffragettes seem to bring out the very worst in our gender."

"True, but for an officer to set upon a group of women like that, women who were clearly middle class or better...To muffle them with their own scarves..." Rayley broke off from that train of thought and abruptly changed the subject. "Where will you be traveling with the Queen?"

"Russia."

"Russia?"

"That's what I said."

"Good God, man, you might never come back. Why would she want to go there?"

"She doesn't. But it seems the Grandmother of Europe is now focused on the fate of a particular granddaughter. One of the girls from the German branch. Alix of Hesse, the youngest surviving child of the Queen's dead daughter Alice, and thus a bit of a pet, or so I take it. And the girl has her heart set on marrying the tsar's oldest son."

Rayley snorted. "English girls, even those come by way of Germany, have no business marrying Russian boys."

"Precisely as the Queen sees it."

"The solution seems simple enough. The Queen orders the girl to find someone else."

Trevor shrugged. "I can only assume the situation is more complex than it appears on the surface. Another granddaughter is already over there, remember, Alix's sister Ella."

"Indeed. That's probably what set the whole plan in motion, the older sister playing matchmaker for the younger. And can I assume that the tsesarevich is equally smitten with the idea of Alix?"

Trevor raised a questioning eyebrow at the unfamiliar word.

"Tsesarevich," Rayley repeated. "It means the oldest son of the ruler, the boy next in line for the throne. Like our Prince of Wales."

Trevor puffed out his cheeks and sighed. "The affection is almost undoubtedly mutual to have caused Her Majesty this much consternation. Of course she didn't summarize the totality of the family drama for my benefit, she just told me to pack my bags. And I bowed and backed from the room."

There was a knock on the doorframe even though the door stood open. The two men looked up to see Davy leaning in.

"Another summons to the Palace, Sir," he said.

"Again?" Trevor frowned. "I was just there yesterday."

"Perhaps this foolish trip has been cancelled," Rayley said.

"Don't think so, Sir," Davy said, so quickly that Rayley realized Trevor must have confided in Davy before he'd said anything to him. "Because this time the request is for both of you."

London - Windsor Palace

10:33 AM

The Queen looked dourly down upon the two documents on her desk. The first was Ella's letter, the one begging her to send Alix to Russia and offering enthusiastic but vague assurances that all within St. Petersburg was well. *You may have heard that the people in the streets grumble,* the letter insisted, *but the serfs are like children. When any member of the royal family appears in public a cheer goes up so loud that seems it would rattle the carriage off its wheels. They love us just that much, you see.*

The Queen didn't believe such mawkish prattle for a minute and the only real question was whether or not Ella did. Her brother-in-law's formidable personality may have swayed the girl somewhat, but the Queen still had trouble believing any grandchild of hers could truly be so foolish. Tsar Alexander III ruled his citizens with the proverbial iron fist, bringing it down upon them at intervals which seemed to be dictated more by his personal moods than the demand of circumstances. And no people – even an impoverished and illiterate one – would bear this sort of casual disregard forever.

And then, on top of Ella's overwrought and ridiculous letter, lay a terse telegram which had arrived this morning, and the contents of which had nudged the Queen from merely concerned to openly alarmed. When she had sent Ella a British lady in waiting, she had chosen a very specific woman, one ideally suited for her task: persistent but discreet, experienced in the ways of the word, yet British to the very bone. Cynthia Kirby's sole function within the Winter Palace was to observe and report. The Queen did not think in terms of intelligence or surveillance. She certainly would not have used the ugly word "spy" to describe the tasks which the respectably widowed Mrs. Kirby had been sent to perform. After all, this was her own flesh and blood she was speaking of, the beautiful and much-loved Ella. But if Ella had ceased to tell her grandmother the truth about circumstances in St. Petersburg, someone had to, and this latest telegram had only confirmed what Victoria had long suspected. That her granddaughter was sitting atop a very ornate powder keg. Royal carriages were on the verge of being rattled, it seemed, but not by the cheers of the people.

And finally, on the other side of the desk lay a much larger stack of papers, her notes for the meeting with the Prime

Minister. The Queen did not personally care for Gladstone, whom she considered a pompous prig, prone to lectures so far-reaching that they were even sometimes insinuated toward her royal person. But you do not have to like a man in order to use him, and in her absence, whether it was the three weeks she hoped for or the six weeks she feared, Gladstone's already sizable base of power would broaden, so they must consult on any number of issues before she set sail. It was exhausting to even contemplate. Most pilgrims must only pack their bags to travel, but when one is the Queen of England, one must pack up an entire country.

The Queen pondered the slow tick of the clock on the desk. Gladstone at eleven, the two detectives from Scotland Yard at noon. For she now knew that merely taking Trevor Welles would not be enough. Mrs. Kirby's telegram had informed her that two dead bodies had been discovered in the Winter Palace that very morning. Not in the streets of St. Petersburg, where one could only assume that corpses were piled in every gutter, but within the palace itself. And the mindless brutes surrounding the tsar had called their deaths a double suicide.

Victoria knew better. The tsar had his people and she had hers. The dead boy was not merely a dancer, but also the brother of Gregor Krupin. How someone with his family connections had ever been allowed within the walls of the Winter Palace at all was a troubling question, followed by the even more troubling one of why he had been killed there. And since this one young radical had gone undetected for so long, what others might likewise have penetrated the gates, might be, even now, within striking distance of the imperial family? The family which included Ella. If she were to find the answer to these questions, Victoria knew she would have to travel to Russia with reinforcements.

St. Petersburg – Nevsky Prospekt

1:47 PM

Nevsky Prospekt was by far the longest, widest, and busiest street in St. Petersburg and the word that citizens most often used to describe it was "fashionable." This was an arguable point, especially for anyone accustomed to the more consistently elegant shopping districts of London and Paris, but it was undeniable that Nevsky Prospekt served as a perfect microcosm of the city. Wealth and poverty squared off like duelists in the broad white street. Outside a butcher shop, blood seeped onto the sidewalk, forming wide puddles which the customers of the jeweler next door must wade through in their quest for diamonds and pearls. Furs in one window, guns in the next, then a shop of honey and one of soap. Western fashions and eastern cures for unspeakable ailments, a patisserie and dentist back to back, so that the diners could hear the muffled wails that accompanied extraction as they savored their tarts and rolls. Ladies extending a silk-gloved hand to be helped from a carriage, men extending a grimy palm in a plea for spare coins.

But Vlad Ulyanov saw none of this as he stomped down the boulevard, his hands thrust in his pockets, his head tucked down as if he were heading into a windstorm whose power only he could feel.

Yulian was dead. His body was being held in the Winter Palace this very minute but none of them dared approach to request it. Not yet. The presumption must be maintained that Yulian had arrived in the capital friendless and unknown. That his family was now traveling from the remote village of Simbirks, a journey of two days under the best of circumstances and more likely three. So Yulian would lie alone in his frozen chamber until enough time had passed that Gregor and the others could finally venture through the gates of the palace, their workingman's caps in hand, bowing and scraping and weeping that they had come from a great distance to claim the body of their little brother.

Well, on deeper thought, Vlad conceded that Yulian was probably not totally alone. Presumably that unlucky little ballerina was packed in ice beside him.

Here was the joke of it. One of them, at least. When Vlad had heard that it was Yulian and not him who had been tapped to infiltrate the Winter Palace, he had been jealous.

Granted, Yulian had a rare gift for dance, a talent which Vlad most certainly did not share, and thus a logical vehicle which would carry him beyond the massive gates and to the heart of the imperial enclave within. But Vlad could have been hired as a footman, could he not? Someone who helped in the kitchen, who built the fires or rubbed down the horses? At the time it seemed that Yulian's selection was nothing but the rawest form of nepotism. For Yulian's older brother Gregor held a high rank within the Naronaya Volya, while Vlad's older brother Sasha held no rank at all.

And why did Sasha hold no rank?

Because two years earlier he had been martyred in the same cause which had carried Yulian into oblivion. Yulian had been taken by the knife and Sasha by the rope, but both of them now stood comrades in mankind's only truly egalitarian empire, that of death, and all the while that goddamn bastard of a tsar still lived.

When he learned that Yulian had been murdered, Vlad was immediately sorry for the way he had treated him, all those things he'd said about Yulian being girlish and weak. The two boys had joined the Naronaya Volya the same month, both part of the appropriately-named "little brothers," that segment of the revolutionary group not yet at the university and thus considered too young and inexperienced to participate in any of the truly vital work. They ran errands, fetched coffee and bread and vodka, absorbed the opinions of the older boys without question. They were kept in the dark about anything that mattered, which is why Vlad had been one of the last to learn that Sasha was involved in a plot to assassinate the tsar. The idea had been to kill Alexander III on the precise anniversary of the date his father Alexander II had been killed. Even the notoriously stupid imperial family could not fail to grasp the meaning of that.

The symmetry of the plan had been perfect; the execution, less so. Fifteen university students were caught within minutes of leaving the grounds of the school. Ten of them had talked, and lived. Five of them, including Sasha, had refused to divulge particulars or name comrades, and thus had swung from the gallows.

Sasha's death was the first horrible thing – perhaps also the first significant thing - which had ever happened in Vlad's life. He had adored his brother, so much so that their mother loved to tell the story of how when Vlad was merely four she had asked him if he would prefer to take his oatmeal with butter or milk and he had replied "Like Sasha." No matter what the question, throughout the subsequent years this had always been Vlad's answer. He would do it like Sasha.

Having approached the perimeters of the palace some blocks back, Vlad paused at one of the gates and considered the iron bars. The bottoms were thick and utilitarian while each top was sculpted into the shape of a Romanov eagle and dipped in gold. He peered within, pushing his face against the fence like a child. In the summer the copse of trees surrounding the palace created a thick green curtain that was nearly impossible to see through, and yet he knew well enough the size and shape of the building beyond. The guard posted to this particular entrance glanced at him without interest.

The executions had been carried out so swiftly that Sasha had probably never known the lengths his mother had gone to in her efforts to save his life. Vlad hoped he did not know. To plead for mercy in a worthwhile cause is a failure of principle. To plead for mercy unsuccessfully is the ultimate humiliation. But Vlad did not blame his parents. They were bourgeois. French was a disgusting sounding language in general, but he had always considered that word, bourgeois, to be the ugliest of then all, and the revolution had taught him that families of the middle class are susceptible to a very specific type of fantasy: the belief in gradual progress. His parents had been delighted when Sasha was accepted at St. Petersburg University. A move upward, a step in the right direction, a path that Vlad might someday follow. They could not have imagined that the young intelligentsia of Russia had become a fiercely malcontented lot, more concerned with dismantling the world than prospering in it, or that Sasha, more through kindness than in sham, would be careful to hide his evolving political beliefs from his affectionate mama and papa. So when the police had come knocking at the door on that spring morning two years ago, shouting that their oldest son had been arrested in a botched assassination attempt, this unexpected news was more than Vlad's parents could grasp. His father had gone into his study and shut the door. His mother had sat down at the kitchen table and begun writing a letter to the tsar.

A letter to the tsar. Only the most innocent of women would believe such a missive would ever be delivered or read and besides, what would it have said? *Yes, my son tried to shoot you, but he's a good boy, really. He just fell in with the wrong sort of crowd at school.*

Fifteen year old Vlad had silently stood among the weeping, and for the first time had seen his own life clearly. His parents believed that history was linear, that events moved at a steady pace, much like a military parade. They believed that those who ruled deserved to rule and thus that the world they created was understandable and fair. They may has well have believed in fairy tales. After her letter to the tsar had been posted, Vlad's mother had wrapped a loaf of the dark rye bread that had been Sasha's favorite in a cloth and gone straight to the jail, begging to see her son, pleading for an interview with the panel which had condemned him.

Neither request had been granted. The bread had gone uneaten. They would never have rye in the house again.

Vlad moved closer to the guard and said something about being a student of botany, a statement aimed at explaining his apparent fascination with the trees around the palace. This was not true. It was Sasha who had studied botany, who had spent his boyhood exploring the banks of the Neva and the broad meadows outside of town, looking for particular types of ferns and flowers. Calling them by their Latin names, pressing them within the pages of the family Bible. It was Sasha who had the gift of seeing the whole world in a single leaf, who claimed that the happiest moment of his life was when he had first looked through a microscope in the university laboratory. The guard might not have been so blasé had he known that the young man whose hands were gripping the iron bars, the one peering so intently through the railing, was instead in his first year of law school at the university which had so thoroughly schooled his brother, or that he had not drifted mindlessly into the great maw of politics, but rather had sought out the Volya on the very day he had registered for his first class.

For Vlad was filled with regret, sickened with it like a fever that refused to leave his body. Regret that he had not tried harder to understand Sasha's love of nature, even regret that he had mocked Yulian's passion for dance. When Yulian had brought that girl, his Katya, to the café Vlad had been the only one of the comrades who had not walked across the room to shake her hand. That young poet who was always with them, whose name he could not now recall - the boy had claimed to know fifty of Shakespeare's sonnets by heart. He had quoted one for the occasion of Katya's first day among them as Vlad had sat there scowling, in the far dark corner where he generally sat. He had such contempt for the scene before him - the sonnets, the pressed leaves, and most especially Yulian turning his little Katya first one way and then the other, showing her off just as he likely did when they were dancing. Smiling with pride, as if he were the first boy who had ever found a girl, as if he had invented them, as if the fates of two people could matter more than the fate of the revolution. Blasphemy.

The men in the café that day were a very specific type of Russian. The kind who believed in poetry and beauty and love and already, his puberty barely behind him, Vlad well knew that he was not that sort of man. Women were either whores or comrades – or, in some rare and exceptionally convenient cases, both – but they would never be his weakness. And so Vlad had felt superior indeed on that day as he had watched Yulian making a fool of himself over Katya, spinning her before the others as the poet said some grand words in English, and Vlad had leaned his chair against the wall, smoking his cheap cigarettes.

They were all dead now. Yulian, the poet, even the spinning girl. In retrospect he was sorry he had not shaken her hand.

Vlad had no doubt there would be many more martyrs before this business was finished and he also knew that the best men would go first. The idealists would fall in the earliest days while the men like him – those who preferred whores and newspapers to ballerinas and sonnets - would survive a bit longer. Perhaps he would even live to the end. What sort of world was this, he sometimes wondered, where the better men went out in an early blaze of glory while the lesser ones trudged on? For Vlad knew he was one of these lesser men. He knew this in his heart and if he ever had doubted it, the world around him stood as a constant reminder that he was but a pale echo of his handsome, brilliant, heroic older brother. His parents kept a religious shrine to Sasha at home, candles and a host of icons, all those flat faced Orthodox saints who had collectively failed to save him. And the Volya maintained a tribute of a different sort, flags and pictures of the dead boys, their school portraits clustered on a wall in a shabby room. But both the godless and the god-fearing were in agreement upon this one point: that Sasha Ulyanov had been entirely too fine for this world.

A carriage approached the gate and the guard stiffened to attention. Vlad and a few other curiosity seekers stepped aside as the bars were wrested apart to allow entrance. The carriage rolled to a stop slowly and there was a bit of business with the horses, one of them proving reluctant to turn. Plenty of time for Vlad to look through the glass window and observe the three passengers inside: a laughing boy his own age, his amused attention directed toward a younger girl who had her face screwed up in some sort of crude jest. She was imitating someone - mocking them, Vlad realized. A governess or schoolmistress most likely, some thankless imperial servant who had failed to earn the approval of her spoiled young charge. And one of her brothers was entertained by her brattish outburst while the other, the solemn young man positioned on the seat across from them, was not. This was the tsesarevich, the heir, as handsome as he was claimed to be and dignified too, observing his younger siblings with the world-weary tolerance of the first born. It was an expression Vlad had seen before, on the face of Sasha.

They are a family, he thought. They are, when it is all said and done, no more than a family.

The tsesarevich was the same age as Gregor Krupin, the same age Sasha would have been if he lived. Twenty, perhaps twenty-one. A man on the brink of owning the world. And just as the gates finally finished their slow yawn and the carriage rumbled back to a start, the tsesarevich glanced out the window. The eyes of Nicholas Romanov locked, very briefly, into the eyes of Vlad Ulyanov and Vlad saw in those eyes a sort of resignation, an implied shrug. A Russian is not supposed to look directly upon the tsar. It is too bright, too dangerous, like looking directly into the sun and yet the eyes of the two young men met, even if just for a second. What was there to be done about it now?

A church bell chimed twice. It was time to return to the small dark room where they all met. It was in the back of a bank, yet another irony, but the comrades were largely just like Vlad, the sons and daughters of the middle class, and the father of one of them worked in this building, had gotten them the room under the foolish impression they were using it to study. The Volya met every afternoon and Gregor would be there, even today, even as his brother lay dead, for to mourn one human life above another contradicted everything in his philosophy. On the day before he got the news of Yulian's murder, Gregor had just returned from one of his recruiting trips to the nearby farms. Vlad had sensed that the trip had been a colossal failure, although Gregor had not used the word. Instead he described how he and the others had worked side by side with the farmers, intending to show them that their hopes lay in joining the Volya, the party, that the goals of collectivism should be their future too. But the farmers had shown little interest in politics. They were tired at night. They wanted to eat their bread, drink their vodka, tumble their wives, and go to sleep, not to talk of revolution. They were not interested in a glorious tomorrow. The real one would come soon enough.

Gregor had laughed as he told Vlad these stories. He had held out his fine white hands, a student's hands, now covered with cuts and blisters, and he had said "The revolution is for them but it shall not be by them," and then he had thrown back his head and roared, as if it were all a great joke. For it was, in a way. The students of the Volya would have to save the peasants who would not save themselves. They were simple souls, really, and in dire need of rescue by men like Gregor and Vlad. These boys from the university – for yes, the ironies are now stacked like firewood, are they not, leaned one upon the other to make this great blaze – it was the boys from the university who could see what the men in the fields could not. That progress is not a slow and steady thing, the result of years of careful planning. It comes in sharp, thrust upon us all at once. The only sound that truly changes the world is the sound of a bomb.

Gregor had said this and Vlad had nodded. Their brothers may be saints but they were survivors, and survivors must make their strange alliances. There were times when Vlad thought he hated Gregor as much as any Romanov, because on that horrible day two years before when five bodies had swung, Gregor Krupin's had not been among them. Vlad did not know for certain and would never know, but he suspected that Gregor had been one of the ten boys who had talked.

The carriage had rolled to a stop before a great entrance, high blue doors at the top of marble stairs. Through the wall of leaves Vlad could catch glimpses. The girl jumped from the door of the carriage, not waiting for assistance from a servant and the younger of her two brothers scrambled out after her. She was wearing a white dress with a red sash around her waist and the ribbon in her hair was the exact same color. There was laughter coming through the trees and Vlad closed his eyes at the sound. This was where his hate belonged, on these pretty parasites with their sashes and ribbons.

Vlad knew that someday he would supplant and dispose of Gregor, and that he would take pleasure in that shedding, but for now he must keep his focus where it mattered. You do not have to like a man to use him. Besides, the betrayal of a whole race of people was a greater crime than the betrayal of a single man. It had to be. Evil was numerical, measurable, subject to the same laws of math as a crate of apples. Each day these royals were allowed to live, a hundred peasants died in their place. In the mine shafts, the sewers, the factories and the fields, they sputtered and coughed and bled and died, casually sacrificed to support the Romanovs and their world of elegance and ease.

Through the blanket of the trees, Vlad could hear the girl laughing and he knew he would not rest until he had completed the task that his brother had begun. He would devote his life to the sanctity of the revolution. Just like Sasha.

Chapter Five

St. Petersburg – The Winter Palace

June 14, 1889

4:45 PM

There were those who considered dance to be the greatest art of Russia, far outstripping any national accomplishments in music or literature. The supremacy of Russian ballet, of course, went uncontested – so much so that it was rumored that in the academies of Paris, French girls had begun adding an "-ova" to the end of their last names in a misguided effort to imply they had been born in the east. But while ballet was the pinnacle of the form, all Russians considered it their patriotic duty to know at least a few steps of a folk dance, and it would have been unthinkable for any lady at the tsarina's court to be unskilled in the waltz.

This was how Tatiana met Konstantin. He served as one of a cadre of imperial dance masters, and if Tatiana's position within the palace required an odd balancing act, Konstantin's was even more demanding. For to dance with someone is an extraordinarily intimate act. More intimate than lovemaking in many ways, and it was Konstantin's professional duty to take a variety of women one by one into his arms, to push his thigh between their knees and slip his palm into the small hollow beneath their shoulder blades. He was required to transform them into larks and gypsies and tigers in turn, as they moved throughout the nuances of a dozen different tempos. And, most challenging of all, he must perform these transformations before the watchful eyes of their husbands, fathers, brothers, and sons.

It was not a task for the faint of heart.

In the stratified world of the Winter Palace, Konstantin was one of the anomalies, a man who belonged neither here nor there. On the dance floor he was the undisputed master of his realm; even the tsarina must follow his lead. He moved among the numerous court parties as an honored guest, one invited specifically to pay attention to the ladies at dinner. Otherwise, they were often ignored by the men, especially when the talk drifted to hunting or war, and in this role Konstantin quickly became as adept at navigating a flirtatious conversation as he was at navigating a crowded dance floor. But at the end of these long evenings, he would return down the hall which led to his quarters, unfastening the cuffs of his tuxedo as he walked, loosening his tie and cumberbund, sometimes even slipping out of his shining black shoes and carrying them, dangling lightly from his fingertips. The hall was long, but, when he finally got to the end, for the first time in his life he had a room of his own.

Konstantin was introduced to Tatiana the first week he came to the palace. Filip had just been granted his most recent promotion, and Tatiana had thus been invited to join the tsarina's court of ladies. She had learned with a remarkable swiftness, despite her utter lack of experience with dance. There is not much waltzing in a slaughterhouse.

Theirs was not a case of love at first sight or even at twentieth sight. Nor did they have that sort of instant antipathy that often masks sexual attraction. Instead they began with a matter-of-fact appraisal of their role in each other's new life: She must learn to dance and he must teach her. Tatiana could not have named the precise day when she became aware that her excitement about the next lesson might truly be an excitement at seeing her dance master. Konstantin understood only in hindsight that at some point he had begun to put on his best shirt on the days he was to instruct her, that he took the time to rub powder into his palms before he led her to the floor, that he remembered her favorite waltz song and would request the pianist play it for their practice sessions. But a passion that develops over time has a unique sort of magic - it comes not with bells and fireworks but rather with the slow awareness that assumptions once taken for granted are now no longer true. Falling in love slowly is like awakening one morning to find that the sun has risen in the west.

They laughed about it later, their initial disregard. Konstantin's tutelage had been polite but firm; her willingness to practice - even on five days a week when he had suggested only three - had been nothing more than conscientious. Tatiana's position in the tsarina's court would require her to learn many skills, and she had been relieved to find that at least one of them came easily to her.

Her talent was a relief to him as well. He was one of many dance masters and eager to make his mark. Because he was the most recent addition to the royal contingent, he had been saddled with the most hopeless of the Romanov ladies - the tsar's squirming young daughter Xenia, the ancient and arthritic Princess Louisa, and Ella, who looked as if she should be able to dance like an angel, but whose reserve made her awkward on the ballroom floor. These were women for whom no amount of instruction would improve their musicality or grace, women destined to clatter their heels to the marble floors with each step, to clutch his shoulder as if they were drowning, to grow dizzy in the spinning and thus require their partner to constantly step in to smilingly rescue them from their own ineptitude. Konstantin feared that if people judged him by the progress of these three pupils he would be sent back to Siberia on the next train.

At least when he danced with Tatiana people could see that it was not his fault.

4:40 PM

The rude detective had been as good as his word, for despite the fact that the day had dawned with the unpleasantness of the double suicide, the afternoon waltz practice commenced at the usual time of 4 PM.

As part of the series of performances scheduled for the upcoming ball, the imperial ladies and their attendants were presenting what was known as a formation waltz, an elaborate patterned dance which began and ended with twelve couples on the floor. But during the long central movement, each couple would move in turn to the heart of the circle for a brief moment in which they were featured in a particular step or – if the female dancer in question was especially unsteady - a held pose.

They had been practicing for weeks and it was still a disaster. It had been announced at the last rehearsal that half of the ladies should come to the next session at the customary time of four and the other half at five, the discrepancy being explained as some challenge of choreography or blocking. The ruse fooled no one; the real reason was that the four o'clock ladies were in need of an extra hour of practice and the five o'clock ones were not.

Tatiana, of course, was a five o'clock lady and when she arrived at 4:45 she went back to the platform where she had stood earlier that morning and considered the scene before her. There was the customary swirl of activity in the theater - various couples in their places all about the stage, the trio of musicians who came to such rehearsals noisily warming up, some of the ladies standing to the side having costume fittings. Konstantin was dancing with Ella, which was not surprising, but as Tatiana squinted down at them, she could see that they were talking, which was.

It is not easy to converse while you waltz. The woman holds her head back and to the left in an exaggerated curve and the man is likewise also looking to the left, although his arch is not so extreme. But their faces are turned in opposite directions and the music is often very loud and besides, dancers are expected to have expressions of paralyzed rapture. Their mouths should not move. Elegant silence is the goal, with communication between the couple flowing exclusively through their bodies, a gesture as slight as the pressure of a palm directing the lady's shoulders or the most subtle shift of his hip easing her own into a turn.

But the reality was that the dance masters talked to their students constantly. Granted, it was mostly a matter of counting out the beat or saying "Slow" "Hold" or "Left," "Right," or "Now," but most of the instructors had acquired the skill of ventriloquists, carrying on these primitive conversations without moving their lips. The students rarely spoke in return, and were thus the dummies, Tatiana supposed, but as she watched she could see that Ella was openly talking and that Konstantin had tilted his had gracelessly close to her in an attempt to listen. He noticed Tatiana above them at some point and their eyes met briefly. Impossible to read his expression or to guess what news the grand duchess might be so determined to convey under the guise of a waltz.

Tatiana sat down in one of the small chairs and began to lace up her dancing shoes. It would not do to show any more interest in one of the swirling couples beneath her than the others, but she could not help but notice that Ella, while by no definition a skilled dancer, was one of the ones who loved it. You could tell by the way she finally stopped talking and tilted her chin back, closing her eyes as they moved. Konstantin often instructed his partners to close their eyes. The better to hear the music, he would say. The better to lose your embarrassment at performing under the watchful gaze of others.

But it was also romantic, Tatiana thought. This voluntary self-blinding made it easier for the woman to submit to the movements of the man, to be truly swept away, to slip off the confines of her everyday self. Not being able to see where you were going or how close you were to other couples on the floor certainly made it easier to follow, for really, under such circumstances what other choice does one have? Ella had settled back into Konstantin's arm, and it was abundantly clear to Tatiana, if to no one else in the room, that she liked this feeling of a man's arm around her waist, drawing her steadily in, and the gentle pressure of her hand in his. Even if the man was but a lowly dance master, even if they were surrounded by dozens of other people in the middle of the day.

Something is missing in her life, Tatiana thought. Perhaps it is the same thing that is missing in mine.

She was not jealous. When a woman is married to a powerful man and having an affair with a less powerful man, and when she is playing her dangerous game in a well-lighted room, then jealousy is an emotion she cannot afford to indulge. Besides, Ella was not a threat to her. No woman, not even a woman possessed with Ella's pedigree, would risk dishonoring the Romanov family with an indiscretion. Not in word, not in deed, not even by implication. If Tatiana's ankle was in a trap, Ella was buried alive, and had been since the day she first touched Russian soil.

Tatiana knew she had been staring too long. That was always her challenge when Konstantin was in the room - to remember to periodically break the spell, to sometimes look up and away. When she did, she saw that Cynthia Kirby was also on the balcony level, also looking down at the dancers, and that she too had fixed her gaze on Ella and Konstantin. The lady in waiting had seen it all: their conversation, followed by this, followed by these tight powerful swirls of the formation and Ella's head, thrown back too far for balance, thrown back in a type of ecstasy.

I don't like this Mrs. Kirby, Tatiana thought. She has never wanted something that she knows she cannot possess, never sinned nor broken rules and she has no compassion for those of us who have. I bet her eyes have never closed, not even when she danced or when she made love. I doubt they close when she sleeps.

The theater was often chilly, kept deliberately cool for the benefit of the performers and Tatiana always brought one of her large silk scarves with her when she came to rehearsal. She reached down to her bundle and pulled out the red one, draping it loosely around her shoulders. Konstantin looked up again, spied it, and smiled, not at her but at something above her.

She had two scarves, one red and one white. They were not only a means of keeping warm while she waited her turn to dance, but also a signal. The white one said no. But the red one said yes, that she would meet him later.

7:20 PM

"Do you like the velvet britches, or the satin? Which ones show my legs to their best advantage?"

It was two hours after the rehearsal had ended and Tatiana and Konstantin were lying in a heap of bright colored clothes, costumes that needed cleaning. The pile of discarded finery was relegated to the darkest and most hidden corner of the prop room and they had trysted here many times before. It was a luxuriously quiet and private place, for once the rehearsals were over, the dancers and musicians always emptied the theater en masse, leaving it with that strangely exaggerated emptiness that only comes after a flurry of activity has departed.

It never failed to surprise Tatiana how quickly the bubble could burst.

Besides, Konstantin liked the costumes. They not only provided a serviceable bed – albeit one that contained an occasional jab from a wayward sword or crown – but they allowed him to come to her in many forms. In the ten months of their affair, Tatiana had been ruthlessly ravished by a gypsy, coldly claimed as a spoil of war by a Prussian general, seduced by the exotic rituals of a prince of India, and thrust heavenward in the arms of a Greek god.

Today he was wearing the plumed hat of a French aristocrat, red velvet riding britches, and one boot. She sat up on her elbows to consider his latest manifestation.

"The velvet is fetching, and more practical too. The trouble with satin is that it's so hard to grab hold of. And I don't wish to slide off."

He grinned and flopped down beside her, the grand hat tumbling to the side as he did so. "I can find a way to travel to the coast this summer, you know. It isn't impossible."

"It is."

"All I must do is send a message to the tsarina saying that the littlest grand duchess needs extra practice. That my progress with Xenia has been so hard-won and tentative I fear two months without any dance lessons at all might knock her right back to the starting point." He shrugged. "It's true enough, in a way."

"Most lies are."

He looked at her from the corner of his eye. "You're in a strange mood today. What's wrong?"

What was wrong? Only a man could ask such a question, half-naked, in that particular tone of voice.

"The thought of you coming to the coast for the summer scares me," she said. "St. Petersburg is big and busy with lots of places for us to hide, but you can't imagine how different the Crimea will be. It's a small world and everyone is far too aware of what everyone else is doing." Tatiana settled back into the soft nest of ball gowns. Her own red dress was in here somewhere, among all the others. "Filip does not have so many duties in the Crimea."

"Giving him more time for his wife," Konstantin said flatly.

"You know I hate it," she said. It was true. But on this trip in particular, more than ever, she must at least make a show of keeping her marriage together.

They lay for a moment in silence. "Besides," she finally added. "A single summer is not so long."

Now this was an outrageous lie, perhaps the worst Tatiana has ever told. A single summer could be forever. Whenever she stopped to consider it, she was not sure she would survive nine weeks trapped in the villa of her husband. Konstantin suddenly sprang up, as if the same mental image had struck him at the same time, and began to dig once again into the pile of clothing.

"I cannot seem to find my gypsy costume," he said ruefully. "Which is a great tragedy for the mood of the day seems to require a gypsy. A snarling knife-wielding king of the gypsies, to be more precise."

"I suppose," she said. This was possibly their last time together before she left, and Tatiana knew she was ruining everything with her mood. He was trying very hard to entertain her, was he not? He pulled on the rough woolen traveling robe of a monk – most likely Friar Lawrence from the abandoned Romeo and Juliet ballet - and turned toward with a wicked grin.

"And what of this? Perverse enough to please you?"

"Quite perverse. Shall I dress as a nun?"

"No, too much the cliché. You shall be the grand lady who confesses her sins to the holy brother and then allows him to lead her into many more. Put your red dress back on. It's beautiful, you know. I can hardly stand to see you in it."

"You must be careful. Someday when we are dancing your face will give you away."

"Or something shall."

She laughed and fished a single red sleeve from the pile of costumes, draping it across her chest like a military sash. She would give him this much, but she would not obey him completely. She was not in the mood for costumes today. "It's the nicest dress I've ever worn."

"You'll have nicer things yet when we're in Paris."

She gave him a half-hearted smile. Paris, always Paris. Whenever things were tense between them, Konstantin would talk of Paris. The only place in the world where dancers were held in as high esteem as they were in St. Petersburg, so when he fantasized about them escaping, of course he would imagine them there. He claimed that he would get a job on the stage or perhaps instructing in the most exclusive academies. If he could teach hopeless Russian girls, then surely he could teach hopeless French ones, and then Tatiana would have dresses even more elaborate than the costumes of the Winter Palace.

Tatiana never challenged these dreams, since they brought him such comfort, but each time he said the word "Paris" it deepened her despair. He was so young. Not just in years, but in experience. Konstantin had spent his childhood within the walls of a ballroom, his young adult years in a theater, and he knew little of the cold and storyless outside world. He sincerely believed that a man could become whatever he pretended to be.

And now he misread her hesitation. "Perhaps you won't have fine things at first," he conceded. "At first we shall be poor."

"I've been poor before," she said.

"Then why do you look so sad?"

"You know the reason. Filip."

"He ignores you."

"He owns me. And each time we take this chance, the more likely we are to be caught."

"That isn't true, you know. At least not in a mathematical sense. Each time one spins the wheel of fortune, the odds of success or disaster are precisely the same, no matter how many times one has played that particular game before."

"Spoken like a true gambler. Or at least like a man who has spun the wheel of fortune many times."

It was a jibe. He was three years younger than her but, for his age, he had known many lovers, and often, she suspected, they had been his students. Married women – lonely, ignored, ripe for the picking.

He looked at her somberly. "I've never played a game quite like this one."

"What was the Grand Duchess Ella telling you while you waltzed?"

"Are you jealous?"

"At one time she was called the most beautiful princess of Europe."

"At one time perhaps she was," Konstantin said. "She asked me if I knew the ballet dancers who were found dead this morning. Which I did, but only slightly. I'd seen them in rehearsals. They were good."

"Why would she even suggest that you knew them?" Tatiana asked sharply.

"You know how these people think as well as I do," Konstantin said. "They assume that all dancers must know each other, just as they imagine one German of course must be related to another or that if a man has taken to sea he must have met every other sailor in the world. Life beyond their own small circle is a bit of a blur to them."

"I was there, you know."

When he frowned in confusion, she tried to explain. "Filip told me two dancers were dead, this morning while we had breakfast. He meant to frighten me, because he suspects something between us, and I don't care how many times you tell me I am being silly, I know that he does. He tells me that two dancers are dead and then he smiles this horrid smile with egg all over his teeth. So when he left, I went to the theater and I saw them lying there on the floor. The guards were cleaning up."

Konstantin was still frowning, but more gently. "You thought one of them might be me? Why should I be dead?"

"I don't know. I suppose I panicked. But the Grand Duchess Ella was there too, with that ghoul of an Englishwoman that she drags about with her everywhere she goes. She and I discussed the situation."

Konstantin softly laughed. "Discussed? I was not aware that Ella discussed anything with anybody."

"She discussed it with you."

He ignored that. "The guards said it was suicide. The dancers playing Romeo and Juliet become too absorbed in the story, then have some sort of tiff and kill themselves. Rather sad and silly but what more could there be to it?"

"The Grand Duchess Ella thinks they were murdered. And I agree."

"Come here," Konstantin said, pulling her to him and they leaned together back into their makeshift bed. He draped the rough woolen cloth around her and pressed his knees into the hollow of hers. The robe was scratchy but warm, and familiar in a way that all the satin of the world would never be, and they often rested like this, between bouts, in this position that always reminded Tatiana of twins tucked in the same womb. She knew that he was trying to comfort her and she also knew that lately this had been an impossible task.

"Why would you think they were murdered?" he whispered into her ear.

"I don't know," she admitted, her own voice trembling. This morning the world had seemed very sinister to her - the knife in the girl's hand, the careful positioning of the bodies. But here and now, in this darkened room, in the holy embrace of an unholy monk, the danger didn't seem quite so likely. "I'm not thinking clearly. I suppose I'm just unhappy." Tatiana set up, pushing the clothing aside, exposing her legs. "She took a picture of the bodies, you know."

He shrugged. "All the royals are mad for their cameras."

"I know. But it seems rather sad, don't you think, this mania for photographing every element of their lives? It's as if they don't expect anything to last."

He dragged the back of his hand up her thigh, the knuckles grazing against the muscles of her leg. It was a dancer's trick, this stroking of not just the skin but the muscles beneath it and the motion had a French name, although Tatiana couldn't think of it now.

"Perhaps the Grand Duchess is unhappy too," he said. "Unhappy women are quick to believe unhappy stories."

"That's what she told you while you were waltzing? That she is unhappy?"

"In a way," he said. "But I already knew."

"You know us all better than we know ourselves, is that what you're saying?"

He looked impossibly young when he smiled like that, like a boy and not a man, someone proud of himself for all the wrong reasons. "Whatever a woman whispers in my ear," he said, "it is my job to have already known it."

Chapter Six

The Royal Yacht the Victoria and Albert - Skagerrak Strait

June 16, 1889

7:28 PM

If there was anything more startling than the beauty of the afternoon it was the fact that it seemed it would never end.

Their second day aboard the royal yacht The Victoria and Albert was coming to a close and the ship was slowly making its way from the fretful waters of the North Sea into the Baltic, which was rumored to be more tranquil. "Nothing more than a big lake," one of the sailors promised Emma and then he had pointed a short calloused finger toward a distant land mass and added "Denmark."

She wanted to believe him. Perhaps the worst was literally behind them now. The crew all swore that as they sailed deeper into the waters of Scandinavia that the last three days of the voyage would become ever more scenic and pleasant, a gentle drift through high-walled fjords and charming fishing villages. That was when the team would have time to confer, to gather their forces and make the many decisions necessary if they were to convincingly carry out this masquerade.

The ship carrying Queen Victoria and the others had left the harbor of London at two in the morning. Yesterday morning, Emma supposed, although it was hard to think of time in that way. It had been instructed that the royal colors would not be raised until midday, when they would be far from the city, somewhere off the rocky coast of Scotland. Victoria did not like for her subjects to be made aware of the fact that the Queen was not in London. She felt her absence gave rise to anxiety among the citizenry.

For the majority of the first day Emma had not left her cabin. She had been placed in what was called the Princess Royal's room, a lovely if somewhat overwrought little nook tucked behind the stairs with pale salmon walls and a ceiling fashioned entirely in plaster imitations of shells. The high maple bed was bolted to the floor and there was reliable electricity and a modern toilet, which she had made use of with regularity as they pulled away from the coastline of Great Britain and entered the North Sea. She was fortunate indeed compared to the men, who were apparently making do in the cramped berths where the sailors slept and had not even a porthole to help them keep their perspectives righted. When she had opened her door last night to set her tray of barely touched food into the hall, she had seen Rayley pacing. He'd reported that Davy was suffering the most and that Tom and Trevor had dragged him up on deck for a bit of light and fresh air. Staring at the horizon, Rayley said. It's the only known cure for seasickness.

Before leaving London, Emma had bought a white blouse and slim white skirt specifically for the nautical part of the trip, the outfit purchased under the romantic impression that everyone at sea wore white, even the passengers. She now saw that – like undoubtedly many more to come – her assumption had been almost laughably faulty. Ships were dirty places, spewers of coal dust. The chairs on deck had been covered with soot when she had ventured out this afternoon, but an obliging sailor had stepped forward with a woolen blanket and draped it over the chair so that she could now sit without danger of smearing her virginal clothing, staring off in the direction of the dim coastline what was rumored to be Denmark.

Although the hour for supper was fast approaching, the intensity of the sun was enough to fool someone into thinking it was still midafternoon. They were high on the globe – certainly higher than Emma had ever traveled – and nearing the summer solstice, when the sun would be visible for a remarkable twenty hours a day, fading only to a dusklike glow during the middle of the night. One of Emma's favorite childhood books had been about a girl from a Viking village titled "Land of the Midnight Sun," but no amount of reading could have prepared her for the complete disorientation of a day which refused to end. She wondered what it would feel like in winter, when the opposite trick of light took hold. Endless night. A pale and watery daylight breaking through for a only few hours at noon. No wonder people went mad in such sustained darkness – drinking, weeping, killing each other, killing themselves. The fabled Russian temperament with its wild extremes of behavior, Emma thought. Perhaps much of it is the result of mere geography.

Emma glanced around, but there was no one else on deck and finally she opened the files in her lap and began to skim, once again, the notes she had been studying since Trevor had announced they would be accompanying the Queen to St. Petersburg. Their first collective meal was scheduled to begin in the dining room within the hour and if she was going to play schoolmistress to Her Majesty the Queen, she had better be prepared. The implications were terrifying. But Trevor had insisted she was the only one fit for the task and, even while she recognized he was using flattery in a clumsy attempt to win her cooperation, she also realized he was probably right.

The lecture Emma would be required to give had two parts: a brief summation of the last few years of the history of Russia and an even briefer summation of the Russian imperial protocol, specifically the "Order of Precedence" which dictated, among other things, who must bow to whom. The former was straightforward enough but the latter was profoundly confusing, since the social structure of the Romanov court, to put it charitably, was far less linear than that of Great Britain. So much so that even Victoria apparently needed to refresh her memory before her visit and had requested that Emma – whom Trevor had evidently portrayed as some sort of general consult on all matters arcane – should stand before them all and outline the rules of the Winter Palace.

It would never do for the Russians to realize they were being spied upon, so back in London they all created some plausible role for themselves, some way to explain why they were traveling with the Queen. As detectives, Rayley and Trevor could easily pass as bodyguards. Davy was a bit trickier, but since the Queen maintained excessive correspondence, even while abroad, it might be plausibly explained that she traveled with her own messenger boy to handle the post and telegrams. They decided to place Tom in the circle as royal physician. He was suspiciously young, but they concocted a story that Victoria's primary physician was too elderly to travel, so his assistant had stepped in for this particular journey. Despite her age and her girth, Victoria was remarkably healthy and did not customarily travel with a doctor of any sort, but the Russians certainly didn't know that.

But Emma, how to explain the presence of Emma? Serving as a maid was the most likely ruse, but such a role would severely limit her usefulness once they got to Russia. The Queen had confided to Trevor she already had a Lady in Waiting in surveillance, so a second would be superfluous. Trevor eventually declared that Emma would pose as the governess of Alix, a role which would allow her to interact across a broader social spectrum once they were inside the Winter Palace.

Emma shifted in her chair and took a big gulp of air. Brisk and refreshing, just as promised. Salty on the tongue. She wished that Gerry was traveling with them. There was no way they could explain an elderly heiress as a true member of the forensics team and Geraldine herself had quickly pointed this out, thus saving Trevor the discomfort of raising the issue. But without Gerry among them, Emma mused, the entire forensics team seemed a little at sea. Geraldine was possessed of no practical skills whatsoever but still somehow managed to be one of the most useful people Emma had ever known, and her presence would be missed in many small ways. Gerry is my family, Emma thought, pulling the blanket around her and taking another deep breath in an attempt to steady her nerves. By the age of twenty, Emma Kelly had buried her mother, father, and sister and her brother was somewhere in America, likely never to be seen again. Gerry had stepped into the void, serving as an unorthodox but unfailingly compassionate parental figure in Emma's chaotic life.

And perhaps these men are my new brothers, Emma thought soberly. We make our family where we find it.

At precisely nine o'clock the doors opened and they were all ushered into the dining room. For a moment the five of them stood without speaking, as awkwardly silent as if they were in a cathedral. Davy, Emma noted, was pale but otherwise appeared to be in control of himself. Trevor seemed distracted, Rayley anxious, and Tom was precisely as he always was. He winked at her as he wandered over to look at the portraits on the walls.

The dining room was like all the other public spaces Emma had so far seen on the yacht – neither lavish nor ostentatious, but designed instead for comfort and the most practical usage of space. The checkered linoleum floor was covered with a red carpet, which, judging from its slight undulation, was probably rolled up and stored somewhere when the Queen was not aboard. There were various settees around the wall, all crammed with cushions. Emma was somewhat surprised to see a profusion of potted plants in each corner but the green leaves offered a spot of land in the midst of the sea and were quite pleasing. Above the table dangled a large brass candelabrum of nautical design, which was brightly lit despite the fact that a nearly undimmed sun was still streaming through the windows.

"Surprising to find seamen on the walls," Tom said, breaking the silence.

"I beg your pardon," Trevor said.

"The portraits," Tom said. "Every one of them shows a former captain of the vessel. Fitzclarence, Denman, Seymour, Campbell, and finally Thompson, who according to the dates below his picture, must still be at the helm. Will he be joining us tonight, do you suppose?"

"I doubt it," said Trevor. "Princess Alix of Hesse will be present for the meal and then she will retire and we shall converse with the Queen about her expectations of the time in St. Petersburg."

Davy shuddered.

"Steady, lad," Trevor said. "Her Majesty's presence can be intimidating at first, as I'll freely admit, but I urge you all to speak just as you would if we were sitting around Gerry's parlor. Tom, you might want to hold yourself to five glasses of wine and keep your boots off the table, but otherwise, we must follow our normal routes of inquiry."

"Mustn't we wait for the Queen to speak first?" Emma asked.

Trevor shook his head. "Not in this case. Her Majesty has specifically requested that we conduct our briefings as we would do in London and raise any questions that come to mind."

"Then I shall begin by asking her why the four of us are rolling about in bunks when perfectly fine cabins stand empty," Tom said.

"You'll do no such thing," Trevor snapped. Even after several months of close acquaintance he was never entirely sure when Tom was joking. "Those cabins are held for Lords and we're servants of the crown, not titled gentlemen."

"But Emma has her own room and she isn't a Lady," Tom said with a grin. "No offense intended, darling."

"And none taken," Emma said.

Just then the double doors wrenched open and, with no announcement, the Queen entered. A few steps behind her came a young girl who was presumably her granddaughter Alix and thus the source of all this extraordinary bother, followed in turn by a servant. Although Emma dropped into a quick and awkward curtsy, she had time to note Alix's serious expression, her eyes slightly downcast and her mouth slack in a way that seemed vaguely mournful.

"We shall sit," said the Queen, and so they did.

The sole attendant who had come in with the Queen held out one chair at a time, pointedly looking at the person meant to occupy it as he did so. Emma found herself beside Alix, which pleased her. If she was to convincingly pass as the girl's governess, they should become companionable with each other during their brief time at sea. They were all scarcely seated when the first course, a shellfish soup with cream, was served with admirable promptness and the meal began.

Thank God for Tom, Emma thought. He might tease Trevor about the seamen and the bunk beds and he might be a bit mercurial in mood, but he can talk to anyone about anything. He immediately gestured toward the portraits and asked the Queen about the various captains the vessel had employed and soon had her reminiscing over past voyages. As a family, the Bainbridges had two inborn gifts – wealth and what Emma's father used to call the gift of gab. Both came in handy on a regular basis and as Tom and the Queen chatted, a collective calm settled over the table. The soup was finished and replaced by a terrine of vegetables. Wine was poured and poured again. Trevor ventured a comment or two and Rayley chimed in behind him and, although silent and a bit subdued of appetite, even Davy seemed to relax. When the server brought around the bread with tongs, he took a second roll and the Queen approvingly said "Best thing for seasickness, you know."

"Yes Ma'am," Davy croaked. "That's what me mum says, not that she's ever been on a boat."

Under cover of the chuckle that ran around the table Emma turned to Alix. "How have you passed your time these first two days at sea?"

The girl hesitated. "Reading."

"I like to read too," Emma said. Despite their difference in rank the girl was clearly shy and the task of sustaining any sort of conversation would therefore fall to Emma. Her face was pretty, her dignity remarkable for her years, but yet it was hard to look at her and immediately imagine what the tsesarevich would see that was so unique and compelling that it would sustain an infatuation over a separation of four years and a thousand miles. "What were you reading?"

"Paradise Lost."

Emma raised an eyebrow. "By Milton?"

"Is there another?"

Well that was something. An attempt at humor and, if she were indeed reading Paradise Lost at leisure, the girl must have at least a bit between the ears.

"I very much admire the poem," Emma said. "What do you think it means?"

Alix hesitated again and Emma realized the girl was behaving as if she really was her governess, not a dining companion, and as if this were all some sort of test.

"Myself, I consider it an analysis of how we each must take personal responsibility for our actions," she hastily added, to establish that this was a conversation and not an examination. "I most adore the line where God says that he made humans 'sufficient to have stood, but free to fall.'"

Alix nodded slowly. "I see it as a tale of forgiveness," she finally said, glancing self consciously around her at the various servants in the room, who were coming and going with their pitchers and plates of food. "Adam and Eve were the first humans to sin and thus to require the grace of God." She raised her rounded chin, suddenly looking much like her grandmother. "It is my opinion that salvation is the only proper theme of literature."

Emma smiled. It was a very basic interpretation of the text, but not an inaccurate one. The young princess indeed had more possibilities than were evident at first glance.

"It's an admirably challenging reading choice," Emma said, aware that she herself also sounded a little too adult and pious. "Most girls favor romances."

"I read those too," Alix whispered, as a steaming plate of veal was placed in front of her.

"Salvation of a different sort," Emma whispered back, picking up her wine glass.

"Nicky loves the sea," Alix said, with a return to her normal tone and a rather abrupt change of topic. "He wears the uniform of the Russian navy for all state occasions."

The Russian navy, Emma thought. Founded by Peter the Great, the design of their ships all allegedly based on that of a single skiff the first tsar had brought back from a visit to England, thus giving rise to the theory, at least in the universities and shipyards of London, that the success of the Russian navy was the result of science stolen from the British. Emma had been so immersed in reading eastern history over the last three days that these facts slid back to her unbidden. But she merely nodded encouragingly, and Alix went on.

"His family yacht is far larger and grander than this one," Alix said, with a guilty look in the direction of the Queen.

Emma made a noncommittal sort of murmur, wondering if Nicholas possessed the skill to actually captain a craft, even one the size of Tsar Peter's original skiff. She suspected he did not, which made his pride in wearing a nautical uniform rather affected, like a child playing dress-up. But it hardly mattered. For when she had said the name "Nicky," Alix's face had suddenly become alive with light and animation. She was one of those women who could be transformed by joy, who could fly from merely pretty to compelling on the wings of sheer emotion.

"He is so dashing in his naval uniform," Alix said. "The trousers are white and the jacket is blue with gold braid on the shoulders and an insignia —"

"I say," Tom said, calling down the table as if they were all patrons at a boarding house. Rayley startled with horror but the Queen seemed completely nonplussed. "What holds you ladies so deep in conversation?"

"We're discussing Paradise Lost and the nature of salvation," Emma replied.

"Good heavens, such gravity," said Tom with a mock frown. "If your thoughts grow any more ponderous, I fear the very ship shall sink beneath us."

"We shall continue our conversation later," Emma said quietly to Alix, and, on impulse she reached across the table and squeezed her hand. It was doubtless an inappropriate gesture, to touch royalty without their bidding, but the girl flushed with pleasure, clearly happy to have a new friend or at least a sympathetic tutor. She's frightened too, Emma thought. Unsure of what she'll find in St. Petersburg or all the changes the years might have brought to her Nicky. To write a passionate letter from afar is one thing; to have something to say to the person when you meet them is an altogether different matter, and Alix knows that she is sailing into an uncertain future. Going to one of the few places on earth where the flag of her grandmother may not protect her.

And then a violinist began to play from the corner and any further discussion was unnecessary.

An hour later the table had been cleared, the servants had departed, and Alix too had gone to her cabin, presumably to dream of salvation and men in white trousers. The true business of the night was about to begin.

"We shall not concern ourselves with talk of the order of precedence until some later evening," the Queen said. "For Alix will need to be present at that lecture as well. From what I understand from Ella, a German princess is expected to curtsy to a Russian grand duchess, so she will need some direction."

A British Queen is expected to curtsy to a Russian tsarina as well, Emma thought, but she supposed the arrogance of the Russian court was indeed a subject best suited for another day. They had enough to cover tonight.

"Miss Kelly," the Queen continued, with the tone of one long accustomed to being in charge. "Will you now give us your summation of Russian history? Not the entire dreadful subject but rather just the most recent facts, the ones most pertinent to the matter at hand."

"Certainly, Ma'am," Emma said. "I suppose we should start with the current tsar's father, Alexander II?"

The Queen nodded. "A good man, if memory serves."

"He accepted the need for reform," Emma said, striving to keep her voice measured and matter-of-fact. A week ago she had been mending Gerry's underdrawers and she could hardly fathom the turns of fate which had brought her to this place and time, sipping sherry on the royal yacht and giving a history lesson to the Queen. "The Russian serfs are abysmally poor, which I suppose goes without saying, and Alexander II signed a bill early in his reign giving them the most basic sorts of rights and freedoms. Before that, the serfs were thought to belong to the land they worked and thus could be bought, sold and traded, much in the manner of American slaves. The reforms, limited as it may seem to outsiders, established the reputation of Alexander II as a tsar who was sympathetic to all classes of people and somewhat of a progressive. But many of the serfs did not think the reforms went far enough and, especially in the rural regions, the new rules were not sufficiently enforced. Over time resentments began to build again."

"Eventually leading to the tsar's death," the Queen said tonelessly.

Emma paused and took a deep breath. "Yes, Ma'am. The assassination of Alexander II was undoubtedly the most pivotal event in recent Russian history and I believe it would be a mistake to underestimate the impact it has had on the psychology of the present royal family and thus the matter at hand. "

"The imperial family," the Queen corrected her. "We are royal, but they call themselves imperial."

"Yes, yes of course," Emma said. "A distinction we must all take care to remember."

"The particulars of the assassination?" Trevor prompted.

"It's a sad tale," Emma said. "One morning the tsar was traveling by carriage through the streets of St. Petersburg. A homemade bomb was thrown at his entourage but missed its mark, in the sense the tsar himself was uninjured. He insisted on stopping to offer aid to wounded members of his guard and as he exited the coach, a second bomb was thrown. This one found its target and the tsar suffered dreadful injuries. The loss of both legs, great gashes on his torso and face." Emma glanced at the Queen, who sat immobile. "Begging your pardon, Ma'am."

"No need to apologize," Victoria said calmly. "We are speaking of Nicky's grandfather and, as you say, an event that informed the current state of the Romanov court. Please continue."

"The tsar was mortally wounded," Emma said, "and requested to be taken to the Winter Palace to die. That was just as it happened, two days later. The irony is that Alexander II had not only granted basic reforms twenty years before his death but had also, on the very morning he was attacked, signed an additional bill into law granting further freedoms to the serfs, such as the right to own private property and elect representatives in their rural districts. You might say he was attempting to start Russia on the road to modern government and yet…"

"He was killed by the very people he was trying to help," Tom said simply.

"As is often the case," the Queen said. "His kindness was his doom. He would have lived had he stayed in the royal carriage and not insisted on disembarking to offer succor to his guard."

"His reforms would have lived as well," Emma said. "For when he learned that his father had been murdered, the tsar's son and successor, the man we know as Alexander III, went into his father's office and ripped up the freedom initiative his father had signed that morning. He proclaimed that in attempting to help the serfs Alexander II had tried to pet a rabid wolf and vowed to never make the same mistake. And he has thus been an autocratic and unrelenting ruler, not only recalling his father's reforms but pulling Russia back into a more feudal way of life. We are speaking, of course, of the present tsar and the father of Nicholas."

A silence fell on the table. Trevor noticed that the Queen's lips had grown thin and her jaw was tense. She had certainly been aware of the events Emma described but revisiting the details seemed to have stirred up a variety of emotions. Victoria had been fortunate enough to escape an assassination attempt early in her own reign and had from that time nursed an unhealthy interest – some might say obsession –with the subject of murdered politicians.

"Is there any way of knowing where young Nicholas stands on these matters?" Trevor asked the Queen. "His grandfather was a reformer, his father a traditionalist. It seems the boy would have to lean one way or the other."

Tom reached to splash a bit more sherry into his glass. Very bad form in front of the Queen, but the servants had all been banished from the room and she did not appear to notice. She was frowning at the tablecloth before her, evidently deep in thought.

"There is no way of knowing what, if anything, Nicky thinks," Victoria finally said. "I gather he is rather sheltered, young for his age, and that his father has done a remarkably ineffective job of preparing his eldest son to rule according to any political philosophy at all."

A slight but awkward pause fell across the table and Rayley's eyes briefly met those of Trevor. The precise same charge had been laid against Victoria herself, that she had allowed the fiftyish Prince of Wales to remain a gadabout schoolboy, not to mention his son, the even more wretched Bernie. There's something about these monarchs with all their power, Trevor thought. This power that they are reluctant to release even to their own children. Perhaps they believe that if they never acknowledge their mortality, it shall never come to pass.

"They call the tsar "The Bear," do they not?" Tom asked, knowing that sometimes an awkward silence is best smoothed by asking a question to which everyone already knows the answer.

"They do indeed," Emma said promptly, "and the assassination of his father has stamped the entire reign of Alexander III. He is the proverbial iron-fisted ruler - suspicious of outsiders, preoccupied with the idea that his father's cruel fate might await him or other members of his family. His fears are undoubtedly warranted, for social unrest in Russia is extraordinarily high and the poverty of the serfs is more profound than ever."

"Yet in her letters my granddaughter Ella assures me that all is safe and calm in St. Petersburg," the Queen said. "I know this to be untrue, both from an awareness of the facts Miss Kelly has so neatly summarized and from my own intelligence sources around the city." The Queen gave a bark of laughter, a sound with more anger than humor. "And sometimes Ella herself slips up in her letters, providing details which clearly show the excessive precautions which are undertaken in an effort to protect them all. Guards in such number that I sometimes suspect the entire imperial family lives under a type of very well-appointed siege, all but hostages within the walls of the Winter

Palace. Then, as if I needed any more proof of my suspicions, this came." She reached for a pile of papers on the table beside her, evidently placed there by a servant before departing, and slowly brought her eyeglasses to her face, carefully tucking the wires around her plump ears.

In the silence that followed as the Queen flipped through the papers, Emma was aware they were all holding their breath.

"Will you read this aloud for the group, Detective?" the Queen asked, handing what appeared to be a telegram to Rayley. "It arrived two days ago from Cynthia Kirby, the British woman serving as lady-in-waiting to my granddaughter Ella."

Although startled to have been singled out, Rayley adjusted his own glasses and unfolded the thin yellow paper.

Two ballet dancers from royal troupe found dead this morning in theater of Winter Palace. Stop. Playing Romeo and Juliet. Stop. Throats cut. Stop. Royal police treating as double suicide. Stop. Boy is Yulian Krupin, brother of Gregor. Stop.

"And what do you think of that?" asked the Queen. "Please speak without inhibition, and Detective Welles, we wish you to lead the discussion."

"It's odd," said Davy, surprising everyone by going first.

"What's odd about it?" Trevor asked.

"It's more than twenty words."

Laughter ran around the table. "Our young officer Mabrey has a mania for holding his telegrams to twenty words," Trevor explained to the Queen. "If the crown is ever bankrupted, I can assure you it won't be because Scotland Yard is sending overly long messages."

"May I ask if you know who this Gregor Krupin is, Ma'am?" said Rayley. "That's obviously the key part of the telegram."

"Of course I know who he is," the Queen said, folding her arms across her ample stomach, "as I suspect Miss Kelly does as well." She looked directly at Emma. "Would you illuminate the gentlemen?"

"Indeed, Ma'am," Emma said, her mind racing as she attempted to collect her thoughts. Much of her study over the last few days had come from the extensive notes of Britain's foremost expert on Russia, a professor at Cambridge who often served as a consultant to the Yard. He had produced two files at Trevor's request, one marked "The Official History" and the other "The Real History." Both had been bulging, full of long, unpronounceable Russian names and Emma had struggled to digest the information within. But the lines about Krupin leapt up from her subconscious mind, like trout from a stream.

"As we've suggested, Alexander II was right to be concerned that the same revolutionaries who murdered his father might take aim at him as well," she said calmly, her eyes flitting around the table at the kind and familiar faces of her friends before at last settling on Trevor, who was nodding with a small encouraging smile. "Gregor Krupin was one of several revolutionaries who were arrested two years ago in an assassination attempt on the present tsar. It was a band of university students and very badly planned, so much so it is doubtful the tsar was ever in significant danger. Five of the plotters were hanged, convicted on testimony provided by Krupin."

"So he's a turncoat to his own cause," Trevor said. "Was he jailed?"

"No," the Queen said shortly. "They do things differently there. Our understanding is that he is still free in the streets and still involved in radical causes. His surviving comrades do not appear to know that he is the one who – what is the phrase, Detective?"

"Sold them out?" Trevor guessed.

The Queen sat back. "Indeed."

"So the dead ballet dancer is the brother of a known revolutionary," Rayley mused. "No one in the tsar's guard was aware of that fact before he was allowed inside the gates of the Winter Palace?"

"From what I gather from Ella's letters, the guards are shockingly inept," the Queen said, with a slight quaver in her voice. "They seem to arrive just after a crime has occurred but never before. And the Russian authorities do not keep the sort of records that are kept by the London police."

Trevor nodded. "This is part of the problem we shall face in St. Petersburg. Your Majesty, everyone at this table knows the frustration I felt during our time in Paris last April, when our efforts to apprehend an escaped British criminal were thwarted by the lack of continuity between Scotland Yard and French police. Shared intelligence and records among all nations is absolutely essential to the future of investigative police work."

"Truly, Welles? I've never heard you mention such," Tom said drily. Laughter went around the group and even Victoria smiled. Trevor's obsession with the idea of an international police intelligence agency rivaled the Queen's obsession with assassinations.

"Very well," Trevor said, holding up his hands. "I shall save the sermon for Sunday. But the point is that the situation in Russia is even worse. The police forces in various cities do not communicate with each other and even the districts of a single large city like St. Petersburg act each as an independent unit. Which means that if a criminal escapes capture in one district he could simply walk a few blocks and begin his nefarious activities anew. I'm surprised the entire country isn't in chaos."

The Queen slightly lifted one eyebrow but remained silent.

Rayley leaned in. "May I ask, Ma'am, if the tsar's own guard was unaware of this young ballet dancer's suspicious family background, how a lady-in-waiting would come to gain this information?"

She nodded. "As you have undoubtedly guessed, Mrs. Kirby is more than simply a lady-in-waiting. Because of our concerns for our granddaughter's safety there are a certain number of people in St. Petersburg who have been sent by the crown to guarantee –" Here she broke off, as if suddenly struggling with emotion. "No one can guarantee the safety of anyone else," she said, correcting herself. "But we have taken steps to lessen the degree of risk."

"And may I ask if your granddaughter is aware of the true purpose of Mrs. Kirby's presence?" Trevor said.

'She is not," said the Queen, her composure swiftly restored. "Ella believes Mrs. Kirby to be nothing more than a British widow, traveling to escape the sadness of her husband's death. In fact in her letters she complains that the woman is tedious and ordinary. She would be surprised to learn that Mrs. Kirby is...what did you call her, Detective?"

"A crack shot with a pistol," Trevor said.

"A crack shot," the Queen repeated slowly. "We have learned so many marvelous new phrases during our consultations with Detective Welles. At times one almost feels like an American."

"Is there any chance that the fact Gregor and Yulian were brothers is coincidental?" Tom asked. "It's possible that the ballet dancer wanted nothing to do with the revolutionary's sordid past as evidenced by the fact he assumed a quite different line or work."

The Queen's eyes flickered. "The Crown does not believe in coincidence."

"Nor does Scotland Yard," Trevor hastened to assure her. "Especially now that the boy has been found dead. I wonder that the guard, even if they are as inept as Your Majesty suggests, were so quick to deem the deaths as suicide."

"The fact they were playing Romeo and Juliet does suggest it," Tom said, seemingly unembarrassed even after being refuted so thoroughly in his last theory. "I'd be very curious to hear how the bodies were found, what sort of knife was used, which of them appeared to have died first."

"You shall have the chance," said the Queen. "For this is why we have asked you all to travel with us." She looked steadily at each person in turn as she spoke. "When we arrive in St. Petersburg you must appear to be our personal guards, our doctor and messenger, and Alix's governess. We must observe perfect protocol and do nothing to contradict the theories and beliefs of our hosts." She grimaced. "When the time comes for it, I shall even curtsy to the tsar and his wife. But our true mission is to learn how a violent revolutionary group managed to get one of their members within the gates of the Winter Palace and living in the midst of the imperial family. We must uncover what Yulian Krupin's hidden purpose was inside the palace, why he was killed, how, and by whom."

A stunned silence fell on the group. Trevor and Rayley looked at each other and Rayley shook his head. They had spent the last three days speculating on Her Majesty's true reason for insisting the entire forensics team accompany her to St. Petersburg. The crown had dozens of trained bodyguards she might have more logically brought along if her only aim was self-protection, so obviously Victoria anticipated a different role for the men from Scotland Yard. They had imagined it to be something along the lines of digging up dirt on the Romanovs, giving the Queen more ammunition to shoot down Alix's desire to marry Nicky. But to now hear that they were expected to solve a double murder in a land not their own, one where they had no authority and no logical reason to be asking the kinds of questions a murder investigation would require…

"What of the bodies?" Trevor ventured.

"By now they have mostly likely been claimed and buried," the Queen said with a quick nod. "Which we appreciate is a disadvantage from a forensic standpoint."

"It's the ultimate disadvantage," Tom said bluntly. "We're starting with no physical evidence at all."

"And since they deemed them as suicides, any police reports we should manage to lay claim to would be cursory and incomplete," said Trevor. He was obliged to serve the Queen, but this seemed like an impossible request.

"Then you shall have to be very clever indeed," the Queen said. She looked around the table with understanding, even compassion. "I know the task sounds daunting, but it is not required that you build the sort of case which would be strong enough to bring a killer to justice in a British court. These deaths are a Russian matter and not our concern. Instead we are asking you to make an evaluation. Russia is a dangerous place, but just how dangerous? If the revolutionaries managed to place one man within the palace could they do it again?"

"You want to know if it's safe for Alix to marry Nicky and live there," Emma confirmed.

The Queen looked at her with such intensity that Emma blinked and dropped her own eyes. "Alix is most certainly not going to marry Nicky and live there," she said. "Upon my life, she shall never be Tsarina Alexandra of Russia with the insupportable burdens such a title implies. The question is whether or if will prove necessary to extricate Ella as well."

"We shall devote ourselves to finding the answer," Trevor said. For once he felt he was reassuring a grandmother, and not a Queen.

"You must," Victoria said, and her enormous blue eyes drooped nearly closed, as if she no longer had the heart to look at the world around her. "For my blood runs cold when I think of what could happen to my girls in Russia."

Chapter Seven

St. Petersburg, the Winter Palace

June 18, 1889

2:27 PM

It is not a difficult thing to be an imperial spy. If one wishes to gain details of the intimate lives of powerful people, all one really must do is befriend their servants. Cynthia Kirby had not been in St. Petersburg for a week before she knew that the Grand Duchess Ella's personal maid liked apricot jam, and was furthermore vulnerable to the charms of French cologne and American tobacco. In the afternoons, when Ella napped, her British lady in waiting and her Russian maid would sit in one of the courtyards located adjacent to her suite of rooms, sometimes sharing a cigarette, sometimes just talking. By the time April had gone to May and then to June, they had swapped all the stories of their girlhoods and of their long departed husbands, and moved on to the gossip of the present. Gossip which primarily circled around the lady they both served and, most specifically, the sad state of her marriage.

The halls and rooms of the Winter Palace were so numerous and labyrinthine that when she had first arrived, Cynthia had despaired that she would ever learn her way around them. So it had been a shock to realize that there was an additional unseen structure within the visible one, an entire second layer of halls, tunnels, and staircases, vital passageways concealed like veins beneath the skin. Sometimes these passageways served a utilitarian function, such as allowing food to be transferred swiftly from the great kitchen to the private suites, or to permit soiled laundry and other refuse to be carted away without its foul presence assaulting the sensibilities of the people who had created it. Sometimes these halls served as conduits of intrigue, the means by which a man might visit his mistress or his wife slip her own lover from her apartments upon his return. They also provided an extra buffer of protection, being the primary means by which the imperial guard came and went, keeping them unobtrusive and yet close to the tsar and his family.

In fact, one could argue that this network of tunnels, halls, and stairways – which the servants collectively called "the web" - was where the true drama of the palace was played out. It was the route by which Katya and Yulian had been carried away on the morning their bodies had been found, transferred from the theater to the icehouse where they were now entombed. It was how Tatiana Orlov had first found a way to meet Konstantin Antonovich, how the young grand dukes were routinely escorted back to their rooms by their attendants after an especially raucous night of gambling and drink.

And it was the way that Ella's husband Serge left her bedroom every night.

The three acts of their evening theatrical followed as such: First, Serge would approach the door of Ella's apartments through the public areas, often taking some special pains to announce to anyone within earshot that he was off to bed with his wife. His twenty-four year old wife with the red gold hair and large blue eyes, a woman both beautiful and imminently suitable for a man of his exalted rank, herself being descended from royal blood on both sides. The sort of woman any man would be proud to escort by day and eager to claim by night. Once within Ella's private apartments – which were also blue, very nearly the exact shade of her eyes – he would continue to walk, sometimes exchanging a word with his wife but more often not, until he had crossed through all three chambers and stood before a large panel upon which hung a seascape. The picture had been chosen prior to Ella's wedding by some well meaning relative who had thought that a painting of the sea might remind the young bride of the British coastline, and thus serve as a comfort to her undoubtedly homesick heart.

But alas, the sandy gray shores of the Crimean' Sea look very little like the rocky cliffs of Dover and it was thus behind a flat and foreign sea that Ella watched her husband retreat every evening. He would push aside the curtain of the wall, his fingers groping for the familiar lever, and then throw it, causing the sea to slide from view and a great void to open in his place. Serge would step into that darkness and, within a few seconds, the panel with the painting would return.

"But where does he go?" Cynthia asked the maid. She was named Alina, and her darting, gleaming eyes indicated that she was the sort who would always take joy in recounting the troubles of others.

"To the gentlemen's enclave," Alina said.

Well, that didn't sound so bad. Cynthia had heard that the imperial men had an entire wing set aside for their private use, where they played billiards and cards and displayed their gap-mouthed trophies of sport - including, it was rumored, a stuffed bear posed for eternity in the most vulgar of all possible postures. Guns on the walls, brandy in the glasses, pipe tobacco in the air. Cynthia's British heart had not disapproved of such an arrangement, even though it was mysterious that Serge would leave his pretty young wife for so many nights merely to indulge in these gunmetal-and-leather sort of masculine pleasures.

"It is a long series of rooms," Alina said, then added, "with halls which lead on one side to an exit through the stables, and on the other side to a dock. They have their own bathhouse there and a steamroom and sauna. Where the gentlemen sweat out their poisons and beat each other with rushes."

"Two exits, do you say?" Cynthia inquired, her ears perking up at the most relevant part of the description. This was scarcely good news for the wives. "So the men can travel unseen by either boat or horse to visit their mistresses, I presume? Or are the pleasure women brought into the palace instead?"

Alina laughed, blowing out a great puff of smoke.

"The pleasure women," she said. "I've never heard them called anything quite like that. If they're the pleasure women, I wonder what that means for the rest of us."

Cynthia waited for more, but it was not forthcoming.

There was a great deal of speculation within the palace as to why after four years of marriage, Ella and Serge had yet to produce an heir. She was of the perfect age and constitution. He was older, past forty but still a fit figure of a man, capable of riding and shooting with the best of them, or so it was said. Therefore, wagged the tongues, where was the baby?

If there was to be one, the servants would have known before the royals. The maids were aware of which bedsheets had dried smears on them in the mornings and which did not, and they certainly knew which ladies produced monthly pads for disposal and which did not, and thus could generally predict the impending arrival of heirs long before their fathers were privy to the happy news. In fact, there was protocol around even this aspect of imperial life. The cloth pads were placed in a special container once they were bloodied, then carried away not to be washed and returned but burned, since palace etiquette dictated they were never to be used again. The other discarded items from the Romanov women – the dresses and gloves and shoes and even their lingerie - were passed on to their personal maids, but not these. The Russians were too superstitious about blood, especially aristocratic blood, no matter how it had been rendered. The pads collected from the elite apartments were merely burned, but those from the chambers occupied by the family were furthermore burned by a priest, in a ceremony not unlike that of a funeral, a ritual of mourning for a child who was not to be. Cynthia was too accustomed to Anglican logic to accept the folkloric roots of Russian Orthodoxy or to understand how these people who looked so elegant on the surface could indulge in such primitive rites without batting an eye. She could only speculate on the thoughts of the low-ranking cleric assigned to this thankless task, who was required to solemnly pray for the souls of even nonexistent Romanovs.

"The Grand Duchess Ella remains incorrupt," Alina said, leaning back against a stone wall and exhaling another great puff of smoke.

"Incorrupt?" Cynthia asked in some confusion. Her Russian was adequate but there were still times when she was unsure she had full understanding, and this was a word she had only heard in connection to the church. The body of Christ had never decomposed, and thus was incorrupt, but a human? And then, with a sick thud to the chest, it occurred to her what Alina was truly saying. "You mean that she is still a virgin?"

The woman nodded.

"You're quite sure?"

"We see him come, and we see quickly him go," Alina said, with a shrug so exaggerated that it bordered on being French. "On their wedding night and each one after, without fail. He goes to the men's enclave, just as I said." And it was this time, the pointed way she said "men's," that Cynthia fully grasped her meaning, and her horror grew.

"If this is true, then why would he marry her?"

"Men such as him need a wife." Alina gave a wicked grin. "More than the other kind, wouldn't you say?"

"But he was in the army," Cynthia said, aware that such a remark was foolish but still struggling to understand. "A military man during his youth."

The woman rolled her eyes. "Ah, yes. The army."

Cynthia sat back too, the stone wall behind her striking her shoulder blades, knocking the breath from her lungs. "How many people know this?"

Alina paused to consider. "A dozen servants, but we don't add to the count. Within the imperial family, perhaps only the two of them can say for sure, but many more suspect. And the more time passes without a child, the worse it shall look."

"The worse it shall look for him, you mean," Cynthia said.

"It is hard to say who they might blame."

And in that remark, so benign on the surface but with so much implied, Cynthia at last saw the full of Ella's situation. It was quite clear which of the two was dispensable. Not the brother of the tsar, but a princess from a minor German principality. If the marriage were to fail, all blame would fall to the blameless Ella. The real question was whether or not Cynthia should share this tale with the Queen. She had been sent to collect a very specific type of information, only relevant to whether or not Ella was in danger. Would an unconsummated imperial marriage count as danger? How long would the dynastically-obsessed Romanovs continue to tolerate a barren bride?

Alina ground out her cigarette on the sole of her shoe and then tossed the stubby remains over her shoulder, into a nearby rose bush. They had dallied for some time already and should return. Ella loved her naps but no woman, not even a royal one, could sleep forever.

Cynthia wanted to ask Alina why she thought Ella would stay in this sham of a marriage. Ella who'd had so many options, who had been courted by so many men, who could run home to her grandmother at any time. But perhaps that was the very reason she stayed. How humiliating would it be to return from her marriage childless, rejected, a virgin? After she had defied Victoria, refused so many suitable suitors to marry this man, to cross this great distance, to insist upon this cold and empty bed over every other one in Europe?

She will never admit her mistake, Cynthia thought. She would rather live out her life without love than without dignity. This information went a great way toward explaining the woman's personality – the cool reserve with everyone around her, punctuated only by her inexplicable fondness for that dancing master, the handsome one with the dark ponytail and the Asian slant to his eyes. The excessive gaiety expressed in her letters back to London. Why she did not flirt at the balls and grand dinners but sat instead with the sort of vague, far-away stare that one generally only sees on the face of saints in church paintings.

Cynthia tossed her own cigarette and the two women stood. Alina was still smiling, proud of the potency of her gossip and the effect it had had on the obviously shaken Cynthia. News of this weight was worth another pot of jam at least, for this was surely the most interesting story being swapped in all the back rooms and courtyards of all the elite chambers in the Winter Palace that day.

But she was wrong. For down another hall and in another courtyard, this one smaller and less carefully tended, two more maids had also brought their heads together. One of them was whispering to the other that it had now been nine weeks since she had last burned the pads of Tatiana Orlov.

The Streets of St. Petersburg

3:14 PM

In the meeting room of the Naronaya Volya they were beginning the funeral of Yulian Krupin. It was not a simple matter to plan a funeral for a young atheist, especially one with parents who remained profoundly faithful to the orthodox church. But fortunately or unfortunately, depending on how one chose to look at it. the members of the Volya were quite experienced with such diplomatic delicacy; this was the eleventh funeral they had planned in the last two years. At a stage in life when most young people were attending weddings and christenings, the comrades of the Volya were far better versed in the ceremonies of death.

Vlad endured the hypocrisy for as long as he could – the speeches from the men, the weeping of the women, Yulian's poor, bewildered mother reminding him so much of his own – before he escaped outside. It was a mockingly beautiful day and he found himself walking down by the river. He took pains to turn before he got to the expanse of the Neva which led to the Winter Palace. He could not bear seeing it on this particular afternoon.

He walked until his legs ached, his feet stumbling a bit in the marshy land by the river. The effort of pulling his boot from the mud with each step quickly exhausted him and finally he climbed higher on the bank, where he could sit looking up at the billowy clouds.

A formation of geese flew overhead and their presence excited a cadre of men on the opposite riverbank, men whose presence Vlad had not noted until now. St. Petersburg fell from a bustling city back into a fetid marshland within the course of an hour's walk and the Neva had always been a working river, drawing fishermen and hunters to its banks. Two men stood up from their huddled group and pointed their long guns toward the sky.

The geese flew in a perfect vee, their symmetry so precise as to be militaristic. There is always a plan, Vlad thought. Even birds have one. The silence here on the banks of the river was almost deafening. He was aware of the pounding of his heart, and - even greater weakness – the sadness that lay there as well.

A shot rang out, and then another. One of the bullets must have found its mark because the lead goose in the vee dropped from the sky, spiraling down as gracefully as a ballerina before hitting with a splash. A shrill blast of a whistle goaded a pack of dogs into motion, and they galloped into the water, the alpha male paddling to the center of the river to retrieve the goose. The racket they made was appalling but Vlad's attention remained heavenward, where, within the formation, another goose had moved forward to take the place of his fallen leader. The geese flew on, their symmetry slightly less perfect, but their pattern essentially undisturbed.

Such is nature, Vlad thought. One life barely gone before another replaces it. Order restored before the dog can even carry the body of the dead goose back to shore.

And so it was with the imperial family.

This has been our great mistake, Vlad thought, watching the geese move across the sky until they were nearly out of sight. We killed one tsar and another took his place, and if we kill this tsar his son will move forward, and the formation shall remain unchanged. The Romanovs shall simply fly on, far above us, until the end of time.

To kill one was not the answer.

You would have to kill them all.

Vlad knew such a plan would not be readily accepted by his comrades. Even Gregor, whose bile sometimes rose to match his own, focused his fury solely upon the tsar. It was easy to hate a tyrant who thundered out his edicts, who, with his barreled-chest and thick beard, fully looked like the bully that he was. Any man on the street would happily take a crack at such a beast. But to accept the necessity of dispatching of the whole family, including the blue-eyed children and the inconveniently pretty women, required an entirely different turn of mind.

Vlad knew that he could see the truth – this had been the curse of his life, his almost singular ability to see the truth – but he also knew that his comrades did not yet have the stomach for true revolution. They wanted to overthrow the imperial family, not obliterate them, and it would be years before they would grasp the necessity of his ultimate solution. Enough time for a different sort of man to rise to the helm of the revolution. Vlad's thoughts stuttered back to the image of the girl with the red sash, joking with her brothers, and then leaping from the carriage before it had fully come to a halt. How old would she be? Twelve, perhaps thirteen?

    The dogs paddled back to the far shore, the alpha dropping the goose at the feet of his master and earning a hearty pat. The others shook water and lay back down on the bank while the men resumed their position in the blind. One goose would not feed the families of five men.

    But both the hunting and the fishing would have to wait for a while, because to the left a boat was coming into view. A large one, with both the flap of sails and the dull drone of an engine, boasting a deep navy hull and sparkling white fittings. It bore no flags, but the craft was too fine boned and graceful to have been designed for any practical purpose. A yacht, a pleasure ship of some sort, and across the bank the hunters all shifted to watch it pass. One of the fools even saluted, although there was no evidence of whom the vessel might carry or what purpose it might serve. Just as it passed Vlad, a figure appeared on the deck. A young woman with red hair, dressed entirely in white and then, emerging from behind her, a plump pigeon of a man, raising his hand to squint into the sunlight, a gesture the cheering hunters mistook for a return of their salute.

They don't look like aristocrats, Vlad thought, but who could tell? Oppression, like the devil, had the ability to assume many forms.

Vlad lay back on the bank. More of the titled and wealthy seemed to come to St. Petersburg every day, with their tennis rackets and valises, their crates of champagne, well-starched servants, and small yapping dogs. These people thought differently from the members of Volya – they were frightened and pleased and motivated by different things. It was beginning to occur to Vlad that, at least for now, the energies of the revolution were perhaps better spent looking for ways to influence the tsar than for ways to replace him. Alexander was not a man to be shaken by petitions or riots or strikes. He would be controlled only by a different sort of means.

We must take something that he loves, thought Vlad. Something that not even he will find so easy to replace.

A kidnapping. A hostage from within the inner circle. The bear will not bend his ear toward his people even if we bring a thousand petitions, Vlad thought. But will he bend it if he knows we have the girl in the red sash?

The Royal Yacht – The Victoria and Albert

4:12 PM

"Do you waltz?" Trevor asked Emma.

"Why on earth would you ask that? I don't hear a band."

He chuckled. "I am asking on behalf of the Queen. We were just discussing Ella's last letter in which she spoke of rehearsals for an imperial waltz, one featuring the ladies of the court and some of their attendants. Her Majesty had the very inspired suggestion that you and Alix might join in this presentation."

Emma leaned against the ship railing. The sailors had said they were within minutes of St. Petersburg now and the yacht had been held back to a fraction of its power. Trunks and valises were beginning to be brought up on deck, stacked all around them. It still seemed unreal, perhaps because there were no clear signs that they were indeed approaching a city. Marshland stretched all around her, as far as the eye could see. Young green reeds poking up from blue water, pine trees clinging to small spits of land, the loud and hopeful birds trailing the yacht, screaming out as they dove and rose in the still air.

Emma wrinkled her nose. "It smells."

"So it does."

"All this stagnant water. It seems the entire city would be full of contagion."

"You can mention your concerns to the tsar when you meet him." Trevor leaned over the railing too, clasping his hands close together and bringing his shoulder to where it almost touched hers. "But in the meantime, I believe we were talking about the waltz."

"I waltz well enough, I suppose, at least for a schoolteacher. But I don't understand what she's asking."

"There's a grand ball scheduled in a just a few days. To mark the summer solstice and the return of the composer Tchaikovsky to his motherland after a triumphant tour of the continent. There will be performances of all sorts, including some sort of exhibition waltz featuring, just as I said, the imperial ladies and their attendants. Her Majesty believes it would be a simple matter to get you and Alix invited to join them."

"But why should we do that? If Ella wrote her about rehearsals, presumably they've been going on for weeks, which suggests a rather elaborate presentation, does it not? And yet the princess and I are to arrive at the last minute and join the troupe?"

"Heavens, Emma you're not thinking clearly at all. This isn't about whether or not you're the star of the show. If you join in the rehearsals, this will give you an excuse to be in the theater. To get to know the other dancers, and that is really what we will need." Trevor looked down into the swirling water beneath them, the hosts of dragonflies hovering just above the surface. "If you're afraid you will dance badly you can pretend to roll an ankle on the last day of rehearsal."

"'I never said I was afraid I'd dance badly."

"Then what are you afraid of?"

"It just seems rather implausible."

"Well if we were to enumerate all the things about this journey that seem implausible I hardly think you waltzing would be at the top of the list." Trevor darted his eyes to the side and noted the freckles on Emma's nose, more visible in this light than they ever had been in London, and quite enchanting. "Look, dear, it's Her Majesty's suggestion and I think it's rather a good one. Alix is quite keen to show her waltzing skills in front of Nicky and play at being a Romanov for a day. And it's the best chance we have of getting someone backstage at the theater and within the circle of the dancers. They may know nothing of Yulian's true background and they may know quite a lot."

"Why has she lowered her standard?"

"What?"

"The Queen has taken down the flag bearing her royal standard."

"Hmmm… I hadn't noticed," Trevor said, squinting up at the mast. "I suppose it's because she wants to make it clear from the moment of arrival that this is not a state visit but a personal one. Look….there it is."

And indeed there it was, as they eased around a small bend, the beginnings of a city. They called St. Petersburg the Venice of the east, Emma thought, all the random facts and details from her files still coming back unwarranted at strange times. Or at least the Russians called it that. She doubted the Italians would concur. But she was beginning to see a bit of what they meant, as the ship nosed its way along the bank and toward a city built on islands, bridges slowly coming into view and the number of boats along the bank increasing with each minute they sailed. She wondered if the real Venice smelled like this.

As she and Trevor stood at the railing and watched the city grow before them, Tom soon came up, and then Davy, followed by Rayley. Finally the Queen and Princess Alix, whose agitation showed on her face. She wasn't looking at the scenery, which she doubtless remembered well enough from her visit four years ago. She was straining only straight ahead, waiting for her first glimpse of the Winter Palace. She was also trembling, Emma noticed. Not just her hands but her whole body. Alix's dress was pink, elaborate and overdone in Emma's estimation, with a high collar composed of silk roses, so many and so large that she seemed lost in a mountain of organza petals. The hat was even worse, with the back ludicrously puffy and the brim so deep that her plump little face seemed to have receded within a hollow of silk. She had tried very hard to be glamorous and failed. It made Emma sad.

The Queen's affect was the opposite. Her Majesty opted to arrive wearing the same sort of black broadcloth mourning gown that she had worn for decades, and pointedly devoid of ornamentation. Victoria is sending a signal as well, Emma thought. She wants the Russians to know that for her this is all nothing more than another day of work.

And then it was there, the Winter Palace. Enormous gates, grand swathes of iron fencing and behind it, a light blue building the size of which Emma had never beheld. They approached a dock and sailed past it.

"Not this one," the Queen said in terse explanation.

They continued to sail. Another dock came and went.

"Nor this," the Queen said.

"The palace has four separate docks along the river," Alix whispered loudly to Emma, a statement which caused Davy's jaw to literally drop open.

It's bigger than Buckingham, Emma thought. Bigger than Windsor and Sandringham and, as the third dock also slipped past them, she thought, Dear God. It is bigger than Buckingham and Windsor and Sandringham all together. It is the biggest structure I have ever seen, or ever will see. Bigger than any building in Britain. Perhaps the biggest in the world.

The five members of the Thursday Night Murder Games Club remained motionless and silent as they continued to sail and the Winter Palace continued to stretch. Davy was still openly gaping and Tom seemed on the verge of letting go a series of the sarcastic quips he always used to hide any unease. Rayley and Trevor were managing to maintain a sense of professional reserve, but Rayley had begun his nervous habit of blinking rapidly and, perhaps because she was standing close to him, Emma was aware that Trevor had stopped audibly breathing two docks back.

She could only assume that the others were thinking thoughts along the same lines as her own. What the hell have we gotten ourselves into? How far off the earth have we fallen this time? We are too small to be here, too insignificant and too utterly out of our element.

And finally the boat began to slow even more until the engines were screeching with the effort. They pulled parallel to the fourth dock. It was the largest and most ornate so far, with a wall of white marble dotted with sculpture, and evidently was the entrance point reserved for honored visitors such as themselves. Although their Russian hosts could not have know the exact hour of their arrival, a contingent of guards and workers stood ready to receive them. The Victoria and Albert, which had seemed so stately when it left London, occupied scarcely a third of length of the landing berth. A swarm of men spring into action and the yacht was quickly secured and the gangplank lowered.

"Granny?" Alix said with uncertainty.

"Come along, my dear," Victoria said. "You and I must go first." She took her granddaughter's hand in her own, a plump black glove firmly grasping a trembling pink one and the two moved down the gangplank. Just as they reached the bottom, Victoria paused briefly and turned to look back up at the others, who were still waiting on deck.

"I know it seems very grand," she said. "But at least I'm not afraid to live in mine." And with that her foot descended to the ground and they were in Russia.

Chapter Eight

The Winter Palace – Ella's Lounge

June 18, 1889

6:27 PM

"There is no need to fight the inevitable, Granny. I am Russian now."

"You are not and never shall be."

"It's true. Your simple German princess is no more."

"You're not even German," Victoria said, the tremor in her voice suggesting that the Queen was on the verge of actually losing her temper. But Ella, standing haughtily before her, clearly had no plans to retreat.

They had been welcomed in a flurry of hugs, squeals, and tears. Ella had greeted them halfway down the long promenade leading from the dock up to the palace and her joy at seeing her sister and grandmother had been touching to behold. The young grand duchess, whom Trevor considered even lovelier in person than in her portraits, then had escorted them to her private apartments for a late luncheon and it was there – amid tassels, gold gilt, great dangling prisms, and, in short, the rather flashy sort of glamour that made the very roots of Trevor's teeth ache – that the conversation had devolved from reunion to argument with shocking haste. Now the entire group sat awkwardly in chairs scattered about the cavernous room, holding their tea cups too tightly and striving without success to ignore the royal tempest brewing around them.

"A woman becomes whomever she marries," Ella said. "The virgin is sacrificed on the altar of marriage and reborn as a wife. I was taught that from earliest childhood and let us think, who might have been my council on such matters? Why, I believe it was none other than you, Granny dear, and if this is true, it must also follow that a woman becomes a citizen of whatever nation she marries into. So when my mother married my father she became German, as were all the children from that union. I was German until I married Serge, and now I am Russian. Whatever position or influence I have within the walls of this palace stems from that singular fact. It is not a difficult thing to understand, no matter how determined you are to not understand it."

"You are the one who is being willfully foolish," Victoria said, with ever the slightest hiss to her voice on the word "foolish." "Your pedigree trumps that of anyone within this palace and yet you have somehow let yourself forget from hence you sprang. Heaven knows, on your father's side you can trace your lineage all the way back to Charlemagne and any present power you have, any at all, stems from the fact that your grandmother is Queen of England."

"And you may as well know that I have at last made the decision to convert to Orthodoxy," Ella plowed on, ignoring the fact that at, at least in the eyes of Trevor, the Queen was scoring the majority of points in the debate. "For it is the faith of the realm and thus the people expect it of me, especially on the high holy days. Oh, and don't look at me like that, Alix," she added a bit guiltily to her sister, whose mouth had dropped open at this latest declaration of defiance. "It is not really all that different from being Lutheran. We worship the same God and the same Christ, do we not? And is that not what truly matters?"

"It is as different from Lutheranism as two faiths can possibly be," the Queen said. She had grown so angry that Tom was staring at her and his own hands gripped the sides of his chair. Whether he was merely surprised to find his normally stolid monarch in such agitation or feared for the health of an elderly patient, Trevor could not say. "The rituals of Orthodoxy," the Queen continued, "are contrived to dazzle a peasant populace, not to encourage the development of a rational mind. You may as well announce that you intend to throw you head back and bay at the moon."

"When we are in England, you control us all and you marry us off to suit your needs," Ella said coldly. "But what you fail to realize is that once we are indeed married, in that very instant we move beyond your control. The continent of Europe is not your personal chessboard."

A beat of silence. And in it the Queen's face changed from angry to sad.

"If I saw the continent as a chessboard," Victoria finally said, with a tender simplicity, "do you honestly imagine I would set forth you and Alix as pawns?"

At the softening of her grandmother's voice, Ella's shoulders slumped, as if all the fight had suddenly gone from her as well. She paused in her pacing and considered the small, round woman seated before her. "Darling Granny," she said. "I'm so happy you're finally here and I don't wish us to open our visit with this sort of distressing discord. But you simply must accept that Serge is my husband and that Russia is my home." Then she turned abruptly toward the others and said "But I fear I have been rude. We've been so caught up in our family tussles that I have neglected to formally greet your traveling contingent."

They went through the circle of introductions with teacups clattering into saucers and bows and curtsys all around. It seemed a bit silly to resort back to such pageantry just after having witnessed the sort of row one might more reasonably expect from a working class family, but Trevor supposed that being in private service to the royals would be much like working behind the scenes of a theatrical. Like it or not, they were about to witness the machinations of the magic, and to see the principals devoid of their costumes and props.

"Emma Kelly," Ella said thoughtfully, pausing in the round of formalities to consider the girl more closely than the men. The unexpected attention seemed to fluster Emma, who blushed to the roots of her hair.

"Emma has been tutoring me in Milton," Alix said, surprising Trevor by even speaking. During the argument between her sister and grandmother she had sat still and ashen, undoubtedly aware that beneath this clearly well-worn debate, what the two women were truly discussing was the possibility of her own future in Russia. Besides, Trevor had never been entirely sure how Alix felt about being accompanied to St. Petersburg by three members of Scotland Yard or the ruse of presenting Emma as her governess. The necessity of their presence was an implied insult to the court her cherished Nicky would someday rule, so it seemed she might resent them all. But instead she had now leapt to her feet and had linked her arm through Emma's as if they had been devoted companions for years.

"Milton," Ella said vaguely. "Most excellent. You must illuminate us all at the welcoming banquet, which I'm sure my family will be holding within a day or two in honor of our British guests." If these last lines, especially the pointed emphasis on the words "my family," were designed to take a final jab at the Queen, they fell short of their mark, for Her Majesty had turned her attention back to the luncheon and was merely prodding suspiciously at some sort of overblown pastry with her fork.

"Emma will be dancing at the Tchaikovsky ball," Alix said. "As am I."

"So I understand," said Ella, smiling at her little sister. "This means you shall both meet Konstantin and your lives shall be instantaneously transformed." Her large blue gray eyes flickered back to Emma. "But I find your name inconvenient," she said. "Emma and Ella? Far too similar and it shall leave us all in confusion. For the remainder of your time in St. Petersburg, you must be known by your surname of Kelly." And she laughed, but in a way that made it impossible to tell if she was truly joking, and then the royal women – Alix, Ella, and the Queen – abruptly recessed from the room into Ella's private parlor, leaving the members of the Thursday Night Murder Games club flattened against their seats like the survivors of a hurricane.

"The Grand Duchess is quite something, is she not?" Rayley finally said. "It's hard to think of the exact word."

"Oh, I can think of several," Trevor said, shaking his head. "I never would have believed the Queen would have accepted such impudence from anyone."

Tom winked at Emma. "And what of you, Kelly? I thought you were going to faint when she turned the full force of her personality in your direction. I suppose the Grand Duchess is like Eve in the Garden of Eden – she's been given divine authority to name us all to her liking."

Before Emma could reply, another set of doors swung open – Trevor was already beginning to suspect a building of this size and design would be next to impossible to guard – and a small dark-haired woman in spectacles walked in.

"My name is Cynthia Kirby," she said. "And the Queen has instructed me to brief you at once."

Trevor and Rayley exchanged a look. If being held hostage to the unfolding dramas of the royal family was not bad enough, it appeared they were now about to be lectured on their duty by a lady in waiting. The four men had leapt to their feet as she entered. Or perhaps "leapt" was not the proper word; so many women had been coming and going and the Russian divans were so demonically soft and deep that Trevor found himself growing increasingly ridiculous with every arrival. He rolled, he foundered, he flopped his way up from the cushions and onto his feet and then he struggled not to openly gasp for air in the face of the Kirby woman, who had evidently elected not to sit herself. She stood before them in the manner of a general, her legs planted far apart, her arms folded across her chest.

"Please sit," she said. "I shan't, for there are only a few points to be covered. Mr. Mabrey?"

"That's me," Davy croaked. "I mean, Ma'am, that is I."

The woman studied him over the top of her spectacles. "You do indeed look like a schoolboy, which is just as I hoped. The revolutionary group with which Yulian Krupin was affiliated, and which his brother Gregor still dominates, is rooted in the University at St. Petersburg. We have a friend there – a man by the name of Elliott Cooper who serves as a teaching assistant in their government program. He shall be your liaison."

Complete confusion covered Davy's face. "Liaison, ma'am?"

"Good heavens, haven't they told you anything? Perhaps this meeting will not be concluded as efficiently as I had hoped." Mrs. Kirby dropped gracelessly into a chair. Her appearance was oddly all of one note, Trevor thought, with her hair, eyes, and dress the same color of dull brown. But he supposed such blandness could prove useful in her line of work.

"We do know that the Volya originated in the University," Trevor said, sitting once again too, with his intrusion into the conversation earning him a look of profound gratitude from Davy. "But our understanding was that during this visit Davy would pose as the Queen's private message boy."

"And so he shall," Mrs. Kirby said. "Cooper, as his name suggests, is most thoroughly English and presented himself to the University as a visiting professor from Cambridge, which on one level is precisely what he is. But alas, the Russian universities are like everything else in Russia – insular, suspicious, and riddled with ceremony. Despite Professor Cooper's stellar academic credentials, or perhaps because of them, it has taken him two years to gain the position of assistant to a professor named Tomasovich." She paused, as if to give them time to assimilate her barrage of information. "Tomasovich is a mentor to the students in the Volya, for his field of expertise is Marx and the Communist Manifesto. I assume you are all familiar with the Communist Manifesto."

"Of course we are," Emma said quickly. At least she was. The file marked Unofficial History had been full of it. For the benefit of the others, especially the horrified Davy, she gave a brief summary. "It advocates a completely egalitarian society and thus the overthrow of all existing governments. In this case, I presume the emphasis is on overthrowing the tsar."

Mrs. Kirby nodded, tossing Emma a look of grudging respect. "Tomasovich can hardly advocate revolution from his lectern, but he comes close, and Cooper, who poses as a communist sympathizer, has successfully gained the trust of both the professor and the young members of the Volya. He is prepared to introduce Davy as a student he knew back in Cambridge who is also sympathetic to their cause."

"You're suggesting that our Davy is to infiltrate the Volya?" Trevor said in true disbelief.

"Of course. Cooper is older than the boys, separated from them by both age and his position as an instructor. But this lad before us seems quite the proper sort, does he not? If they believe him to be a British comrade, they shall perhaps more readily confide in him."

"And why would they talk openly to a complete stranger come from a country they most likely despise?" Trevor asked. The idea not only sounded mad, but it could place Davy in the most extraordinary sort of danger.

"Two reasons. Cooper is an accepted adjunct to the group and he will vouch for him. Secondly, the Russians brag. They can't help themselves." Mrs. Kirby took off her glasses, immediately stripping a decade from her appearance, and once again looked at Davy. "All you have to do, my young friend, is claim that your fellows back in England are cowardly and slow to action, nothing at all like the true revolutionaries of St. Petersburg, and then sit back and let the Russians tell you everything they know. The whole nation falls to flattery, especially if you contrast them favorably with the rest of Europe."

"But how am I to pass a university student?" Davy protested. "I barely made it through my primaries."

"I assure you that is not a problem," Mrs. Kirby said. "Cooper reports that his Russian students speak English quite well, but certainly not well enough to notice any nuances or errors in grammar that might betray your class."

It was a slap, but Davy took it without flinching. "Nonetheless," he said with dignity, "it seems that Tom would be better suited for this assignment."

The same thought had occurred to Tom. "We had no idea we were expected to infiltrate a revolutionary group," he said to Mrs. Kirby, with the sort of smile which generally won him ground with women of any age or temperament back in London. "It seems a lot to put solely onto Davy's shoulders. Perhaps your spy, this Cooper chap, could claim to know two students —"

"Elliott Cooper most certainly is not a spy," Mrs. Kirby snapped. "The word implies an ongoing conflict between two nations and Russia and Great Britain are of course friends and allies. Cooper is...an observer. He listens and takes notes and reports to the Crown what he learns." She frowned and replaced her glasses. "'Spy' is a crude word, and one that no proud Englishman is willing to claim. And as for your duties," she added, with a swift look to Tom, "you are the medical student posturing yourself as a doctor, are you not?"

"I suppose I am," Tom said coolly.

"Then I have a quite different sort of challenge for you," she said. "One involving such a personal and delicate matter that I trust you all will forgive me for not sharing it with the rest of the group. Shall you and I meet privately tomorrow to discuss the particulars?"

"I most eagerly anticipate the event," Tom said, turning to consider the clock on the mantle and trying to figure the difference in time between St. Petersburg and London. It was not yet a civilized hour to pour a cocktail in either city, but surely under the circumstances he could be forgiven for requesting something more bracing than tea.

"Emma Kelly," Mrs. Kirby continued briskly, for she was evidently immune to sarcasm and as deaf to conversational nuance as the Russian students she had mocked. "I take it your turf in this particular battle is the grand ballroom?"

"Yes. I am to be instructed in the waltz by a man named Konstantin Antonovich."

"Something is up with that one," Mrs. Kirby said. "Keep your eyes sharp. And learn what you can about another of his students, this petite little doll of a woman named Tatiana Orlov. She was there when they found the bodies of the ballet dancers and for some reason she felt compelled to disturb the tranquility of the Grand Duchess with the theory they had been murdered."

"But they had been murdered, had they not?" Trevor asked.

"Almost certainly, but how would she know this? And why would she care? There was no reason for her to have been present at the investigation and even less reason for her to have engaged the Grand Duchess in conversation. I don't like the Orlov woman. I don't trust her. Oh, and her husband is a member of the tsar's private guard." Here Mrs. Kirby broke off and her face twisted with regret as she turned to Trevor and Rayley. "The private guard is the one area of the palace in which we have made no particular progress in our efforts to gather information. But perhaps now that the two of you are here and posing as Scotland Yard, we can rectify that oversight."

"We aren't posing as Scotland Yard," Rayley said sharply. In her systematic efforts to insult them all equally, Mrs. Kirby appeared to be a bit of a communist herself. "We are Scotland Yard."

"And now we have a question for you," Trevor said quickly, before his friends could all rise as a group to maul the woman. She was inordinately tactless, but then again so was Ella. Did Russia coarsen women, he wondered, or was it that only the boldest of them ventured into this vast and incomprehensible land in the first place? If it were the latter, then the meek little Alix was in trouble. He could scarcely imagine the young girl he had met on the yacht functioning in this world which seemed, even in the first hours, one of the most chaotic places he had ever seen.

"I shall enlighten you if I can," Mrs. Kirby replied, her tone clearly indicating she preferred asking questions to answering them.

"Is the Grand Duchess Ella in danger?"

The question, while being both the simplest and the most obvious one he could have asked, seemed to catch the woman off her guard. She sat for a moment staring down into her own lap.

"Her husband," she finally said, "is not affectionate."

Well, that was certainly an interesting tidbit of information, but Trevor failed to see how it applied to the matter at hand.

"You mean he doesn't value her?" Rayley ventured. For if Serge saw Ella as a mere trophy or as some sort of necessary diplomatic compromise, this could be good news. Victoria's granddaughter might be more willing to flee her marriage than she appeared on the surface.

"As I have written to the Queen, he is rumored to be a man of curious tastes," Mrs. Kirby went on, actually blushing, which caused Rayley and Trevor to exchange yet another pointed look. Good God, they both seemed to be thinking, are we back in Paris again?

"And you believe that the Queen understood what you meant by that phrase?" Rayley asked. Victoria may well have thought that the term "curious tastes" referred to the man's butterfly collection or a passion for harpsichord music.

"I cannot say."

"So the marriage is possibly in danger," Trevor said slowly. "Which could be pertinent in the long run. But what I am asking you now is if you have any reason, any reason at all, to believe that Ella's life may likewise be in danger."

"Of course not," Mrs. Kirby said staunchly, once again rising to her feet, this time to indicate that their extraordinary briefing session was finally at its end. "The Russians will always be an eternal mystery to the British mind - prone to violence and hostage to the sort of emotions which leave us mercifully untouched. But they would never harm an Englishwoman, and certainly not the Queen's granddaughter. Even they would stop short of that."

Chapter Nine

The Streets of St. Petersburg

June 19, 1889

10:40 AM

"Where are we going?" Alix asked Nicky. The rumblings of the carriage were so loud that she was forced to all but shout the words, which was unfortunate. She wished to appear feminine, dignified, and remote, not like a child shrieking questions.

She had journeyed six days and nearly two thousand miles to see him, but it had taken nearly as much effort to arrange this brief bit of time alone. Or at least relatively alone, for Emma and a stern-looking guard were wedged on the bench at the back of the carriage, staring straight ahead, while Alix and Nicky sat facing each other on the red velvet seats at the front. With a chaperone and a guard in attendance, and a noise level more suitable to a bull fight than a courtship, it was not the most perfect setting for romance, but a girl must seize her chances in whatever form they are offered.

"I am taking you to the place where my grandfather was killed," Nicky shouted back, with what appeared to be a reassuring nod. Or perhaps he was merely being jostled by the movement of the carriage.

Emma could not help but overhear this exchange, and Nicky's planned destination struck her as a most improbable choice. She peered out the window at the passing scenery, which was a jumble of people, animals, vehicles from various centuries, and shops, the chaotic nature of the city evident as once. There were all manner of citizens standing in the street, quite heedless of traffic, as well as others who were sitting squat on the sidewalks, smoking, drinking, and conversing. The carriage had slowed in acknowledgement of an inconveniently placed cart and the rattling inside diminished to the degree that she could more easily hear the rest of the conversation between Nicky and Alix.

"My grandfather was a good man," Nicky was saying. "I want to be a good man."

"But you are a good man," Alix said.

The remark must have pleased him, for he flushed, but he evidently had more to get off his slender chest.

"The last time we had a ball at the palace," he said, "it was the birthday of one of the girls who had been invited. Everyone wanted to dance with her. All the men, I mean. Of course it was the men who wanted to dance with her."

Alix nodded politely, as if this were a perfectly logical sequence of thought, to move from stories of ancestral murder to recollections of the latest grand ball.

"And so I lined up with the others to take my turn," Nicky said, "and later my father berated me."

Alix notably swallowed and Emma became abruptly aware that she was gaping at the two young lovers and turned her gaze back to the street. It was terribly wrong that they could not even have this brief exchange – nonsensical as it seemed to be – without witnesses, but then again she supposed that royalty never has true privacy and neither Alix nor Nicky seemed embarrassed by the presence of outsiders. To his credit, the guard wasn't eavesdropping at all, but was rather focused on the action outside his own window, where the potato cart had now overturned and the vendor was waving at the carriage to wait while he scooped up his wares from the cobblestone street.

"Why did he berate you?" Alix asked.

The guard is worried, Emma thought, sensing more than seeing the tension which moved throughout the man's body. The overturned cart could be a ruse, some way to disrupt the progress of this grand carriage with the Romanov eagle painted so conspicuously on its side.

"For standing in line with the others," Nicky said. "Papa told me that the future tsar of Russia does not wait for anything. That if I am going to rule a great land that I must learn to take what I want. He said I should have walked directly up to the girl and claimed her, pulled her from the other men and led her to the dance floor."

The carriage began to move. Slowly, and swaying unevenly as it crushed the heaps of potatoes still in the street. Emma watched the infuriated face of the vendor slide from view as they passed.

"Why do you tell me this?" asked Alix.

Yes, thought Emma, shifting slightly as the guard settled back in the seat, why do you tell her this?

"Not to make you jealous, my love," Nicky said quickly, leaning towards Alix, bringing his head closer to hers. "It was a special day for the girl and I was simply trying to show her courtesy. I don't even recall her name. I tell you this story only so you understand that I wish to be a tsar in the manner of my grandfather, and not my father. I wish to bring back something of the Winter Palace I remember as a boy, a place of elegance and compassion."

Elegance and compassion, Emma thought. Two unlikely qualities to mention in the same breath and it seemed, when one thought of it, that when elegance and compassion came together it added up to nothing more than basic good manners. How extraordinary that Nicky would so willingly confess that his father's court lacked them.

"And what I most need is a partner in this quest," Nicky added, his body still straining toward that of Alix. "I have prayed daily to God to bring me such a woman."

All in all it was a strange appeal for a young man to deliver to the girl he loved, Emma thought. No declaration of affection, no flattery or persuasion, and certainly not an attempt at an embrace. Sitting across from each other on the red cushions, it looked as if Nicky and Alix were playing chess, and they were, in a way. It was her move now.

Alix might have found this to be a rather passionless sort of proposal, but, on the other hand, Emma supposed Nicky's words might just as easily have warmed her heart. They were if nothing else a bold declaration that Nicky was taking her seriously as a potential consort, and Alix was by nature so solemn and bound to duty that she might actually be charmed by a rendezvous which began with a visit to the scene of an assassination. Certainly no one could accuse Nicholas Romanov of trying to misrepresent the challenges of his situation. It would be Alix's situation too if she opted to be his wife, although Emma was still not entirely sure what form that Nicky's elegant and compassionate empire would take. He could be speaking of bringing back the sort of reforms his martyred grandfather had sought for the serfs, or he might have been merely planning to reconfigure the dance protocol for royal balls. Either way, his words had made one thing quite clear: Nicky resented and feared his father as much as the rest of Russia.

Alix had not yet answered.

"This is it," Nicky said abruptly as they rolled toward a bridge. "The very place where my grandfather was struck down."

"And are we to pause at the spot?" Emma quietly asked the guard. "To allow the tsesarevich and the princess to pay their respects?"

He did not turn away from the window to look at her as he answered, his shoulder so twisted that she could barely see past it to the pale gray world beyond.

"This carriage makes no stops," he said.

The Streets of St. Petersburg

10:53 AM

Had Emma crooked her neck a little further she might have noticed, at a cafe sidewalk on the far side of the infamous bridge, Davy Mabrey sitting with his cap pulled low over his forehead, deep in conversation with the man named Elliott Cooper, the professorial assistant with ties to the Volya.

"This is a significant place in the city," Cooper was saying, gesturing toward the bridge. "I've always found it odd that the lads would choose to meet so close to the spot where Alexander II was killed, but they're strangely sentimental for a group of revolutionaries. Or strangely superstitious is perhaps more like it."

Davy studied the bridge, which looked precisely like the seven others they had crossed on their journey from the university to this workaday part of the city and took a cautious sip of his coffee. Turkish, Cooper had called it, and it was black and bitter on his tongue. "But that was better than eight years ago, wasn't it, Sir?"

"True, but they still look upon it as their finest hour." While Davy had been taking in impressions of his surroundings, Cooper had been taking impressions of Davy and he added, "You shall pass well enough as a former student from my time teaching in a British boarding school."

"Good to hear that you think so. Mrs. Kirby said my class was evident and then went on to say not to worry, that the Russian lads wouldn't be able to tell the difference."

"Our very dear Mrs. Kirby," Cooper said, blowing on his coffee. "She is quite the charmer, is she not? But, as usual, her statements are correct. The British all look alike to the Russians."

Cooper was a strange man, Davy thought, while taking peripheral note that an elaborate carriage was bumping past them, with squashed bits of produce caught in its wheels and a huge gold eagle embellished on the door. Although the day was temperate and on its way to genuine warmth, Cooper was not only bundled in a scarf and jacket but had insisted on stopping for a coffee. With his chubby cheeks bearing the slight remains of a pockmarked youth, he did not look at all like Davy's notion of a university professor or indeed like any sort of authority figure at all. If the members of the Volya would not talk to him, why was everyone so sure they would confess their intentions to Davy?

"Don't worry," Cooper went on, slurping the syrupy coffee with a slight shudder and misinterpreting Davy's frown. "If I introduce you, they will accept you as anything I claim you to be. The Russians believe that their suspicion of all outside influence is what keeps them safe, but they fail to see the dangers that lie on the other side of the street. For if a boy has been taught from childhood to fear strangers, the inverse of that prejudice often makes him too quick to trust the people he thinks he knows. Membership in the Volya is less about understanding the principles of communism and more about being a friend of a friend of a friend. You look like one of the little brothers, you know, and Vlad, I suspect, will be especially quick to take you under his wing."

"The little brothers?"

"Just as it sounds," Cooper said, distractedly digging out a few coins to leave on the table. "The younger members, sponsored into the group by a relative or an older friend. Vlad is a little brother and Yulian was one too."

"Yulian Krupin, the dead boy?"

"One of them. The Volya can claim several dead boys."

"And you haven't heard anyone venture a theory on why Krupin and the girl were murdered?"

Cooper gave him a sharp look as he pushed against the table to stand. "Don't give yourself away by being too analytical," he said. "Or too Scotland Yard. In London, people die for a reason. Here, they just die."

The Winter Palace – The Private Room of the Orlovs

11:22 AM

The realization that she was pregnant had come upon Tatiana Orlov all at once, in a single wave of nausea.

She had tried, with a fair amount of success, to ignore the possibility for weeks, a self-deception made easier by the fact that she had never fully stopped bleeding. For the last two cycles, her courses had been far lighter than usual, but she had passed it off to the grief she felt about the impending summer and her enforced separation from Konstantin.

Speaking of Konstantin, he must not know. They had used precautions. Ineffective ones, as it turned out, but who was to say how he would react to this news? He might be driven to do something drastic, to assert some sort of claim on her, especially if he knew the child she carried was definitely his and not Filip's.

And speaking of Filip, he absolutely without question must not know. Two years ago, as they had traveled from their small village of Sugry to St. Petersburg, grains of rice from their hasty marriage still sticking to her hair, he had looked at her and said, "If there are no children from our union, you will understand this?"

"I will celebrate it," she had told him. "I don't like children."

And he had thrown his head back and roared with laughter, saying "We shall suit each other well, little bird."

Precisely what he had meant with the remark about the children, at the time she did not know. Perhaps his manhood had been compromised by the injuries he had suffered in his service to the tsar. This too she might have welcomed - Filip and Tatiana were scarcely a love match - but their overnight stop at an inn on the outskirts of town had repeatedly and emphatically proven that such was not the case. Filip still had his virility, but evidently not his potency, for, just has he had predicted, two years of marriage had produced no pregnancy.

Until now.

Tatiana leaned against the wall of her bathroom, pressing a towel to her mouth and staring at her splotched face in the mirror as if it were the image of a stranger. This could not be. There were ways to end the process, dangerous and bloody ways, but to find them she would need help. Help that would most likely come in the form of a servant, a servant who would have to be bribed into cooperation, and who might still talk when the deed was done. She would have to find a way to put her hands on money and then she must select someone who was utterly discreet, for if such a thing was ever –

A knock at the door.

The face in the mirror frowned at her. Whoever could that be? No one ever came to her apartments save for servants and Filip, and they certainly would not bother to knock.

Tatiana hastily splashed water from the basin on her face and smoothed her hair. She crossed through the bedroom and sitting room and into the small foyer, tossing the soiled towel in a refuse basket as she walked, and finally pulled open the door to find the Grand Duchess Ella Feodorovna standing in the hallway, her hand raised as if to knock a second time.

Stunned, Tatiana bobbed a curtsy. "Your Imperial Highness."

"You are surprised."

"Yes. I was made to understand that your family had recently arrived."

"And that is why you are surprised to find me here?" Ella inquired with a twist of her mouth. "Because you expected me to be with my British family? I assure you that no one has noticed my absence. Granny is locked away with her papers - she works every day, you know. Being a monarch, and not a consort, must be a terribly tedious role for a woman to play. And Alix is out for a carriage ride with Nicky."

"Congratulations."

"Are my motives that obvious?"

Tatiana gripped the doorframe, suddenly hit with another wave of queasiness, but through sheer force of will she managed to quell it. "I meant no disrespect, Your Imperial Highness. I can only imagine it would bring you great pleasure to have a sister living in the palace."

"Indeed it shall. Might I be allowed to enter your rooms?"

"Oh yes," Tatiana said, jerking back. What was wrong with her? How could she leave the Grand Duchess standing in the hall while she weaved on her feet like a drunkard, clutching both sides of the doorframe? "Please do enter. And please, would you like to sit?"

The smile still playing around her full lips, Ella circled the small sitting room before electing to perch herself on the tallest chair. Tatiana frantically glanced about, seeing her cast off robe tossed across another seat, a pair of Filip's boots in the corner, the remnants of breakfast still on the tray.

"I would of course welcome a match between my sister and my nephew," Ella said smoothly, as if she had not noticed the disarray of the room. "And I have hopes that any opposition to their union will melt away when the Russian side of the family finally manages to throw their welcoming dinner for the British side. As of now, the plans are for Friday evening. The summer solstice. The longest day of the year. It is shockingly late, waiting three days after their arrival to formally welcome guests, but you know how they are."

The use of the term "they" was telling. Tatiana felt like a perpetual outsider within the Winter Palace, but it was a surprise to hear that the Grand Duchess felt equally disenfranchised. Surprising too that she would confide anything at all suggesting a riff between the British and Russian factions of her family. But surely none of this was what had brought Ella to Tatiana's doorstep, to a part of the palace so removed from her own apartments.

As if reading her thoughts, Ella reached into a satchel she had wedged beside her on the chair and said. "We are alone, I presume."

"Yes."

"Excellent. There is something I wish you to see." Her graceful white hands withdrew a file from the satchel and then a square paper from the file. Moving to accept it, Tatiana saw it was a photograph.

"What do you make of it?"

Just as expected, it was the photograph Ella had taken on the morning the bodies had been found. Tatiana studied it. Considering the distance from the balcony to the floor, the images were quite clear.

"The knife," Ella prompted impatiently.

"Clamped in the girl's hand, just as we noticed and commented upon."

"Indeed. And does the shape of the blade look familiar?"

"Curved and long. The handle is not–"

Tatiana broke off, horrified. How could she have failed to notice this earlier, on the morning she had gone to the ballroom? It seemed she was failing to notice any number of things of late, as if her famously clever mind had deserted her just when she needed it most. But from the angle the camera had taken, it was obvious that the knife in the dead girl's hand was most unusual, a weapon which was in fact designed to draw notice to itself, to attract the attention of someone sitting even in the highest tiers of the theater.

"It is his, is it not?" Ella asked, her tone indicating she well knew the answer.

Tatiana looked down into Ella's face. The photograph in her hand was trembling. "Anyone in the theater could have gained access to that knife."

It was true. The props used in the theatricals were not locked away. Konstantin had even remarked upon it their last time together, that he couldn't find his gypsy costume, that it was likely lost somewhere in the laundry. If the costume had been taken, then the knife certainly might have gone missing too. And while most of the knives and swords and pistols used in the entertainments were fakes, the long curved dagger of Konstantin's gypsy costume was the real thing. At the climactic moment of one especially vigorous scene, he was expected to climb a rigging of an improvised ship and use it to release a flag. Everyone involved with the performances for the Tchaikovsky ball knew this – knew that the curved knife carried by the gypsy king was both dangerous and commissioned to Konstantin Antonovich.

"Marriage is very difficult, is it not?" Ella said, fiddling carelessly with the edge of her glove.

Tatiana only could look at her mutely.

"When one is a girl, just on the brink, you hear the older women talk of the necessity of compromise, but of course at that time you have no way of understanding what they mean," Ella continued with a low, soft voice. "And by the time one understands the true nature of these compromises, it is too late. You are trapped and must seek solace wherever you can, even in the most improbable places. I believe it was Alexandre Dumas who said that the chains of wedlock are so heavy that it takes two to carry them, and sometime three."

Was this meant as a joke? As a threat? Tatiana forced a weak smile. Ella did not smile back, but rather pulled off her glove and considered the pale gold ring on her left hand. "You care for him. That much is obvious."

"Yes, Your Imperial Highness."

"As do I, which is why no one must know this picture exists. The man who developed it is disinterested. He develops many pictures for me, roses from the gardens, the family at ease, that sort of thing. It is unlikely he will remember this one."

Tatiana blinked but said nothing. She thought it was quite likely the man would remember this particular picture, murdered bodies being intrinsically more interesting than roses and photographs of families at ease.

"And Cynthia Kirby is sworn to secrecy on the matter," Ella continued. "Other than that, you and I are the only ones who know it exists, so as of this moment, it does not." With a theatrical flourish of her own, Ella tore the picture once, then again, and stood to toss the pieces into in the same woven basket which held the cloth Tatiana had used to clean away the traces of her nausea.

So this is how the powerful dispose of inconvenient facts, Tatiana thought. They rip them, place them in a basket, and believe that this act alone is enough to make the truth disappear. Perhaps they are right. Suddenly weak again, she pressed her fingers to her lips and weaved slightly on her feet.

"Why are you so pale?" Ella asked, turning toward her. The question was accusatory in tone, as if Tatiana's continued obvious distress was a challenge to Ella's ability to manage the situation.

"Begging your pardon, Your Imperial Highness, but there were many members of the guard present when you took that photograph. Any one of those men might remember the event and inquire after the resultant image."

"The guard was more than willing to dismiss the murders as a double suicide," Ella said with a shrug. "I don't anticipate trouble from them."

"But the person who did this…who used Konstantin's knife and then left it in the dead girl's hand. It was a very direct effort to draw attention to him, is it not?"

"Indeed, the most obvious of clues, which the men cleaning up the crime nonetheless managed to ignore."

"This person must be furious that his plan has failed. That he left, as you say, the most obvious of clues, and they still were not noticed."

For the first time Ella hesitated. "Do you have any idea how our boy might have made an enemy such as this?"

"No," Tatiana said.

"For you know what we are on the verge of suggesting, do you not?"

Tatiana shook her head. She desperately wished to sit before her legs gave way, but it was impossible to do so with Ella still on her feet.

"What we are suggesting," Ella continued, "is that there is someone within this palace who is so cruel that he will kill two innocent dancers simply to pin the crime on his true enemy, which is Konstantin. But it appears this person has failed. The bodies have been carted away with only the most perfunctory of examinations and the weapon, while presumably being stored somewhere, has to date attracted no attention at all. No one within the guard has cared enough to notice that the knife in question was part of Konstantin's gypsy costume and not the plaster cast knife used in the Romeo and Juliet scene. So it would appear that this elaborate message, this switching of the props, has gone undetected and thus our villain's plans to incriminate Konstantin have fallen to ruin." Ella frowns. "But one thing does bother me."

"That whoever is determined to destroy Konstantin might try again?"

Ella responded to this rather obvious suggestion with surprise. "Yes, I suppose there is that chance. But I was about to say that my grandmother has traveled from London with two bodyguards, and that the British police are quite different from the Russians. Bulldogs, every last one of them. I would imagine that if Granny's Detective Welles and her Detective Abrams gained possession of that picture their eyes would go to the knife at once. But of course…they won't."

"Mrs. Kirby might not tell them that the photograph exists?"

"Why ever should she do such a thing? Or talk to them at all? She works for me."

"And she is loyal to you?"

"Of course she is loyal to me. All my servants are loyal to me," Ella said, her head jerking with exasperation. "And whatever is wrong now? I have offered you every assurance and yet you remain so pale."

"I am unwell, Your Imperial Highness."

Ella tilted her chin. "What sort of unwell?"

Chapter Ten

The Winter Palace – The Premiere Ballroom

June 19, 1889

3:45 PM

"You fight me."

"I promise you that I do not."

The dance instructor dropped his hands from Emma's waist and stepped back so that they stood for a moment in silence, each considering the other. She had never met a man quite like him. Eurasian, the term was. His straight black hair, pulled taut and knotted at the nape of his neck, certainly gave him an Oriental look, as did his high cheekbones and deep set brown eyes. But his height and pale skin were undeniably Russian. He told her he came from Siberia, that part of the map which lay between the finely-detailed countries of Europe and the blank empty expanse of Mongolia. His features, like the land, were a bit of a compromise.

He frightened her. Or perhaps it was the waltz itself. When Emma told Trevor she knew how to waltz, she had anticipated a dance quite different from this. The English version of a waltz involved standing straight up, with the man bracing the woman at arm's length, the two of them moving at a slow and measured pace through the shape of a box. She had not been in the ballroom of the Winter Palace for ten minutes before she realized that what Konstantin expected of her was something else indeed. Something swift, whirling, unpredictable in form and powerful in execution. The Russians claimed their women like they claimed everything else – hips thrust forward and in the pace of a gallop.

"The imperial family," Konstantin said, pointing to the balcony level, "sits there. Everything we do is to entertain them, so your face must be tilted upward. You know what this means?"

"I must lean backwards."

A displeased toss of the head. "This is a myth, you know. The myth of the waltz. The woman does not actually lean back. It is a trick of the eye. I will show you. Come here."

Emma stepped toward Konstantin, wondering why she was so nervous. No one was there to witness her clumsiness. They were the only two people in the theater.

He took her hand in his and pulled her close. "Flex your knees," he said, "and push your hips into me. No, not straight in, not like that. You stand a little to the left of me. It is so we will not knock knees or step each on the other one's feet." Emma bent her knees and pushed her hips toward him. It was a most extraordinary position to be in and they were having an even more extraordinary conversation.

"Now," he said, "the woman remains to the left of the man during the entire dance to accommodate his sword, which hangs on his own left hip. I do not have a sword, but try to imagine." He looked down at her, his eyes narrowing a bit over the bridge of his substantial nose. "If it is done correctly, there's a bit of a hollow there, just right for you to slip into. No. Closer. You must not be so afraid. It is all very natural, is it not?"

Was this natural? If so, why had she never felt it before?

"So you see," he said, when she had finally edged herself close enough for his satisfaction. "We are not bending the tops of our bodies away from each other, we are pushing the lower bodies closer to create that illusion. Keep your arms high, if you please. I do not want a drooping flower." He turned her slightly to the left and then to the right but did not move his legs, which was a relief. Their four feet were so close that she was afraid if she moved even one of hers, she would topple.

"Are you comfortable?" he asked.

"I am miserable."

"Good," he says. "Do not straighten your legs."

"I don't think you understand. I have just arrived here. I am a stranger in your country and entered into this pageant at the last minute, as some sort of courtesy to the Queen. No one expects me to be good."

"Will you be dancing with me?"

"Evidently."

"Then I expect you to be good. If you have finished talking, we shall now attempt to waltz."

We are all but fused, Emma thought. It is impossible to clang against each other when we start out so close, and I won't lose him in the turn, and there's some comfort in that, I suppose. They had only been working together for a few minutes and already she could tell her back would be sore when she climbed into bed tonight, and her legs exhausted from keeping her knees so unnaturally forward, wedged between his.

But when Konstantin began to move, Emma could see at once the wisdom of this strange position he had bullied her into, for their turns felt simultaneously easier and more dramatic. Was he pleased that she had managed to hold on, to stay with him through these initial revolutions?

Three turns in, he stopped. "Don't drop your chin."

"I did not drop my chin."

"You looked at me," he said. "You must not. Not to me or to the other couples on the floor or those in the audience. Look to the ceiling."

"The ceiling? How will I know where I am going?"

"You are a woman. You do not need to know where you are going. I will take you there." His narrow eyes narrowed more. "You do not trust me?"

Trust him? She did not know him. The women who trust strange men, she thought, those who close their eyes and lean back…they are carried away on any number of dark waves, some of them never to be seen again. Her sister Mary's face flashed through her mind, unbidden as it always was.

But he had already accused her of fighting him, so it would be pointless to argue further. Not in the grand ballroom of the Winter Palace in Russia of all places, when she was so very out of her element and so far from home. She was here to protect the Queen and her granddaughters, after all, not to argue with some strange man about how to waltz. With a sigh that Emma hoped Konstantin would take as evidence of compliance, not exasperation, she lifted her arms as wide as they would reach, tilted her hips towards him, and raised her chin.

As if satisfied by her surrender, he began again, the turns wider and more vigorous. For a moment she was dizzied, but quickly realized that it helped if she directed her gaze toward something specific with every turn. Fortunately, the top of the theater had no end of things to attract the eye. Each corner of the room held a stage set, presumably for the upcoming ball. A peasant cottage in one, looking like something from a child's fairy tale book and nearly complete. A balcony in the next, presumably for the lost scenes from Romeo and Juliet, and then a half-finished ship with a mast and riggings, and in the final corner there was a canopy of green branches that were evidently the beginning of some sort of forest. These four environments, each so strange to behold, gave Emma something to spot as she turned, a way to orient where she was on the enormous floor. Cottage, balcony, ship, and forest.

For a few minutes, it worked. And then he began to take her into a series of reverses which scrambled the sequence she had come to expect, and she began to lose her form. Her hand dropped from its dainty perch on his shoulder and dug desperately in. The chin dropped as well and she turned toward him, her eyes beseeching. He stopped.

"I am sorry," she said.

"Why do you not trust men?"

"What do you mean? Of course I trust men."

"Close your eyes."

"What?"

"You look around the room with your head swinging back and forth, trying to guess where we are going next. If you close your eyes, you will trust me." He smiled as they began to move again and Emma allowed her eyes to flutter closed, just as he had asked.

"For I know something about women, you see," he whispered, bringing his mouth close to her ear. "They only trust men when they find they have no other choice."

The Streets of St. Petersburg

4:35 PM

Davy and Vlad were sitting at the precise same café where he had braved coffee with Elliott Cooper that morning, although this time the drink at hand was even more potent. They should call this place the Café of the Revolution, he mused, but perhaps it was really not so strange that the members of the Volya would choose to congregate there both before and after their meetings. Humans were habituated and self-limiting creatures, Davy had noted. Even in a large city with innumerable options, they tended to return to the same places over and over.

"Do you have brothers?" Vlad inquired.

"Three."

"You are lucky. A couple of spares."

"You'll forgive me if I do not see it that way."

"My brother Sasha was killed in the revolution," Vlad said without emotion. "But I suppose Cooper told you that."

"He did."

"I am not surprised. This is the first thing that anyone ever knows about me. That I am the brother of a martyr."

Davy sat back as a serving girl approached and plopped, without comment or ceremony, two squat glasses of what was apparently vodka before them. Vlad had not ordered them, at least not in any manner Davy could identify, so he could only assume that promptly delivered glasses of unornamented vodka were standard procedure at the Café of the Revolution, along with the sort of short harsh cigarettes that Vlad was now lighting.

"A man needs brothers," Vlad said.

"I noticed the members of the Volya use the term 'brother' as often as 'comrade,'" Davy said. "At least you have Gregor and the others there."

"I meant real brothers," Vlad said, cutting his eyes at Davy as he took the first draw on the cigarette. "Gregor…trivializes me."

"He told me that since you had lost Sasha and he had lost Yulian, that he considered the two of you to be-"

"Shit. Pure horse shit. You saw the way it was as well as anyone. I raise my hand to make a suggestion and he sends me to check the lock, or bring him cigarettes, or on whatever other senseless errand has struck his fancy. Speaking of which, will you join me in the smoke?" He sent the paper package of cigarettes, with a match tucked inside, spinning across the table and Davy deftly, if somewhat reluctantly, caught it.

"Older men often play that game with younger men," Davy said, striking the match against the heel of his boot. In the nine months he had been with Scotland Yard, Davy had developed his own brand of interrogation and had found that the best way to get someone to confess to something was to first make a confession of your own. "There are two men ranked above me where I work and there are times when I think they see me as comedy, the way the actors bring a dog or donkey on stage during a play." He brought the match to his cigarette and puffed, pulling in a wave of smoke so dark and acrid that he coughed and grabbed for the vodka, which only turned his cough into a strangled sputter.

Vlad watched this scene with the slightest hint of amusement. "You are not accustomed to smoking? Or drinking?"

"Not accustomed to smoking these or drinking that," Davy gasped when he caught his breath.

"Nothing in Russia ever goes down quite as smooth as one expects," Vlad said. He had a thin face, with a pointed chin. A look of hunger played about his features, and Davy suspected that his brother's death had not turned him into the malcontent creature he now was, but had rather merely accentuated his inborn nature. Vlad Ulyanov had most likely been unhappy even back in the sand pile, a sniveling disgruntled toddler who always wanted whatever toy lay in the hands of another.

Nonetheless, Davy's story seemed to have earned him some ground for Vlad was now looking at him with sharpened interest. "These men who trivialize you, they also work for the Queen?"

Davy nodded, glancing at an earthenware pot to his left which held a clump of geraniums. The next time the man was distracted, he would have to toss his vodka into it, for if he consumed too much he suspected he would find it impossible to keep his senses. "They found me doing a nothing job in the streets," he said. "A less than nothing job. Trained me, gave me my first promotion. Are good to me, by all measures."

"And they never quite let you forget it."

The tone of voice was sardonic, but Davy recognized the genuine emotion behind it. This shaming sense of having been the last one invited to the party, allowed in as an afterthought, and expected to be perennially grateful for the chance. Yes, he too understood well enough how it felt to be the least among men but loyalty would not allow him to demonize Rayley or Trevor, not even to further gain Vlad's confidence.

"They do not always seem to welcome my ideas," he conceded. "But they have given me some chances. At times I feel they have even placed me in situations that are somewhat out of my depth."

"Out of your depth? As a messenger boy?"

Well, that was a bit of a error, was it not? Davy had never totally believed Mrs. Kirby and Elliott Cooper when they had blithely claimed that the Volya would accept the notion that a lad who was wealthy enough to have attended boarding school would then accept the paltry job of being a messenger boy. Not to mention the other incongruity, that he was expected to pass as a political revolutionary in service to the Queen. He would have to divert the conversation at once or risk making an even greater error. Someone – was it Rayley? – had once told Davy that the secret of a successful lie was to keep it as close as possible to the truth.

With a short, shallow puff of the cigarette, Davy leaned back in his chair, consciously mimicking Vlad's own pose, and said, "Messenger boys see many things in the course of a routine day. My work has taken me from the homes of the most wealthy and privileged into the most desperate parts of the city."

"And witnessing this divide is what has turned you into a revolutionary?"

"You might say that," Davy said. "I remember one afternoon I saw a woman, maybe just a girl, digging around in the muck for the core of a fallen apple and then the next place I was sent was a kitchen so large and fine that there was a cook going through a great sack of apples, tossing aside any with the slightest mark. You know, any flaw which meant they were not good enough for milady's daily tart. I asked if I could take the ones she threw away and she laughed at me and said yes. So I went back to the street where I had started, but the girl was gone."

Vlad's face revealed nothing. "What did you do with the apples?"

"Gave them to the next person who passed. Everyone in that particular street is likely hungry."

"You never saw the girl in the mud again."

"No."

Vlad shrugged. "Such is revolution. The fruits, if you will pardon my pun, never seem to fall to those whose needs prompted the fight in the first place, only to the strangers who come behind." He glanced down at the empty glasses. "So shall we drink again? To the girl in the mud, wherever she may be?"

"Indeed," said Davy, raising his glass. "To the girl in the mud."

The Winter Palace – The Grand Ballroom

5:02 PM

When Emma emerged into the hall after her dance lesson, she found Tom approaching from the other direction. "What are you doing here?" she whispered.

"Sleuthing, of course," he said, whispering too, but loudly, as if for the stage, and he finished off the pantomime with a bit of an exaggerated tiptoe toward her. "The laudable Mrs. Kirby agreed to meet me in the theater at five and describe exactly how the crime scene was situated, although at this point I imagine it will be more of a history lesson than anything forensically useful. And apparently there is some confidence she must share as well, something so dark and dreadful it's meant for my ears only. How was your first lesson?"

"Most unusual," she said. She hesitated a second, but it was Tom, after all. They kept no secrets, at least none of this sort. "He asked me to close my eyes."

"While you were dancing?"

"Of course while I was dancing. He said I was struggling against him when I should be following. And you know, it did help."

"Did you like it? This sense of being overpowered by a faceless stranger?"

"Oh, stop looking at me like that, and stop smirking. You turn everything into a joke and I really want to do well in this waltz. Not disgrace England and the Queen and that sort of rot."

"So you liked it."

"I didn't dislike it."

"It reminds one of the Scottish rapes, you know."

"I'm sure I don't know."

"The crime we were discussing at the last meeting of the Murder Games Club. You truly don't remember? Of course that assailant used a scarf to disorient his victims and you seem to have been an enthusiastic participant in your own self-blinding."

"The rapes in Scotland," Emma said, tilting her head. "That seems a year ago doesn't it, and not just last week? But I was hardly Konstantin's victim and it didn't make me disoriented. In fact, if anything I was uniquely oriented, more so than I've felt for some time." She cut her eyes to his. "When did you say you were supposed to meet Mrs. Kirby?"

"Five," said Tom, looking over his shoulder. "And I'm rather surprised not to find her here already. She struck me as the punctual type. But perhaps she's inside." He pulled against the heavy door. "Come along, I wish to be introduced to this Siberian with his mysterious methods of instruction."

"I'm sure he's gone," Emma said, hoping that this was true as she walked through the door. For some reason she was not eager for Tom and Konstantin to meet. "He said I was his last lesson of the day. Here's the ballroom," she added, with a half-hearted sort of gesture.

"I never would have deduced as much."

"But it's huge, is it not?"

"Everything in this country is huge." Tom walked to the middle of the dance floor and made a slow circle, taking in the series of balconies, the imperial boxes, the half-finished sets in the corners of the performance level, the orchestra pit, the marble staircase leading from the wardrobe rooms to the ballroom floor. "There are so many points from which people can enter and exit this room."

"My guess would be that the two victims at least came down the stairs," Emma said. "The performers are perhaps accustomed to entering from the second level, where the costume and props and dressing rooms are located. Konstantin both arrived and departed by that level today. They most likely do not use these lower doors, on the audience level, at all."

"I agree," said Tom. "Although Trevor would be in despair if he could hear you use so many words like 'guess' and 'perhaps' and 'most likely' all in sequence. Let us look upstairs."

"And what is our explanation if we're caught snooping around the performers' area?"

"That you forgot something after your lesson, you silly girl."

"I wouldn't have left it up here," she muttered, as they climbed the broad staircase which led to a changing room for the dancers. Adjacent to it was a prop room, larger in itself than many theaters, and then a small sitting room with any number of settees and even a small daybed.

"Not a bad situation," Tom said. "A little home away from home for the performers."

"Given what most of them have come from," Emma mused, "it's hard to imagine they'd be inclined to risk losing their position within the tsar's troupe."

"What makes you say that?"

"I don't know," she confessed. Even though they had left the ballroom, they were still whispering. "But the young ballet dancers who were killed, they were meeting here at night, were they not? Which implies a forbidden sort of liaison."

"Or just a desire for more privacy than their own rooms provided," Tom said, pushing aside a set of curtains and considering the walls of boxes behind it. "Heaven knows, this place is full of enough nooks and crannies to accommodate an army of forbidden lovers. But it makes me wonder – had they decided in advance to meet and if so, how would their killer have known their agreed-upon time and place? Or was the tryst a last minute decision, with the man perhaps luring each of them here with a note that they believed was written by the other?"

"More likely their killer overheard them planning to meet," Emma said. "It's easy to eavesdrop in this theater. The acoustics are extraordinary."

"Which implies that our murderer is part of the dance troupe," Tom said. "Or perhaps even someone in their confidence. Their own Friar Lawrence, so to speak."

"Rayley and Trevor got the pages from the police report after luncheon, did they not?"

Tom rolled his eyes. "No plural needed, darling. The report was a single page. And the police had collected no weapon, no samples of clothing, nothing at all. That's why I need to talk to the Kirby woman. At least she was at the scene before they moved the bodies and, who knows, those eagle eyes may have noticed something. Odd she still isn't here. Perhaps I should go back down and check the hall again."

"Saying you would meet her in the theater was a rather imprecise location," Emma said. "But wait a second, there's only this one last room. It appears to be costumes too, or some sort place where they do the mending and sewing…"

She had walked three steps in when she saw them. For a moment she thought they were unreal – dummies used in a play, perhaps, or dressmaker's models. And then, judging by their prone position, cast among the garments on the floor, she thought that perhaps they were dead. It was this last thought that prompted her scream and the fact that she spun on her heel, crashing directly into Tom, who had entered the room no more than a few beats behind her. But the sound roused the lovers from their distraction and they leapt apart, thus proving, even in the shadowy darkness, that they were both quite real and very much alive. Konstantin sprang to his feet instinctively, causing Emma to give another small exclamation, this one more of a yelp. Tatiana, prompted by another sort of instinct, went scrambling beneath a nearby pile of clothes, but not before catching a glimpse of the expression on Tom's face.

"We beg your pardon," he said smoothly, backing out, pulling Emma with him. She had once again closed her eyes, offering further proof of Konstantin's theories, for she followed Tom's lead without question back into the lighted prop room where they stood for a moment before bursting into a sort of muffled laughter.

"That was Konstantin," Emma said at last, wiping the nervous tears from her face.

"Truly? Your dance master? He seems uniquely qualified for his post."

"Don't you dare make a joke of this," she said. Her heart was pounding and her face was hot. She had never had cause to study a man, fully naked, except perhaps in statuary, and somehow none of it was arranged quite as she had imagined. "How will I ever be able to dance with him again after witnessing such a thing?"

"And who was the lovely lady?"

"I have no idea. Was she lovely?"

"Oh, I assure you."

"At least Mrs. Kirby wasn't with us, which would have been the only thing that could have made the situation more appalling." Emma shuddered at the thought. "She has already declared that Konstantin is up to no good. Come, we must find her and waylay her long enough to let them escape, for if she even suspects-"

"She will what?" Tom said, taking Emma's arm and leading her from the performance rooms back toward the staircase. "Mrs. Kirby has no authority over the dancers or indeed anything that happens in the palace. We must not let her haughty manner bamboozle us all into thinking she holds more sway than she does." But as they moved closer to the well-lit staircase, the look on Emma's face softened his tone. "I suppose you're right. There's no reason to give her aging eyes this particular shock, so we will intercept her, at least long enough to allow our lovers to escape."

They hurried down the staircase, Emma still flushed and Tom still chuckling, then across the broad ballroom floor to the door where they had entered. But Mrs. Kirby was not in the hallway beyond, nor in the next one they tried, nor the next. Finally they returned to the ballroom and stood in the center of the floor, slowly circling, looking at all the entrances.

"Strange," said Tom. "She was insistent that we talk in private."

"See that rope," Emma suddenly said. "Was it there before?"

"I don't know," Tom said. "But it's some sort of prop. Meant to look like part of the ship's rigging, is it not? See, they have the shape of a hull beneath it."

"It wasn't like that when I was dancing," Emma said.

"How would you know? Your eyes were closed."

"Not the whole time," she said irritably, starting toward the rope. "I was looking up at the performance level for most of the lesson. I know what was in every corner."

"Leave it be," Tom said. "You might bring a full model of a ship crashing down upon your head."

But Emma was already in the corner, looking up, frowning at a wad of fabric wedged up near the top of the stage set. It appeared to be a rolled flag, evidently meant to be unfurled when the rope was cut, but there was more there too, something else crammed beneath the shape of the hull. "Do you have a knife?"

"What are you talking about? We can't go cutting up theatrical props because something doesn't seem right to you."

"I swear to you that someone has altered this set."

"Look, Emma," Tom said, his voice lower and kinder, "you're rattled. We both are, and the others as well. We've all traveled a great distance with little preparation and come to such a different sort of place. Even Trevor has been set on edge. And now this day…this day in itself has been quite extraordinary."

"If you don't have a knife, we'll have to pull it," she said. If she went up the steps to the very top, if she stood on one of the seats… She would still be at least four inches too low. She looked at Tom expectantly.

"Very well," he said, stepping onto one of the chairs and indicating with a turn of his hand that she should move closer to the wall. "But I will pull it, certainly not cut it, so that you can behold your flag and then we shall depart this bizarre place and go take a rest. I really think that the sight upstairs –"

A single yank was enough. With the sound of an exhalation, an enormous Russian flag was released. It unfurled towards Tom and Emma's upturned faces and, halfway through the process, released the dead body of Cynthia Kirby. She dropped past them and then began to roll down the steps, her head bouncing cruelly with every increment of her descent until she at last came to rest on the edge of the dance floor, sprawled with comic gusto beneath the great lights. She was dressed as the king of the gypsies.

Chapter Eleven

The Winter Palace – the Kitchens

June 19, 1889

10:20 PM

"The cause of death is a broken neck," Tom said.

"And there is no chance it was broken during the fall to the ballroom floor?" Trevor confirmed.

"Absolutely none. For one thing, it's a clean snap right at vertebrae C2, known as the hangman's fracture, since it generally brings about instantaneous death." Tom looked up from the body of Cynthia Kirby, which was lying swaddled on a long wooden table. "Someone knew what he was doing. Also, there's bruising around the front of the throat. She was likely grabbed from behind, choked into unconsciousness, and then the neck was broken."

"Which would indicate that the killer was a man of strength," Trevor said, bent forward on his wooden stool and steadily scribbling in his notebook.

"That's one way to look at it. But it's just as important to know where to break as it is to use great force. My guess would be we're looking for someone who knows how to most efficiently dispose of a life – a former military man, a member of the guard, or a doctor, of course."

"Possibly a dancer?" Rayley ventured, from the other side of the room. "They make study of the human body too, do they not?"

"There's a thought," Tom said.

They were in a room off from the kitchen, although not in the same meat locker where the ballet dancers had been stored. Presumably Mrs. Kirby would be moved there after the autopsy, but that was a cold, dark, and airless place. For now, they were conducting their examination in a brighter room which, from the profusion of white flour around, evidently was used each morning for the making of the palace bread and pastries.

It was hardly a sterile environment for an autopsy, but under the circumstances, Trevor supposed they must take what they could get. When Rayley had asked Viktor Prakov, the bald man who headed the palace police, if they could examine Mrs. Kirby before his unit, the man had readily agreed. "Since the woman was English…" Rayley had said vaguely, which was all it had taken for Prakov to nod. Examine anything you want, seemed to be his unspoken response, just so in the end you turn her body back to us. And so they had been escorted to this distant part of the kitchen and left alone. In the larger rooms, the staff was finishing the final cleaning from the evening meal and a young maid had most considerately brought them a tray of pork sandwiches as they worked.

"Funny that a place this size doesn't have a proper morgue, isn't it, Sir?" Davy asked.

"Very odd," Trevor agreed. The Palace may function like a city, but it was a city which strained to maintain the illusion that no one within it ever died. His request to do the autopsy within the Palace infirmary had met with an abrupt refusal, as had his next suggestion, that they might conduct their exam within the woman's own bedroom. So instead Mrs. Kirby had been carried here, stripped bare among the rolling pins and ladles, then wrapped in a tablecloth. None of them had particularly liked the woman, but Trevor doubted anyone present would have wished her this ignoble end.

At least they had plenty of room. Tom was examining the body with Davy's help, as they systematically lifted each limb and section, going over it with a magnifying glass. Tom called his observations out to Trevor, who served as secretary, while Emma and Rayley stood at another table going through the woman's clothes and the boxes of her possessions, which they had snatched from her room in an effort to get hold of the evidence before the palace police. Emma had draped the gypsy costume over a chair and was studying it dubiously.

"This loop of cloth on the hip," she said. "What purpose would you guess it to serve?"

"It appears to have been designed to hold some sort of weapon," Rayley said, glancing up from a box of books and papers.

"So I thought," Emma said. "It's on the left hip where an officer wears his sword."

"The loop isn't large enough to support a sword," Rayley said. "More likely a dagger of some sort. Was there one with her when she was found?"

"I don't see anything of the sort," Emma said. "This costume is quite elaborate. Look at the way this vest ties and all the buckles on the britches. How on earth would a woman begin to know how to get into such outlandish clothing?"

"How on earth would her killer have gotten her into it so quickly is a better question," said Tom, peering into the hollows of Mrs. Kirby's left ear. "I keep thinking of the time frame."

"Spell it out for me," said Trevor, pencil in hand.

"You start, Emma," Tom said, absently, turning the corpse's head to inspect her other ear.

"My lesson with Konstantin concluded at precisely five," Emma said, folding the pants of the costume as she spoke. "I know, because we heard the chapel bells strike. He told me I was his last private lesson of the day but that I should get some rest and have something to eat, for the group rehearsals would begin at seven. At the time he and I parted company, there was no body wrapped up in the flag hanging above the pirate ship. I am certain because he was scolding me to look upward as we waltzed, so I was paying particular attention to the top of the room. There are sets located on the second level of the stage, what they call the performers' level, and one of them was this ship. I assure you that during the time I was dancing, the flag at the top of the mast was furled neatly."

"But then you closed your eyes," Tom said.

"Closed your eyes?" Rayley inquired, looking at Emma over his glasses. Judging by the number of books in the box, Mrs. Kirby had evidently been a great reader. Rayley was shaking them, one volume at a time, but so far nothing had fluttered out onto the floor.

How like Tom to say something both so embarrassing and so off the point, Emma thought, and she hastened to explain. "It hardly matters, but my dance instructor suggested that I close my eyes while we were waltzing so that I might be better able to follow. But they remained so for only a minute or two. Certainly if someone had hauled a dead body by rope to the top of the ceiling I would have heard the commotion and opened my eyes."

"I doubt the body was pulled up from the floor," Rayley said, mercifully not becoming distracted by the idea of Emma waltzing with her eyes closed. "More likely lowered from the balcony, I would guess."

"Either way, Konstantin and I would have heard it."

"You waltzed without music?" Trevor asked.

"Yes, he counted the beat. That's the way practicing often is," Emma said with authority, as if she had been taking formal dance instruction all her life. "But the point is that when I stepped out of the ballroom at a few minutes after five there was no dead body in that flag. Once I exited into the hall, I promptly met Tom, who was waiting there for Mrs. Kirby and wondering why she might be running late for their appointment."

"And from there," said Tom, who was now stooping to look into the dead woman's bloodshot eyes, "we went together back into the ballroom and did a slow circle of observation. So I can confirm Emma's claim that the body was not in its cruel position dangling from the ship's mast at just after five o'clock."

"If you could confirm my timeline, why did you make me start?" Emma said in exasperation.

"I just wanted to hear you tell everyone about how that Siberian got you to close your eyes," Tom said cheerfully, gently pushing Mrs. Kirby's own left eyelid closed. "He told her she'd be more submissive to his burly masculine will if she couldn't see, and, against all odds, our girl agreed."

"Moving on," Trevor said.

"We went up the grand staircase that connects the ballroom floor to the performance level and spent just at twelve minutes poking around the costume and prop rooms behind the curtain," Tom said. "Like Emma, I am quite certain of the time, for I looked at my pocket watch just after we found the body. Thus it seems that whoever placed Mrs. Kirby in the flag did it with an amazing rapidity, almost as if he knew that we would be coming back into the ballroom within minutes."

"Was she killed there in the theater, do you think," Davy asked. "Or killed and moved?"

"What would your guess be?" Trevor asked mildly.

"Killed and moved," Davy said promptly. "Obviously Mrs. Kirby was not going to her meeting with Tom dressed in a gypsy costume. So while he was in the hall waiting for her, she was late because she was either already dead or was being murdered at that very moment. Then the murderer dressed her as a gypsy and took her to the theater."

"Quite right," Trevor said. "Although it's nearly impossible to imagine that anyone could murder a woman, strip her of the clothes she was wearing, and then dress her in this rather complex and outlandish outfit, and still have the time to hide her body all within twelve minutes. So most likely she was already dead and dressed when Emma and Tom went up the stairs to explore the costume and prop rooms."

"The choice of the costume is bewildering," said Rayley. "It's meant as a message, obviously, the sort that would be impossible to ignore, at least if you were the person to whom it was being sent. The killer garbs the poor woman as a gypsy and rolls her in a flag, for God's sake. A flag placed in a position that is guaranteed to not only be found, but be found and released in a most spectacular fashion. What we have is the opposite of trying to conceal a murder. Our killer wished to show off his work, to turn the unveiling of a dead body into a theatrical flourish, staged for maximum dramatic impact."

"Much like the Romeo and Juliet we began with," Trevor agreed, still scribbling. "But at least there the message was clearer. Why the deuce was the Kirby woman dressed up as a man? Or a gypsy?"

"Whose costume is it?" Davy asked. "Who wears it in the show, I mean?"

"An excellent question to start with," Trevor said. "Although the answer is more likely to tell us who the message is intended to frighten rather than who sent it."

"The killer was in the room the whole time Konstantin and I were waltzing, wasn't he?" Emma said dully, still holding the shirt in her hands. She had left Rayley to contend alone with the task of going through Cynthia Kirby's worldly possessions, which was unlike her, and seemed instead singularly preoccupied with the gypsy costume, which she had now folded and refolded several times. "Hiding in the balcony just above the pirate scene with this poor woman's dead body. Waiting for us to leave. Waiting for his chance."

"Perhaps not," Rayley said, for she seemed genuinely distressed at the thought. "It is possible, of course, but it seems to me far more likely that most of the people connected to the theatricals, perhaps even many more people from all sorts of walks within the palace, knew that the dance lessons ended at five and that there was generally a lull before the group practices began. So he might have entered the ballroom from the top floor with the body, which had already been killed and dressed just as Davy and Trevor say, and believing himself to have a leisurely two hours in which to stage his grand unveiling. The idea was most likely that when any number of people were assembled for rehearsal that someone would notice the alteration in the pirate scene and pull the rope. And thus the shock of finding Mrs. Kirby's dead body would be witnessed not merely by two inconvenient foreigners poking about, but rather by the entire dance troupe, including a coterie of the imperial women and their attendants."

"Excellent," said Trevor, writing with increased fervor. "Whatever message implied in the choice of costume was meant to be delivered to someone the killer expected to be in that room during the group rehearsals at seven. Our man believes he has two hours to do his work but then is startled when Emma and Tom, without warning, enter the room and begin to explore. When they disappeared into the dressing rooms, he seized the chance to finish his task, no doubt more clumsily than he intended, and escape."

"We must examine the balcony above the ship scene," Rayley said. "If the killer waited there, whether it was for the full hour of Emma's practice or merely the few minutes she and Tom were exploring the theater, he may have left some evidence of his presence."

"That's it," Tom said, standing back. "I doubt the body has much more to tell us, at least not at this point."

"And we must talk to your Konstantin," Trevor said to Emma. "He and everyone else that was in the theater this afternoon or who might have been expected to be at the group rehearsals at seven."

"Why Konstantin?" said Emma with surprise. "I am his most perfect alibi, am I not?"

"Only if your time line is correct and the killer was hiding in the balcony between four and five," said Trevor. "I'm more inclined towards Rayley's theory that whoever intended to hang the body waited for you to leave the ballroom before beginning the task. And who knew the precise time you left the ballroom better than Konstantin? If the Kirby woman was already dead and dressed, then during those twelve minutes he could have –"

"Oh I assure you, he has a most perfect alibi for those twelve minutes as well," said Tom, matter-of-factly pulling the tablecloth over Mrs. Kirby's face.

"Is there really any need to go into that?" Emma asked.

"But don't you see, my dear? What began as your teacher's condemnation has now become his defense." Tom removed his apron and wiped his hands on it before turning to Trevor. "Because while Emma and I were exploring the costume and prop rooms we happened to come across–"

"Dear God," said Rayley.

"What is it?" said Trevor.

"The very last book in the stack," Rayley said. "I shook it and this flew out." He advanced toward Trevor, holding an object very lightly between his fingertips. It was a photograph of the dead ballet dancers.

Chapter Twelve

The Winter Palace – The Gentleman's Enclave

June 20, 1889

1:20 PM

"Would you like me to beat you with rushes?"

"I beg your pardon?"

"Bulrushes brought up from the river," Filip said. "Once the sweat begins to flow, a steady tapping helps to bring the blood to the surface of the skin and aid in the purification process. The blows are very light, of course," he added, noting Rayley's skeptical expression. "But the raising of the blood is an important part of the sauna ritual."

"Seeing as how this is my first sauna," Rayley said, "perhaps I should content myself with only the most basic sort of purification."

"Truly? Your first sauna?"

"I'm English."

"Yes, I know who you are," said Filip, holding out a beefy hand which Rayley clasped and shook in an ineffectual manner, their sweat-slicked palms sliding from each other at the first touch. "One of the queen's bodyguards, which means that you and I are in the same line of work. I similarly serve the tsar."

Rayley nodded slowly. When the invitation had come this morning suggesting that Trevor and Rayley might enjoy the services of the gentlemen's enclave, they had been temporarily flummoxed. It was undeniably an opportunity to observe a new part of palace life and also undeniably some sort of trap. The cream colored piece of paper sitting on a heavy silver tray bore no clue as to who might have sent it. A brief conference between the two men had led to the conclusion that Rayley, whose time in Paris had left him with a greater proclivity for foreign cultures, should accept the invitation while Trevor, along with Tom and Davy, explored the theater balcony where they believed Mrs. Kirby's body must have been hidden.

At the appointed hour there had been a knock at the door of their apartments and a silent servant had arrived. Rayley had followed him down a series of hallways until he had arrived in a large dressing room where the man had handed him a red silk robe and simply disappeared. It had been a strange matter indeed to strip off his gray suit and don the robe, quite uncertain what, if any, garments were meant to be left on beneath, and to venture across the broad stone floor toward the cave-like entrance of the adjoining room. A blast of hot damp air had engulfed him before he was fully over the threshold, filling the room with hisses and fogging Rayley's small round eyeglasses so thoroughly that he had been forced back into the dressing area where he pulled his spectacles off and peered nervously in the direction from which he had just come.

This was surely what the gates of hell must be like. Minus the silk robe, perhaps.

It was just then that the servant had reappeared and surprised Rayley by addressing him in English. "Steam or sauna?" he had asked.

"What is the difference?"

"Steam wet, sauna dry."

Ah, so that moist and hissing cave must have been the steam room. Anything would be better than that, and at least in the dry room he would be able to see his hand before his face.

"Take me to the sauna," Rayley said decisively, wiping his spectacles on the robe. "And would you be so kind as to tell me who sent the invitation you delivered? I am uncertain as to how I might thank my host."

But the man's English appeared to be limited to the distinction of "Steam wet, sauna dry," for he had looked at Rayley blankly, then turned and walked toward a second hallway. Rayley had little choice but to follow, which had resulted in his arrival in this place, a long and thin wooden room, the walls of which smelled quite pleasant in the manner of a cedar forest and were lined with benches. Seven or eight men were already seated, all of them alarmingly nude, causing

Rayley to wonder if the ability to see detail was really an advantage.

But when in Rome, he'd supposed, and unknotted the red robe. Due to the slick texture and elegant weight of the garment, it had fallen to the floor decisively, leaving Rayley as naked as the others and announcing his Judaism and thus his outsider status in one fell swoop. And so he had sat, trying desperately to look nonchalant, and noting that while the heat of a sauna did not rush at one all at once in that sort of breath-snatching, skin-flushing assault of the steam room, it was still a formidable enemy. A film of perspiration was slowly growing across his chest and the wire rims of his glasses were beginning to burn against his temples and the bridge of his nose. Just as Rayley had been about to flee the sauna and return to the relative sanity of the dressing room, he had been approached in conversation by Filip Orlov.

"Your English is very good," Rayley said.

"It is one of the languages of the court," Filip answered with such notable modesty that it was evidently a point of great pride.

"The court appears to have many languages."

"We are not so uncivilized as the westerners think."

Just then the definitive sound of a slap filled the sauna and one of the naked men let fly with a muffled moan. He was bent over one of the wooden benches and two of his fellows were merrily pounding away at his buttocks and back with bullrushes. By now there were a dozen men in the room, most of them sitting sedately on the benches with towels folded beneath them, staring straight ahead in the disinterested manner of passengers on a train. One of them looked a good deal like the photographs of the Grand Duke Serge, which Rayley had seen scattered around Ella's apartments on the day they had arrived in Russia. Yes, the more Rayley observed his handsome but haughty face, the more convinced he was that this was Ella's husband and, judging by the mottled quality of his skin and the sheen of sweat across his chest, the Grand Duke had been sitting in the sauna for some time. Personally, Rayley wondered how much longer he would be able to endure this bizarre environment. The heat was oppressive, but the growing claustrophobia even more so, and Rayley had struggled to maintain his composure in small spaces ever since the time of his captivity in Paris.

"Yes, we are in the same line of work," Rayley said, reaching to adjust the tangled robe which he had thrust under his buttocks as protection from the slowly advancing warmth of the benches. "Is this why I was invited to the gentlemen's enclave? As a professional courtesy?"

"We are comrades, are we not?"

"I suppose we are," Rayley said, thinking that a more unlikely pair of comrades would be hard to find. He was pale and thin, his ribs slightly sunken, while Filip's torso was broad and hairy with a scar which ran diagonally across his side like a military sash.

"Wounded in duty," Filip said, noting that Rayley's eyes had settled on the scar. "I took a bullet for the tsar two years ago."

Rayley's eyebrows shot up. "In the famous assassination attempt?"

"It is famous? As far away as London? That is surprising. As assassination attempts go, I assure you this was a very feeble one." Filip looked down reflectively. "The bullet did not strike anything vital, which was fortunate. I tell people that it hit me in my fat."

Rayley smiled. It sounded like something Trevor would say. "Then you were fortunate indeed."

"It was my lucky bullet," Filip said, "for it won me the tsar's unfailing trust. See, I keep it close to me like a saint," and he leaned toward Rayley abruptly, startling him as their chests almost touched. Filip turned a thin silver chain that had been hanging down his back, revealing the crushed shape of a bullet. By the way he dangled it before Rayley, he was expecting some sort of reaction, so Rayley extended a fingertip and recoiled immediately. The metal of the bullet was nearly sizzling to the touch, explaining why Filip had turned it from his chest. Filip smiled, pleased at the intensity of Rayley's reaction. "I was one of many before this bullet, and now I am head of the private guard."

"Such a post must be deeply gratifying."

Filip considered Rayley through narrow eyes. "You also have suffered wounds in your work?"

"I fear that my scars lie deeper inside."

The heavy man sat back with such a definitive gesture that the bench they were both sitting on trembled. "Yes," he said quietly. "I have this kind too."

A surprising degree of subtlety coming from someone who looked like such a brute on the surface and Rayley inclined his head to study the man more closely. If Filip, who had been suspiciously quick to deem the British bodyguard a "comrade," had truly been the source of this invitation, he must have had a reason. A reason beyond showing off his bullet and his English.

"My partner Welles would have found all this most invigorating," Rayley said, as one of the men tossed a ladle of water on the coals and the room was shrouded in a subtle but most welcome mist. "But since that business yesterday with Mrs. Kirby, the Queen refuses to be without one of us constantly at her side."

A bit clumsily stated, but at least the door was open. Would the Russian walk through?

As it turned out, he was more than ready. Filip leaned back toward Rayley in his confidential manner and said "Our suspicious lie with a dance master from Siberia, a man by the name of Konstantin Antonovich. He was already our most likely suspect for a previous double murder of two young ballet dancers. We believe the Kirby woman may have also suspected him of this crime."

"Any what if she did? An aging lady in waiting would hardly confront a strong young killer, would she? If she had any information linking this Antonovich to the first murder surely she would have taken her suspicion to the authorities."

"She was British as well, you know."

"Yes, of course I know."

"In service to the Queen's granddaughter."

"All of which goes without saying. What are you really getting at, Orlov?"

In true police fashion, the man answered the question with a question. "So does the Queen wish for you and Welles to investigate this second crime, this killing of a British woman on Russian soil?"

Rayley paused and took a deep breath of the dry, punishing air. It is hard to measure a man's degree of anxiety in a sauna, he thought, and hard to gauge the degree of hostility which might be lying beneath the surface of seemingly civil discourse. If everyone is flushed and sweating, with a pounding heart and shallowness of breath, how is a detective to gauge the level of anger or fear? Rayley glanced around them, but none of the other men appeared to be taking even the slightest degree of interest in his conversation with Filip.

"The Queen is concerned about the murder, just as I mentioned," Rayley finally said. "It would be unnatural if she were not, given that Mrs. Kirby was British, a respectable widow, and in service to the royal family."

"The woman was a rash," Filip said bluntly, but with no apparent rancor. "Everywhere at once. All over the place with her camera and she liked to talk to servants."

Mrs. Kirby had a camera? This was significant, since it indicated she most likely was the source of the photograph which had been in her possession at the time of her death. As for the rest, servants often talk to other servants and gossip is the currency of life within any palace, but Rayley did not wish to contradict Filip or make him question the wisdom of such extraordinary candor. So Rayley merely nodded and said "Private citizens who take it upon themselves to snoop about and ask questions are the bane of lawmen around the world, are they not?"

Filip nodded back with great enthusiasm. "The Kirby woman was seen in the ballroom on the morning the bodies were discovered. Perhaps she was there earlier too. If she happened to know something - or even if Konstantin Antonovich thought she did - he may have felt the need to…the phrase escapes me."

"Hush her up."

Filip smiled, his eyes glittering with pleasure. "Yes. Hush her up."

"The costume she was found in—"

"It is his. Which makes the matter easy to understand, does it not?"

Actually, no, it did not. Unless Filip was implying that Antonovich was foolish enough to kill a woman and then dress her in his own clothes, his theory made no sense at all. Surely even the palace guard would have to realize that the use of Antonovich's costume served to exonerate him. Glancing at Filip's self-satisfied face, Rayley tried another tack.

"What would this dance master's motive be? Not for killing Mrs. Kirby, I mean, but why would he have wished the two dancers dead?"

"They were going to Paris, part of a grand tour." A groan rang through the sauna as another man bent forward to take the beating of the rushes and Filip observed the scene with a placid expression. "You are quite certain that you do not wish to give our small custom a try? I assure you that the rushes will not hurt you very much, at least not once you get used to them, and the results are quite invigorating."

But Rayley was frowning, too intent on the Russian's last words to be distracted by the scene before him. "You cannot be suggesting that Antonovich killed the ballet dancers through professional jealousy. No sane man would cut the throats of two children simply because he was envious of the fact that they were going to perform in Paris."

"You forget you are in Russia now. We are a passionate race. Quicker to act on our emotions that the British criminals you perhaps are accustomed to. But shall we continue our conversation in the smoking room?"

"Gladly," said Rayley, scrambling to his feet. As he followed Filip toward the narrow door he considered that he was talking to a man who had caught a bullet meant for another, a man who had undoubtedly seen any number of innocents slaughtered for the causes of love, ambition, politics, or God. As they paused in the foyer outside the sauna to once again don their robes before moving on to the next room in the dimly-lit hall, Rayley wondered at the reasons behind Filip's eagerness to suggest Konstantin Antonovich as a suspect for all three murders. No doubt this was why he and Trevor truly had been invited into the gentlemen's enclave – to make sure they got a generous dose of the Orlov's propaganda against the Siberian dance master.

Rayley was relieved to find the smoking room a more conventional affair, with deep padded chairs around a fire. Despite the fact it was June, Rayley chose one close to the hearth for now that he had left the sauna he was chilled by the return to normal air. Filip plopped down beside him and opened a cigarette box.

"Try one," he said. "They are treated with opium. Just a touch, so there's no need to fear the loss of your senses."

Opium? Rayley observed the slender cigarettes with interest, including the brightly lacquered box which held them. "Where do they come from?"

"Another part of the homeland," Filip said airily, causing Rayley to once again reflect that this monstrosity of a nation stretched from Europe to the Pacific, enveloping a dozen distinct cultures along the way. "Pleasures you cannot imagine can be found in the east," Filip continued, his voice already dreamlike, as if the even the idea of the opium or the feel of the small cigarette in his large palm was enough to impart an anticipatory intoxication. "Those oils the men rubbed on themselves back in the sauna, did you happen to notice the aromas? Each was rendered from a different exotic plant, all with unique properties of healing, and most of them from Asia. The plants of the east….and their women…" He abruptly jerked a thumb toward the door. "Later I shall show you the passageway we use to bring them in and then, of course, back out. Have you by chance ever lain with a woman from Japan?"

"Never," Rayley said. 'I'm not sure I've even seen one. At least not up close."

"The sensations they evoke are extraordinary," Filip said. "Their feet are corrupted in the most intriguing way. Twisted, you know."

"Yes, I've read about it. I always thought the practice was cruel."

Filip shrugged, as if the statement was undeniably true but inconsequential. "All human pleasure comes at the cost of another creature's pain."

"What an extraordinary suggestion."

"Remember it the next time you sit down to dine," Filip said, finally striking a match and lighting the cigarette in his hand, then taking a deep drag before putting it aside to light a second one for Rayley. "The next time you sink your teeth into a leg of chicken pause for a moment to consider the final seconds of the chicken's existence in this earthly realm and you shall see at once what I mean. But somehow I've found that contemplating the suffering of the chicken doesn't make her leg any less juicy." Filip gave a quick consult to the clock on the wall. "We do not have much longer until you will see what I mean."

"The women are on their way now? So early in the afternoon?" For some reason, Rayley found this the most depraved detail of all.

Filip smiled. "But what difference does the hour make? Why should anyone care if it is day or it is night?"

"I must confess, the longer I remain here, the less I can distinguish them myself." Rayley looked at the lit cigarette with suspicion then took a tentative puff. He was not immune to botanical pleasures and had dabbled in a few back in London, but had always made it a policy never to mix this particular indulgence with work. Still, considering he had already witnessed the sauna and the oils and the slapping of bullrushes and was sitting here, nearly naked, discussing philosophy with some manner of a hairy beast, he supposed such a small smoke couldn't hurt. He had been commissioned by Welles, after all, to explore the rituals of the men's enclave in their entirety.

"The passageway which leads to the docks is quite cleverly designed," Filip said. "I believe the detective's part of your mind will be intrigued. And as your host I must insist that you make the acquaintance of one of the eastern women before our time together is past. You've only had British, I presume."

And not so very many of those, Rayley thought wryly, feeling the first puff of the opium curl down his throat and through his chest, unloosening everything, each tension and doubt that it found there. It was sweet to the smell and the taste but, he suspected that, like most sweet things, it had the power to sting.

"I was with an American whore once," he told Filip.

"Ah," said Filip. "I cannot claim that particular pleasure. And how was it?"

"A bit like your sauna. Bizarre at first. but in the end, most invigorating."

The two men laughed and then, in unison, they raised the small dark cigarettes to their lips and pulled the velvety smoke in yet again.

The Winter Palace – Guest Quarters

1:30 PM

Their search of the balcony in the west-facing corner of the ballroom had revealed little. Certainly nothing that would suggest that a woman had been killed there, even by the bloodless method of strangulation followed by a twist of the neck. They had been ready to write the entire venture off as the waste of a morning when Davy had spied a lone thread, tucked beneath a chair, its wiry texture indicating it most likely came from a rope. With it reverently folded within a piece of paper, Tom, Trevor, and Davy returned to their rooms where they sat down in straight chairs and stared at each other wordlessly.

"We're missing quite a lot," Trevor finally said.

"Indeed," said Tom. "As in witnesses, suspects, a murder weapon, and a motive. Other than that we're well on our way."

"I would not say we're entirely missing motive," Davy said. "Mrs. Kirby was most certainly killed because she knew something about how or why the ballet dancers died."

"Agreed," said Trevor. "Something that for some reason she neglected to mention to us."

"Oh, and we're missing a table," Tom said. "It feels rather strange to sit here in straight chairs without one, does it not?"

"None of the rooms in this part of the palace seem to have desks or working tables," Davy said. "They have angels on the ceiling and flowers on the bedposts but they don't have tables."

"I hadn't noticed, but you're quite right," said Tom, looking thoughtfully around him. "I suppose it's because no one who has stayed in these rooms before us has ever felt the urge to do any sort of work."

"You know when the Queen first described Mrs. Kirby to me she said the woman was a crack shot," Trevor mused. "Certainly a unique trait in a female of her age and background, and it implies she was the owner of a pistol. Yet we found no such weapon among her things, nor did she have one with her when she died."

"Two possibilities come to mind," Tom said, idly slapping out a rhythm on his thighs as he talked. "The gun is still in her room and well hidden, which implies she did not perceive herself to be in danger, at least not of the type which would prompt her to carry a weapon wherever she went. Certainly not when meeting me. The other scenario is that she did have the pistol with her when she was attacked, but since she was likely jumped from behind, did not have the chance to use it. Her killer could have disarmed her after death, which leaves us with the unsettling possibility that a man who used a knife the first time, and his hands the second, now has a brand new and far more efficient toy with which to play."

"I do wish Mrs. Kirby had been more forthcoming about what or who she was onto," Trevor said, leaning forward onto his own thighs and frowning. "I have never understood private citizens who come to the police and say 'I suspect something, but I dare not tell you what it is.' It has always seemed to me rather like announcing that they wish to become part of the evidence, and not part of the investigation."

"But she left the photograph," Davy said. "It must have some meaning, else she wouldn't have gone to such great pains to hide it."

"Perhaps whatever is in the photograph is what she wanted to discuss with me in our meeting," Tom said, now slapping out a new tune with a bit more energy. "Although of course she didn't have it with her when she left her room either, did she?"

"Fortunately, she did not," said Trevor. "Or it would now be in her killer's possession and not in ours. It isn't much, but it appears to be all we have, so let us go over it again."

The night before they had spent hours taking turns peering at the photograph, but it had as of yet yielded nothing beyond the sad sight of two beautiful young people, both dead. Trevor now placed it on a small serving table and the three men stood around it, gazing down.

"The significance of the picture almost has to be the knife in the girl's hand," said Tom, pulling his magnifying glass from his coat pocket and bending to squint at the center of the photograph. "But she is clutching it so tightly, that the shape of the handle is all but invisible and the blade is lost in the folds of her nightdress."

"Can we make the image bigger?" Davy asked.

"Sorry, my friend," said Tom, shaking the magnifying glass at him. "This thing has sadly limited powers and I left my microscope back in London at Aunt Gerry's house. Dear Aunt Gerry. I wish she was with us now. She would have gotten every gossipy detail from that wretched Kirby woman in three minutes flat."

"No, I don't mean looking at it through a microscope or magnifying glass," Davy said. "If this picture was found within these palace walls, then the negative is likely also close at hand. Are there not ways to make pictures larger, expand them, so that details become more clear?"

"Bravo, Davy," said Trevor. "So they can. We have no idea who took the picture but presumably it was developed somewhere here at the palace. These people don't leave for any reason at all, including birth, death, and everything that comes between. We simply must find where the photography is developed and see if the negative still exists."

"I shall do it, Sir," said Davy.

"And I shall go with him," said Tom. "Four eyes are better than two and we may have to study the expanded image within the dark room."

"Good lads, for I" – and here Trevor paused to check his pocket watch – "am within minutes of my two o'clock audience with the Queen."

The Winter Palace – Ella's Parlor

2:02 PM

"I am dreadfully sorry, Your Majesty," Trevor said. "And may I extend my condolences to you as well, Your Imperial Highness."

He stood before the settee which held the Queen and a bewildered-looking Alix while Ella walked back and forth behind it, staring down at the rug and wringing her hands.

"We do not understand how this might have happened," the Queen said, perhaps slipping back into the royal "we" through agitation and perhaps simply speaking for both herself and her granddaughters. "You say she was found dressed in a stage costume? Why on earth should that be?"

"We do not know for certain," Trevor said, "but we imagine that the gypsy king costume is some sort of message. Perhaps things will become clearer when we have had the chance to interview the dancers and know whose costume it was and how the assailant might have come to possess it."

"I can save you the effort," Ella said, still not meeting his gaze as she continued to pace. "The Gypsy King is a role played by Konstantin Antonovich in one of the sketches planned for the ball. I have seen him wear the costume in rehearsals many times. Everyone has."

"Alix most certainly shall not waltz with that man," said the Queen.

"But don't you see, Granny?" Ella said, stopping at last and facing the settee. "All this contrivance, this ridiculous theatricality, only serves to prove that the killer is anyone on earth except Konstantin."

"The Grand Duchess is most likely correct," Trevor said. "Not only is the costume a rather extreme gesture, but we have narrowed the time frame during which Mrs. Kirby might have been placed among the ship rigging to a mere twelve minutes and Antonovich appears to have an alibi for that period." He lifted his eyes to Ella. "You said you had seen him in the costume. If I bring it here, to your apartment, will you be able to confirm it is the same one you have seen before? That no parts of it are missing?"

She frowned. "I suppose so. But why do you suggest that parts of it might be missing?"

"We don't know for certain that any are. There is a loop on the hip of the sort where men often place a sword or a dagger, but no weapon was found on the person of Mrs. Kirby. Do you perhaps recall if some such was part of the original costume?"

She hesitated, but only for a moment. "There was a rather large knife and it hung, just as you say, from a loop on his hip. He was to climb the rigging and use it to release a flag at the climatic moment of the scene."

"Then the knife is missing," Trevor said. "And since we are speaking of the rehearsals, I must ask you one other thing, Your Imperial Highness, if you will kindly grant me just one more minute of your valuable time." He was aware that his courtesy was exaggerated, a behavior he sometimes unconsciously adapted when speaking to someone he did not truly admire, and hoped that it would not be seen as sarcasm. Ella seemed accustomed to such sugary speech and the Queen was too deep in thought to notice. But Alix, of all people, regarded Trevor with a certain acuity. *Do not mock my sister*, her expression seemed to say. *No matter who you are or what news you bring, you shall not mock my sister.*

"Of course," Ella said. "Mrs. Kirby was my lady in waiting, after all. I shall do all I can to assist you."

"What is the pattern of the day in the ballroom? Especially now, with so much preparation for the ball?"

"Private lessons begin around noon and go to generally five in the afternoon. The Winter Palace is not full of early risers, Detective, as you have likely noticed. The group rehearsals generally commence at seven, and are finished by nine, when everyone goes to supper." Ella paused, considering her own words. "So if you are asking who might know that the ballroom was likely to be empty between the hours of five and seven, the answer would be many people. Certainly anyone connected to preparations for the ball and most likely their spouses and their servants, if they have any."

"Do you have any suspicions of your own?" Alix asked. She spoke so rarely that, as always, anything she said seemed to carry more import than the words of others. Trevor supposed such a trait might serve her well some day as a tsarina. "Is there any evidence indicating why Mrs. Kirby might have been killed?"

"We have a photograph," Trevor said.

The Queen looked up, her heavy-lidded eyes suddenly alert. "What sort of photograph?"

Was it just Trevor's imagination, or had this news also shocked Ella? She had finally stopped her agitated walking about and chosen a chair, giving him her full attention for the first time since he had entered the room.

"A photograph of the dancers who were killed, Your Majesty," Trevor said. "Posed as they were left after their deaths and shot from a position high above their bodies, presumably from one of the theater's many balconies. If you will forgive me, your Imperial Highness, do you know why Mrs. Kirby might have had such a thing within her possession?"

"I do not," Ella said. "She was a curious person. Some said she stuck her nose into places where it did not belong. That is most likely what led to her death, is it not?"

"Ella..." the Queen said warningly, and her granddaughter stopped and slumped in her chair like a scolded schoolgirl. "Whatever the gossips may have said about her character, Mrs. Kirby died in service to the crown." The Queen shifted in her chair to address Trevor. "She will be transported back to London by us, when we leave, and there given a full and proper funeral. You must promise me that her body will not fall into the hands of the Russian police."

"We will certainly reclaim her body before we depart, but as for the palace guard... I regret to say that they are examining her as we speak, Your Majesty," Trevor said. "I fear it was unavoidable. After all, the crime did occur within the palace and not even the Russians can pretend that a woman might manage to break her own neck and then wrap herself in a flag and lower herself over the side of a balcony. To be more precise, it is impossible for the authorities to brush aside this most recent death as a suicide. The crime not only says 'murder,' it exclaims it."

"I don't wish to dance at the ball," Alix suddenly blurted out. "I don't want to go into that horrid room at all, into that place where three people have died for reasons that no one can understand. I must go to the chapel. I must pray for the souls of the dead."

"Of course you must, darling," Ella said soothingly, slipping an arm around her younger sister's shoulders as her eyes locked with Trevor's. "And I shall come with you. For prayer is all we have at this point, is it not? The science of detection certainly seems to have failed us."

Chapter Thirteen

The Winter Palace – The Grand Ballroom

June 20, 1889

3:40 PM

"You are here early."

Emma looked up at Konstantin, who was walking slowly down the marble staircase.

"I wished to practice before our lesson," she said. It was strange, she thought. Because he spoke simply, as does any man using a language not his own, so did she. And somehow these short sentences, with their limited choice of words and directly-stated thoughts, were allowing her to express herself more freely than she had done in years.

"I am surprised you have come at all."

There were several things she could say in response to this. Perhaps he was speaking of the last time they saw each other - the evening before, that scene of bedlam and tears, with scores of dancers arriving for practice, only to be turned away with the news that there had been yet another murder in the ballroom. The British police and the Russian, literally circling each other as they examined the ridiculous form of the fallen

Mrs. Kirby, looking heavenward with an expression of angry surprise as she lay sprawled in her blue silk britches and yellow hose. Or perhaps he was referring to the next-to-last time they had seen each other, in the costume room, he and Tatiana caught in a tangle of clothing and her clutching Tom's hand and willing the image away.

It was impossible to guess to which of these things, if either, he had been referring, but it was less awkward to be standing face to face talking with him than she would have guessed. He did not appear to be embarrassed or frightened by the events of the previous day, so she decided to move on as well. "Your four o'clock lady is not here?"

"Nor was my three o'clock. Or the one before or the one before." He looked down his great nose with a sad smile. "They are all frightened. This ballroom began as a place of peace for me. My church, how do you say? The sort of church where one can hide."

"Your sanctuary."

"Yes. My sanctuary from the world." He looked around slowly, in the manner of a man who is saying goodbye to something. "Within these walls, I could be whatever I wished to be. But now…"

"It is a room of death."

"The other ladies do not come," he said. "And yet Emma Kelly is here. So it does not frighten you, this room of death?"

"I used to be frightened of everything," Emma said. "And then the worst thing I could ever have imagined happened. My sister—" He was looking at her expectantly, but she shook her head. "There is a strange gift that comes to you after the worst thing you can imagine actually happens," she said. "You find yourself with nothing left to fear."

He smiled, a movement of the mouth but not the eyes. "Would you like to talk or would you like to dance?" he asked.

She raised her arms. "There is nothing to say. I have come to dance."

The Winter Palace – The Guest Quarters

4:57 PM

"So that's it," Trevor said irritably, as Rayley wrapped up an abbreviated description of his conversation with Filip Orlov. "The only reason you and I were ever invited into the inner sanctum was because one of the tsar's bodyguards wished to implicate Antonovich as their prime suspect in the murders of three people." In anticipation of the group meeting, Trevor had ordered up the Russian equivalent of a British tea, which turned out to be a tray of elaborate confections and a hot beverage so strangely sweet that Trevor suspected they would all have trouble getting it down. But privacy within the Winter Palace was proving to be elusive, so he was glad to have this chance for them all to confer together, no matter how different from their customary leisurely evenings in Gerry's parlor.

"That's all I took from it," Rayley admitted. "He theorizes the dancers were killed out of professional jealousy and that Cynthia Kirby was killed because she somehow learned Konstantin was to blame and had gone to the theater to confront him." Rayley raised his palms at the barrage of objections certain to come his way in the wake of such an illogical statement. "Don't shoot the messenger. I'm only repeating what Orlov shared with me. I was braced for him to query me about the extent of our own investigation into the matter, but the conversation never took that particular turn. Where is Emma? She must have a more distinct impression of Konstantin Antonovich than any of the rest of us. In fact, where is everyone?"

"The boys have gone in search of the chemist who developed the photograph you found last night, all on the theory that it might be possible to expand the image and give us a better view of the knife in the dead girl's hand," said Trevor. "And Emma is presumably bidding adieu to the murderous Mr.

Antonovich as we speak. She was quite insistent that she keep her scheduled lesson and I may have erred in indulging her."

"I don't see any harm in the notion," Rayley said. "The use of Antonovich's costume is too clumsy to be taken seriously and, let us be frank, the motive put forth by Orlov for the slaughter of the ballet dancers is likewise nothing short of ridiculous."

A rap at the door and Emma entered, her dance shoes in hand. "Don't rise," she said, pulling up a chair and glancing without enthusiasm at the tea set on the far table. "I'm sorry that I'm late, but it appears I am not the latest. What have I missed?"

"Just this," said Trevor. "The Grand Duchess Ella has informed me that the gypsy king costume worn by Mrs. Kirby at her time of death belonged to one Konstantin Antonovich and is indeed missing a knife. A member of the palace guard named Filip Orlov has furthermore suggested to Rayley that Antonovich is their primary suspect."

"Well, that's convenient," Emma said drily, sinking to her seat.

"You know more of him than anyone else," Rayley said. "Do you think there's a possibility he could be involved in some way, even if he is not the murderer? After all, he does seem to have access to everyone and everything involved in these two crimes, as well as intimacy with Ella, one of the people we are sworn to protect."

"Yes, yes, of course he teaches Ella and the tsar's aunt and his daughter as well," Emma said. "Social intercourse with the imperial family is part of his job. But as much as it pains me to say it, I believe Mrs. Kirby was right in suggesting that it is another of his students who is at the root of this issue, someone with no royal blood at all. He dances with Tatiana Orlov, the wife of the very same Filip Orlov who has served him up on a platter as he perfect suspect."

Trevor raised an eyebrow.

"And if you substitute another verb for 'dance' and I think the matter should become even clearer," Emma said. "Konstantin and Tatiana are lovers. Ask Tom if you don't believe me."

"Well, that indeed is quite the coincidence," Rayley said. "The wife of a member of the private guard, in a tryst with the private guard's chief suspect in the murders."

"How on earth did the two of you discover this?" Trevor asked Emma. "And why did you not mention it earlier?"

"We learned that they are lovers in precisely the manner you are now imagining," Emma said. "Although it seemed inconsequential in comparison to our discovery of Mrs. Kirby's body a few minutes later. But if Konstantin and Tatiana were indiscreet enough to have been caught by Tom and myself backstage at the theater in the worse possible moment, it's possible that they have given other people reason to speculate along the way. Mrs. Kirby perhaps, or Tatiana's husband."

"This explains a great deal," said Rayley. "For now Filip Orlov has every incentive to frame Konstantin. It provides him with a neat and elegant solution to all his problems. Konstantin hangs, guilty or not, while Filip retains his wife and earns another commission for service to the tsar."

"Hangs?" Emma asked sharply. "He may be guilty of a romantic indiscretion but hardly murder. In fact, between me and Tatiana Orlov, his every moment is accounted for during the time the body must have moved." She looked from Trevor to Rayley. "I don't know about the ballet dancers, but he certainly had nothing to do with the Kirby affair, and whatever evidence they've collected against him is unlikely to be enough to convict him in a court of law."

"If we were in London, I would agree with you," Trevor said. "Here, who can say?"

"We've only begun our investigation, Emma," Rayley said with sympathy. "Until we get our answers and thus the Queen gets hers, we won't be leaving St. Petersburg anytime soon."

"True, true, true," Trevor agreed. "All quite true. But even if Konstantin is a somewhat unlikely suspect, we must exhibit caution around the man and indeed everyone else until this matter is sorted out. The one thing I'm inclined to agree with Filip Orlov about is that Cynthia Kirby was most likely slain because of something that she saw or knew. Which means that we have a killer who won't hesitate to kill again in order to cover his tracks. A killer who may well be in possession of both Konstantin's knife and Cynthia's pistol."

The door opened again, this time without even a perfunctory knock, and Davy and Tom burst in, a file in Tom's hand.

"We've got it," Tom said. "Or at least we have something. Good God, but we do need a table, don't we?" He pushed aside the three empty cups and the teapot and deposited the file in the middle of the plates. "The chemist was able to provide us with several enlargements of the original photograph."

They scrunched together and collectively studied the new photograph.

"It image is far from perfect," Tom said. "Apparently photographs grow ever more blurry as you enlarge them, who would have guessed? But it's enough to show that the blade is curved, rather dramatically so, which leads me to suspect....Well here, I shall show you." He shuffled the pictures to produce another closely focused section of the original photograph, this one showing the gash at the boy's throat. "As you can see for yourselves," Tom continued, "the cut which killed Yulian seems to be a rather short straight one, probably made by an assailant who knew precisely where the jugular would be found and who dug in deep, just at that point, most likely with a dagger shaped weapon. While in contrast a curved knife, especially if used in an attack from behind, creates the sort of broad, level gash that has the power to nearly decapitate a victim. It's a shame that the amount of blood obscures the wound to the degree it does, but I think any sensible man would agree with me. The knife the girl is holding in her hand is not the same knife that was used to cut the boy's throat."

Trevor was frowning at the picture. "It's quite blurred."

"Yes, yes, the chemist said that enlargements always are," Tom said impatiently. "But anyone can certainly see that their heads are in the normal position people's heads would be. Not nearly severed. It suggests –"

"I agree with you as far as it goes," Trevor said, "and I'm happy to have these enlargements in our possession. But whoever is determined to frame Konstantin Antonovich would not let a few blurry photographs and a mere suggestion put forth by a foreigner, no matter how apt it might be, derail his plans."

"The dance master?" Tom said with a frown.

"The woman we found Konstantin with yesterday was Tatiana Orlov," Emma said shortly. "And now it seems that the Tsar's private guard, or at least her husband Filip, have seized on him as a suspect in all three deaths."

"Then the poor bastard's done for," Tom said. "Remind me to never publically make love to a policeman's wife in the middle of a murder investigation."

"All right, let's wrap this up quickly," Trevor said, closing the file and indicating they should return to their seats, "for our time is limited if we wish to interview the dancers at seven. Davy, I trust you've made inroads with the student group?"

"Not invited to a meeting yet, Sir. But at least one of them seems to have warmed to me."

"Excellent. And you believe you will be able to carry the role of a disgruntled schoolboy, ready to toss aside the constraints of an unjust political system and snatch away the privileges of your societal betters?"

"Of course, Sir."

"That was a suspiciously swift answer," Tom said with a laugh. "Perhaps Davy is not as gruntled with his lot in life as you assume, Trevor."

Davy's ears turned red with what the others assumed to be embarrassment. "He brags a lot, just as Mrs. Kirby predicted they all would. A fellow named Vlad Ulyanov, brother to Sasha Ulyanov, one of the students hanged two years ago in that unsuccessful attempt on the tsar. Thus central to the Volya leadership, but he's one of the younger members. Claims the others don't take him seriously."

"His brother died while Gregor Krupin lived," Trevor said. "His resentment of Krupin's authority must be profound."

Davy nodded.

"For a group of self-proclaimed revolutionaries these lads do not appear very cautious," Rayley said. "Perhaps this is why their plans have been so easily broken up in the past, even by the notoriously inept local police. But it also occurs to me that, just as Filip undoubtedly invited me to the men's enclave in order to plant suspicions about Konstantin, that this Vlad may be pretending to accept Davy in order to feed him misinformation."

"Possible," said Trevor. "We seem to have two theories in front of us about how to best deal with the Russians. One is to take them at face value and thus conclude they are playing clumsy psychological games with us, so clumsy that one could safely call them stupid. The other is to consider them diabolical masterminds who play at being stupid so that we will discount them too easily as worthy adversaries."

"There's a third possibility," Emma said. "We may be confounded because they are in reality neither more nor less intelligent than we are, they simply think differently."

"The most likely theory yet, I would say," Rayley nodded. "My afternoon in the gentlemen's enclave felt a bit like Alice down the rabbit hole. We cannot assume they approach life, much less matters like guilt or innocence, in the same manner that we do. To apply British motives to a Russian crime scene would be the most foolish mistake of all."

"So while we are in St. Petersburg, we are to readily accept all offers of friendship on the surface but privately remain skeptical of the sincerity behind the offer," Tom said airily. "I like it, for this is pretty much my philosophy with all new acquaintances, no matter what their nationality."

"We don't have to do any of this, you know," Davy blurted out. "It isn't our fight."

The others turned toward him, their faces showing different variations of inquiry, but all of them confused.

"We are behaving as if we've been brought here to solve a crime," Davy said. "But that isn't the case at all. I remember the Queen's words on the ship most specifically. She wanted us to determine whether or not the Winter Palace was a safe home for her granddaughters. Asked us to find out if the revolutionaries could get their people in. Well it seems to me that question was answered within hours of us getting off the boat, before we even had the chance to do anything. Mrs. Kirby's murder proved the earlier two weren't suicides, so what more do we need to know? It is only pride that makes us so determined to push further when we have no authority in this country. Trevor wants us to finish in time to talk with the dancers at seven but why should they bother to speak to the likes of us? We are outsiders."

A silence followed this. Emma glanced to see if Trevor was offended by Davy's words, but he didn't seem to be. He actually seemed to have been rendered momentarily shamed by Davy's quite accurate assessment of the situation.

Tom spoke first. "We didn't have any authority in Paris either, but that didn't stop us."

"That was different," Davy said. "Detective Abrams had been kidnapped, and of course we would move if one of our own was in danger. But in this case…Mrs. Kirby might have been English, but beyond that, I cannot see why we owe her the same level of loyalty we feel toward each other. And even if we find her killer, who is to say what the palace police will do with that information? There is no way this can come to a satisfactory outcome, at least by the standard of Scotland Yard."

"You're right," Rayley said. "At least as far as you and Emma and Tom are concerned. Your responsibilities begin and end with the question put forth by the Queen and, just as you say, that question has been answered. But Trevor and I are bound by a different level of duty. If we are aware of a crime, whether it lies within our jurisdiction or not, we are compelled to follow the trail."

"That is just the sort of thing the revolutionaries say," Davy said, once again speaking recklessly, for Rayley's cheeks flushed with irritation. "If there is an injustice anywhere, any time, they believe they must correct it. And so they will always fight."

"Your point about knowing the limits of our power will be duly noted," Rayley said, this time more sharply. "But men of the law do not cease to be such because they have crossed an international border. Trevor and I do not expect the rest of you to necessarily heed the same call."

It was a bit of an indirect scold toward Davy, who was also a man of law, and he tension in the room thickened. Emma gamely waded into the mix. "Davy is quite correct in that we are behaving as if the Russians want us to help solve these crimes," she said. "While the truth of the matter is that they likely wish we would all go away and leave them alone. And he is also right to remind us that we didn't know the ballet dancers and had scarcely met Mrs. Kirby, who appeared to be roundly disliked and justifiably so. But it is hard to remember areas of jurisdiction and limits of power when one is in the middle of this sort of situation, is it not? Now that you tell me Konstantin is being framed, I find that I too must remain involved. I feel a personal loyalty to him which has nothing to do with nationality."

"My motivations are different as well," Tom said. "Mrs. Kirby was on her way to meet me when she was killed and her body dropped at my feet. It is not that I feel responsible for the fact that curiosity ultimately killed this cat, but her killer came very close so I feel that I too must–"

"Of course," Davy said. He was flushed. "I did not mean to suggest that any of you were wrong to want to see justice done, or to wish to protect innocent people, no matter what or who they are. I was just saying that we answer to the Queen, no one else. I think we should admit that as we proceed

– and I will keep helping as well – that this is not an official case. We are all doing this for reasons of our own."

"You have changed, Davy," Trevor said. "You have begun to think for yourself."

"I have always thought for myself," Davy said, this time a ghost of a smile coming to his mouth. "It's just that I have now begun to speak for myself as well. But I have taken enough of our time, haven't I, Sir?"

The "Sir" seemed to once more establish equilibrium within the group. Emma poured herself some tea, and the men all leaned back once again in their seats.

"Yes, still moving on," Trevor said, with a glance at the clock on the mantle. "While you have all been gadding about waltzing and taking saunas and joining the revolution, I have spent the last hour going through the diary of Mrs. Kirby."

"She kept a diary?" Rayley asked with surprise. "An odd thing for a spy to do, is it not?"

"There's no such thing as a British spy, remember?" Trevor said. "But unless there's some sort of embedded code I have yet to break, the diary appears to be merely the ramblings of an older woman spending time abroad. What she wore, what she ate, palace gossip, that sort of thing. Only one line jumped out at me as potentially significant and I don't know quite what to make of it. The day before her death she wrote this: *Alina said she is immaculate.*"

"Who is Alina?" Tom asked.

"Ella's personal maid," Trevor said. He pulled the thin blue book from his folder and consulted the last page again, as if to make sure.

"So Alina is a good maid who keeps things clean," Tom said. "An odd thing for Mrs. Kirby to note in her diary, but I scarcely see what it has to do with her death."

"The 'she' is not necessarily Alina," Rayley said. "The pronoun could refer to another woman. I'd say most likely the Grand Duchess Ella, considering that both of the women served her."

"So Ella is immaculate?" Tom asked. "Once again, a pointless statement."

"She might mean immaculate in the religious sense," Emma said, setting aside her scarcely touched tea. "Immaculate is also what they say of a virgin."

"The Grand Duchess has been married four years and yet remains a virgin…" Rayley said. "That seems unlikely."

"But possible," Emma said. "Not every marriage is consummated, and royal unions are often more a matter of politics than passion." They all sat back, each absorbed in their own thoughts.

"Even if it's true, does it matter?" Tom finally asked. "I mean, as gossip goes, it's quite fascinating, but how could an unconsummated marriage have anything to do with two ballet dancers being killed?"

"I don't know," Trevor admitted. "I don't even know if we're interpreting the line correctly. There are no children from the union of Ella and Serge, which I suppose somewhat supports the theory."

"There are many explanations for why a woman might fail to bring a pregnancy to term," Tom said. "Especially a woman from this particular lineage."

"Ah yes, the royal disease which no one acknowledges," Trevor mused. "Do you think that the Hanover bleeding disorder could possibly play into this riddle?"

"Hemophilia taints the royal bloodline," Tom said, "and thus, I would imagine, the bedrooms of the royal marriages. I shall do a little research and make that report on the morrow as well."

"So here is what we have," Rayley said. "A dance master who instructs and thus is connected to several women within the Romanov family and who also is having a love affair with the wife of the tsar's personal guard. A revolutionary group which seems suspiciously willing to accept outsiders but who also managed to get the brother of one of their high ranking officers into the Winter Palace where he was subsequently killed. A lady in waiting to the Queen's granddaughter who has also been murdered, most likely because of something she learned in her unofficial capacity as a royal spy, and who was dressed after death in the costume of the aforementioned dance master. This Queen's younger daughter wishes to marry the son of the tsar while the Queen's older granddaughter is married to the tsar's brother. That marriage may be unconsummated and this fact may be known among the couple's servants or it is also possible that she has been unable to conceive due to a hereditary illness which no one within either royal house is willing to acknowledge. And then we have a palace police force and private guard who function as separate units but which collectively seem quite happy to beat each other in saunas, procure Asian whores and opium, and accept ridiculous explanations for the three dead bodies that have been found on their watch within a single week. Am I leaving anything out?"

"Obviously you're leaving quite a lot out, but we don't know what any of it is yet," Tom said.

"Let us all continue down our separate lines of inquiry and we shall resume at the same time tomorrow," Trevor said. "Perhaps the connections between all these facts will be a little clearer then. And Emma, under the circumstances I'm not sure it's wise for you to continue your lessons with Antonovich."

"Under what circumstances?" Emma asked. "The circumstances that he's been put forward as a suspect in the most unconvincing manner possible? Such a charge gives me greater incentive to stay close to the man than ever, does it not?"

"She's right," Rayley said. "There's no reason to abandon our stronghold in the theater, especially not now, after a third body has been found there."

"Very well," Trevor conceded. "But at least promise me you will exercise precautions. Perhaps one of us should come with you to the ballroom during your lessons."

"On what pretense?"

"On the pretense of guarding your virtue," Tom said, with a wink. "That is, assuming that you wish for your virtue to be guarded."

"Oh, I think everyone's time is better spent guarding my virtue," Rayley said, laughing and gathering his notes. "Given the events of my afternoon in the gentleman's enclave, it would seem that I am the one whose moral fiber is in danger."

"Tell us everything, Sir," Davy said with enthusiasm. He seemed quite returned to his normal self. "Vlad says the boys in the Volya all claim that the Palace has bucket loads of depravity."

"And depravity should indeed be served up by the bucket load," Tom said.

"Just grant me this one courtesy," Trevor said quietly, leaning forward, so that under cover of the men's guffawing and the scrapes of their chairs being pushed back, only Emma could hear him.

"And what is that?"

"Dance with the man if you must, but don't tell him that he is a suspect."

Chapter Fourteen

The Café of the Revolutionaries

June 21, 1889

11:20 AM

Vlad watched Gregor's face carefully. It was almost impossible to tell what he thought of the plan.

"Despite all that has happened, the Tchaikovsky Ball remains our perfect opportunity," Vlad repeated, hoping that his tone of voice was not desperate or, even worse, presumptuous. "All of the imperial women will be there and Yulian assured us on several occasions that the confusion backstage before a performance will create the ideal backdrop for our intentions. Dozens of people rapidly coming and going through any number of entrances, half of their faces obscured by costumes or masks, carrying props, some of which may even look like weapons. An unprecedented mingling of citizens from every class, at least while they're waiting in the performance areas. When shall we get another chance like this?"

"At the time we made those plans we had Yulian on the inside," Gregor said tersely. "Now we do not."

"True," Vlad said. "But we still have his drawings of the theater, including all the private performance areas normally closed to outsiders. These maps are his legacy to us. Not to use them would mean that his death was in –"

"Enough," Gregor said. "It has only been days, after all."

"The timing is regrettable and I mean no disrespect," Vlad said, staring down into his coffee cup. "But the date of the ball is fixed and after that they shall all go to the seaside for their summer holiday and no one can say when the next such opportunity will present itself. Besides, the details of our plan can be altered to accommodate Yulian's absence, just as we have discussed."

Vlad paused here. It was well known throughout the Volya, even before his death, that Yulian Krupin's resolve had been weakening. Life within the palace walls seemed to have dampened his enthusiasm for destroying the place or perhaps it had been the girl, her soft arms entreating him toward a different sort of life. There had even been talk that Yulian was on the verge of deserting the cause entirely and decamping to Paris. Paris, of all frilly, inconsequential places. Gregor had of course denied these claims and steadfastly defended his brother. He had always sworn that when the time came and the oppressors were trapped within the theater row by row, Yulian would not hesitate to throw the bomb into the imperial box, just as planned. Gregor had said that Yulian's spoken reservations about doing so were only the natural nerves of a boy his age, a claim Vlad had found ludicrous. Yulian had been seventeen, not twelve. The perfect age for a soldier: old enough to have stepped away from his family of birth but too young to have formed a new one through marriage.

"I was not aware that changing the plan was under discussion," Gregor said, lighting a cigarette. "You have stated that you wish the plan to change, but that is all. No decision has been made."

Vlad continued to stare at his coffee. "Without Yulian, it may prove easier and more effective to take a woman out than it is to get a bomb in."

"Kidnapping is crude. A clumsy way to strike at the heart of the beast."

"And you're suggesting that a bomb thrown in a crowded theater would have been precise? This is a strange time for you to become squeamish about the notion of women and children being involved, but even if you are, you must conclude that seizing a hostage is more morally defensible than bombing the theater. We won't hurt the girl, at least not if her father cooperates."

"And that's another thing," Gregor said, with a shake of his sandy-colored curls. "Why are you so fixated on the tsar's daughter? She is but a child. Her youth and her sex make her sympathetic, which is the very last thing that we want in a victim. Should she be injured in the process, trust me, the resultant street gossip will not play well to our cause."

"It has to be someone very close to him. Someone he loves."

"This Xenia is undoubtedly too well guarded."

"On any ordinary night, you would be correct. But backstage, awaiting her turn to dance at the ball, she will not be. Look, Gregor, you know what we have in our hands. Yulian's notes, telling us not only the particulars of key locations but also who will be where and at what time. The Imperial Waltz in which Xenia dances is the first item on a program which begins at eight in the evening. She enters from the left hand side of the stage. She will be wearing a red gown, a gold headpiece on her brow. When else will we know precisely where one of the tsar's children will be at a specific time, of having the cover of the performance as distraction for our entrance and exit? If Yulian was here with us, I assure you he would approve of this plan, even over the original."

This last jab struck vulnerable flesh. Gregor looked at him, his expression pained. They waited.

"We should focus on someone else," Gregor said, seemingly unaware that in discussing a variation in the victim he was indirectly conceding to Vlad's overall strategy. But Vlad was aware of what this small objection meant, and a sense of victory coursed through him.

"Who might you suggest?" he asked mildly.

"Perhaps that British bitch. The one who's too proud to bow her neck to the true mother church. No one would care if she got a bit roughed up in transit."

"Agreed. Including the tsar. Rather than the ransom, he would probably send us a note of thanks."

The two men contemplated their coffee cups, tilted back in their small black chairs. The day was fine, sunny and fair, with a breeze carrying the sugary aromas of childhood up from the bakery next door. They each thought for a moment of their mothers, standing at stoves, calling out that supper was almost ready, although neither man shared this memory with the other. They were not friends, after all.

Gregor sighed. "Your point is sound. I suppose the little one must go."

The Winter Palace – The Guest Rooms

11:40 AM

Fortunately, Tom had brought his most recent textbook from Cambridge. He had stuffed it in his black bag, along with some other hastily-gathered accoutrements of the medical profession. At the time he had viewed these instruments as no more than the props an actor would use in a play, but now he was grateful that he had them close at hand. Especially the textbook.

Emma had interpreted Mrs. Kirby's diary as suggesting that Ella's marriage was unconsummated. If so, this certainly explained why she and Serge were childless, but there were other possible explanations as well. Tom had spent the morning going back and forth between his medical textbook pages on hemophilia and picking certain pertinent facts from the bulging file Trevor kept on the royal family. This was a tricky matter, since the Queen had never directly acknowledged that hemophilia, most often passed from mother to son, was present in her family history at all. And she had certainly never entertained the suggestion that through her penchant for marrying her daughters and granddaughters as advantageously as possible, she thus had been instrumental in spreading the disease into half the royal houses of Europe.

Through the Hanover family tree Trevor had supplied, Tom could surmise that not only the Queen but two of her five daughters were carriers, including Ella and Alix's mother, the Princess Alice. Hemophilia was a mercurial disease, and there was no known explanation for why some siblings were cursed and others were not. Just as not all of Victoria's daughters appeared to be carriers, not all the boys born of carrier mothers were stricken with the disease. Alix and Ella's brother Ernest was one of the lucky ones, apparently hale and hearty and next in line for their father's German title. But their brother Frittie had not been so fortunate. He had taken a tumble from a window when he was but three years old. The fall had left him with no apparent serious injury at the time, but that evening he had begun the long slow process of internal bleeding which marked hemophilia. By the next day he was dead.

But despite this tragedy – and similar tales involving three more of Victoria's sons and grandsons – the family remained publically mute on the subject and Tom doubted that they even discussed it among themselves. There was a chance, ridiculous as it may seem to the educated mind, that neither Alix nor Ella fully understood that it was hemophilia and not a fall from a window that had killed their brother or that there was a possibility the same villain slept tangled in the strands of their own genetics, waiting to claim their unborn sons.

The cynical side of Tom wondered if the Queen's silence on the subject was her refusal to lessen the currency she held in her hands with so many grandchildren. If it was known throughout Europe that the Hanovers were, to put it in the crudest possible terms, defective breeding stock, her ability to forge alliances through international marriages would come to an abrupt end. The more sympathetic side of Tom suspected that the Queen simply could not face the truth: that despite her obsessions about assassinations and governmental overthrows and revolution and riots, the single greatest threat to her family actually coursed within their own veins.

Tom closed the textbook and the file and sat staring off into space. All the information he had gathered boiled down to one most pertinent fact: Since their mother carried the gene for hemophilia, there was a chance that either Ella or Alix did as well, or possibly both of them. There was no way to test a woman for this, no way to predict which of Alice's daughters, if any, would also be forced to watch her own sons die young, but Tom suspected that the next generation would suffer more than the present. In many ways, the Hanovers were their own worst enemy. Their tendency to marry their own cousins, this arrogant belief that no one was good enough for a royal except another royal, had only served to increase the risk, multiplying the statistical chance of a familial disease striking each new child that was born.

But then again, horrible but true, hemophilia might also be Ella's way out of her marriage to Serge, should she wish to take it. If Ella's rumored virginity was indeed just a rumor, then the true reason for her childlessness might lie in infertility or a series of early miscarriages as nature struggled to correct itself. Too many lost babies might convince the Grand Duke to abandon her, or at least to readily agree to her return to England. Many high-ranking families followed this pattern, and Tom had also seen it among the landed gentry in the countryside. While divorce might be scandalous, extended holidays were not. Unhappy husbands and wives often opted to live in separate houses – if not separate nations – for years. Ella could go to visit her dear Granny in London and simply never return.

It would be a neat solution. A logical solution. Bloodless and painless and practical, with no unnecessary suffering and no loss of face.

Which is why Tom doubted that anyone involved would choose it.

The River Neva

Noon

"Somehow you and I keep ending up in boats," Rayley said wryly and Trevor leaned his chin against the handle of the oar and laughed.

"Thank you for agreeing to confer with me in such an unlikely place," he said, indicating the broad expanse of the Neva in front of the Winter Palace. "But I felt a need for some fresh air and I've always found that the repetitive motions of piloting a boat have a remarkable power to settle the mind. I row the Thames nearly weekly back in London. Weather permitting, of course."

"Indeed?" said Rayley, with some surprise. For all their professional collaboration, he knew very little about what Trevor did in his private hours. Rayley leaned back against the side of the boat to regard the Winter Palace which, if possible, looked even larger and more imposing from the angle of the water. When the two men had wandered down to one of the docks they had been promptly issued this small red rowboat and Rayley had to admit there was a kind of peace here along the river. Trevor braced the oars and settled back as well, lighting a cigar and letting the current simply pull them.

"Is there more to confide about your evening in the men's enclave?" Trevor inquired with a deceptive nonchalance.

"It's exactly as I told you," Rayley said. "We were invited there apparently for no other reason than for Filip Orlov to impart his heavy handed and self serving theories about who might have killed the ballet dancers and Mrs. Kirby. The fact that his wife is having an affair with the dark eyed dance master only makes Filip's true motives even more transparent. At this point I'm inclined to see Konstantin Antonovich as simultaneously our only named suspect and the least likely person in the whole Winter Palace to have committed the crime."

"But you think Emma is safe alone with him?"

Rayley indulged a slight smile. "I'd agree with Tom that she's precisely as safe as she wishes to be."

Trevor exhaled a puff of smoke, coughing slightly with the effort.

"We can talk of personal matters, you know, Welles," Rayley finally said. "I'd like to think that if my misadventures in Paris served any purpose, it's that the door to greater conversational intimacy now stands open between us."

"Then you must share with me the details of your evening in the men's enclave, even those too bizarre for our young teammates. All I can gather is that you smoked opium, frolicked with women from the orient, and let men oil you up and beat you with bulrushes."

"I assure you no man has ever beaten me with a bulrush and I find 'frolick' a rather imprecise verb."

The two men chuckled, Rayley also digging in his vest pocket for a cigar. All right, so Trevor was as disinclined as ever to speak of his true affections for Emma, an attraction which Rayley feared might be the eventual undoing of their unity as a team. He had tried to bring it up several times in an indirect way, but Trevor always evaded the issue with some sort of joke or conversational redirection.

"Perhaps not in terms of the case, but in general it was a most informative afternoon," Rayley finally said.

"I have no doubt."

"Go ahead and laugh at me. I fear I am on the verge of becoming the fool of the force, but I assure you that whatever degree to which I entered into any alleged frolicking, it was only so Orlov and his men would accept me as a fellow."

"What tremendous sacrifices you make in the name of Queen and country," Trevor said, his hand cupped around his cigar to keep it from extinguishing in the breeze. "Were you able to keep your wits about you well enough to observe the design of the place?"

"Observe, yes. Comprehend, no. The long halls end in a snarl of passageways and small individual rooms which I would deem nearly impossible for any private guard to monitor, no matter how many men they employ."

"I suppose Orlov and his squad would tell us that the numerous halls work to the advantage of the protectors, not any invading force. After all, they presumably understand the design of the maze rather well whereas an outsider would become immediately confused."

"That's what they would most certainly say, but damn it all, Welles, you didn't see the place. Dark and labyrinthine, with business of every conceivable sort being conducted in every corner."

"I suppose you felt the need to brag of your own exploits," Trevor said indulgently, digging for another match.

Rayley had already tamped out his own cigar, for the steady wind over the water had almost immediately proven that smoking would be impossible. He supposed that was one of the key differences between Trevor and himself – Rayley conceded to the inevitable quickly, devising alternative plans within seconds of an initial failure, while Trevor charged on in the face of all obstacles, as if his very will was a battering ram which would eventually shatter any reality he found displeasing. Rayley was not at all sure which of them was the closest to right, but he did know one thing. It was their differences, not their similarities, which made them such a formidable team.

"Yes, I told them of my American whore," Rayley said. "But they were hardly impressed. I take it that what you and I would consider unspeakably exotic entertainments are a daily occurrence in the gentleman's enclave. It was first with the sauna and steam, then on to a lounge for brandies and opium-treated cigars and at one point in the afternoon a gong sounded and we all stood up. An accomplishment in itself under the circumstances. We went to the dock outside the boathouse and saw a profusion of women approaching in a sort of gondola, each dressed in a different hue. The most poetic of colors - deep pinks and purples and golds and that shade which is neither blue nor green, what do they call it?"

"A boatload of Asian women actually sailed right up to the dock?"

"And they then had to be carried out by these big hulking men who were rowing them. I would scarcely have believed it if I hadn't seen it."

"The Grand Duke Serge was in your party? Did you observe him with any of the women?"

"No, but nor did I notice him showing interest to any of the men. He is a distant fellow. More of the type who stands and watches, you know."

Trevor frowned and shook his head as if he was having trouble taking it all in. "The women had to be carried from the boat?"

"Their feet were bound as children, you know. I saw a few of them taking these little hobbled steps but for the most part they were carried."

"A dreadful business."

"Indeed, "Rayley said. "And I never understood the reason for it, at least not fully, until that afternoon. They call their feet their lilies, you know, because the bones have been broken and reformed to curve in the most extraordinary way, rebuilt in such a manner as to emulate…"

"Emulate what? Flowers?"

"Well, you know, Welles."

"I'm quite certain I do not."

"Shaped as they are, it creates a…a secondary sort of ingress."

"Ingress?" Trevor said blankly, gazing toward the shore. Then suddenly the meaning of Rayley's words struck him and he startled. "Good God man, are you serious? You saw this?"

"I believe so."

"And did you participate?"

"Of course not. Despite what you may think, I am still Scotland Yard. Now, look up the riverbank, will you? That must be some sort of chapel."

They had drifted some distance from the original dock, far enough that Rayley had already begun to dread the lengthy row back upriver, and were now passing a chapel and graveyard. It was a lovely little situation designed to a human scale – the only part of the Winter Palace Rayley had yet seen which did not seem to be an overblown and oversized architectural brag.

"Perhaps we should not have left the Queen unguarded," Trevor said, the thought perhaps prompted by the resemblance of the free-growing chapel gardens to those in England.

"Tom is near her rooms if assistance is needed. He planned to spend the morning in study." Rayley watched clouds of dragonflies hovering over the still water, the sun reflecting in brilliant shards off of their doubled wings. "Whatever was driving our young Mr. Mabrey last night? I've never known him to be so contrary."

"A bit of sympathy for the devil, I'd imagine," Trevor said. When Rayley raised a questioning eyebrow, he elaborated. "How long had you been in service when you first found yourself reluctant to arrest a particular criminal? Because you recognized that if you had been in his position you might have done the exact same thing?"

"Oh, I see where you're going. Not long. Some desperately poor man and a bit of petty theft, as I recall. The temptation to look the other way can be quite strong in certain cases. So you think Davy feels an affinity with the students he met at the Volya?"

"I would imagine that he does. And so might you and I if we had met them. In a country which flaunts the appalling inequities between its classes and is ruled by a tsar who shows no heart for his people, it seems any man of conscience might be drawn to the idea of revolution. Especially university students who have means to understand that things are done differently elsewhere." Trevor continued to study the chapel, thinking how different it seemed from the other chapel they had seen, an ornate gilded hall within the palace where weddings and coronations were held. This humble little structure would have been more in place in a rural town, overseen by a kindly pastor, filled with flowers brought from the women of the village. "I am actually quite pleased that Davy felt free to speak as he did in our presence. I would never have been so frank with a superior at his age."

"Nor would I, and now I better appreciate your tolerance with him yesterday. But despite any youthful scruples, he will do his sworn duty to Queen and country when the time comes, I imagine."

"Oh, I haven't any doubt."

They drifted a few more minutes in silence and then Trevor ventured, "Is there any chance you hallucinated the whole affair? The bit with the women in the boat, I mean."

"Perhaps. It was a very long afternoon. I have the impression that I slept at one point and awakened and then perhaps slept again. The light, you know, it's so disorienting. But I don't believe I dreamed that part."

"You say they call them lilies?"

"Yes."

"Sheer barbarism."

"I agree. But Filip Orlov told me that all pleasure is bought at the cost of another being's pain."

"And you believed him?"

Rayley shrugged. "It wasn't my job to believe or disbelieve, it was simply my job to listen to whatever he had to say."

"The Queen is quite right. This whole nation is corrupt."

"Perhaps. But the irony is that my time in that dark little smoking room gave me a better sense of the scope of Russian empire than the grandest halls of the Palace had yet managed to do," Rayley said. "It showed me the variety one can find in a nation that reaches from Europe to the Pacific Ocean, a mix of the familiar and the exotic. Their sense of what is possible stretches, I believe, with the vastness of their land."

His cigar had been out for several minutes, but Trevor still chewed on it. "And who told you this, that great philosopher and whoremonger Filip Orlov?"

"I've never seen you so agitated about a matter completely not related to the case," Rayley observed wryly. "Besides, we're scarcely in a position to judge the Romanovs and their attendants. Most men in London, and I daresay all over the world, have had their share of similar encounters. You have, I have. It may not have been our most shining moment, but it hardly makes us monsters."

"We were with British whores, Abrams. British whores with flat feet and we went to them alone, ashamed, and cloaked in the darkness of night. It's an entirely different matter altogether."

"From a moral standpoint, I'm not sure I follow," Rayley said.

"I just don't understand what's wrong with the old way."

"Good heavens, Welles, stop rolling back and forth like that or you shall pitch us both headlong into this river of contagion. I didn't mean to distress you. Of course there's nothing wrong with the old way. But the salient point of my afternoon is just this: secret halls run the length of the Palace, and empty out at the stable and boathouse. This is how they got the women in… and back out when the debaucheries were concluded, I suppose. You can't imagine the darkness of that maze of halls, the length, the numerous turns and twists along the way. It is a building designed for intrigue. So the question now becomes 'How much of this, if any, do we tell the Queen?'"

Another dock was in view. Unmanned, but Trevor supposed they could simply pull up and abandon their rowboat there. It would be easier to walk back across the broad lawns than to row upstream along the river, and besides, it would give them the chance to enter through another door and explore a different part of the palace. Trevor doubted that, even among the five members of the team, they had seen a fraction of the building whose security they had been charged to analyze.

"We tell the Queen nothing," Trevor said, "at least not now. The welcoming banquet is to be held tonight, bringing with it our first chance to observe the key players in this intrigue. It has occurred to me as we've drifted along that three couples are at the heart of this story. Konstantin and Tatiana, Serge and Ella, Nicky and Alix. Oh and the first ones. Our poor little Katya and Yulian, frozen forever in the posture of Romeo and Juliet. You see, I had already forgotten them."

"The star-crossed lovers," Rayley said mildly, as Trevor began to steer them toward the dock.

"Yes, just that." said Trevor. "Star-crossed. But the more I think of this case, the more I am convinced they all are."

Chapter Fifteen

The Winter Palace - Ella's Apartments

5:20 PM

They were being insulted on at least two levels, perhaps more.

The first slight came in the fact that their "welcoming dinner" was in fact an annual event whose true intent was to celebrate the summer solstice. The details had been planned long before they arrived, and the presence of the Queen of England and Alix would be but one small facet of the celebration.

The second insult came in the form of a gown which had been delivered to Ella's apartments on the morning of the dinner, with a note attached saying it was for Alix to wear. The dress was silver brocade and encrusted with great stones – pearls and rubies, even the occasional diamond – and it was so heavy that Alix's knees had buckled when she had lifted it from its box. Fortunately her excitement over the grandeur of the outfit, coupled with the fact that Nicky would be publically escorting her to the dinner, had kept her from noticing the implications of the gift. Her grandmother and sister had not been so deluded. Alix may have made no formal appearance before the imperial family, but evidently at some time during her singular outing with Nicky or her days confined to her sister's apartments, her wardrobe had been judged and found wanting. This dress was a none-too-subtle indication that, in order to save face, the Romanovs had taken it upon themselves to attire her suitably for her first state occasion.

"Don't get too proud," Victoria said when Alix, with the assistance of Emma, had finally managed to struggle into the dress and emerge from the dressing room to parade before the others.

"I'm breathless," Alix confessed. "Both by the value and the heaviness of the stones. I feel as if I am all but pinned to the ground."

"This is the weight that comes with being an empress," Ella said. "If you truly want Nicky, you may as well get used to it."

"Precisely who sent this gift to you?" the Queen asked.

"The tsarina," Alix said, staring at herself in the mirror in a rather abstracted manner. "It is an extraordinarily kind gesture, is it not?"

"Extraordinary indeed," the Queen said, raising her eyebrows to Trevor. He and Emma were the only members of the team currently in Ella's quarters, but they were all expected to attend the solstice dinner, save for Davy who had seemed relieved rather than offended that the invitation had not included his name. The Queen's look had been pointed, but precisely what she meant by it was a bit of a muddle. The family trees of Europe had always confounded Trevor, but he knew that Nicky's mother was sister to the wife of the Queen's eldest son. These dark-eyed Danish sisters, who had risen through marriage to become Tsarina of Russia and the Princess of Wales, were both rumored to have sharp tongues. The Queen's limited enthusiasm for her daughter-in-law was well known throughout England and now it was clear that Her Majesty was accumulating reasons to dislike the tsarina as well.

"The note says we are to be received at the German Staircase," Alix said, tearing her eyes from the glitter of her own torso and looking upon her sister. "Is that where the most important visitors enter the banquet floor?"

Ella hesitated, just long enough for everyone in the room save Alix to guess the answer. Trevor looked at Emma for guidance. She was frowning.

"The German Staircase," Ella finally said. "It's a very thoughtful acknowledgement of our heritage, is it not?"

Alix was satisfied with this vague response. No one else was.

"My understanding is that the Jordan Staircase is the means by which the imperial family enters the public areas of the palace," the Queen said and Ella's immediate flush was confirmation that this was so. So not only were they to be feted at a party which was not really planned in their honor, but they were to enter via a back staircase wearing other people's clothes. The slap in the face could not have been more definitive.

"Does any of it truly matter?" Ella asked. "As long as we all come to the same table in the end?"

But of course it mattered. Even Trevor, who was struggling to assimilate the implications of a borrowed dress and an inferior staircase, could see that the Russians were heaping one humiliation after another upon the heads of their English guests.

"We shall all come to the same table," the Queen said faintly. "And then we shall see what will happen." Alix nodded and disappeared back into her dressing room, with Emma following close behind, her face already grim with anticipation about the degree of effort it would take to wrest that ponderous gown over Alix's head. Only the Queen, Ella, and Trevor were left in the lounge and the Queen turned to her granddaughter.

"You cannot pretend that this is anything other than what it is," she said. "The Danish Tsarina sends us down the German staircase, when you know as well as anyone how the Danes view the Germans. She sends this grand gown, with each jewel a boulder around your sister's neck. Your family through marriage has chosen to mock your family of birth."

Ella flinched. "Granny, please do not put me in this position."

"You situation is cruel, I realize, but I was not the one who placed you there," Victoria said, looking down into her lap where her small plump hands were twisting a handkerchief with sharp, measured moves. "Someday soon you will be forced to make your choice."

The Winter Palace – St. George's Hall

9:17 PM

They may have entered by means of a minor staircase, but their introduction into the festivities of the imperial dinner was still dazzling. Trevor doubted that anyone other than himself and Emma, who had witnessed the awkward discussion in Ella's apartment, was aware that the British visitors were being in any way marginalized. For in the presence of such splendor, who could find the subtle lines of demarcation? Who could remember that rubies are inferior to sapphires, that the music of Mozart soars higher that of Chopin, or that white caviar is a more valuable tidbit to place upon a cracker than black?

They had descended the German staircase – which seemed perfectly broad and grand to Trevor's eyes - then processed through a series of gigantic galleries, each as humbling as a cathedral, treading on carpets thick enough to make the feet trip and passing beneath a series of brilliant chandeliers, before finally arriving at the banquet hall. As a person entered, he or she was escorted to the appropriate seat by a Cossack guard, each of them clad in scarlet and as stern faced as if a dinner in honor of the summer solstice was the equivalent of a military assault. Trevor, who had been seated relatively early in the procession of guests, watched the others enter the ballroom in their turn: the generals, their chests sagging with medals, most of them likely won in conflict with the Turks. The women, their breasts equally challenged, but this time with the weight of their jewels. Medals of their own kind, no doubt, evidence that they had managed to parlay their youth, beauty, sexuality, or family connection into an alliance with one of the aforementioned generals or perhaps – even better – with some minor relative of the ruling family. For if there was anything that the Romanovs valued more than military strength, it was imperial blood.

Trevor was positioned about halfway down an astoundingly long table and there were a variety of other smaller ones, flanking to either side. How many people would ultimately dine in this room, he wondered, trying to do a quick count in his head of the still-empty seats. Two hundred? Perhaps more? Trevor cast a glance around to ascertain the location of his teammates: Tom a bit forward, Rayley a bit back. Emma approaching one of the side tables on the arm of a Cossack, and looking especially lovely in an amethyst gown with a border of gold. He couldn't imagine her owning such a thing, so perhaps she too had been subjected to the stinging courtesy of a borrowed gown.

The Tsar and Tsarina – he, ridiculously large and she, ridiculously tiny – were seated at the elevated table at the far end of the room with the Queen to the left of the Tsar. Her Majesty wore black, the only woman in the room to do so, making her a solitary raven among so many peacocks. She appeared ill at ease to find herself perched on a raised platform, which did give the effect that the hosts and their most honored guests were actors on a stage. State dinners at Buckingham, Trevor surmised, must be nothing like this.

Ella and a man who was presumably her husband Serge sat at the end of the table, each of them staring straight ahead like faces on a postal stamp. Since there was no one in front of you, a seat at the head table effectively halved one's chances for lively dinner conversation, and it was quite clear that Ella and Serge had exhausted all potential topics for discussion long ago. Trevor wondered once again what Ella might have seen in such a man. Handsome enough, but cold, his eyes focused on some distant horizon, his mouth pressed into a straight and unyielding line.

The rest of the imperial family had been meted out around the room, presumably so that no guest would feel as if he had been exiled to a social Siberia. Trevor was a bit surprised that Nicky and Alix had not earned a spot at the head table, him being next in line for the throne and she a stated guest of honor. But the two young people seemed more than happy to be wedged in close congress at a small table at the base of the raised platform, a situation which gave the suggestion that their parents and grandparents were literally looking down upon them. If Ella and Serge were keeping their decorous distance, Nicky and Alix were the opposite, with every gesture illustrating their mutual affection. They leaned ever-so-slightly toward each other, even when politely chatting with others seated around them, and young Alix was flushed with happiness. Nicky glanced at her frequently, his own pleasure in her company equally evident, and the sight of them made Trevor somewhat ashamed. His function during this entire trip was to collect proof that the country was unsuitable for the Queen's favorite granddaughter and the Russians were making his task very easy indeed. Three murders in a week was scarcely a ringing endorsement for life within the Winter Palace. And the Queen was right, of course, to wish a different future for Alix than the dreary fate which had trapped Ella, and yet the sight of Alix and Nicky sharing shy smiles troubled Trevor. Only a fool would doubt that they were most sincerely in love.

Trevor's own table boasted the presence of the tsar's elder daughter, Xenia, who looked to be barely in her teens. He tried to remember what Emma had said on the ship during her lecture on protocol, and could only recall that a princess, the daughter of a king, must curtsy to a grand duchess, the daughter of a tsar. He wondered how many times Ella had supplicated before this pudgy, nondescript child, and how far she was required to stand behind her husband's niece on state occasions. He suspected that her life was full of such small indignities and was only glad that the obscurity of the German staircase had meant that very few foreign eyes had been treated to the sight of the mighty Victoria inclining her own head - barely an inch, but still - to the Tsar.

Next to pick out the infamous Konstantin, which was simple enough. Emma had described him as "Oriental, but not at all as you'd think," and Trevor's eyes were almost immediately pulled toward a tall, elegant man at a seat a good deal more far-flung than his own. The only Asians Trevor had ever seen were the chaps who ran the tailoring houses of London, and they were small, darting people who seemed to be perpetually looking at the ground. This man's height gave him presence, and the absence of ornamentation on his clothing further distinguished him. And yet it was his strange stillness which Trevor found the most compelling. Nothing in his manner betrayed even the slightest anxiety, which was noteworthy in this room of incessant chattering and high, manic laughter, and Trevor was forced to admit that it was easy to imagine all sorts of women being drawn to him. If Serge seemed perfectly cast as the unfeeling villain in the piece, then Konstantin Antonovich was equally well suited to play the role of exotic lover.

Tatiana was harder to find. Small and blonde and pretty was all he had to go on, and that description could have been applied to a dozen women within his sites. The odds were she would be sitting near her husband, but Trevor did not see anyone fitting Rayley's description of Orlov at all. Trevor turned in his seat to more clearly face in the direction of Rayley, whose eye he quickly caught, since the other detective was also systematically scanning the room. Trevor mouthed the word "Orlov?" and Rayley shrugged and shook his head, then turned his attention back to the woman on his right, a frail and elderly creature wearing some sort of turban.

Trevor's own dining partner was a woman so bejeweled that she looked as if a drawerful of emeralds and rubies had been overturned on top of her. My God, he thought. These people make the French seem understated. The woman glittered. She simpered. She chortled with amusement at jokes she made herself. She even heaven forbid, flirted with him and he knew that politeness required him to meet her thrust to thrust.

"Tell me, Sir," she was saying. "From what you have seen so far, do you prefer the ladies of St. Petersburg to those of London?" It was obvious what answer she expected.

"The ladies here tonight are dazzling," Trevor assured her, which was true enough in its way. The light bouncing from some of them was enough to make a man avert his eyes in fear of blindness. "Tell me, who among us is considered to be the greatest beauty of the court?" Her plump lips immediately pushed into a pout and he hastened to add "Besides you, of course. I realize I have been most fortunately seated."

Good God, but he was bad at this. The woman hesitated, as if wondering how long she should punish him for his small social slip, but quickly relented. They had not yet received the first course of what would likely be a laboriously long dinner; she seemed to decide that there was no need to alienate her traveling companion so quickly in the journey, for her pout gave way to a smile and she leaned forward to whisper in his ear. With this gesture, the egg-shaped ruby wedged between her ample cleavage all but threatened to roll out onto the table and Trevor tried not to gape. He had been taught to staunchly ignore this part of a woman's anatomy, no matter how temptingly it might be presented, but it seemed this was but yet another way in which they did things differently in Russia. Given the calculating manner in which his partner's breasts were arranged, he feared it might be ruder to ignore them, rather like refusing to salute a flag.

She whispered several names in his ear that meant nothing, twisting and pointing at various tables as she did so. Trevor noted that all of the women she indicated as beauties had a similar round-faced large-eyed appearance, making them seem a succession of rather vapid dolls. The Romanov court apparently appreciated a most specific type of feminine beauty. But with the last name, Tatiana Orlov, she directed his gaze toward yet another small, blonde woman and this time Trevor was given pause. On one level, Tatiana was much like the others. On another level, she was extraordinary, with dimples and heavily-lashed eyes and cheeks which glowed without benefit of rouge. She was what the others wish to look like, Trevor thought. She is the prototype they aspire to, the way jewelers cut glass in a doomed attempt to emulate diamonds.

"You like her?" his companion asked sharply.

He had evidently given himself away, so there was no need to lie.

"She is beautiful."

The woman shrugged, and her ruby rose and fell. "Her birth was common."

As was mine, Trevor thought, raising a glass of champagne to his lips and smiling apologetically at his companion. At times like this he often pondered what throws of chance had brought him to these grand and foreign places, so far from the simple village of his youth. Back then he had often announced to his schoolfellows that when he was a man he would go to the city, and they had all jeered at his boast. By "the city," he had of course meant London. A portrait of the much-younger Victoria had hung on the wall of his schoolhouse, a map of England beside her, and this was as far as Trevor's mind could expand. If anyone had suggested he would someday find himself in France or Russia, serving Her Majesty on missions of intrigue, he would not have deemed such a thing possible. The life of the man had exceeded the dreams of the boy, a state of being which may sound marvelous, but which actually had left him adrift, unsure of what to hope for next. He wondered if Tatiana Orlov, raised from her own humble past to become one of the acknowledged beauties of the Romanov court, ever felt the same way.

The first course, thank heaven, was finally being served. Not by the Cossacks, whom Trevor thought might double as footmen, but instead by a host of servants in full livery. They swarmed the tables with serving dishes while the Cossacks remained farther back, lining the walls, where evidently they would remain for untold hours at military attention. As the tureens of soup were circulated around the table, Trevor's dining companion drained her champagne glass and then – or could he have imagined this? – winked at him.

    From there, the procession of dishes was rapid enough to confuse a scholar and the wines were potent and plentiful enough to knock a gourmand to the floor. At one point, an entire fawn, his legs curled beneath him, his eyes bright and trusting, was carried in on a great silver platter and deposited on the head table between the Tsar and the Queen. This grand entrance was meant to signal the arrival of the venison course - the seventh or perhaps the eighth, for it was impossible to keep count in the face of such an onslaught. The one thing that Trevor did note was that the manners of the imperial family and their guests were growing steadily more appalling as the dinner progressed. The men drank at a pace which could only be described as businesslike, and talked far too loudly, sometimes shouting over the ladies seated between them. Down the table, the young Grand Duchess Xenia had done nothing but complain that the Tchaikovsky ball had delayed their normal summer progress to the shore and the pleasures which awaited her there. Trevor had no doubt that she would not have tempered her displeasure with this inconvenience even if she had been seated beside the composer himself. His own dining companion had just sucked a clam from its shell with all the finesse of an East End whore and now sat gazing at him in the manner of one who has seen the worst of the world and fervently hopes to see it soon again.

"Our ultimate aim, of course, is to unite the two shores of our land," the young Nicholas was saying, with such palpable enthusiasm that it rang out to all within earshot. Trevor, with yet one more smile of apology at his dinner mate, had to incline his head and strain to hear him. With his entire table in respectful attendance, Nicholas went on to extol the virtues of the half-completed Trans-Siberian Railway. To hear the young tsesarevich speak, you would think that no previous nation had ever struck upon the idea of building a single continuous track from one end of their country to the other, cutting across deserts, rivers, mountains, prairies, and whatever else it found along the way. Trevor suspected the project was in fact a mimic of the famous railways of the American west and wondered if the Trans-Siberian system, upon its conclusion, would have a similar impact. It seemed that if Russia had truly found a way to create reliable transport from the European-influenced St. Petersburg all the way to the shores of the Pacific Ocean, taking in Moscow, Siberia, and Mongolia along the way, then Russia would be…

Unstoppable.

The word struck Trevor like a thud to the chest. As it now stood, Russia's massive size could be deemed as much a disadvantage as an advantage, rendering the country difficult to govern with borders far too expansive to defend. But what would happen if the country did find a means of marshalling its staggering wealth of resources? If so, they truly would become another America – so vast and rich that no nation in Europe could begin to match their collective power. Trevor was not sure the civilized world could handle a second America. It had barely survived the first one.

"And I shall tell them so the next time the committee meets…" Nicholas was saying. He trailed off at this point, betraying himself by glancing nervously in the direction of his father. It was evident that Nicholas had not yet found a seat on this much-acclaimed Trans-Siberian committee, and was thus not yet in a position to tell anyone anything. But it was just as evident that he fervently wished to be. The boy has a desire to matter, Trevor thought. If not on this committee, then on some other. He needs something to give him a voice, a role, and a man's place at the table of power. Alix had abandoned any pretense of conversation with the gentleman seated on her other side and was straining in her seat toward Nicky, smiling and nodding to indicate she was listening to his every word.

But, unfortunately for the tsesarevich, so was his father.

"Committee?" the tsar boomed. His voice was low and deep, pitched to the timbre of a cannon and it had the unlucky effect of halting conversation all around him so that his words to his son thundered down from the elevated table to those on the floor. At least a third of the room had ceased conversation, making Trevor wonder how on earth the tsar had been able to hear Nicky's words in the din. But perhaps the acoustics of the banquet hall, like those of the theater, were contrived to benefit people seated in certain locations.

"You are not ready for the Trans-Siberian committee," Alexander called out to his son, in the grand and empty silence. "I shall have a set of toy trains sent to your room instead."

And then he boomed with laughter, the sound crueler than his words, and Trevor dropped his gaze back down to his plate, fairly certain everyone in earshot was doing the same thing. No matter what their nationality or politics, Trevor suspected they were all discomforted to see a young man so utterly humiliated in the presence of the woman he loved.

Voices slowly entered back into the void and conversation resumed. Trevor gulped from his glass and stole a sideways look to the table where Nicholas was sitting – silent, but with an odd look of forbearance on his face. Emma was right, Trevor thought. He has not been trained in politics at all, not even the politics of the dinner table, or else he would not have risked such a childish brag within earshot of his father. Nicholas had deep dark eyes and a kind and gentle expression. He has the innocent look of a faun, Trevor thought, and we can all see what happens to fauns around here.

"I am ready for a grand ball," said Xenia. "A silly little dinner like this is a dreadful bore, but a ball…"

And here she drifted off, seemingly unaware of how her words might sound to the British guests, articulating what had previously only been hinted: that the arrival of Victoria, Alix, and their coterie was an occasion worth only a bit more fuss at a silly little dinner which had already been planned. The possibility that the Queen of England might be forced to offer Russia yet another granddaughter was certainly not an event worthy of a grand ball.

"The Tchaikovsky is coming up soon enough," the man beside her said to Xenia, with a wearied air. He had evidently had a long night.

"Good, for I am bored," she said. "I don't like the Winter Palace in the summer." She chattered on about the glories of the Palace in cold weather- grand balls for Christmas, sledding on the hills or ice skating on the Neva- and Trevor reflected that the Romanov family, like most of the royal houses of Europe, were hardly a bevy of intellectuals. They liked to talk about the events of their days, but their days never varied. They liked to talk about their relatives, but their relatives were all alike. Irony was lost on the majority of them, as was humor, unless you counted vulgar jokes. Belches and farts and the like and they did not like to debate ideas, for to enter into a debate was to concede that there might be more than one rational way to look at a matter, and this was something that royals as a species were loath to accept. As Xenia prattled on to her captive audience about toboggans and snowmen, Trevor let his gaze once again move to Alix and Nicky.

"Religion," Alix was saying, "is not a ring that one can slip on and off."

Oh dear, thought Trevor. She sounds so serious, so pious, so much the exception to the rule I have just established. The next thing we know she will be lecturing everyone on the meaning of Paradise Lost. She already has the wrong clothes and she furthermore distinguishes herself as an intellectual, her position at court is fully doomed. Bloody slabs of venison were being deposited on each plate along the table.

"Of course not," Nicholas was responding. "I quite agree. I agree with…I agree, of course, with everything you say."

They could be such a nice young couple, Trevor thought. The boy a little timid, too eager to please, too desperate to be liked. The girl tense and solemn, pitched forward with the weight of her unaccustomed jewels. If they lived in another time and place, if they were not required to become Nicholas and Alexandria, and could remain just Alix and Nicky… He might make a great success somewhere as a greengrocer or a bookkeeper, perhaps a chemist. She would be a devoted mother, the sort who read to her children each night as they drifted to sleep. They'd be lovely people to have as neighbors, a family you smile and tip your hat to on a Sunday stroll.

They would be fine, Trevor thought, just fine if they were average people.

Trevor cut a bite of venison and raised it to his mouth. It was delicious, stunningly so, with the lusciousness of the flesh unchanged even when he looked into the tranquil brown eyes of the faun centerpiece on the high table. What were they all to make of this, of this great dinner with its dozens of hidden implications, not the least of which was that it was not truly so great? That the imperial family was welcoming them with a yawn and not a fanfare, and beyond the wine-dulled drone of conversation swirling over the tables Trevor's eyes moved to the double doors opening into the portico and the glow beyond. It was late, or perhaps early, but what difference could it make? No matter what the hour or what the day, the sky remained the same. The sun visible for twenty hours on this particular date on the calendar. Sunset fading to a milky shade of pearl which would last until morning and then, when one looked to the east, you would see the true miracle of the summer solstice: That before the light of the old order had fully departed, a new day had already dawned.

Chapter Sixteen

The Winter Palace – The Imperial Gardens

June 22, 1889

2:20 PM

"I trust you did not find my invitation for you to join me in my daily stroll untoward," Ella said. "But I wished to speak to you privately."

"Of course," Tom said, as if a summons to an imperial suite was an everyday event. This was the second time in three days that a woman had insisted that they should meet alone and he could only hope this time did not end as badly as the last.

"Is my grandmother well? I have never known her to travel with a doctor."

"It's a precaution only, I assure you," Tom said, offering Ella his arm as they strolled through the small enclosed garden behind her apartments. She ignored it.

"I'm sure the solstice dinner was distressing to her."

"It was an interesting evening for everyone present."

"She has no intention of allowing Alix to marry Nicky, does she?"

"I assure you that I am not privy to Her Majesty's private thoughts."

Ella looked at him out of the corner of her eye. She truly is lovely, Tom thought, suddenly seeing how Ella might have once been proclaimed the most desirable princess in Europe. She's a bit of a tyrant and a bit of a prig, but God knows they all are, and as princesses go, she does have a certain fire.

"What you mean is that you're too ethical to reveal facts to which you are undoubtedly privy, which speaks well of you as a private physician. Tell me, Tom, is there some sort of doctor-patient confidentiality, just as that which exists between a person and his solicitor?"

She was good. The use of his given name, tossed in so casually, and the belated decision to take his arm, to turn her profile only slightly more toward him. Ella was a woman who had been frequently photographed and painted throughout her life and she knew her best perspective was this one, neither fully facing the man nor fully in profile, but somewhere in between. Yes, just like this, with her remarkable eyes regarding him from the side. She was trying to charm him and despite the fact Tom recognized her tricks – despite the fact he himself had used similar ones on countless occasions – he was not immune to her machinations.

He smiled. "I would consider it an honor to serve you just as I serve your grandmother."

"And does my grandmother have to know that you are to be…in service to me as well?"

"Of course not," he said, with more certainty than he felt. Where the devil was this all heading? She had paused before a rosebush, and therefore he had paused with her, both of them considering the blossoms before them, the heady smell of the flowers hovering in the heat.

"What experience do you have in the practice of obstetrics?"

The question startled him. It was the last thing he had expected her to say.

"There is to be a baby?"

"Not mine. I wish you to attend a friend."

"Where is this friend?"

"In her room. Packing."

"So your friend is going somewhere?" It was a nonsensical question, but the best he could muster under the circumstances.

"She will be traveling to the coast. Or at least she will be, with your help. And I intend to go with her."

"This conversation is very obscure, Your Imperial Highness."

"Only by necessity. Follow me."

And so he did. Into the building and down the halls, the damn halls. The never ending halls. Later, in the storm-tossed nights which followed excessive drinking, Tom would sometimes dream of a hell which was very much like the Winter Palace – an eternal succession of hallways, doubling back upon themselves, collectively leading nowhere. Tom and Ella walked through them, their feet sometimes silent on the islands of carpet and then tapping quietly against the wooden floors until Ella at last paused in front of a rather ordinary door in a rather ordinary section of the residential wing of the palace. Tom casually tilted his head and tried to take in the sort of details he knew Trevor and the others would expect to hear upon his return. Judging by the moderate spacing of the doors, as well as the pedestrian quality of the artwork on the walls, he could only conclude that they were in some sort of middle tier of the palace. Not as grand as the imperial wings, nor as dreary as the working staff's rooms, but somewhere in between.

Ella rapped once and then turned the knob. The door swung open. Evidently they were expected.

Tom followed Ella through a sitting room and into a bedroom where a woman was indeed packing. One chest stood open on the floor, another was already locked and strapped on the bed, and her arms were full of dresses destined for a third.

"My friend, Tatiana Orlov," Ella said. "And this is Dr. Thomas – do you have a last name, doctor?"

"Bainbridge," Tom said. Tatiana flushed.

She had recognized him, just as he recognized her. She was the same petite blonde woman he and Emma had found in the theater dressing rooms scurrying away from the arms of Konstantin Antonovich to hide herself under a pile of costumes.

"Tatiana is going to have a child," Ella said.

"This is true?" Tom asked Tatiana, without caring if the question insulted Ella. The woman before him was so small, so impossibly slender beneath her laced corset, that it scarcely seemed possible she was pregnant. She could not have been more than two or three months along and women were often still uncertain in that stage of gestation.

The woman nodded. Her expression conveyed nothing about how she felt in the matter. She may as well have been agreeing that it was lovely weather.

"She is going to have a baby…and then, I am going to have a baby," Ella said. "Do you understand what I am telling you?"

He did. The plan was neither original nor complex. One woman is carrying a child that, for whatever reason, she must not have. Another woman desperately needs a child that, for whatever reason, she cannot conceive. And so a friendship forms between the two, an alliance both unholy and as old as the Bible.

Tom turned toward Ella. "Your husband will accept the baby as his own?"

"Yes. More readily than you could ever know."

His eyes moved to Tatiana. "And I assume your own husband is not aware of your pregnancy?"

Both women flinched at the word "pregnancy," as if he had uttered a vulgarity in their presence, and Tom wondered anew at the peculiar sensitivities of women, how the two of them could calmly plot the brokering of a human life, each of them most profoundly duping her husband in the process, but still recoil from such a simple biological term.

Tatiana shook her head. "Filip has suffered many… many injuries in his service to the tsar," she finally said, and he realized this was the first time he had ever heard her voice. It was low pitched, out of accord with her delicate appearance and thus rather thrilling. He thought back to the scar Rayley had described on Filip's chest in the sauna and wondered if Tatiana was implying that some sort of further unseen damage had rendered her husband sterile. Tom could think of no obvious way in which a shot to the torso could create such an unwelcome complication; if Filip Orlov was unable to father children, syphilis was a more likely explanation than a wound in the line of duty.

Of course, the particulars of how it happened really didn't matter that much to the issue at hand. If Tatiana Orlov believed her husband to be sterile and yet was currently pregnant, then her situation was dire indeed.

"My father is dark," Ella added, "in both hair and complexion." The remark seemed bizarrely off the subject until Tom considered the line of argument the women evidently intended to follow, the argument they were practicing on him. The child Tatiana was carrying was almost undoubtedly fathered by Konstantin Antonovich, and Tom's mind flashed to the images of the man's heavy dark hair and intense almond-shaped eyes, so different in every way from the fair, startled-looking Romanovs.

"Have you been ill?" Tom asked Tatiana.

"A little. In the morning, just as they say."

"That's a good sign. Evidence that the pregnancy is well established and will continue."

She smiled and nodded with evident relief. So, despite it all, apparently at least part of her was happy to be carrying this baby and grateful for his assurances. The plan these two intended was madness, madness in every way, but it was not his place to tell them so. Tom looked from Tatiana back to Ella. "So what do you want from me?" he asked bluntly. "Her baby is obviously not due to be born for many months."

"If you had a patient who was an expectant mother…" Ella said vaguely.

"If you were my patient, you mean," Tom said. It was bad form to interrupt royalty but this was no time to stand on ceremony.

"Precisely," said Ella. "If I were your patient would you advise me to escape the dangers of the city and spend my confinement in the country? By the sea, perhaps?"

"Yes I most certainly would," Tom said. It was perhaps the only completely honest statement which had been uttered in the room since they entered. "Cities are full of contagion as a matter of course and I would imagine that St. Petersburg, which was built on marshland, is worse than most. Especially in the summer. When I was walking in the gardens just this morning I thought I saw a hummingbird which, on closer inspection, turned out to be a mosquito."

Tatiana not only relaxed at this statement but looked almost amused. Ella, however, bristled at this slight to her adopted city.

"We were never meant to summer here," she said icily. "We have remained overlong this year because of the Tchaikovsky ball."

"I'm aware of that," Tom said, his own tone nearly as icy. He was once again verging on the edge of rudeness to a woman of rank, but he couldn't see Ella running to tattle to her husband or her granny about anything he said in the course of this particular conversation. He had always found it an affectation when people used the words "summer" and "winter" as verbs, and he wondered if Ella, who was accustomed to decamping to the sea with the first heat of June, had ever bothered to consider all the citizens of the city, pregnant or not, who were forced to endure the risk of cholera and malaria year round. But just as it was not his job to tell Ella that her plan was mad, nor was it his job to lecture her on her marital family's responsibilities to their people.

"I believe," he said in a more conciliatory tone, "the question before us is whether or not a doctor would advise an expectant mother to go to the country rather than remain in the city, and the answer is yes. The purity of ocean air is most palliative, especially when temperatures climb."

"And you would say this to my grandmother? As general advice, that is?"

"Of course. But I will not lie to my monarch. I will not tell your grandmother I have found you pregnant when I have not."

"You do not have to lie," Ella said, with an impatient shake of her head. "I will tell her about the baby myself. And we shall all leave soon. Just after the ball. Due to the untimely death of my former lady in waiting, I have asked my sister-in-law if she can spare Tatiana from her own court to enter my service and she has most kindly agreed. And so we are an expectant imperial mother and her loyal attendant traveling to a safe place for the duration of her confinement. No one shall find anything odd in it at all."

"Who is this 'we' who will leave soon?" Tom asked. Dear God, she didn't expect him to travel with them, did she?

"Tatiana and I to the coast…" Ella said.

"And Konstantin to Paris," Tatiana said simply.

And with that Tom saw the whole of the situation. In giving Ella her child, Tatiana had bought the safe passage of her lover. Once he was ensconced in France, Konstantin would be far beyond the reach of Filip Orlov, or anyone else inclined to frame him for a triple murder.

"Konstantin Antonovich is a lucky man," Tom said. "He seems to enjoy the most intense loyalty of all the women in his life. You are certain that you're prepared to do this?"

"He must never know," Ella interrupted. "He doesn't like for women to lead him. Just ask your red-haired friend what he's like." She crossed her arms across her chest and gave a slight, definitive shudder. "Russian men are proud, Siberian men even more so. He leaves us no choice but to dissemble, for he would never accept the risks that two women are undertaking to guarantee his safety."

Tatiana had resumed packing. It was impossible to see her face.

"I need a baby," Ella said defiantly, as if Tom had uttered some word of protest. "Tatiana needs to not have a baby. Konstantin needs to leave Russia. But all three of these problems are easy to rectify if we work together. We can be, in a sense, each other's saviors. Why do you hesitate?" she added, when Tom did not answer, but rather continued to watch Tatiana struggling to push an armful of dresses into the small valise. "Surely you can see that this child will be given every privilege in life, will have every sort of comfort."

"Are you quite certain you want to stay in Russia?" Tom asked, a question that was directed toward Ella even though his eyes never left Tatiana.

The question seemed to pull Ella up short. "This is where my destiny lies," she finally said.

"Well, you certainly sound Russian."

"Fatalism is the true national contagion," Ella said with a slight laugh. "And I fear I have caught it. This baby will be the salvation of Serge as well, as you have undoubtedly noticed, doctor. Your eyes are very sharp. He and I shall have our child and Konstantin will have his new life in Paris. He is innocent, we all know this, but once a man has been singled out by the private guard, the truth does not seem to matter. Tatiana will concur with this opinion, I believe, and realize that I do not mean it as a criticism of her husband, but simply as a pragmatic analysis of the situation."

She is so like her grandmother, Tom thought. Moving people about to suit her aims. Manipulating the world and calling it fate.

Tatiana had now closed the trunk and was buckling the strap. "And if Konstantin gets his freedom and Ella and Serge get a child, what do you gain from this bargain?" Tom asked her. "You seem the forgotten soul in this grand plan."

"I gain redemption," she said quietly. "My sins have been numerous, Dr. Bainbridge."

"Somehow, my dear Mrs. Orlov, I doubt that your sins have been any more numerous or more damning than those of anyone else."

"She will live in the closest proximity to the child," Ella said, her voice conveying no particular understanding that such proximity might well be a torment and not a relief. "And not just this year, when Tatiana and I must remain inseparable, even after the men have returned to the city in the fall. She will always attend me, and thus my family. Her husband will become guard to mine. It happens all the time you know, this swapping back and forth of servants. And I assure you, Doctor Bainbridge, that Tatiana and Filip shall be rewarded for their loyalty, both of them."

"Yes," said Tatiana. "And besides, life is long, is it not, Dr. Bainbridge?"

"For some of us it is far longer than it is for others," he said. The most painful part of the affair was not the woman's sacrifice, but the faint flash of hope which remained in her eyes. She was clinging to the idea that she might someday yet join her lover in Paris, a dream Tom deemed unlikely. Once the child was born Tatiana would undoubtedly find it impossible to leave, knowing that she would never again see her son or daughter. She would trade away any chance for her own future happiness and remain forever in the thankless role of Ella's new lady in waiting, and thus servant to her own flesh and blood.

"I shall write my grandmother this afternoon," Ella said. "And all you must do, when she asks, is confirm that you did indeed tell me that St. Petersburg is a dangerous place for a woman in such a delicate condition. She will readily believe you. She hates this city and has always claimed that the entire Winter Palace was built on a web of pestilence, ready to split and sink back into the Neva at the slightest provocation."

"You don't wish to tell the Queen your happy news in person?" Tom asked. It seemed Ella was far more concerned with what her grandmother might say or do than she was with the reaction of her husband. The men in their lives cannot possibly be so gullible as these women are betting, Tom thought. If the rumors are true, then Serge will certainly know Ella cannot be with child and even if Tatiana managed to conceal her own condition from Filip throughout the summer, it was unlikely she would be able to avoid all intimacies throughout the autumn and winter, up until time for the child to be born. Some luckless doctor on the coast would have to be taken into their plan, bribed or threatened to attend Ella and then deliver Tatiana. Tom observed the two women in the reflection of the mirror which hung on the far wall. They were in many ways different – Ella tall and russet haired, Tatiana with a bird-like frame and mass of blond curls – but they both were beautiful and he supposed that this singular fact might be the key to their ultimate ability to sell this extraordinarily unlikely story, to somehow keep the illusion afloat. Men believe what they want to believe when it comes to women, especially when it comes to female fecundity, truly the greatest magic trick of them all.

Ella tossed her head. "No, I shall write Granny a note to be delivered only when it is time for her to depart. We have quarreled once already, which is quite enough. Did you know? But of course you do. Everyone in the Winter Palace knows the business of everyone else. Some claim it to be the largest residence in the world but when it comes to privacy, we may as well be a gaggle of peasants living in a one-room hut. But it doesn't matter. By this time next summer Serge and I shall be visiting England with a baby in our arms. And the birth of a child has a way of making everything new and right, does it not? Old discords are forgotten and the future seems suddenly hopeful."

"I hope you are right," Tom said. "For your sake and the sake of everyone involved, especially the child."

"Granny will forgive me when she sees the baby," Ella continued, speaking more to herself than to the others. "The child will come with the new year, which is a good sign. They say the earlier in the year a child is born, the more auspicious its future, do they not?"

"I've never heard that particular theory," Tom said. His own birthday was in late November.

"Tell me doctor, have you ever seen a Fabrege egg?"

Another of her jarring changes of subject, but by now Tom was growing use to them. "I have certainly heard of Fabrege. He is the royal jeweler, is he not?"

Although the room was Tatiana's, Ella confidently went to a bureau drawer and opened it. "I want you to see something," she said. "I had it commissioned weeks ago, on some impulse I could not have explained, and now Tatiana has agreed to hide it for me until the proper time." She unwrapped a cloth of blue velvet and revealed a golden egg, about the size of her hand, the top of it crusted in rubies and emeralds.

"It is the only one of its kind," she said, her voice sinking to a whisper. "They are all individual, you know, created by the master to mark a particular occasion or celebration."

She handed it to Tom, who cautiously turned it over in his palm. There were not only the large jewels at the top, but the egg was covered with a profusion of carefully wrought vines, each one coming to bud in the form of a perfectly-shaped seed pearl. The value of such an item was inestimable.

"You will take it, yes?" Ella said quietly. "To remember your time here in Russia?"

This is a land, Tom thought, in which anything can be bought. A woman's child. A doctor's silence. The passage of a suspected murderer across a national border.

"The grandness of the gift overwhelms me," Tom said. "But I fear I cannot accept. It is my duty and my honor to serve your Royal Highness in any capacity."

"Your Imperial Highness," she corrected.

"It is my honor to serve your Imperial Highness," Tom amended, wondering once again what sort of subtle psychological nightmares awaited Tatiana Orlov during her long dark autumn by the sea with this woman.

"And have you seen this part? It is exceptionally clever," Ella went blithely on, changing mood so rapidly that Tom wondered if she was not merely spoiled and self-centered, but somehow mentally unsound. Ella pressed a panel in the center of the egg and a small golden hen popped out of the top.

"Many of them are like this," she said. "Designed with some sort of surprise inside, whether it is a small portrait of the person giving the gift or perhaps some symbolic message. As in this case, do you see? The hen represents fertility and is thus a subtle way for a woman to tell a man that she is carrying his child."

"Then perhaps this particular egg should be given to the baby's father," Tom said.

"Ah, yes" said Ella. "Yes, perhaps you are right. But see here, this part is clever. You press the panel on the other side and, just like this, our golden hen is gone."

"So it is a trick," Tom said.

"I suppose a trick is precisely what it is," Ella said with a shrug, as she carelessly rolled the egg back into the blue velvet cloth and replaced it in Tatiana's bureau drawer. "But it is a pleasing one, is it not?

The Streets of St. Petersburg

3:54 PM

"You seem to work rather lenient hours."

Davy looked at Vlad out of the corner of his eye. Was this a challenge? Were they onto him somehow? "The Queen does most of her paperwork in the morning," he said. "Any correspondence she sends is likely gone by early afternoon."

"Lucky for you, I'd say."

"Are you about to tell me that the work of a revolutionary is never done?"

To Davy's relief, and somewhat to his surprise, Vlad laughed. He was such a serious sort that Davy found it hard to tell when he would accept a joke on face value and when it might prickle his sensibilities. The two young men were walking in a rather indirect fashion toward the Volya meeting, a stroll which Davy was enjoying, since it gave him the opportunity to see more of the city. The streets of St. Petersburg were broad and beautiful, with space between the buildings and a more modern sense than one found in London. This openness is what you get when you build a city from scratch rather than letting it evolve over centuries, Davy thought, trying to remember all that Emma had told them on their lectures at sea. She had unleashed a torrent of facts on their heads in a matter of days and Davy doubted that a fraction of it had truly sunk in to any of them. He wondered if Emma would be willing to tutor him on history when they returned to London, but at a more civilized pace, perhaps one evening a week in Geraldine's parlor. It would be embarrassing to ask her, an admission of how limited his past education had been, but he suspected she would say yes.

"What is the meeting about today?" he further ventured, since Vlad appeared to be in good humor.

"A licking of wounds," Vlad said. "We had a great plan which fell through when one of our comrades was killed."

"The ballet dancer."

Vlad sighed. "What are they saying of the matter inside the palace?"

"That it was a double suicide."

"They would call it that, wouldn't they?"

"I take it you don't agree."

"Of course not. Yulian Krupin was not the sort to kill himself. In fact, he was disgustingly happy."

Davy raised an eyebrow.

"Oh you know, happy," Vlad elaborated, flapping his hands about like wounded birds. "He had a girl in his bed, food in his belly, a ticket to Paris in his pocket. Besides, even if his life hadn't been such a plum, Yulian didn't have the bollocks to do himself in, especially not with a knife to the throat. My guess is that someone within the palace did the deed for him. Someone who had figured out who and what he was."

"And do you have any notion as to who that might have been?"

Vlad hesitated. "You know the members of the Queen's private guard?"

"We all traveled over together, of course."

"What do they think of security within the Palace?"

Now it was Davy's turn to hesitate. But after running through several alternatives, he decided that the most appropriate response was also the most truthful. "They don't hold it in high regard. The place is so big and spread out that it seems the left hand doesn't know what the right hand is doing. The tsar's private guard is a different group entirely from the palace police and the two entities don't share information. That sort of thing."

"The Russians are all fools. I assume that this is what the Queen's British bodyguards think?"

Davy was conscious that his mouth was dry and his heart seemed to be pounding its way up his throat. How on earth had he, he of all of them, been placed into this sensitive position? "I have never heard them call the Russians fools," he finally ventured. "But they have said that they find the structure of the Palace inefficient, at least from the standpoint of security."

"Which is precisely what Yulian reported to the Volya," Vlad said, his tone of voice once again mild. They were walking across the expanse of a great public square and Davy was suddenly, at the sight of the giant statue of Peter the Great, oriented to where he was in the city. "When he first told us about the plans for the Tchaikovsky ball we scarcely believed him. He described a scene of such confusion, with so many people coming and going in costume, that it was almost as if the tsar had sent the Volya an invitation to attend the event."

"The Tchaikovsky ball?"

"You know of it?"

The street before him seemed to shiver, to tremble in the golden light. Is this what if felt like to faint? He had to at least get off his feet before panic caused him to do something truly foolish, to say something which would bring down the entire political structure of Europe with a single blast.

"Do we have time for a drink?" Davy asked.

"There is always time for a drink, my friend."

There were cafes at each corner of the square and they approached the nearest one, pulling out their chairs with a scrape. Vlad raised a finger to the bored waiter, without bothering to ask Davy what he wanted. Vodka was cheap. Plentiful. The drink of the people and thus the drink of the people's champions. Davy steeled himself for the taste.

"We were speaking of the ball," Vlad reminded him. "And will your Queen be in attendance?"

"I imagine so."

"And you?"

"Of course not. Among her attendants, I'm the lowest of the low."

"That's good," Vlad said, nodding to the man absent-mindedly as the drinks were placed on the table.

"Why is it good that I shan't be there? Is something going to happen?"

"No one has tried to recruit you in London?"

God. Questions and questions from these people, with never an answer.

"I have already told you. The cause in England lags far behind your work here." Inspiration suddenly struck Davy and he sipped the vodka slowly to stall for time. I am hardly a match for Vlad in a war of wits, Davy thought, but Mrs. Kirby was right enough in her description. He is obsessed with his own self importance. "I cannot tell you what my time in St. Petersburg has meant to me," Davy said. "When I return to London I will begin the work myself, modeled on what I have seen within the Volya. So anything you can tell me is worth…is worth a handful of Romanov rubies."

Vlad seemed amused. "What do you mean, begin the work yourself? There's no need to reinvent the wheel. I'm sure a city the size of London has any number of existing groups and that they would all be delighted to take you on. Ask Cooper for a letter of introduction if you need one, although you most likely would not. Your position within the palace makes you an asset. It can take an organization years of painstaking work to get a man on the inside and you come to them with the matter already in hand."

Davy rolled his eyes. "Please. I'm merely a messenger boy."

"And Yulian was merely a ballet dancer. The point is that any revolutionary groups needs within its ranks a spy. Someone on the inside, who can move around the palace without attracting comment." The rim of his glass had a chip and Davy started to warn him of the fact, but something stopped him. Vlad was most likely the sort of man to prefer a glass with a chipped rim. "Do you know what I would be doing right now if Yulian had not existed?"

"Asking me to tell you everything I've observed about the interior of the Palace?"

Vlad gave a bark of laughter. "Precisely."

"So I can only conclude that before his death Yulian had already provided the Volya with the layout of the building."

"The parts that matter. Like the theater."

"Exactly what were you planning to do on the night of the Tchaikovsky ball?"

Vlad took an inelegant slurp of his vodka, his thin lip resting on the chipped part of the rim. "What does it matter? Yulian is gone and with him, our chances."

"And yet you asked me if I was going to be in the theater that night."

Vlad looked at him sharply, his pale eyes cutting from a distant gaze to Davy's face with such speed that Davy jumped. "You flatter yourself, comrade. We would not take you on so fast, not even on the recommendation of Professor Cooper. You think it is this simple? You are introduced and within days become the inside man with all our plans?"

"That isn't what I thought at all," Davy said with complete honestly. Even in his most anxious moments, he had never entertained the thought of what he'd say if the Volya tried to recruit him. "I assumed that you were warning me away from the theater as a friend."

Vlad shrugged with a suspiciously high level of nonchalance, and put down his glass. "There is nothing to warn you away from. Just another night of champagne and waltzing and jewels and idiocy. The incessant feeding of the imperial family and their friends upon the very flesh of Mother Russia. You do well to shun such a place. Absence from their corruption will save your soul, if not your flesh."

Davy sensed that this was far from the total truth, but he was not sure what to do about it. Vlad now he looked at his pocketwatch and winced. Time for the meeting of the Volya, evidently. A meeting to which Davy was not invited and there was no telling when the two of them would meet again.

But the Russians liked toasts, didn't they? They always seemed to be toasting someone or something. There was but a swallow of vodka left in his glass. Davy raised it. "Peace to your country."

Vlad left his own glass on the table. "You insult me, my friend," he said. "True Russians do not want peace. We want justice."

Chapter Seventeen

The Winter Palace – The Grand Ballroom

June 22, 1889

4:50 PM

They had been dancing for nearly an hour when Konstantin took a break. There was a carafe of water on a tray atop the piano and he led her to it, poured a careful glass for her and then himself. Emma took it with pleasure. She had been thirsty for some time, but the fact that he was as well was a type of confirmation that her dancing indeed was getting better. They had spent the last fifty minutes working hard, covering larger sections of the floor. It was the first time a pianist had joined them in their lessons and practicing with music had inspired her. Her small solo within the long and complex imperial waltz lasted no more than twenty seconds, but they had gone over the steps numerous times and there was a faint sheen of perspiration on Konstantin's broad brow. It showed her what she suspected that he would never say – that they were truly dancing now.

"You are not married?" he asked.

The question surprised her. They had never spoken of anything remotely personal. She shook her head and took another sip of water.

"So the man you were with when you opened the door…he was…" He paused, glanced at the pianist. "Who was the man you were with that day?"

She supposed it was natural that he would want to know.

"Thomas Bainbridge," she said. "The Queen's physician."

"And he is your lover?"

"Good heavens," she said. "Certainly not."

He sipped his water too, regarding her flustered response with confusion. "If there is no husband and no lover," he said, "then who protects you?"

Trevor protects me, she thought automatically and the speed with which the name came to her was surprising. Not that she could tell Konstantin this, of course.

"I protect myself," she said. "I live on my salary as Alix's governess and being in service to the royal family puts a very adequate roof of my head, as I'm sure you can well imagine." His surprise irritated her, although she couldn't have said why. The majority of Englishmen undoubtedly felt the same way, that it was impossible for a woman to function without male protection. "I am what we call a modern woman," she added, and for some reason felt ridiculous almost the minute the words were out of her mouth.

"A modern woman," he said slowly and thoughtfully, rolling the syllables around on his tongue like a pit from a cherry. It seemed as if the combination of the two words confused him, as if they had stretched his knowledge of English – or even his knowledge of women, which she knew to be far greater – to its breaking point. But she could think of no way to explain to him why Geraldine and her friends were marching for the vote - not here and now, to this man, who lived in a country where even men did not vote. Besides, even if she could have made him understand, that was far from the whole of it. Suffrage was a very small part of what Emma Kelly expected out of life.

"Modern women," she said tentatively, "or perhaps, now that I think of it, modern men as well, do not look to a church or a government or even their ancestral family to assign them their position in life or instruct them on their fate. They expect to be self-sufficient and have the chance to determine their own destiny."

He looked at her utterly without comprehension. She tried again.

"To be modern is to look at things objectively," she said, "thus trying to see them as they really are. Modern women value science more than faith. They value the future more than the past and friendship more than romance."

"Oh no," he said, with mock seriousness. He thrust his hand to his chest and pretended to stagger about. "But this is terrible. Does it hurt much, to be this modern woman?"

"Sometimes," she admitted.

"That is because in the heart all woman expect to be a princess," he said, in a tone that implied the subject was closed. "They want the man to come and rescue them from the lives they have as children. Like in the folk stories of the ballet, where the duck becomes the swan. This is what we dance, you know. We dance the dreams of little girls."

A few months earlier, Emma might privately have agreed with him, at least with the part about all women wanting to be a princess. But now that she had met Ella and Alix, she wasn't so sure. She thought of Alix, so weighted down in her borrowed silver dress that she could hardly lift her fork, and Ella, far from home and married to a man who ignored her. Their royal births did not seem to have guaranteed them any particular happiness. In fact, you could argue that in many ways these real-life princesses enjoyed fewer freedoms and pleasures than Emma herself.

Konstantin put down his water glass and held out his arm. Practice was evidently resuming and as they walked back to the center of the dance floor it suddenly occurred to Emma why he had really asked if she and Tom were lovers.

"You needn't worry about what Tom and I saw," she said quietly. The pianist did not appear to be interested in their conversation, but one could never tell. "He may not have a mistress himself but I assure you he will keep your secret. I have never met anyone who cares so little for conventional morality."

"So he is this modern man."

"I suppose he is," she said. "I suppose they all are." She realized she had almost slipped with the word "all," so she hastily continued. "Those of us who travel with the Queen, that is. Her bodyguards and messengers and private physicians."

He took a moment to absorb this information, but did not ask why the famously traditional Queen Victoria might have chosen to surround herself with such a pack of godless wolves. "And it makes you happy, to depend on no one or nothing and to always think for yourselves?"

"Trevor and I are the ones who suffer the most with it," Emma said. "We want the whole world to change, or at least we say we do, but I suspect there will always be something in us that will mourn the death of the old order."

Talking with Konstantin always seemed to have this effect on her. She found herself blurting out things she had never consciously thought about, but the minute the words left her mouth she knew that they were true. Tom rushed toward the novel, embracing scientific advancement with every fiber of his being, and in his own way Davy displayed equal aplomb, playing the cards he'd been dealt with the posture of a man who knows he has little to lose. Rayley of course had his characteristic reserve, his constant sense of standing back from a situation and watching it unfold as if all were a play staged for his benefit. This detachment, Emma knew, was the sort of mental state that true modernity required. She and Trevor were the ones in trouble. They could not help reacting to the people and events around them. As many times as they declared themselves to be creatures of logic, they probably fooled no one. In the heat of the moment, they made their decisions based on impulse and emotion.

"If the two of you suffer the same," Konstantin said, holding out his arms, "then this Trevor must be a great friend."

"He is."

"So he is the one who is your lover."

"He most certainly is not," she said impatiently, moving into his frame. "I have no lover. Trevor and I are friends, and that is all."

"Good," he said. He was moving slowly in the shape of a box, as if this were their first lesson. "For people who are similar in character should not be lovers. Your lover should be someone who stands across from you, who sees the world from a different place."

She wondered if he were speaking of his own affair with Tatiana. "We have a phrase for that in English," she said. "We say that opposites attract."

"Opposites attract," he repeated, expanding the scope of their waltz very slightly, beginning only the gentlest of a turn. "As in science, you mean? The, how do you say this, magnum?"

"We say 'magnet,'" she said. "And yes, that is the basic idea. But I have always wondered. Opposites attract…and then what? Does the attraction remain or, after a while, do these dissimilar lovers fall apart?"

He did not answer, at least not with words. He turned his face from hers, stretched his frame and began to dance with more energy, pushing off from flexed knees, covering a greater distance across the floor with each stride, carrying her along like a sail carries a mast. Or perhaps she was the sail and he was the mast – it was hard to say, really. She closed her eyes, more out of habit than anything else, and let herself relax into the repetitive motions of the dance.

At moments like this, when her guard was dropped and her mind was free to wander, Emma would sometimes drift back in time and speculate about how her life might have been different. If her mother had not nursed the town during the cholera epidemic…if her parents had not sickened and died and her brother Adam not gone to America and if she and Mary had never been cast into the dark streets of London…if none of that had ever happened, then who might she be? She probably would have stayed forever in the town of her birth. Been the schoolmaster's daughter who married the cobbler's son. Most likely would have had children of her own by now, as would Mary and Adam. She never would have met Gerry, then Tom, and then all the others. Never would have traveled great distances, baited the Ripper, swam the Seine, waltzed with a Siberian. She would most certainly not have been a modern woman, but would she have been happier? More at peace? For seeing the world in all its cruel glory was changing her, each day after the next, and there were times when she was no longer sure of anything.

"You can do the waltz correctly now," Konstantin said. "And this is good. Soon you will do it big."

She opened her eyes and looked at him questioningly.

"You have learned fast," he said. "Faster than any. Five lessons and you do not make any mistakes. Very good. But there is more to dance than not making a mistake."

Her mouth curved up. "Are you suggesting that I have learned faster than any student you've ever taught?"

"You are smart, Emma Kelly."

He said her name strangely, all the emphasis on the last syllables of the word. Em-mah Kel-lee. He had already told her how to make the dance bigger, at one of the previous lessons. Apparently this was the only part of the affair that was her decision. In the first motion of the waltz, when the woman steps back on her right foot, that simple gesture tells the man how big the dance will be. Her backward step creates the empty space he will step into and he cannot go farther than she allows. The man determines the steps, the rotation, the direction, the timing, the couple's position on the floor. But the woman alone decides how big their dance will be.

He had shown her how to do this. How to bend the knee of her standing leg and push the other one back with confidence, stretching her legs apart like a hurdler, creating a world for him to move into, giving him a large canvas upon which to paint the colors of the waltz. She understood it all intellectually and had even been getting used to the required movements, although it was not an easy thing to step backwards with confidence, to commit so absolutely to a future one could not see. Something was keeping her small and tight, and she knew this, but she could not name this particular fear.

"You have wondered if Tom will keep quiet about the day we found you and Tatiana," she said, a bit breathlessly, for they were moving with more energy now, the pianist having switched from Beethoven to Strauss. "But you have never wondered about me."

"I know you will keep my secret," he said. "You are my friend."

The word "friend" stunned her. It was true, of course, that in their short time together they had formed a type of bond, that she indeed trusted him in any number of strange, wordless ways that she had never shared with anyone else. But it was still the last word she ever expected him to use. They slowed to a stop as the song ended and she glanced at the pianist. He was ruffling through sheets of music, preparing to begin again, and without thinking Emma stretched on tiptoe. Came as close as she could to the elegant length of Konstantin's neck, the shine of his hair, the curve of his ear.

"You must leave the palace," she whispered. "The tsar's private guard believes you are a killer."

The Winter Palace – The Guest Quarters

5:28 PM

The Queen not only received daily updates from London via telegram but also received British newspapers. Granted, the issues were generally three or four days out of date by the time they arrived in St Petersburg by train, but Trevor still enjoyed flipping through them as he took his tea. He was a bit homesick, a condition that was soothed by the familiar pages of the London Star. Even the advertisements for soap and tea and digestive tonics suddenly held a certain charm.

He was on his second read through in the empty parlor of their rooms when his eye fell upon an article about a series of rapes in rural Scotland. He read it, squinting at the small smeared print, and then sat back in his chair with a frown. The story was written, of course, for your average newspaper reader and thus emphasized the more lurid details over the basic facts, but it had still given him a sizable serving of the proverbial food for thought.

"Do you remember the last meeting we held of the Thursday Night Murder Games?" Trevor asked, looking up as Tom and Rayley shuffled into the room for their own tea. "We discussed criminal profiling and what personality type was most likely to commit certain crimes?"

"Barely," said Tom, speaking for them both. "That evening seems months ago."

"Something reminded me of it today," Trevor said. "If you recall, we began our study on that evening with the subject of personality profiling, which raises the question: What sort of personality type is likely to be found in an assassin?"

"A man who imagines he is putting the good of the many above the good of the few," Rayley said promptly. "He likely believes he is chosen in some way, selected by some higher power for a specific task. Called, if you will."

"I would argue that's the prototype of a saint, not an assassin," Tom said, draping himself back into a chaise lounge with an exaggerated languor, his cup sloshing into the saucer as he did so. "Where are Davy and Emma, by the way?"

"Still in the clutches of their various Russians," Trevor said. "And I quite understand what Rayley means. The type of psychology which might drive a man to assassinate a political figure he has never met seems quite different that the psychology of a typical murderer. Most killings are prompted by jealousy, rage, bloodlust and the like – the most primal and personal of emotions. But the urge to kill a stranger must be more akin to religious fervor."

"Look at it this way," Rayley said. "When people kill in service to a cause it suggests that they have put the principles of that cause above the needs, or perhaps even the very lives, of their friends and family, not to mention themselves. You might infer that they no longer are capable of personal loyalty. Which is why the rest of us call them extremists, because we find it extreme that anyone would value an abstract ideal more than he values his individual relationships."

"Truly, Abrams?" Trevor protested. "Here our reasoning parts paths, for I find that an extreme definition of extremism. We all have things we exalt above ourselves or perhaps even those we love. Religion and country are the obvious examples, or in my case, it would be the Yard. Let's say a man leaves his wife and children to go to war to fight for an ideal. By your estimation, that makes him an extremist, even a type of assassin, where most people would argue that it makes him a patriot."

"Davy reports the members of the Volya are all young," Tom said idly. "Perhaps there's some correlation between youth and one's willingness to sacrifice all for a cause."

'Which makes sense, for it is easier to pursue ideals when one is young," said Trevor. "Duty to a wife and children tend to come to a man later in life, making him cautious, less likely to risk himself, and thus their future as well, in pursuit of a vague idea."

"And Davy furthermore says this Vlad he's befriended is certain beyond all hesitation that the revolution is right," Tom said.

"Again, it is easier to be certain when you are young," Trevor said. "As we age, life has a way of heaping examples on our heads, and in many ways, the more examples we have, the harder it is to draw a conclusion. One fact always manages to contradict another." He looked about. "But criminal profiling wasn't all that I hoped to discuss. I was saving the real business of this meeting for the moment when everyone arrived, but it appears Emma and Davy have both been detained. Unfortunate indeed. I feel it's been days since I've had a proper conversation with either of them, especially her."

"She has been preoccupied, it would seem," Rayley mumbled around the scone in his mouth.

"Yes, and solely by the fate of her dance master," Tom said. "In this complicated case, the future safety of Konstantin Antonovich is her overriding concern." For once his voice carried not the slightest trace of sarcasm or flippery. It was the flat clear observation of a man stating a fact.

Trevor looked at the other men with surprise. Surprise that Emma might have changed without him noticing and further surprise that Tom and Rayley must have seen this before he did.

"But the question is, why should he have such a hold on her thoughts?" Rayley asked with a swallow. "She has known him scarcely a week."

"He has no hold on her," Trevor said quickly. "We're all in agreement that Konstantin is most likely innocent but that, unless someone intervenes on his behalf, he may still be arrested. So why is it odd that she might rally to the man's defense?"

"It's not that her desire to protect an innocent man is odd, it's that she's changed her behavior," Tom said. "She hasn't ventured an opinion on anything since she started waltzing with the man. And Trevor, don't tell me that you haven't noticed that she has become rather misty and distant. Like a heroine in one of those novels for ladies, you know the sort, where the hero starts out looking to be the villain but in the end is revealed to be a lord of the manor in disguise. Soon she shall be announcing to us all that the Siberian has touched some previously unexplored part of her soul."

"I haven't noticed such a change because there isn't one," Trevor said, with more confidence than he felt. "Or at least no more of one than could be expected after such a long journey to such a strange place. We are all of us changed by every case and I daresay also changed by the people we find along the way."

"Well, I have something a bit more definite to report," said Tom, pulling to a full sitting position to reach for a sweet roll and abruptly changing the subject as he did so. "The Grand Duchess Ella is expecting a child."

"Good heavens," said Rayley. "This is news. But how would you know?"

"She has been led to think I am a bona fide doctor, don't forget," Tom said. "Oh, and don't look at me like that, Abrams. I certainly didn't examine her imperial person. But this morning she summoned me for a sort of consultation."

"This means Mrs. Kirby was wrong about her marriage being unconsummated," Trevor said.

"Not necessarily," Tom said. "The child Ella is expecting, and is planning to pass off as her own, will be the actual offspring of Tatiana Orlov and Konstantin Antonovich." As he shared the details of his visit to Tatana's apartment, Trevor and Rayley sat with expressions of growing incredulity on their faces and finally, as Tom finished his story and his sweet roll in the precise same second, Trevor sat back in his chair and exhaled.

"It's madness," he said. "Such a deception will never work."

Tom shrugged. "It's a risk, but men are deluded in this manner every day I dare say. And if the Grand Duchess and Mrs. Orlov do indeed remain at the coast until time for the child to be born, their story may pass unchallenged. The women involved are possessed of beauty, power, and money, don't forget, and this combination may be enough to allow them to rewrite history in any manner they please. If there are enough advantages all around the table, no one may feel inclined to question the origins of the single dark-eyed Romanov in the family portrait."

"There are other moral questions to consider," Rayley said. "For a start, is it proper to let the Antonovich fellow escape?"

"Escape is hardly the word," Tom said, "considering he has been charged with no crime and in all probability committed no greater offense than seducing another man's wife. If a Russian dancer decides to immigrate to Paris, I can't see why it's any concern of ours."

"For the record, I agree," said Rayley. "But here is the real poser: Do we tell the Queen?"

The question was directed at Trevor, who was leaning back in a precarious angle in his chair, staring at the ceiling, where a dozen naked cherubs sat perched on clouds, gazing back. He didn't answer.

"I promised Ella that she should be the one to give her grandmother the happy news," Tom said.

"But you didn't take the Fabrege egg," Rayley said.

"No, I most certainly wasn't bribed," Tom said tersely, "but I did give my word. Initially I had all the same doubts you've mentioned, but I've had the afternoon to mull it over and my opinion has changed a bit. Consider this. Ella may be a virginal wife and may be a carrier of hemophilia to boot. Under these circumstances if she wishes to pass off an adopted child as her own, it's a rather understandable sort of lie. And as she herself said to me, it isn't as if the child won't be given every advantage. The big loser in this game is poor Tatiana, but in an odd way she seems the most at peace with her decision. So here is the true question before us: As a unit of Scotland Yard, we are sworn to uphold the law. Or at least you and Trevor and Davy are and I suppose when Emma and Aunt Gerry and I came into the group as volunteers, we agreed to these rules as well. But what we are talking of here aren't matters of law, they're matters of personal morality. The relations between husbands and wives, love affairs, pregnancies, and the most everyday sort of deceptions. Deplorable perhaps, but are these matters really under our jurisdiction?"

The door opened and Emma entered, a little breathless, as if she had run the length of the long halls leading to the guest quarters. Without greeting the men, she dropped the bag containing her dancing slippers to the deep red carpet and went to the table to pour her tea. "What have I missed?" she asked.

"Very little," Trevor said crisply. "I was asking Tom and Rayley if they remembered the last case we discussed at the

Thursday Night Murder Games Club. You know, the Scottish rapes?"

So that is that, Tom thought. If Trevor has decided not to tell Emma about the Grand Duchess and her baby, he certainly doesn't intend to tell the Queen.

Emma came back to her seat, frowning in thought. "There was some question about how the man used the train system to come and leave the crime scene, was there not? And then of course the business with the blindfold. I remember that seemed quite exotic at the time."

"The Edinburg police have proclaimed the case to be solved," Trevor said, gesturing toward the stack of papers on the desk in the corner. "It seemed a detail came to light that opened up a new line of reasoning. The women, you see, reported that the assaults were…multiple."

"Multiple?" Tom said wryly. "Do you mean what I think you do?"

Trevor sighed. "Begging your pardon, Emma…"

"Oh Trevor, we've been through this a thousand times. Do speak plainly," Emma said, pulling her chair into the circle. "I assume you mean each woman was raped more than once?"

"Precisely," said Trevor, slightly flushed. "They reported this to the bobbies of course, but the men investigating were mere youngsters and didn't think anything of it. But as the case remained unsolved and thus bumped its way up the chain of command…"

"I quite see where you're going," Rayley said. "As the case moved under the jurisdiction of older men they found the vigor of the assailant more noteworthy."

"Proving what?" Tom said. "That the rapist was a young enough man to be able to initiate sexual congress twice in rapid sequence? From a medical standpoint, I scarcely find that a persuasive line of reasoning. Assaulting a person, no matter who or why, is bound to raise levels of adrenalin, as does the act of sex itself. So I would imagine that rape, which combines intercourse and violence, creates enough of a surge to make even an older man capable of exceeding his normal limits."

"Maybe so," said Trevor, still flushed. "But apparently in speculating on the dual nature of the assaults, one of the supervising officers made a joke about how it must have been two men. And you know how it is, sometimes a remark made in jest can introduce an entirely new line of thought. Someone began to think what if it truly were two men working together in tandem. It seemed an unlikely notion, for while everyone accepts that crimes such as robbery are most efficiently carried out with a whole contingent of criminals, rapists usually act alone. At least in these planned, methodical sort of rapes. But once the idea of two men had been raised, the investigation took a different turn."

"It explains the blindfold at least," Emma said. "The woman would have no idea, I presume, that she was being attacked by two men."

"Indeed," said Trevor. "And as the story unfolded it seems that the fact it was two men had worked to confuse the time line. While one was busy with the victim, the other made it a point to be seen on the street and vice versa, thus giving each of them an alibi for the time of the crime. For they were local lads, you see. Would have been recognizable to their victims. But they were able to use their proximity to the village station, the coming and going of the trains, and the blindfold to convince everyone from the women to the local coppers that the assailant must have been from out of town. We immediately jumped to the same faulty assumption, as you might recall."

"Fascinating," Rayley said. "And you have a reason for bringing this story up now, I presume?"

"I was wondering if we were perchance making the same mistake as the Scottish police," Trevor said.

"You mean we're looking for one man when in reality there might be two?" Rayley asked.

"It seems at least worth considering," Trevor said. "We have been assuming all this is the work of a single man, and that there is thus a single line of logic to the killings. Yulian must have been killed by an enemy of the Volya, and Cynthia Kirby must have been killed by the same person, who realized she had discovered something – most likely through the photograph she and Ella took on the morning after the crime. But it seems to me that there's an inherent flaw in that thinking."

"Wait...wait," said Tom. "Give us a shot at it. It goes back to the question of why Yulian was killed, does it not? Because if someone within the palace, either the private guard or the police or just some concerned citizen, learned that he was affiliated with the Volya, they wouldn't have had to cut his throat in the dead of night and then taken some innocent girl along with him. They could simply have exposed him and let the law do their dirty work for them."

"Quite right," Emma said. "We've all assumed the obvious – that Yulian was killed by an enemy of the Volya. But the enemies of the Volya are the authorities and they would have arrested him, not killed him. And they hardly would have, in turn, killed Katya and Mrs. Kirby. Poor Katya was probably just in the wrong place at the wrong time, but looking beyond her, our other two murders lie at opposite ends of the political spectrum. One victim was a loyal member of the revolution and the other a loyal servant to the imperial family. Who would have had reason to wish them both dead?"

"No one I can think of," Trevor said. "Which is why the resolution of the case in Scotland so intrigued me. Upon reflection, our quick assumption that whoever killed Yulian must have also killed Cynthia is quite illogical since, just as Emma says, it implies a man who stands against both the revolution and the established order. But perhaps we are not looking for one man with dual motives. Perhaps we are looking for two men."

"I must disagree," said Rayley. They all turned toward him, Trevor nodding encouragement. Disagreement, not runaway accord, was the purpose of these meetings.

"In this huge edifice, with more than a thousand rooms, both crimes were committed in the same space, were they not?" Rayley said, pushing back his eyeglasses and clearing his throat. "Even more significantly, they were both staged in precisely the same theatrical manner. Yulian and Katya posed as tragic lovers, Mrs. Kirby as the king the gypsies. No, I feel both crimes had to have been committed by the same person, and that they are both designed to relay a message, albeit one we have yet to fully crack."

"Come now, Rayley, everyone in Russia is theatrical," Emma said, setting down her cup with a careless clatter. "You're right, if this crime took place in London, in a shop or a school or a hospital, the elaborate staging would be noteworthy. Some great clue to the killer's mind. But these are Russians, and dancers, and revolutionaries, and what seems excessively dramatic to us is more or less the way they all think."

"So have we come to an impasse?" Trevor said, after a moment of silence. "Yet once again?"

"Not at all," Tom said. "I find your mention of the Scottish case most apt. It reminds us to question every assumption. There may be two killers afoot, and not one, and they may be connected to a joint cause or acting on completely different motivations. The murders may be less connected that they appear. Yulian may not have been the only member of the Volya to have infiltrated the palace."

"I find that last thought the most chilling," Emma said. "For you're quite right. If Yulian Krupin managed to dance his way through these iron gates and into close congress with the imperial family, there could be others."

"One other point," Rayley mused. "Yulian had been part of the imperial ballet corps for nearly a year. Why was he killed now?"

"Rayley is returning to his training," Trevor said, nodding toward Tom and Emma. "When the Yard cannot discover why something has happened, we busy ourselves with the timeline, the 'when' of the crimes. For the 'when' often leads us to the 'why.'"

"Perhaps Yulian's killer only recently discovered his identity," Tom said.

"I think it's more likely there's some sort of ticking clock we aren't aware of," Rayley said. "Some upcoming event which is forcing the killer's hand."

"Quite a few events are converging," Emma said, her voice also slow and speculative. She seemed to be talking as much as ever and sifting through the discussion plenty well, at least to Trevor's point of view, and he wondered about this misty, distracted manner that both Tom and Rayley had commented upon. She certainly wasn't showing it to him.

"There is of course the great ball," Emma was continuing. "And the customary closing of the Winter Palace just afterwards, so that the imperial court can retire to the coast. You might also argue that our own arrival is a significant event, even though no one appears to be treating it that way. A visit by the Queen of England is inherently significant, is it not? And of course, except for Ella, no one seems to want Alix to marry Nicky."

"Another thing - Yulian was shortly to be leaving for Paris," Rayley said. "He and Katya had been granted an exalted and apparently rather rare opportunity to dance there. Filip put this out as part of the motive during our afternoon in the saunas, when he suggested that Antonovich killed Yulian out of professional jealousy."

"Then perhaps young Yulian's loyalty to the Volya was not truly so unswerving," Tom said. The energy of the room was picking up again and they had all leaned a bit closer into the center of the circle. "The chance to dance in Paris with Katya may have tempted him away from his duties to the cause."

"Now we're onto something," Trevor said with enthusiasm. "I'm not sure which, if any, of these notions is the closest to correct, but I feel in my bones that this is a fruitful line of questioning. For the one assumption we cannot be foolish enough to make is that Yulian was the only member of the

Volya within the Winter Palace. We cannot assume that all threats to the imperial family died with him."

"The Tchaikovsky ball is in two days," Emma said. "Everyone will be there. Not just the imperial family and Ella, but Alix and the Queen as well. If I were a revolutionary I would consider it …the last day of hunting season."

"Quite right," Rayley said. "Even with the loss of a man on the inside, the Volya may be prepared to continue whatever scheme they'd conceived. We can't say for sure it would be the ball, but the timing is suspicious, is it not?"

"Damn suspicious," Tom said, slapping his thighs. "Especially in light of the fact that, just as Emma says, all the birds will scatter the day after the ball. Once the imperials and their consorts are at the seashore for the season, they're beyond the reach of anyone, the Volya included."

"Just how desperate would you guess these revolutionaries to be?" Rayley asked. "Enough so that they'd be willing to alter a plan at the last minute, even if they have lost a key player?"

Trevor winced. "If anyone should have a word to say on the subject, it's Davy. But where could he be? I expected him some time ago."

The Streets of St. Petersburg

6:48 PM

    Davy had been wandering the streets of St. Petersburg ever since leaving Vlad. Not only was it a beautiful city, but now that his nose had finally grown accustomed to the smell of the marsh, he found that the most enchanting vistas were those from the bridges. Heaven knows there were plenty to explore. The city was a compilation of nineteen separate islands, all connected by a series of arching bridges, spanning the ever-present Neva at regular intervals.

    The city is a silent place, he thought suddenly, as he stood at the arc of one of the bridges, staring down into the ribbon of steel-grey water below. At first the streets had seemed noisy, noxious, and fulsome – just like the streets of London. But here, just the middle of the bridge, high over the Neva, he realized a different aspect to St. Petersburg. A silence so profound that for a moment it unsettled him.

    The heat had grown with the day and at some point in his walk he had removed his cap and stuffed it in his jacket. At another corner of another street he had rolled up his shirt sleeves and finally now, here on the bridge, he unclasped his collar. Such dishevelment would never be allowed on the streets of London where at any moment he might have crossed paths with someone else from the Yard or perhaps, even worse, some public citizen who knew his function there and considered him a representative of all that was proper with Queen and country. Representing the crown could be burdensome at times, especially for a man who had not yet left his twenty-first year, and Davy now rubbed his throat and neck, seeking the promise of a breeze and enjoying the freedom that came from being anonymous, just another faceless man in the streets.

This is why people travel, he thought. So they can loosen their collar and roll their sleeves in every known sense of the words.

A church bell rang. Even this sound was muted by the water and his elevation on the bridge but his mind automatically counted the faint bells. Seven. Dear God, he thought, jerking to attention, pulling his elbows away from the railing. He had walked for hours, he had missed teatime, and thus the chance to confer with Trevor and the others. Returned to himself immediately, he loped down the slope of the bridge and onto the sidewalk, trying to calculate the fastest route back to the Winter Palace. He suspected the path he had taken with Vlad – the Nevsky Prospect which ran beside the Café of the Revolutionaries and required transit over the bridge where Alexander II had met his famous end – was not the most direct option but that was the street he knew best. It would perhaps be faster to follow along the Neva itself, which would eventually lead to the palace but rivers could undulate and waver, thus limiting their usefulness for a man navigating on foot and who knows how many of the steep bridges he would be required to cross between this spot and the palace?

Striding briskly, Davy decided to take the Nevsky Prospect. If nothing else, traveling a well-known street would allow his mind the time to work on excuses for Trevor and to practice his report, late though it would be, in his head.

He was halfway there, merely a block or two shy of the Café of the Revolutionaries – he really needed to stop thinking of it that way lest he make a slip in the presence of the Volya – when he saw Vlad himself. He was coming up the sidewalk from the opposite direction as Davy and walking with another man. A large and hulking beast whose brown jacket was buttoned to his throat despite the heat and whose facial features seemed ludicrously lost in the vastness of his flesh. Small eyes, small nose, small mouth. He looked like a snowman who was melting, Davy thought, whose coal eyes and stony mouth were being slowly engulfed in his collapsing face.

Vlad had seen Davy too and, judging by his guilty, exasperated expression, some sort of battle was going on in his mind. He is leaving the meeting, Davy thought, in the presence of a fellow Volya member. And here, as luck would have it, he encounters me. He would prefer not to introduce me to this man, but what choice does he have? We are walking right toward each other and it is too late for either of us to pretend we have not noticed the other or to change direction. He must either introduce me to his companion or, by neglecting to do so, know that he has incited my curiosity about the man even more.

"Hello there," Vlad said as they all three came to stop on the street. "Where have you been since we parted?"

"Walking," Davy replied, reflecting upon how sometimes the most honest of answers could also sound the most evasive. "Admiring your beautiful city."

"Ah," said Vlad, looking around with some surprise, as if it had been years since he had closely observed the streets he walked every day. "We have been in our meeting, as you know."

"Yes," Davy said, glancing at the man beside him. Almost all the Russians he had met spoke some degree of English but perhaps this fellow did not. His face was convincingly blank, as if even this banal discussion was beneath his understanding.

But evidently not. With a slight grimace, Vlad accepted the social realities of the situation. "This is Davy Mabrey," he said to the snowman. "He is a British revolutionary in service to the Queen but in sympathy to our cause." The man's small eyes darted to Davy with sudden interest and Davy flushed.

"And this is one of the senior members of the Volya," Vlad continued. "May I present my comrade, Filip Orlov."

Chapter Eighteen

Here was the secret that very few men knew: The attempt on the life of the tsar two years earlier had been a fake.

Well, that is, at least somewhat of a fake.

The events of a political revolution may seem to move like lightning to those watching from outside, but the planning of them requires patience. Placing Filip Orlov within the tsar's guard had been a necessary first step, but the guard employed so many men that the guard was a virtual army. The Volya knew that in order to utilize Filip's unique talents to their fullest potential, they would have to find some way to differentiate him from the dozens of others serving a similar role.

It had been decided that the simplest way to do this would be to have Filip throw himself between the tsar and a would-be assassin. The tsar, like many gruff men, had a profoundly sentimental aspect to his nature; he might reward a detective who had thwarted a murder through clever investigation with some jewel-encrusted trinket, or decorate a guard who had acted quickly to subdue a threat by pinning any number of festoons upon his chest. But his most profound gratitude would be reserved for a man who had suffered in his stead, the one whose body absorbed the bullet which had been intended for him.

And thus the Volya had launched a two-tiered initiative. Most of the lads believed that the mission was to shoot the tsar. And so it was, although the senior and more experienced members of the group knew that this plan, without irony, was a bit of a long shot. The marksman understood that if his first bullet went astray, he was to cut his losses and fire the second one into Filip; that way, if the Volya couldn't manage to assassinate Alexander III on the anniversary of his father's murder, then the entire mission should not fall to ruins. It would at least buy them a comrade placed high within in the tsar's private circle.

The assassination attempt may have been a fake but the bullet, unfortunately for Filip, was real. As it ripped into his well-cushioned side, expertly placed there by the Volya's best marksman, he had been surprised not only by the pain – somewhat different in actuality than it had been in theory – but also by the sense of violation. As he had wailed and stumbled and collapsed in the middle of the street, his grief had been unfeigned.

From there, events had happened exactly as planned. The stretcher, the doctors, the recovery in an elevated suite of rooms within the Winter Palace. The news that several of his comrades had been arrested – that some of them had talked and others had been hanged. Fortunately none of the ones who broke under pressure had known that the shooting of Filip had been part of the overall plan, but still, one never could never predict what details might emerge under questioning, especially the sort of highly persuasive interrogation the private guard was known to employ. Each day in his starched white hospital bed Filip had lain with both physical pain and a far more tormenting sense of anxiety. Any hour could bring the sound of advancing steps, the guard coming to tell him that he had been revealed and was thus to hang with his comrades.

The days turned into a week, then two, as contagion swept the infirmary and his recovery was delayed. But still no such steps rang down the hall and eventually Filip relaxed.

When he eventually expressed a desire to return to his ancestral home for the remainder his rehabilitation, this small request had been graciously granted – so graciously, in fact, that Filip had traveled in one of the tsar's own carriages. His mother had wept at the sight of him, although he had never been entirely sure if it was the size of the wound or the size of the carriage that had brought about such an uncharacteristic reaction. He announced his promotion to the elite guard casually, while smoking in the garden with his brothers, but word spread fast, just as he knew it would. Before he left to assume his new post, his village had bestowed upon their favored son the greatest gift such a humble town had to offer: Tatiana.

She did not love him. He knew this, but was not offended by the fact. One might argue that, other than the enchantment of her beauty, he did not particularly love her either, at least not at the time of their wedding. But despite the surface differences between them, he knew that they were similar in the core. They were pragmatists, cursed to spend their lives among people who did not think clearly, who likely would never be able to do so. They had both noticed, at some point in their miserable youths, that the only road out of town led to St. Petersburg, and they also shared a certain cold ambition – he for his politics and she for a better life. Tatiana did not know about her husband's involvement with the Volya, nor the fact that his marriage to her was a way to accelerate his plans. Being shot in lieu of the tsar might have moved him into the inner circle, but Filip knew that to stay there, it would take more. A beautiful wife who proved a quick study in the ways of the court was an asset. Yes, he was rescuing her, but she brought advantages for him as well.

That was the part that happened quickly. The rest of the plan had taken more time. For the Volya was also, in its way, a slow moving force for change, their plans hampered by the comings and goings of the members. A university was by design a transient place. Young men were trained at great effort and great expense, sometimes of funds and sometimes of life. In most cases, the investment did not pay off. The young men married or took up professions and became caught within the maw of personal ambition. They moved on, their revolutionary days a mere memory, something they would brag about behind closed doors and after much drink. Only a small percentage of the boys recruited remained long enough to progress within the group and even they could not always be trusted.

Yulian was the perfect example. At Gregor's insistence they had gotten him inside the palace and through the boy's own gift for dance he had thrived there. But then came the girl, the damn girl who wanted nothing more than to dance in that whore of a city called Paris, and Yulian's head had been turned. We will kill the tsar after the tour, he told them. Katya and I must go to Paris first. It means so much to her. Yes, this was the impudence of the boy. He looked into the face of a man who had offered his body up to a bullet and said that yes, he would help them, but that he wanted to go to Paris first.

Paris first.

That is what the boy said.

The revolution could wait until his holiday was complete.

And then he had added casually, almost as an aside, the remark which sealed his fate. "Katya understands I must someday return and do my duty. I tell her everything, you see."

Here was the secret that only one man kept: the death of Yulian Krupin came at the hands of the cause he served.

The day he decided he must eliminate one of his own was a dark day indeed, but Filip had long ago accepted the need to make difficult decisions. You could hardly take the boy without the girl; the two had argued quite convincingly to everyone within earshot that their fates were linked. Yulian had died as he lived – blindly - and Katya had followed with remarkable ease, almost cooperatively, almost as if she understood that for Russian women, romantic love was generally a death sentence.

Even when one is a member of a collective there are times when one must act alone. Filip understood that no one in the Volya could ever know of his decision, and nor could anyone within the palace. Keeping his secret had already proven difficult, for Gregor had many unanswered questions about his brother's death. At the memorial service he had approached Filip and held out a handkerchief saying "So that you might weep for my brother, comrade."

The statement was probably nothing more than a rebuke over the fact that Filip had remained dry-eyed among the wailing of the others, but for a moment Filip's blood had run cold. He had taken the handkerchief and nodded briskly, a gesture which seemed to satisfy Gregor, but then Filip's gaze had fallen on the equally dry-eyed Vlad who was leaning against the chipped plaster wall. Watching and listening, just as he always did. A pesky mosquito, that one.

Within the palace, the death of the dancers had attracted little interest from his fellow officers, who had either been fooled by the flourishes of his staging or too unimpressed by the stature of the victims to care. Just the damn British woman, another of those watch and listen types, another mosquito begging for the palm of a hand. Her interference had been unfortunate and her death, he feared, might still arise to haunt him, especially in light of the nearly simultaneous arrival of a contingent of her countrymen. If the British should decide to investigate…

Which is why he had decided that attention must be deflected to Konstantin Antonovich at once.

There were those, he knew, who liked to gossip that Filip's pretty little bird had flown. He had heard the guffaws behind his back, the suggestions that his wife and the dance master waltzed below the bedsheets as well as above. But Filip knew these whispers were not true. There were few certainties in life, but he was sure that Tatiana would never betray him. She was too grateful. Too aware of what awaited her if he should ever decide to send her home in disgrace. She had married him in a gown with its hem stained a dark rust color, for when a woman is the daughter of a butcher, even her best dress has absorbed the blood of the slaughterhouse floor. No, his Tatiana had seen no end of dreadful things before she turned ten years old. A woman who goes to the altar in a blood-soaked dress is, if nothing else, a realist. She would do nothing to risk his wrath or to jeopardize her hard-won position within the palace.

Most people would have found it surprising that a man like Filip should have ever joined the Volya in the first place, much less remained loyal for enough years to rise in their ranks. He was not typical of their membership. Older than most, as broad as a wall, and from some hopelessly obscure little town in the countryside. But appearances can be deceiving, so they say, and Filip knew that his lumbering form and graceless lack of manners gave off the impression he was stupid. He was not. When he had first entered the tsar's guard he had learned the three additional languages of the court with a rapidity that he knew was not typical of his fellows. This is what had inspired him to go to the university, where those in service to the imperial family were allowed to sit spectator to the classes, an advantage few within the Romanov court pressed. What act of fate had carried him into the classroom of Professor Tomasovich and first brought him into contact with the words of Karl Marx? Filip could not say, but his mind absorbed the logic of the revolution just as a dry sponge expands with water. Filip Orlov was that rarity: a man who came to politics by way of his head rather than his heart.

When he had offered his services to the Volya, they had initially laughed, which didn't surprise him. The Marxists were as snobbish as the Romanovs in their way and Filip knew he didn't look like the others. Didn't have their middle class background or university polish. Only one boy had seen through this to his potential and asked "But must we all be cut from a cloth, comrades?" Sasha Ulyanov had shown him respect, Sasha alone had opened the door to admit him, and Filip had never forgotten this. Perhaps that was why, even now, he tolerated Vlad, as a gesture of respect to his dead brother.

The first time Filip had killed, it was to protect the cause. The second time, it was to save his own skin. And so again it would be with the third, but the one thing he was discovering, as his career as an assassin progressed with dizzying speed, is that murder is much simpler if you kill people who don't matter. After an initial flare of interest, the deaths of the ballet dancers were almost forgotten and it appeared to go even better yet if you killed people who were not well liked. No one, not even her own countrymen, seemed particularly distressed by the absence of Mrs. Kirby.

And so it would be with Konstantin Antonovich. Filip knew he was not the only one who had noticed the man's arrogance, his extraordinary sense of entitlement, the sheen of his red trousers and dark hair. The way he put his hands on other men's women as if they were his own. The women by all appearances liked these presumptions. They seemed to become whatever their dance master commanded them to be. They seemed to transform within his arms and move for him in ways they did not move with their husbands, and thus he was ideally suited as a suspect. One might even say he had practically stepped forward and volunteered to take the blame.

For no matter what his nationality, rank, or political persuasion, there would not be a single man within the Winter Palace who would be sorry to see the Siberian fall.

Chapter Nineteen

The Winter Palace - The Breakfast Room in the Imperial Suites

June 23, 1889

10:45 AM

"They are all preoccupied with plans for that silly ball," Nicky whispered, his eyes darting around the sparsely filled room. "This could be our last opportunity to meet."

Alix knew he was right. The halls around the imperial suites had been unusually empty all morning and she could only assume that the area around the theater was correspondingly abuzz with activity. Tonight was the rehearsal, tomorrow was the ball, and her grandmother had informed her that they sailed for home the next day.

"It is a chance," she conceded.

"And one worth taking," he responded. "No one ever goes to the graveyard. We will be alone."

Alone. The word sounded in her head like an oriental gong. Alix had been alone very few times in her life and never alone with a man.

"You will find the chapel out across the lawn," he said, slightly inclining his head in the general direction of the windows, and thus the river. "It stands in the center of the graveyard where the servants are laid to rest."

"A chapel?" she repeated. She had only been in the enormous chapel within the palace with its golden altar and columns of cobalt and jade. She had found it, in fact, quite difficult to pray amid such a cacophony of earthly splendor.

"And I have something for you," he went on in a low voice as he pressed an object in her hand. It was hard and flat and she recoiled when a sharp edge jabbed into her palm. "It stands proof of the seriousness of my intentions."

She looked down and found a diamond brooch in the shape of a single flower, large and bursting with brilliants. A simple gift, no doubt, by the standards of the Romanovs, but it was the grandest piece of jewelry she had ever held. Fifth-born princesses from minor German districts did not customarily wear such items about the house.

"Granny will never let me accept it," she whispered, glancing about. They were the only two seated at their end of the enormous table. Her grandmother had already departed the breakfast room but quite a few members of the imperial family remained, dawdling over their sausages and soft boiled eggs. From the corner Ella was watching them like a hawk, but Alix knew her older sister would completely approve if she chose to accept the brooch from Nicky. In all likelihood, Ella had been the one to pick it out.

"You don't have to wear it publically or at least not when she is present," Nicky said. "Just keep it and know…" He trailed off here, as if this was the one part of the speech he had not rehearsed. "It is a gift," he finished weakly. "Nothing more."

But gifts have meaning, Alix thought, closing her fingers around the diamond and noting that the brooch was entirely too large to be concealed in her hand. Sometimes the things a woman accepted from a man marked her even more clearly than the things she gave to him.

Nicky smiled, as if the very fact she held onto the brooch rather than letting it clang to the floor like a wayward fork, was somehow proof of her answer.

"Meet me in the graveyard at five," he whispered. "No one will look for us there."

The Winter Palace - The Guest Quarters

10:50 AM

At another breakfast table, down another hall, Davy was finishing up his story along with his eggs.

"I feel like a fool," Rayley said. "I sat talking with the man for hours in the smoking room and not once did it occur to me he was some sort of turncoat." He took his glasses off and wiped the lenses in a somewhat compulsive manner. "We must inform the authorities of course, but which ones? How can we be sure that Filip is the only revolutionary within the guard? It seems that we could easily tell the wrong person and thus turn him in to his own comrades."

"For once I am glad that the imperial guard and the palace police are separate units," Trevor said. "Since he is with the guard, our best option, I suppose, is to take this news to the police."

"They plan to do something at the Tchaikovsky ball, don't they?" Emma asked. "The Volya, I mean."

Davy wiped his mouth. "No one has said it quite so plain as all that. But Vlad did ask me if I was going to be there, and the Queen, and I can't think of any other reason he would have made such an inquiry. Or known there was to be a ball at all, for that matter."

"True, true, all true enough," Trevor said. "The very fact that a self-proclaimed revolutionary knows the schedule of entertainments within the Winter Palace is alarming and we can only assume that this information came to him courtesy of either Yulian Krupin or Filip Orlov."

"We shall have to be on high alert," Rayley said. "Starting tonight, for this evening is the dress rehearsal, is it not, Emma?"

"High alert?" Trevor shook his head just as Emma was nodding hers. "When this news is revealed, the ball will be canceled. I'll see to that much at least."

"You'll see to it? I understand your sentiments completely, Welles, but this isn't London." Rayley replaced his glasses and studied Trevor with sympathy. "We can certainly suggest that Her Majesty and Alix remain in their rooms and perhaps even Ella, if it comes to that. But we hardly have the authority to cancel a ball within the Winter Palace."

"Nor are the palace police likely to do so," Tom said. "Such threats are apparently such a common occurrence that everyone is quite blasé in the face of them. I suppose that if the imperial family avoided every public event with the potential for violence, none of them would ever leave their rooms. Besides, there isn't so much to go on when you break it down. The fact Yulian was a dancer, the fact the murders happened in the ballroom, even the fact Vlad asked Davy if he would be there. These details imply much, but prove very little."

"Besides, when you think of it, the situation bears as much opportunity as crisis," Rayley said briskly. "The ball is our chance to flush the traitors out, to see what other Volya members may reside unsuspected within these walls."

"I agree," said Tom. "They've had, what…less than two weeks to adapt to the sudden absence of Yulian, whom they were evidently relying on a great deal if for nothing more than a diversion. Any plan they've created since then would have to be rather slapdash, would it not? Besides, if we're to catch them, our own clock is ticking at the same speed. Forty eight hours from now the Romanovs will be packing for the coast and we shall be sailing for London."

"Very well," Trevor said with a sigh. "Draw the traitors out we shall, but I refuse to use Her Majesty as bait. I shall advise her not to attend the ball and to keep Alix away from the theater a well. And in the meantime I suppose I must consult with that bald man, what's the name? That Viktor Prakov who appears to be head of the palace police. I doubt he will welcome my visit."

"I shall come with you," Rayley said. "For I've met him just a bit, you see. He was one of the fellows in the sauna that day."

"Good god," said Trevor. "Who wasn't in that ghastly room? Next you'll be telling me that the tsesarevich himself was in attendance."

"Most certainly not," Rayley said with a quick grin. "I don't have the feeling Nicky Romanov is that sort at all. He sticks to his room, does he not? And prays for the strength to be a better man."

"Poor Alix," Emma said. But she said it softly, and none of the men heard her.

The Café of the Revolutionaries

11:20 AM

"I cannot imagine why you felt the need to introduce me to that little British pip," Filip was saying in irritation as he finished his beer. His first beer of the morning, but certainly not the last. The day ahead would likely prove challenging, the evening even more so. "It was not as if we were at some sort of dinner party."

"If I did not introduce you, he would have been far more suspicious," Vlad said, his face flushed.

"So why did you not make something up?" Gregor snapped. He had not made such steady progress on his own beer and Vlad's, he noticed, sat completely untouched. No man in Russia could outdrink Filip Orlov, especially when he began before noon, so there was probably no reason to try and keep pace with him in a show of solidarity. "Just say the first name that came to your mind?"

"I am not good at making things up," Vlad said, refusing to meet either of the older men's eyes. "But why is it forbidden for me to confer with Mabrey just because he is English? Cooper vouched for him and neither of you thought anything of it two or three days ago. Meanwhile Filip here is in consort with British policemen, inviting the Queen's private guard to sweat with him in the saunas."

"An entirely different matter," Gregor said with a wave of his hand.

"Yes," said Filip. "For I am, you see, quite good at making things up."

If possible, Vlad's flush grew even deeper, mottling his pale skin and, to his horror, even his eyes were beginning to water. Gregor and Filip had never been so openly displeased with him, and his disgrace could not have come at a worse time. Not now, on the day they had decided they must make their move. He had been the one to point out that the dress rehearsal would be the perfect time to snatch Xenia. For while she - and indeed everyone else involved with the presentations for the ball-would be in their appointed places, the absence of an audience would mean that the theater would be relatively unguarded.

"Davy is a nothing, a mere messenger boy," Vlad said, when he had regained his composure enough to trust his voice. "The odds are that he does not even know the detective you met in the gentlemen's enclave."

"Don't be an idiot," Gregor said. "They all came over on the same boat."

"Here is the first rule of revolution," Filip said, seemingly either unaware or uncaring about the slight crust of foam that was forming within his mustache. "Assume that everyone knows everyone. Assume that the woman on the bench is the sister of the man stepping off the train. Assume the grocer is the lover of the woman in his shop and while you are at it, assume that he is also the lover of the man getting off the train because the world is full of its surprises. This I know, comrades."

Gregor grimaced and turned to Vlad. "If this messenger boy of yours happens to see Filip within the palace –"

"He won't. He said he won't be anywhere near the ball and I believe him."

"Then let's hope he's not one of the ones who are good at making things up," Filip said, shaking his empty beer mug in the general direction of the serving girl. "For his sake and for yours."

Chapter Twenty

The Streets of St. Petersburg

1:50 PM

It was bad luck to question good luck. He knew this and yet he could not help but wonder why she had agreed to meet him here, in the center of town, far beyond the palace gates. St. Petersburg was a large city, as he had reminded her many times before, and size afforded anonymity. The chances they would be observed strolling the parks or drinking wine in some café were slim, and in fact one could quite reasonably argue that it was safer to tryst in the crowded streets than within the walls of the palace. And yet she had always hesitated, as if the very act of seeing him in the full light of day would force her to recognize that their affair was real.

But this morning a note had come. A suggestion they should take luncheon together, in a most public place, Senate Square. And she had further surprised him by announcing – announcing it abruptly, before the menus had even been brought to their table – that she was prepared to leave Filip and run away with him to Paris. He must go at once, she said. In fact, he must leave this very day. He could get a job in a French dancing school and she would follow in a few months, after enough time had passed that no one would draw any correlation between his absence and her own. Money was no longer the problem they had always assumed it to be, nor were the tickets, or travel papers or even the letters of introduction. The Grand Duchess Ella Feodorovna had seen to all that.

His initial reaction was disbelief. He had been dancing with Ella for some time and had never noticed her heart to be within the clutches of any particular altruistic impulse. He knew that he and Tatiana had been far from discreet, but the last person he would have worried might guess their secret was the notoriously self-obsessed Grand Duchess, who was so disinterested in the stories of others that she had never inquired about the village of his birth, the source of his training, or whether his parents still lived.

She certainly had never asked if he would like to go to Paris.

Tatiana slid a piece of paper across the table. A brief glance revealed it to be a train ticket. He placed his wine glass over it, so that the paper - so that his very freedom – would not blow away in a passing gust of wind. Of course Ella had chosen Tatiana for her court. Tatiana's beauty made her a jewel and the Romanovs, even those who had entered the family by marriage, collected jewels compulsively, amassing too many to count. But it was certainly strange that the Grand Duchess would be willing to forfeit both her dance master and her lady in waiting in one swoop, even if she knew the depth of their shared desperation.

"Why would she help us?" he asked, not noticing that the base of his wine glass had leaked a perfectly-formed red circle onto the railway ticket.

She is willing to help because we have, quite by accident, created something she is unable to create for herself, Tatiana thought. She is helping us because I am giving her the most precious thing I have in exchange for your safely. Because I am willing to trade my child for this ticket you treat so carelessly, this piece of paper you slosh wine upon, as if it were a rag. But Tatiana understood that Konstantin's pride, as vast and cold as Siberia itself, was forcing him to feign this nonchalance and she bit the words back. Instead she merely said, "The Grand Duchess can be very kind when she chooses…and is this not the most glorious day that has ever existed?"

"The most glorious," he agreed, looking around them. The café where they sat was small, but prettily situated. There was a flower market across from it, and petals wafted through the air. A cat, too sleek to be a stray and evidently the pet of the owner, had insinuated his way around their legs as they sipped their wine. Tatiana had been the one to choose the bottle. It was French, and undoubtedly more expensive than any he had ever tasted. It was velvet to the tongue, just as everything Tatiana was saying was velvet to his mind.

"I will go in two days," he said. "After the ball."

She shook her head. Her hair was not pinned up as it usually was, but rather pulled to one side in a fat loose braid, a style very different from what the ladies wore in the palace. It made her look younger, almost like a school girl, and he supposed it was evidence that no one knew she had slipped from the palace to meet him here, that she had dared not ring for the services of her maid.

"You must go now," she said, "when no one expects it. Their attention is diverted to the ball."

"I am expected to dance. My ladies -"

"There are other dance masters who can lead them in their waltz. I must insist. My husband –"

"Do not call him that."

"All right then. Let us be in agreement. I will not speak of my husband if you do not speak of your ladies."

He smiled and sipped his wine. She did not smile and did not sip hers.

"The imperial guard believes you are connected to the murders in the ballroom."

"So I understand. But who told you this? The Grand Duchess?" When she did not answer, he pulled in another great gulp of wine and stared into the distance. "Of course it was the Grand Duchess. But I am not connected in the least to any of these crimes. You believe this, do you not?"

"I would hardly go to Paris with a murderer, would I? Of course I know you are innocent, and so does Ella. But if my husband –"

"Do not –"

She looked at him sharply, raising a glove to shade her eyes as he did so. "Listen to me, Konstantin. If the imperial guard intends to arrest you, they will wait until the ball is over and the tsar's entourage has moved to the coast for the summer. And who shall come to your defense then? What friends shall you find in an empty palace? No, of course you must go today. The ticket is already dated and stamped." And when he still hesitated, she added, "Besides, you know the temperament of the Grand Duchess as well as I do. She cares for us now. We are her distraction of the hour. But who knows how long her interest will remain fixated on our troubles?"

The fullness of the situation struck him at last. "You have brought me here to say goodbye."

"Only for a while. I shall be in Paris by the time the first leaves fall, I promise it."

He sat in silence for a moment, absorbing this extraordinary rash of news. She had finally agreed to leave her husband, to come with him to France. Apparently half the palace knew him to be a murder suspect. Time was of such essence that he must leave at once, so he had unknowingly slept his last night in his bed, eaten his last meal in the palace, taken his last steps within the ballroom. There would be no chance to say goodbye to all his ladies – those he liked, those he did not. His parents, for they indeed did still live, would never see him again. Tomorrow he would awaken in a new land.

But the most extraordinary fact was that his patroness in this complete reinvention of his life was the Grand Duchess Ella Feodorovna.

"All will be fine," Tatiana said, now more calmly. "Ella assures me that if she introduces you to the owner of the Ballet Clausse he will take you on immediately and help you find a place to stay. I take it they are some measure of old friends. So I will know, you see, precisely where to find you in October."

"It seems I have no choice."

"True. At least not in the timing. But this is our chance to begin again. And very few people are given such a chance."

"We must have a picture," he said, abruptly pushing his chair back from the table. "A picture to commemorate this most extraordinary day."

She followed his gaze to the sight of a street artist in the corner of the square, a man painting a patch of daisies. Konstantin waved him over and he moved toward them at once, dragging his easel and palate of paints. "For a year," Konstantin said, "we have taken such pains to leave no evidence of our love. But today there is no need to be careful. Today we must have a memento."

She nodded. The waiter had brought their food and they ate as the man painted them. And at some point, without comment, Konstantin picked up the train ticket and put it into his pocket. When the clock in the square struck three, he waited for her to react. She was always extraordinarily aware of the hour and he had thought on many occasions that this was what having a love affair meant. For if a woman possessed of both a husband and a lover knows anything, she knows what time it is. But she said nothing and he found this so uncharacteristic that he had to ask.

"When must you return to the palace?"

"There is no need to rush," she said. "The Grand Duchess wishes to speak to you one last time before you depart and after that we have the whole afternoon. At least until it is time for you to catch the launch to the train station." She looked up at the sky, which had shifted during their luncheon from dark blue to light, as a low flat cover of clouds had moved in. "The day is changing," she said.

"Everything is."

The drawing which the street artist presented to them was not bad. Tatiana's bright rose colored dress shouted its presence from the center and, beneath the café table, the man had taken note that their knees were touching. Their feet were perhaps touching as well, but given the central location of the cat this was impossible to verify. Their faces were turned away from him, as if both of them were looking at something in the far distance. Konstantin was charmed by the conceit, which showed the yellow braid of Tatiana and his own darker hair, similarly curved, stretching across their shoulders in the manner of two question marks. He believed their facelessness cast them into as archetypal every couple, two lovers determined to squeeze a lifetime into a single afternoon. Tatiana, when she beheld the drawing, only suspected that the artist turned them away because he was not skilled at drawing faces, but she only nodded and smiled.

Pleased with her tacit approval, Konstantin poured the last dregs of the wine into his glass and handed it to the artist, who bowed with great solemnity before drinking. Their last bits of chicken and potato were tossed to the cat. And then they watched as the street artist wrapped brown paper around the drawing, crisscrossing the bundle with twine. Layer after layer, making a loop large enough to serve as a rough handle. Konstantin paid him, and Tatiana paid the café bill, and then he stood and held out his hand to her. After a moment of hesitation. Tatiana took it. He slipped his other hand through the loop of string and they left the café, the carefully wrapped painting brushing against Konstantin's leg with every step he took.

They have done everything a man and woman can do to one another. They have done things that Tatiana previously had not known were possible, things she believed might stop her heart and rip her soul from her body. They have broken every law of god and man and likely ruined each other in the process, but the one thing they have never done together is walk a city street arm in arm. They did so now as the clock struck once for the half hour and as they moved into the stream of people, Tatiana half-expected the city to freeze and for all of its citizens to stop and stare at them. To shout insults at this couple, these sinners walking arm in arm, bearing brazen witness to their love.

But no one did. St. Petersburg moved and they moved within it, walking silently until they reached the palace gates.

The Café of the Revolutionaries

3:30 PM

Among the thousands of people taking no note of Konstantin Antonovich and Tatiana Orlov walking through the streets of St. Petersburg were three men who also happened to be sitting at a café table. It was a far humbler place, lacking artists and flowers and even the rustic charm of a napping cat, and beer rather than champagne was the order of the day. They had sat there for hours, so many that the serving girl had long despaired that they would ever vacate the table for the use of more prompt and generous patrons. But at least the length of their meeting had given enough time for the discord between them to settle and for Vlad to regain his confidence in the face of the more experienced men.

"The place where we hold her must not be too comfortable," Vlad was saying. "It must be a common room with common food and with no particular accommodation against the heat or the stink of the docks. That way when she is returned to her fond papa she can report to him the conditions in which his people live. Give her a pallet and a tin cup of water and let us see what the tsar's daughter makes of that."

This speech both amused and annoyed Filip, but he took care to make sure his expression revealed neither emotion. The younger men in the Volya often argued for extreme measures in dealing with the aristocracy, declaring that they must be forced into the lowest of conditions in order to understand the need for reform. Conditions that most of them had never experienced themselves, mind you, and certainly not Vlad or Gregor, who had enjoyed the comforts of a middle class boyhood and university education, furnished courtesy of their own fond papas.

"But we must be practical," Filip said calmly. "It may take some time before the tsar enacts the reforms we will request and thus our hostage can be released. We can scarcely toss the child into a warehouse like a sack of potatoes and lock the door.
"

"Why should it take time?" Gregor asked. "Her father can sign anything he wishes into law with the stroke of a pen."

Their plan was to demand the right for the serfs to form collectives on the farms where they worked, collectives which would allow them to bargain for a greater percentage of the profits. The idea had occurred to Gregor during his brief and unsatisfactory attempt to organize the rural workers. Filip considered this a rather ridiculous goal, largely because there was absolutely no evidence suggesting that the surfs wished to form collectives. In fact, Filip, who unlike the others had spent a good deal of time in the countryside, strongly suspected that if you walked out into a muddy field and asked the nearest farmer if he wished to form a collective allowing him to negotiate with his land owner over profit distribution percentages on future harvests, the man would simply stare at you. He would be more likely to tell you he wanted a woolen scarf or a bottle of vodka or a new rope for his wagon. But when Filip had suggested to the Volya in their last meeting that they should use the kidnapping to force the tsar to distribute free grain from the country's vast storehouses, this idea had been met with derision. Gregor had said that their aim should be a lasting change in the law, not a one-time gift, and the others had nodded, with Vlad going so far as to give Filip a look of open contempt.

"It takes but a stroke of the pen to sign a law," Filip conceded. "But to create a force of officers spread out across the rural district ensuring this law is actually carried out will take far more time. Especially in light of the fact that the farmers have not requested these collectives and may have to be educated as to their long-term advantages. "

"You're saying we must keep the little duchess the whole time?" Gregor said with audible distress. "Administration is a tedious process."

"I'm saying that you are acting under the illusion that we must hold her for only a few hours, while her frantic family scrambles to meet our demands. But we are not requesting a simple ransom. If you are seeking true reform, including a system to assure that it continues, this could take weeks or even months. The child must live somewhere. Perhaps Vlad can take her home with him. Turn her into yet another little sister."

Vlad scowled, just as Filip knew he would. "She will eat potatoes, half rotted potatoes, so that she knows how her people struggle."

"And this what your mother served at the dinner table last night? Half rotted potatoes?"

Vlad's scowl deepened. "What my family ate for dinner last night is not the point."

"Is it not, comrade?"

"Well we certainly can't hold her for weeks," Gregor said, wearily wiping his brow for the day was warm and he had long ago lost track of how many times the serving girl had refilled his glass. "Perhaps Filip is right that we are better off demanding merely the law and a payment of money. That way, we have means to fund the collectives ourselves, rather than depending upon the government."

"That does seem more prudent," Filip said. "A law and a great wad of money. Things the tsar can produce in an instant. With any luck Xenia will be home by the break of dawn and the Volya will have funding for a year's worth of good works."

"Do you know her?" Vlad abruptly asked.

"Of course. I guard the entire family."

"You have sympathy for her. Perhaps that influences your recommendations."

Filip shrugged. "I have no particular sympathy for this girl. No more than I have for any of them."

"What is she like?"

"Actually, comrade, her character reminds me of your own."

Vlad bristled. "I find it hard to believe that the daughter of the tsar bears any semblance to a son of the revolution," Vlad said.

"She has the impatience of youth," Filip continued, as if Vlad not spoken. "And a certain air of entitlement that most people find –"

"All right, all right, this is getting us nowhere," Gregor said quickly, sitting up in his chair, for Filip had pushed too far and Vlad could be impulsive when angered. "We shall take the girl to the warehouse as planned, with the understanding she cannot remain there long. And we ask for…how much money? It must be enough to fund our work with the collectives, just as Filip said, but no one must ever know the ransom was paid to the Volya. So what is the right amount? Perhaps twenty thousand rubles?"

"Thirty thousand," Vlad countered.

"But is that too much?"

Vlad shook his head. "We must be bold. He will surely pay it. She is his daughter, after all."

"You are right. Thirty thousand." Gregor looked across the table at Filip. "And why do you chuckle? What do you find so funny?"

"Make it a hundred," Filip said. "Thirty thousand rubles is less than the tsarina spends on a gown."

Chapter Twenty-One

The Winter Palace – The Chapel of the Mournful

5:05 PM

"Please don't tremble," Nicky said. "Everyone is so preoccupied with the ball that they won't even notice we are missing."

She was indeed trembling, so violently that her small pearl earbobs bounced against her cheeks. She had run through the rain from the palace to the chapel, which, just as he described, stood free and separate from the Winter Palace and was surrounded by a graveyard. Nicky had been waiting for her there, his thin frame pressed inside the enclave and he held out his hands as she approached, pulling her under the protection of the arch.

"Come in," he said, refusing to release her and thus reduced to awkwardly pushing against the door with his shoulder. "It's the last place they'll look."

She entered the chapel, then, after a quick look around to make sure neither of them had been followed, he went in behind her. The room was terribly dark, but from what she could see, the wooden floor and plain glass windows reminded

Alix of the humble country churches of Germany. She turned to him in wonder.

"It's beautiful," she whispered.

"Shall we light a candle?"

She nodded and tiptoed to the altar where a box of the thin white tapers lay. When she had safely reached the table he closed the door, and they were engulfed in gloom.

"Here's one for my mother," she said, striking a match and bringing it to the ragged strip of cotton at the top, then pushing the candle into the pile of sand. "And I must add one for my sister and my brother."

Nicky moved beside her. She has had much loss for one so young, he thought. His parents and his siblings were all alive, a condition which suddenly struck him as blessed and rare.

"For my grandfather," he said solemnly, picking up a candle of his own. "I pray I will be even half the tsar he was."

"Light it from the one for my mother," she said. "For hers is the soul I most want to emulate."

He dipped his own candle to the tremulous light of hers. "Then they shall be our personal saints," he said. "I feel their blessing pouring down on us already. Do you?"

But before she could answer, they heard the sound of footsteps approaching, feet running across the cobblestone courtyard leading up to the chapel door. Nicky grabbed Alix's hand and pulled her into the priest's alcove behind the altar. It was dusty and full of cobwebs, with a window smudged by so many months of neglect that it no longer functioned as a window, letting in little light and allowing only a partial view of the yard. The dimensions of their hiding place were so small that they were pressed together and she looked at him with wide, questioning eyes.

The door swung open, bringing with it a gust of damp heavy air, which extinguished the candles, leaving Alix and Nicky saintless and Konstantin and Tatiana laughing and dripping on the threshold of the chapel.

"I told you," he said. "No one ever comes here."

"It's dark," she said. "There must be some sort of illumination?"

Konstantin dropped the sack he carried and then wedged the wrapped package holding the painting into the doorway, propping it open to give them a bit of light. "I don't think so," he said. "It looks too old and rarely used."

"They call this the Chapel of the Mournful," Tatiana said. "How did you hear of it? It's where those who have lost something stop to pray."

"Where do those who have found something pray?" he whispered, sliding his hands around her waist. He was happy, shaking the raindrops from his hair like a dog. He has the ticket in one pocket, she thought. And the letters of introduction from the duchess in the other. He shall catch transport from the servant's dock into town, and then the train, and then, on the morrow, he shall walk the streets of France.

"I want to light a candle," she said abruptly, pulling from his embrace and walking toward the altar. "Shall you?"

"No, for I can think of nothing to mourn," he said, squinting up through the murky light at a portrait of an especially regretful looking prophet, who had pressed his long thin fingertips together and rolled his flat dark eyes toward the heavens.

From behind the panel Nicky and Alix relaxed a little. Neither of them knew who was in the chapel, but it was clear enough that these people had not come searching for them but rather seeking some sanctuary of their own. Alix pushed back her scarf and in the shadows Nicky saw, twinkling below the lace, the diamond flower pinned to her dress. Despite all of her protests, she was wearing this gift. He reached out, touched it with a fingertip and she smiled.

"Why are you so solemn?" Konstantin asked.

"Shh," said Tatiana. "I am trying to pray."

"The angels above you are broken."

"So they are," she said, looking up at the chipped plaster faces. "Now be silent, or lightning shall strike you for being such an infidel."

Tatiana closed her eyes, exhaled, and tried to concentrate. She asked for forgiveness first, as she always did, and then for clarity. Don't let me forget this day, she prayed. Push it into my memory. Everything here. His face, his smile, the dust, the raindrops on his jacket, the ashes from the candles.

His hands were back, around her again. More demanding this time, pulling her from the altar with more determination.

"Come," he said. "There will be time to pray when I am gone."

She let him steer her away from the altar and lead her across the wooden floor. Good, she thought. Let him take me. Let me go. He is so innocent and so hopeful, and may I remember that as well. Tatiana found herself suddenly weak with emotion, uncertain if she could exist another minute without blurting out the dark truth. That this was the last time he would touch her, the last time she would hear his voice. That she was not coming to Paris and he must enter his new world alone.

The chapel only had two doors and he led her toward the back one, tucked into an even dimmer and dustier corner, far away from the angels and the candles. Away from the altar which concealed the hidden forms of Alix and Nicky. Nicky had now removed the brooch from Alix's dress and was using the point of the largest diamond to etch their initials into the window. He was sawing the letter A into the glass with a concentrated fervor and she was thinking that if they married, she would wish for them to marry here - in this chapel, which was so simple, so sincere and so sweet. But of course that would never be allowed. When the tsesarevich of Russia married, it would be in the grandest church in the land, with a procession of thousands. His tsarina would be draped in ermine, not a veil of cobwebs.

The door creaked as Konstantin closed it behind them and Tatiana found herself in the base of the bell tower, looking up a steep flight of stairs. The wooden steps were rotted and bowed and she wondered what brave soul had last ventured to climb them. At the top of the tower a rusty bell was tilted at such a sharp angle that she could not see its tongue. A rope, rough and frayed, extended down the staircase, so long that the end lay coiled at her feet. The light at the top of the tower promised a view of the river, a vision fit for a saint who might pause, mid-assumption, to consider the pretty, inconsequential world below.

Why had they come to this tower? Did he intend for them to climb it?

But no. No. Of course not. She knew from his first touch that he had brought her here for some other purpose. Something wilder and darker and more desperate and Tatiana was tired of fighting her fate. Tired of beating back grief. She sank down to the rough steps and lifted her skirt. He pulled the layers of garments which lay beneath in one direction and then the next until her naked hips and thighs slid into that gentle trough that exists in all steps, that indentation that has been worn by centuries of patiently climbing feet. It was as if the spot was designed for just this purpose.

"Are they gone?" Alix whispered.

"I don't know," said Nicky.

"Should we leave?"

"Not yet." The A was finished and he had begun the second line of the N.

"Yes, finish the initials," Alix said, sinking back against the wall. "For this way you will always remember me, no matter what happens."

"Don't say that," Nicky said, his own voice rising above a whisper, causing her to press her palm against his lips and shake her head in warning. Whoever had been there might come back again "You will return soon to St. Petersburg," he whispered, when she pulled her hand away. "And next time we meet we shall be married. Promise me."

There was nothing to say to this, nothing at all. She pointed toward the half-finished initial. "Hurry," she said. "We don't have much time."

"Hurry," Tatiana was saying. "We don't have much time."

Konstantin knew this too, even better than her. Her undressing had been somewhat ceremonial but his own clothes had been dropped or lifted or yanked aside so fast as to defy understanding. He put his knees on the bottom step and leaned into her, pushing her back into the splintered corner of a higher step, causing her to cry out. A sound he either misinterpreted or translated into some higher tongue because he did not stop kissing or pushing against her. Tatiana collapsed into the staircase, throwing back her head, looking up the dark shaft of the tower to the lightness at the top.

"Hurry," she whispered.

He thrust into her. One move, direct and – despite everything – rather surprising. Her back arched and then slammed once again into the step. I shall have bruises, she thought vaguely. Scrapes. How shall I explain them and is this how the angels in the chapels got broken? He lifted her hips up and began to move in a steadier rhythm and when their eyes met, they both laughed with sheer hysteria, the laughter that comes when relief and grief and desire all meet, the sound the body makes when the mind can no longer find the words. The inevitability of finding each other, the inevitability of losing each other, and Tatiana blew him a kiss through the dusty air and then dropped her head back again. I don't care, she thought, how many times my head is pounded against these steps. I don't care if I am knocked insensate and left to die in the foot of this tower. They can bury me outside with the others. The nameless and the mournful. I will lie with them forever.

He pulled out of her and she looked up, startled. Had the door opened, had they been caught? But he was only moving lower as he did sometimes in his Asian way and the sight of his head nuzzling its way down her legs burned into her mind so clearly that she knew the memory would never fade. It seemed as if someone high above them was crying and then Tatiana, her gaze moving upward, saw that it had begun to storm. The sky at the top of the tower has grown grayer and wilder. The wind wafted a diffusion of raindrops down onto them. Onto her upturned face, onto the back of Konstantin's head.

"Hear the thunder," Nicky whispered, pulling Alix's hand to his chest.

Alix nodded, her eyes bright. "Granny says that when it thunders, it means God is angry."

Tatiana knew that it was here. That it would lift her, possibly not gently, and carry her away. She dropped one hand to his head, braced her feet, and cried out. Her other hand struggled to grip the wall because the intensity was frightening, so beyond anything she had ever experienced that for a fraction of a moment she wondered if she might actually be dying. She was certainly falling from a greater height than ever before, and just then her hand found the rope and tightened around it and the world became filled with sound. A single clang that reverberated through the tower, through the chapel and into the graveyard. Every hair on her arms has risen, every bone beneath her skin shuddered. Even the roots of her teeth seemed to move a little and she has been left flushed, pure, and covered with rain.

When she opened her eyes, Konstantin was staring down at her.

"Shit," he said. "We've got to get out of here."

"Run," Nicky shouted, but Alix had already sprinted past him, had already fled from behind the priest's alcove and was across the wooden floor, knocking the wrapped package which had been bracing the door open and sending it skidding out into the rain-soaked courtyard. Nicky had no choice but to chase her. The storm was great now, howling around them and there would be no acceptable explanation for where they had been, why they would have ventured from the palace in such weather, how they might have gotten so mussed and so wet. He caught up with her just beyond the gate to the graveyard and grabbed her hand. He still held the brooch. The great diamond bounced between them, caught in the hollow of their clasped hands, cutting first into her palm and then into his.

"Do you think anyone really heard?" Tatiana asked. They were still clutching each other in the bell tower.

"No," said Konstantin. He was laughing, wiping the rain from her face. "We're too far away. I just panicked."

"But it is time for your boat."

"Yes. Soon."

They crept back through the chapel, with a single glance up at the angels who observed them with no change of expression. They paused at finding the door closed and the package outside, but Konstantin decided he must not have wedged it well and it had been blown free by a gust of wind. It lay in a sad state on the cobblestones, leaking puddles of green and pink, which ran together into larger puddles of gray.

"Leave it," Tatiana said. "It must be ruined."

But Konstantin reached to grasp the rough handle that the artist had made, and they walked across the lawn, down toward the river, not bothering to rush. When one was thoroughly soaked, there can no longer be any fear of getting wetter.

The servant boat was waiting in its dock. He turned to her. He dared not kiss her, not here so close to the dock where workers from all functions within the palace were huddled under the small shelter, where anyone might recognize them. It would be the most unpleasant sort of irony to be caught now, during his last moments on the soil of the Winter Palace.

It is lucky that it is raining, he thought. Rain hides tears.

"I don't know how I shall be able to live until we meet again," he said. And then he picked up his sack and the painting, ran to the dock, and lightly leapt onto the barge. He did not look back.

"But live you shall," she whispered. "And so will I."

The Winter Palace – The Gentleman's Enclave

5:36 PM

"Good God, that thunder," Trevor murmured as a particularly distressing rumble shook the air. They were standing in a covered portico connecting the rooms of the gentleman's enclave to the private dock, awaiting their meeting with Viktor Prakov, who was running slightly late. A condition which was rare in policemen, but apparently quite common in Russians.

"My mum always says that thunder means God is angry," Davy said, his eyes darting around the opulent surroundings, for even the dock was fitted with statuary and carvings and the two small boats in the slips had padded seats and canopies, and resembling no rowboats he had ever seen.

"Then God must be angry in the extreme," Trevor said. "What do you remember of the place, Abrams?"

"At the risk of stating the obvious, this is the dock," Rayley said. "The last in the line of docks used by the Winter

Palace and thus any watercraft leaving from this location will not have to pass the others, or indeed many of the windows of the palace. And through those doors," he added, gesturing back toward the building, "you will find the smoking rooms, dressing rooms, sauna and steambath, places for billiards and the other games that gentlemen enjoy."

"How many rooms?"

"Impossible to guess."

"Not so impossible," came a voice from the side and they all turned to see Prakov approaching from the lawns. He was walking through the downpour with little regard for personal discomfort – there was no hat on his head, nor boots on his feetm and when he stepped under the portico he made no attempt to wipe the water from his brow.

"What matters the number of rooms if there are only two exits?" he continued. "The enclave is designed so that it is easy for a man to hide, but not so easy for him to escape. You are the British Queen's bodyguards, I understand?"

"Trevor Welles, Rayley Abrams, Davy Mabrey," Trevor said as hands were shaken all around. "We appreciate you taking time to meet with us."

"Not much time. The next two days will place many demands on my unit."

"Indeed," said Trevor. "If you could just tell us a bit more about these two exits." He hesitated, as if wondering if he should explain why he asked, but Prakov did not inquire. The Russian did not ask the "why" of anything very often, Trevor had noticed. It was as if cause and effect were somehow severed in their minds.

"This exit is the dock as you have doubtlessly noticed," Prakov said brusquely. "The palace has five – one for bringing the staff in and out, one for bringing goods in and out, one for recreation, one for exalted visitors and the imperial yacht, and this one, for the private use of the gentlemen."

"Not guarded, I presume," Trevor said neutrally.

"Most certainly guarded, but not in any manner one would notice. We do not wish to make the imperial gentlemen self-conscious, after all, at least not in their hours of leisure. Come with me."

Mulling it all over, Trevor followed Prakov through the doors with Rayley and Davy trailing wordlessly behind. The men moved up the plush carpets along the narrow hall, struggling not to gape at the portraits of ladies in various degrees of dishabille along the walls. Davy was trying to count the doors as they walked, but abandoned the plan when the number passed twenty.

"And here," Prakov said when they finally arrived at the point where the hallway branched off into another angle, "is the route to the private stable."

"Also guarded in a discrete manner, I assume?" Trevor said and Rayley almost simultaneously asked "How many points are there within the palace where people might come or go by carriage?"

"Twenty-two," Prakov answered promptly. "Four meant for public entrance, such as visitors arriving for a ball, seventeen for utilitarian purposes. This is the only one which is private."

Trevor nodded. Viktor Prakov was scarcely a talkative fellow, but he was certainly more professional and confident than anyone they had met in the bumbling private guard, the majority of whose members had probably been placed there on the whim of the tsar. Trevor wondered what the bald man thought of the second force within the palace, whether he resented them, envied them, struggled to work with them, or merely ignored them.

"We did not simply ask you to meet us to provide a tour," Trevor said, "for such a simple task could have of course been carried out by any of your subordinates."

Prakov waited.

"We have two pieces of information about Filip Orlov, one of the members of the tsar's private guard," Trevor continued. "He invited Detective Abrams to the gentleman's enclave three days ago and told him that one of the imperial dance masters, a man by the name of Konstantin Antonovich, is his primary suspect in the ballroom murders."

Still no change of expression on Prakov's face.

Trevor fumbled for words. It was hard to talk to a man who was so utterly non-reactive. "Might I ask if the palace police share the theory that Antonovich is involved in the murders?"

"The first two deaths were deemed suicides and the bodies have already been accepted by the families for burial," Prakov said without emotion, or even without any particular cadence to his voice. If a machine could speak, Trevor thought, this is how it would sound. "And our investigation into the death of Cynthia Kirby is likewise drawing to a close. We intend to have her body ready for release into your custody by tomorrow, just as your Queen has requested."

Interesting, Trevor thought. Not only had Prakov avoided answering the question, but he had also avoided even using the word "murder." Apparently the palace police not only lacked a suspect, but they also lacked suspicions.

"You said you had two pieces of information, I believe?" Prakov prompted.

"Tell him, Davy," Trevor said.

"Filip Orlov is with the revolution," Davy blurted.

For the first time Prakov's eyes showed a flicker of a response.

"Which revolution?"

"The Naronaya Volyaka," Davy said. "The Volya, for short. I have been associating with the students who claim allegiance to its cause and one of them introduced Orlov as a high ranking member. The ballet dancer who was killed was one of them too. You know, Sir. The boy, Yulian Krupin."

An almost agonizing silence followed. They were telling the man his business, Trevor knew. Telling him that he and his police force had allowed not one but two revolutionaries close access to the imperial family. One of them even within the tsar's private guard. But now that his brief spasm of reaction at the name "Volya" had passed, Prakov was once again completely composed. What sort man hears bad news so calmly, Trevor wondered. He is either an idiot or a saint.

"If Krupin and Orlov got in, we think there may be others," Davy said, perhaps pouring additional salt into the wounds of the man's pride, but it was hard to tell. Prakov did at least finally answer.

"If what you are telling me is true, then Orlov must-" Prakov said. "There is a grand ball tomorrow night, with hundreds –" He broke off and took a slow breath. "Why should I trust you?"

"We have no reason to lie," Davy said.

"What we have learned," Rayley added, quietly and with extreme courtesy, "I assure you we learned only in service to our Queen."

Prakov looked toward the far door, the one he had indicated led to the private stables. "If what you say is true, Orlov must be arrested immediately."

"Perhaps not quite yet," Trevor said. "For you see, we have come to you with a plan."

The Winter Palace – The Private Rooms of the Orlovs

5:52 PM

Women would be the death of the revolution.

Not because they were not good fighters. There is nothing on earth so fearsome as a woman who had lost what she holds dear. Her children, lover, husband, parents… a woman so deprived would fight without hesitation, like an animal, often evidencing a ferocity few men could match. Filip had even thought that someday there would be a revolution with nothing but women and that when this day came, it would mark the end of the human race.

No, women would be the death of the revolution for an entirely different reason. They disarmed men. A man in love was a man distracted, a flawed comrade, a poor soldier.

Throughout the centuries, sentiment had slain more men than cannons, and Filip knew his great failure was his sentiment for his wife.

He did not wish to ponder this overmuch. To do so would be to risk acknowledging he shared the same weakness as Yulian Krupin. Perhaps that was what had truly driven his rage toward the young dancer, why he had killed in the boy what he knew he could not kill in the man. Filip told himself once again, for the thousandth time, that his marriage to Tatiana was one of mutual convenience, and yet this morning, when he had heard her in her toiletette, the unmistakable sound of her retching…

She carried his child. She did not have to tell him this. He simply knew. And this, of course, was a miracle. For during his recovery in the overcrowded infirmary following surgery for his gunshot wound, Filip had contracted the humiliating disease of measles. The rash and the scratching had tormented him more severely than the pain from his side, and then, final blow, the doctor had told him that the disease had most likely stolen his potency as well as his dignity.

"There is a chance that you might someday be a father," the man had said. "But it is slight." And now this child – conceived against all odds – must be protected.

As Filip waited for Tatiana in their rooms, he smoked his cigar - another small token of gratitude from the tsar - and struggled to convince himself that what he was about to do was only a small betrayal. Unlike Yulian, he would not let his heart take him completely away from the cause, but he would find a way to keep his wife safe from the events that were unfolding. The events which would likely go badly for him and his comrades. Whatever the hours ahead held, he must save Tatiana and the bud of life within her.

She came in just as the clock chimed six. She was drenched straight through to the skin and the sight of him sitting there startled her so badly that she let out a small cry of surprise.

"What are you doing here?"

An odd question. These were his rooms, after all.

The same thought had occurred to her and she amended her question. "Why have you come at this hour?"

"I am here to talk to you," he said. "But you should take off those clothes. They are wet and you will catch a chill."

She looked at the tumbler of brown liquid on the table beside him. "You have been drinking?"

"What if I have? We must get you into something dry."

"I will ring for the maid."

"Don't. I can help you. As I said, I wish for us to talk. Alone."

She hesitated. She was miserable in her clammy gown but to undress in front of him would only lead to an encounter she did not want. An encounter she knew she could not endure. Not with the smell of Konstantin still on her. She would not allow Filip to erase the last vestiges of his presence, to so quickly blot the memory from her skin. A woman who sleeps with two men finds her morality where she can, and it had been a point of honor with Tatiana that she had never lain with both Filip and Konstantin on the same day. She would not break her rule now, especially not now, when all she wanted to do was lie in her bed and weep over the events of the past hour.

"I am unwell," she said. This excuse had not always stalled him in the past, but it was worth a try.

"Yes, I know, and that is what I have come to talk about," he said, rubbing out his cigar and standing to move toward her. "You must leave St. Petersburg at once."

Chapter Twenty-Two

The Winter Palace – The Guest Quarters

7:12 PM

"I fear I do not have the legs for this costume," Tom said, turning one way and then the other to study his reflection in the long mirror.

"If it is any consolation," Rayley said, "I would imagine few men do."

"It is a matter of calf definition," Tom muttered, looking critically at his lower legs which seemed to him thin and rather boyish when encased in the bright yellow stockings. He tried not to ponder the fates of the previous two occupants of the gypsy king costume – the unfortunate Konstantin Antonovich and the even more unfortunate Cynthia Kirby. The shirt hung a little too loose as well, and he wondered if it was folly to imagine he might be able to convincingly pass as the Siberian dance master.

As if reading his mind, Rayley rushed to reassure him. "The mask and the hat will hide your hair and face," he said, "and the cape will conceal any differences between your frame and Antonovich's."

"What of the difference in height?" Tom said. "Everyone speaks of how admirably tall the man is and I am barely north of average."

"If you are costumed and masked, nothing else will matter," Rayley said, silently thankful that his own spindly frame had ensured that he wouldn't be the one tapped for this particular ruse. "You've read the reports from the Yard. Most people see only what they expect to see and nothing more."

"So they claim," said Tom, plunking the large plumed hat over his blond hair. "But we are betting rather heavily on that, wouldn't you say?"

The Winter Palace – The Servant Wing

7:14 PM

When Emma had asked the young man in the hall for directions to Konstantin Antonovich's room she had received little more than a vague pointing gesture and a rude smirk. There was only one reason, she supposed, that women living in her part of the palace came to visit men living in his, and she wondered how many of the imperial women had indulged in flirtations with their dance masters. Flirtations and perhaps more.

After a few more inquiries she finally found the room, but he did not answer her knock. The door was actually a bit ajar, so she knocked again, waited, then pushed it open.

The room was as plain as a monk's cell. A bed, table, cot, and chest of drawers. Two of those drawers were pulled open and the bed was mussed. Emma noted how few personal possessions the room held, and she looked especially for the red satin bag in which Konstantin carried his dance shoes. They were his most prized possession, he had told her, ordered from the west when he had begun his career within the Winter Palace and he only put them on at the last minute, just as they were about to step onto the dance floor. The minute their lesson was complete, he likewise took them off.

It would not take long to search a room of this size. She pulled open the remaining two drawers, threw back the blankets, looked under the bed. No red satin bag. With a sigh, Emma sat down on the narrow cot and stared straight ahead at the wall.

If his dance shoes were gone, so was Konstantin.

The Halls of the Winter Palace

7:42 PM

Trevor's thoughts raced even faster than his feet as he hurried up the steps leading to the imperial suites. Rayley was helping Tom into the gypsy king costume, which had been retrieved that afternoon from the palace police, and Emma was off somewhere in the direction of the servant quarters. Her purpose was to warn Konstantin Antonovich of their plan so that he would not appear at that night's dress rehearsal and thus shatter the illusion they were straining to create. Davy had been dispatched to the theater to procure information on all of the entrances and exits, especially those most likely to be used by the tsar and his family.

And Trevor was on his way to see Ella. For while it would be nice to solve a Russian crime, he had not been distracted from his main function, which was to protect Victoria and her granddaughters. The Queen, when informed of the situation, had readily agreed to stay in her suite along with Alex and Prakov had sent an entire contingent of the palace police to stand guard in the halls beyond. But Ella was temperamental and determined to prove to her grandmother that the palace was safe. Persuading her to abandon the rehearsal would likely prove to be more of a challenge.

Trevor rapped gently on the door leading to Ella's parlor and waited. In their past visits to the royals, the group had always been ushered in by Ella's private maid, a dour looking creature named Alina, so Trevor was shocked momentarily speechless when the door opened to reveal none other than Ella's husband, the Grand Duke Serge. He regarded Trevor with an expression that managed to be simultaneously bored and suspicious.

Trevor stammered out his rank and the reason for his visit while the Grand Duke surveyed him coolly.

"I do not report to my own bodyguards," he said. "And most certainly not to those of my wife's grandmama."

Irritation stirred in Trevor, but he suppressed it. "I only wished, Your Excellency, to suggest that your wife might avoid the rehearsal theater this evening. We have reason to suspect there may be some sort of trouble."

"Some sort of trouble…" the Duke said, sarcasm dripping from every syllable. "Could you possibly be more specific?"

But Trevor had scarcely begun when the Duke waved off the very explanation he had requested and said, "It doesn't matter. My wife has left today for our villa by the sea. I bade her goodbye just minutes ago." And with that he would have shut the door if Trevor had not managed to slip in the toe of his shoe at his last minute.

"She traveled alone, Your Excellency?"

"Of course not," the Grand Duke snapped, his limited patience at an end. "A lady in waiting and her maid are with her."

"Her new lady-in-waiting? Tatiana Orlov?"

"Why should I know the name of a servant? There was a carriage with ladies, headed for the coast and my wife was among them. If you have anything more to say, I suggest you say it to your own Queen. Good day."

And with that the door between the Romanovs and Scotland Yard was closed for good.

The Grand Ballroom

8:18 PM

His first mistake was his promptness. The rehearsal was scheduled to begin at eight o'clock and Tom had entered at 7:55 only to find himself standing in an empty lounge, waiting for the rest of the performers. It was the same room he and Emma had been exploring just before they had stumbled upon Tatiana

Speaking of Tom, he had entered the main ballroom as well and Emma internally winced as she watched him cross the dance floor. With the plumed hat he was nearly as tall as Konstantin, but Tom had little of the dance master's natural grace. He made his way to a distant edge of the room, one of the four shadowy entrance points for the waltz, each tucked behind the base of a stage set, and stood on the periphery of a group of ladies who were all wearing the same red dress as Emma. He seemed to sense her gaze for he glanced upward toward the balcony and made a stiff little bow in her direction.

It seemed to be going well enough from what she could tell. He wouldn't try to dance, of course. When the music began, it was a signal that the performers had a few minutes to warm up before the rehearsal. Tom and Emma had agreed they would find each other at the sound of the first note from the pianist, grandly parade to the center of the floor, and that Tom would pretend to roll an ankle almost immediately. Since their feet and legs were their livelihood, the dancers took even the slightest injury seriously. No one would be surprised if Konstantin quickly retreated to his room to pack his sore ankle in ice.

After all, this was merely the dress rehearsal. The rehearsal for the dancers and for the forensics team as well. If there were truly danger on the horizon, it was unlikely to come to fruition until tomorrow night, when the theater would be packed with an audience full of aristocrats. Tonight was the team's chance to get a sense of how the performers moved around the ballroom, where any lulls or points of drama were likely to occur in the program. Tomorrow they would be back in their places with more information, and the palace police in full force as well.

Emma gave a final quick look around the room before pushing to her feet. The costumes and matching dresses made it a little harder to tell, but she had not so far seen anyone whom she could not identify as one of the dancers, musicians, or performers. There were a few workmen adding last minute touches to the four theatrical sets in the corners and it struck her that this might be an easy way to gain access to the theater. Props were being carried in, while tools and pails of paint were being carried out, and around the cottage set were piled a virtual wall of burlap bags, evidently holding soil in which someone would plant flowers. But Trevor had noticed all this as well. He was leaning against the gilded doorframe of the entrance he was guarding, his eyes flickering from one set to another.

The musicians had entered. The pianist was seated, sifting through his papers. Emma turned to head downstairs and – despite the fact nothing was likely to happen tonight, despite the fact this was little more than practice – her heart was pounding. She must hurry. She must guarantee that she would be the first of Konstantin's partners to reach Tom's side. Because, God knows, they couldn't let him try to dance.

The Halls of the Gentlemen's Enclave

8:53 PM

It was strange to walk through halls that he had only seen in drawings. Strange to see Yulian's careful blueprints brought to life.

Yulian had suggested the idea of bringing in the flowers through the docks and Vlad had to admit it was genius. He had said that one of the theatrical sets was a cottage in the woods and it would be crammed full of flowers. For the sake of freshness, they would only be planted the night before the grand ball. So the dockworker on duty had not been surprised when Vlad and Gregor had rowed up in a boat full of lilies.

"Somebody has already come through with one load of flowers," he did remark, flicking a cigarette in the water. "How many damn posies do they need?"

"Twice as many as you'd think," Gregor had cheerfully answered. "Got another of those cigarettes? The wife won't let me keep them on me. Says I'm sending money for the baby's food right up in smoke."

The man had laughed and Gregor had tossed him a rope. Thus they had been literally pulled to the dock by one of the palace faithful, who had then furthermore lit Gregor's cigarette off of his own while Vlad scrambled to unload the flowers. They had gotten them from a florist whose son was an ambitious Volya recruit, a boy who'd had little conscience about helping his comrades burgle his own father's shop, and they had a subtle waxy smell which reminded Vlad of death. He watched Gregor out of the corner of his eye, admiring his coolness, his ability to share a smoke and a joke with the enemy.

But Gregor had always told him, if you want a man to trust you, ask him for a favor. Most people get this part wrong. They try to win people over by offering something to them, but humans instinctively recoil from those who help them. They like the people that they help far better, even if the favor granted is as small as a cigarette. Gregor and the dock worker smoked and laughed while Vlad advanced upon the palace with armloads of lilies.

The Private Stable of the Gentleman's Enclave

9:02 PM

Inside the carriage, Tatiana was ready to pound her fists with frustration. They had been sitting there for over an hour, while Ella had thought of one excuse and then another to delay their departure.

When Filip had instructed her to leave the Winter Palace, Tatiana's mind had reeled. The entire household was expected to pack and depart for the coast by the end of the week, so his insistence that she remain not even for that brief amount of time meant that something was brewing. She could not imagine what. She did not want to even try. She was already half in shock. Minutes earlier she had said goodbye to the only man he had ever loved, and now Filip was confronting her with the knowledge she was pregnant.

"The noises from your toilette in the morning," he'd said. "And little changes in your body. They tell a man what he needs to know, do they not?"

She had numbly nodded. She would not have guessed he paid so much attention, but he did, and his plan was already in motion. He was making arrangements for her to leave St. Petersburg. Not tomorrow, nor the next day, nor the next, but now.

And so Tatiana had gone knocking on Ella's door for the second time that afternoon. Ella had listened to this new complication and then briskly nodded. They would both go, she said. If they arrived at the seaside villas before everyone else, it would be easier to create the fiction that Tatiana had miscarried. She could send a wire to Filip with the sad news that the carriage ride had unseated her pregnancy.

"It is not a change of our plans, merely a small variation," Ella assured her, and then she had rang for her maid and begun to pack. A carriage was called for and it was furthermore arranged that this would leave from the private stables, the one near the gentleman's enclave. It was a part of the palace Tatiana had never seen, a part Ella had presumably never visited either, and as they walked the long halls, the men with their luggage trailing behind them, Tatiana had wondered at the secrecy of their leave taking. They were dashing off at a strange hour, from a hidden exit, as if they had committed some dreadful crime, as if their departure was not only unexpected, but illegal.

Their husbands had each come down to the stable to bid them farewell. Tatiana had watched as Ella's fifteen trunks and her two were strapped to the top of the carriage. As silken wraps were loaded into the interior, along with bolsters and pillows. They would ride straight through the night, it would seem, and Tatiana glanced up at the driver who had drawn this thankless assignment. Filip had kissed her forehead and departed. Serge had kissed Ella's and followed suit.

And then, just as Tatiana had expected they would simply climb into the carriage, close the doors, and roll through the gates, Ella had begun to think of a dozen things she had forgotten. A special pair of shoes. Her Bible. Some sort of medication. A note for dear Granny, explaining her abrupt departure. Another for darling Alix. For darling Alix must be made to understand. Ella insisted upon personally viewing the food arranged for their trip, so the hamper had to be located and

and Konstantin, he noted, and was evidently the hub of any number of theatrical activities. He paced around nervously until he finally heard the sounds of others arriving downstairs, their voices growing louder as they climbed the stairs, and Tom wished, for the hundredth time in the hour, that he spoke even a smattering of Russian.

At least the first person through the door was someone he recognized. Xenia, the tsar's daughter, and Emma had briefed him that she was the first person Konstantin was scheduled to dance with during the imperial waltz performance. Tom supposed he must greet her, and he sank into an exaggerated bow, holding his cape out to one side.

"Good evening, Milady," he growled, attempting an accent so outrageous that she would not recognize that it was not the voice of her dance master. "Welcome to the hidden lair of the Gypsy King."

She laughed and responded to his English with English of her own. The vast majority of those within the Romanov court were multilingual and at times the palace seemed a virtual Tower of Babel to Tom, with any number of languages being spoken almost interchangeably. But he had noticed that whoever spoke first seemed to dictate the language of the conversation to follow and this time was no exception.

"Why are you dressed so silly?" Xenia asked. "They said we would practice the waltz first and then the theatricals."

"There have been a change of plans, my gypsy princess," he said, noting that she was indeed dressed for the waltz, in the same spangled red dress that Emma wore. Presumably all the women in that performance would be wearing the same costume, along with silk masks and feathered headbands, which would only make his task more difficult.

But Xenia appeared to take him at his word, merely nodding before turning to admire her reflection in one of the room's many mirrors.

Nice job, Bainbridge, Tom thought. You have at least managed to fool a twelve year old girl.

8:34 PM

Emma bunched the voluminous red skirt beneath her and perched on one of the balcony seats. It was the perfect vantage point for studying the ballroom below. She could see Davy at one set of doors, Trevor at another, and Rayley at the third – postings which might have seemed suspicious at any other time, but there was so much hubbub in the ballroom that no appeared to be taking note of their presence. Between the three of them they would get a good look at anyone entering from the public floors. It was up to her and Tom to monitor the entrances from the performance level.

unpacked. Unsurprisingly, she had been displeased with the contents. Another note, this one to the kitchen asking for pate.

In short, the hour had chimed nine and they were still sitting in the pebbly courtyard, waiting for Ella to finally proclaim them on their way. Why does she hesitate to leave the palace? Tatiana thought. Is it merely that those born to privilege never develop a talent for doing anything quickly? Or is something holding her here - some guilt or indecision masquerading itself as a request for an obscure kind of pate?

The Grand Ballroom

9:10 PM

"But I want to dance first," said Xenia, with a pout.

"My gypsy princess must dance last," Tom said, still swirling his ridiculous cape and using his ridiculous accent. The surveillance had gone well. He and Emma had made note of where each of the imperial ladies would be entering the dance floor and the Scotland Yard team presumably had explored the audience level in its entirety. Tomorrow they would enter the ballroom with far more information in their hands.

"He's right," Emma said desperately. The child had gripped one of Tom's arms and she had gripped the other. "The last lady to warm up is in the most advantageous position when the waltz begins."

Xenia seemed to ponder the statement, while Emma noticed that Trevor had ventured farther down the stairs and was looking in their direction. With a strategic toss of her head she saw that no, he was actually not looking at them but was rather observing something just past them, the base of the cottage scene, where several workmen were still arranging flowers and stones into a garden far too ornate to adorn any real peasant's home.

"I promise," Tom said to Xenia. "I dance with you last, and longest, and best."

Trevor was now moving faster and with more purpose, Emma noted, although Tom was still facing the sullen Xenia and did not seem to be aware that something was unfolding. And just then Emma saw the danger, come in the shape of two young workmen. They had turned in unison away from the stone cottage, almost as if they were doing some dance of their own, and they were behind Tom and Xenia in an instant. The taller one tossed a swath of burlap over her head and lifted the girl, hefting her over his shoulder while the smaller man threw his weight against Tom, knocking him nearly off his feet. He stumbled into Emma, his hat and mask flying off and Emma screamed. Trevor was now running, following the man who had snatched Xenia, while the smaller man, the one who had pushed Tom off balance, ran out another door.

Amazingly, no one around them seemed to have noticed what had just happened. They had been standing off the ballroom floor, in one of the little alcoves that rested nearly behind the theatrical sets. It was the location from which Xenia was to enter for her part of the waltz, and she had evidently pulled Tom to the spot while insisting that he warm up with her. Had she by accident played into the hands of the workmen? Were they prepared to grab any of the ladies in the red dresses and was her abduction thus random? Or had they known who would be in each corner of the room and pretended to work on the cottage scene precisely because it gave them close proximity to the tsar's daughter? The music had begun, and with the full orchestra it was far louder than it had ever been in rehearsal, loud enough that no one had heard Emma's cry for help.

Tom sprinted after the man who had struck him while Emma shouted again, this time toward the doors where Rayley and Davy were posted. But neither man heard her, so she ran up the steps - first to Davy, who upon hearing her frantic description of the events of the last minute, looked helplessly in one direction and then the other. There were so many passageways leading to the theater that presumably Trevor and the first assailant had gone in one direction and Tom and the other had fled via some different route.

We could run these halls forever and not find them, Emma thought, but by then Rayley had joined them. From his vantage point of the central door he must have seen more of what happened, for he had already concocted a plan by the time he reached Emma and Davy.

"Stay in the theater," he barked to Emma. "Don't argue with me and don't try to follow. Find the tsar's guard, for there must be some of them around, and tell them the littlest grand duchess has been seized. Send them in the direction of the gentleman's enclave. Which is where we are going as well," he added with a gesture to Davy. "There are only two ways they can get her out, by boat or on horseback. You take the dock and I shall take the stable."

Davy nodded and the two of them disappeared. Emma leaned against the doorframe and yanked her dance shoes off, blinking back tears as she did so. She looked around but saw no one who looked like a member of the guard, even though there were a dozen or so ladies of exalted birth in the ballroom, moving about laughing, chatting, or preparing to dance.

We are fools, she thought. We knew this was going to happen and yet, with all five of us in attendance, it still happened. A movement from the door across the expanse of the ballroom caught her eye. It was the door where Rayley had been waiting and now another man stood there, a man three times the size of her friend. A man who was looking directly at her in her red dress. A dress like the one Xenia wore, like Ella owned, and a dozen other ladies, including his own wife. Emma screamed again, this time at the sight of Filip Orlov. But that sound, like all the others, was absorbed into the persistent rhythm of the waltz.

Chapter Twenty-Three

The Halls of the Gentlemen's Enclave

9:20 PM

An angry twelve year old girl in a burlap sack is not a particularly easy thing to carry. When Gregor had practiced the choreography of the abduction, Vlad had played the role of the grand duchess and through repetition, Gregor had become quite confident in his ability to throw the sack over the head of his victim, then turn and hoist her to his shoulder.

But of course Vlad had stood cooperatively still and the real-life duchess was kicking, squirming, twisting, and doing everything in her power to express her profound displeasure with this turn of events. He had gotten her down the main hall – which had been cleared of all traffic by the order of Filip – and into the more obscure passages leading to the enclave, but it had been a struggle and he was already tiring with the effort. Xenia was emitting a seemingly never ending series of yelps and squeals which were muffled by the thick cloth but still entirely too audible for his liking. Gregor could only pray that they would not encounter anyone else along the hallway.

And then, of course, there was that business about the man chasing him.

This was not supposed to happen. The enclaves behind the sets had been precisely as Yulian had described them and Xenia had been waiting to enter the dance floor where predicted. The music was loud, the room was crowded, and all had been going according to plan. Yulian had told them to expect few guards within the theater, at least not during rehearsals, and had said that if Xenia was to be found with any man in attendance, it would most likely be her dance master. Vlad had done an admirable job of taking that fop off his feet, but then, out of nowhere, descending down a flight of stairs like some vengeful god, had come an entirely different fellow. No, not at all part of the plan. And now the fat fool was chasing Gregor and shouting in English.

Gregor knew he held advantages in the areas of youth, athletic prowess, and of course the fact he knew where they were going. But none of his bobs and weaves had so far fooled the fellow, who seemed, in fact, to be gaining on them. His gasping and rasping were becoming louder, and Gregor found himself stumbling as the Grand Duchess – who was frankly far less ladylike than one would expect – managed to strike the dead center of his chest with her knee, thus knocking the air from him and rendering him momentarily disoriented. He stumbled and lost his grip on the sack, her leaden form dropping at his feet with an appallingly loud thump, and then, just as he debated the advisability of trying to lift her again, the man who was chasing him rounded the final corner.

He would be upon them in seconds. Gregor decided it was time to use his final advantage and he fumbled for the pistol in his pocket.

9:20 PM

Emma was angry at herself for screaming, that most useless and classic of all female reactions. Not only had the sound been lost in the noisy ballroom but Filip Orlov had hardly been focused on her. He had paused in the central doorway for the same reason Rayley had been there earlier, because it offered the best vantage point on the entire ballroom, both the upper and lower levels. Judging from the expression on the man's face he had taken the measure of the situation almost at once, and knew that his young minions down on the floor had walked into a trap. He had left the door with the same haste as everyone else, headed for heaven knows where.

She needed to stay focused on her own task. Rayley had told her to find the palace police and there didn't appear to be any of them in the ballroom. Evidently the majority of the men on duty were clustered around the Queen's apartment, stationed there by the dour-faced Viktor Prakov as a courtesy to Trevor. With a sigh, for it was questionable if they would abandon their position based on the order of an English woman in a red spangled dress, she turned in the direction of the guest wing of the palace.

9:20 PM

Filip knew they had failed. The plan had gone with admirable smoothness up to a point, but as he had watched from the balcony he had realized, just before Gregor struck, that the man standing beside Xenia was not Konstantin Antonovich at all, but rather one of the British dandies who had accompanied the Queen. And with this knowledge, it had not been hard to locate the other three men standing in their separate doors. The Welles man in charge of it tall, his old comrade Rayley Abrams from the saunas, and finally that goddam little twit Vlad had introduced him to in the streets. Filip had tried to tell Vlad that boy would cause trouble, but it had never, even in his most extreme moments of paranoia, occurred to Filip that rosy-cheeked Davy Mabrey was Scotland Yard.

He had rushed down to the second level hoping he might intercept at least one of them before they too gave chase, but by the time he had arrived there no one was left but one of the women in the red dresses, shrieking to the heavens. God knows who she was or what she had seen but at least the orchestra was dulling the sound of her cries, the only way luck had played for them yet.

It was time for Plan B. There was always a Plan B and even, for very bad days, a Plan C. Filip could only hope that in their panic Vlad and Gregor remembered it.

9:20 PM

Vlad was lost. He tried to recall Yulian's drawings and Filip's descriptions, for he had certainly studied them often enough in the meeting room. But now it seemed that all the facts had left his head and he was being followed by the Siberian dance master, a man who presumably knew the palace like the back of his hand. The problem was that the halls, each lined with doors indicating rooms which were small and close together, all looked too damnably alike and, judging by the familiar smirk of a whore in one of the tawdry portraits, he feared he had somehow doubled back and was passing the same point for the second time. If he wasn't careful, he was about to run headlong into the man who was chasing him.

In desperation Vlad stopped at a door. A random choice, one of dozens just like it. He turned the knob and it opened.

9:20 PM

Tom was lost. He had been fairly sure that the boy he was chasing had turned off in this direction, but now he was beginning to doubt himself. He had passed the same portrait more than once, that much was certain, and he stopped, bracing his hand against the flocked velvet wall and struggling for breath.

"Tell me, madam," he said to the buxom woman gazing right at him, despite the fact any number of naughty cherubs were attempting to distract her with grapes. "Has an assassin recently passed this way?"

But the lady was discreet, at least in matters of conversation, so after a moment of rest, Tom decided to retrace his steps back to the entrance of the last set of halls. Perhaps something there might indicate the direction to either the stables or the dock. As he walked he pondered the universal truth that, even when under of the most extraordinary duress, a man always has time to notice a woman without her clothes.

9:24 PM

Trevor took it all in. The long hall. The squirming bundle of burlap. The terrified boy, pointing a shaking pistol in his direction.

A Webley, he thought, with the extraordinary detachment that comes over one in such situations. Standard issue, British service. So this is what became of Mrs. Kirby's gun.

The odds are that the boy would have missed him anyway. He was clearly untrained with such a weapon and so agitated that he was having trouble taking aim. But Trevor's luck was furthermore aided by the Grand Duchess Xenia, who by chance chose the moment to give an especially violent heave, one which caused her to strike Gregor's leg and the gun to jerk abruptly upward just as he fired. A chandelier exploded with a shriek of falling glass which rained down upon Trevor. The boy wobbled, as if trying to decide the advisability of firing again, but then simply turned and fled.

Tom, who had run toward the sound, approached from behind Trevor and then, from another direction, came Rayley. "Gad, Welles, are you all right?" Rayley asked.

Trevor nodded, shards of glass sliding down his shoulders. "See to the girl," he croaked to Tom, jerking his hand in the direction of the sack. And then to Rayley he added, "We must hurry. I fear he's trying to escape through the stables."

9:26 PM

Running barefoot, with her dress grasped up in her hands like a farm girl at the village barn dance, Emma made it to the Queen's suite of rooms in record time. If she had worried that the police stationed there would ignore her, as it turns out that concern was unwarranted. Instead they tackled her.

As she thudded to the carpeted floor, the weight of a young man in uniform crashing down beside her, the resultant scuffle caused the palace police inside the suite to open the door. And knowing that the cracked door offered her only chance, Emma shrieked again, for perhaps the tenth time of the evening.

"Your Majesty," she cried. "It's Emma."

She was surrounded by gray boots but there, from her humiliating posture on the floor with some random Russian astride her, she mercifully saw the bottom of a black shirt approaching. And the bell-like voice of Victoria said, with absolute calmness, "Get off that young woman at once."

9:26 PM

When Filip reached the portico which connected the men's enclave to the stable he saw many things which he had anticipated: horses, groomsmen, and various means of transport. But he also saw something which he did not anticipate and which made his heart promptly sink in his chest. The carriage that was to take Tatiana and Ella to the coast was still sitting in the courtyard. The driver, who had obviously given up on the idea of leaving any time soon, was slumbering in his seat on top, his head rolled to the side and his mouth gaping.

Not to panic. Not yet. His cover had not been blown. He strode up to the carriage and wrenched open the door.

"It is so hard to say goodbye, sweetheart," he called inside. "I have come for a second kiss."

The women startled as the door opened. They were waiting for what Ella had sworn to be the last of her endless requests, one of the Fabrege eggs Serge had given her with a miniature portrait tucked inside. Although sunlight still streamed and the night was warm, there were silken robes in bright colors tucked around them and they were reclining against great pillows. His Tatiana was encased in a pod of light green and dark pink, her hair twisted up in a casual but most becoming fashion. As Filip leaned into the carriage, their eyes locked.

The police may have taken him at his word, and possibly the Grand Duchess Ella as well. But his wife was not in the list bit fooled by his claim he had come for a second kiss.

"Why are you here?" she asked.

"Perhaps I shall come to the coast with you," he said.

The Grand Duchess seemed confused by this exchange. "But we are a party of ladies," she said, as if were an impossible notion that a man and his wife might travel together in a carriage.

Filip could see they were a party of ladies. The tangle of silken colors around them made it seem as if his wife and the

Grand Duchess and even the maid had been consumed by some great flower. Tatiana was drinking champagne. Her fingers, tight with tension, gripped the stem of the glass and the bedclothes smelled of lilac.

She belongs in this world, Filip thought. It was made for her.

And then there was a clatter behind him, so that he turned, one foot on the step of the carriage and the other still on the cobblestones, and looked over his shoulder. Gregor, wild-eyed and waving his pistol in the manner of an actor in a very bad play, had also run into the courtyard.

As the groomsmen moved toward him, Gregor gestured with his gun, shouting for them to get back, and they did. And then he looked at Filip and did the last thing Filip would have ever expected him to do.

Gregor smiled.

Plan B was to exit by the stable instead of the docks. To commandeer a carriage for escape and Gregor apparently thought that Filip was doing just that. He smiled and began to move toward the carriage but, from behind Gregor's shoulder, Filip could see the lumbering form of the British detective also approaching the door. The thin one in glasses was with him. And they both knew precisely who and what Filip Orlov was.

Filip had no more than three seconds to make his decision, but under these sorts of circumstances, time becomes elastic. It stretches to accommodate anywhere the mind wishes to go. Filip could almost see himself standing there in the door of the carriage, the ladies with their rose and green silks on one side of him, the wild-eyed comrade with his pistol on the other. It all hung on his next gesture, did it not?

Since boyhood, Filip Orlov had only two fears: that his life would have no meaning and that his death would have no meaning. He could see what Gregor could not. That the infidels had been prepared for them, that they had walked into a trap. To be caught now would mean that their cause had come to nothing and, perhaps more to the point, it would destroy Tatiana's life.

Her life and the life of his child.

Plan B was to commandeer a carriage by any force necessary, including the death of the driver. Gregor now raised his pistol in the direction of the man, who had been abruptly awakened by the commotion and had taken up the reins in one hand and his whip in the other. Despite the fact he had been snatched from slumber, his grasp of the danger at hand was clear, and he seemed prepared to protect his imperial passenger at any cost.

Filip allowed himself one final look at his wife.

And then he sprang. He leapt from the step toward the top of the carriage, straining to reach the driver's seat. It was a gesture which could be interpreted in many ways. But when

Gregor's bullet went into his back, Filip knew how history would judge him.

And in that same moment Trevor was through the door and on top of Gregor, knocking him to the ground and falling over him. The groomsmen, released from their paralysis, surrounded them and inside the carriage two of the women had begun to shriek while the third remained absolutely silent, her eyes staring out the open door into the courtyard. The courtyard where Filip Orlov's blood was running over the cobblestones.

He was not dead. He groaned. His eyes fluttered open. This time, he knew, he had not been shot in the fat.

A face over his, blocking the light. The thin owlish British detective, the one who had come to the gentlemen's enclave. What was his name? They had smoked hashish and talked of love. The man bent low, his head at such an angle that his eyeglasses edged down the bridge of his nose.

"Lie very still," he said. "We will find a doctor."

"No," said Filip. The sky tilted and slid above him, as if God were shaking the world. The palace police were here now, jerking Gregor to his feet, throwing him against the side wall of the stable, and Filip could hear the clang of their handcuffs, their cursing. The hysteria of the Grand Duchess, the low silent reassurance of her maid. No word from Tatiana, but she surely knew what he had done for her. Where his loyalty lay in the end.

The sky seemed less bright now. The voices not so loud and the pain not so sharp, and Rayley's form, still bent over him, was less distinct. Filip noticed, with some distraction, that he could see the reflection of his own face in the detective's spectacles. He looked tired.

"Hold on, man," Rayley whispered. "They're bringing water."

Filip attempted to shake his head and failed. There was no use for water, except possibly to wash the cobblestones. He pulled in his last breath and saved it until he was sure he had the strength for nine words.

"Tell them I died," Filip said, "in service to the tsar."

9:31 PM

Vlad had kept his ear pressed to the door for several minutes and had slowly convinced himself that there were no more sounds coming from the hall. He had found himself in one of the leisure rooms, a place which held a broad couch, a table with a decanter and ashtray, and what Vlad could only assume were various instruments of pleasure. He felt unclean even being there, but his hiding place had at least given him a few minutes to calm his nerves. The dock, he now remembered, would be at the end of this hall and to the right.

He cracked the door open and listened. Still no noise. He leaned his head out and looked in one direction, then the other. Absolute emptiness. Then he slipped from the room and walked in the direction of the docks. It had occurred to him that if he were able to maintain his composure he might not be intercepted. He carried no hostage and no gun. During the pursuit, no one had seen his face. There was every possibility he could return to the docks and reclaim his little rowboat. That he could depart the palace as he entered it, a humble purveyor of lilies.

And that is just what would have happened had Davy Mabrey not been waiting on the docks.

For a moment the two young men simply looked at each other. Then Vlad walked towards Davy slowly, his palms outstretched to show he carried no weapon.

"Ah, comrade," he said. "So you are with them after all."

"Scotland Yard."

"I should have known. The English are always English, no matter what else they try to be. And now you must turn me in, I suppose?"

Davy swallowed. "The girl isn't hurt. One of my group, a doctor, is with her."

"You tell me this why? Because you think I care?"

"Because it will go better for you that she wasn't injured. Better in court, I mean."

"Court?" Vlad laughed harshly, and the ugly cry echoed off the water. "Where do you think you are, comrade?" He looked at Davy with a sudden intensity. "Let me go. As one nothing to another, let me go."

"You must understand that I cannot."

"The revolution is dead to me now, I swear it. My life has run through my hands like water in the last hour and I didn't like the feeling. The feeling that I might die before I have lived. I wish to go home, to sleep in my bed. To eat chicken and potatoes, to hear my mother sing off-key."

At the mention of the word "mother," Davy's face changed. Only for a fraction of a second, but Vlad noted it and seized the opportunity.

"My woman has already lost one son, comrade" he said. "Could you live with yourself if you cost her yet another?"

The Grand Ballroom

10:02 PM

Tom watched her from the top of the staircase, uncertain of how to approach. But with his first footfall on the first step, Emma heard him and turned. She was standing in the center of the empty ballroom floor. She had been crying for some time.

"Did you find Xenia?" she asked.

"Yes. She's a bit shaken and weepy, of course, but she'll be fine. Orlov was shot dead. By his own man, as it turns out."

She absorbed this in thoughtful silence. "Tatiana and Ella? They will be all right?"

"I suppose that remains to be seen."

Any other time she would have questioned his vague comment. Would have demanded he speak plainly and tell her everything that had happened. But for now, Emma merely shrugged and the movement, even through slight, caused the red gown to shimmer. She had never looked lovelier, Tom thought. Had never worn a gown as spectacular as this one, perhaps never would again. She tugged at his heart, standing there so alone in the center of the dance floor, like a fairy princess whose prince must have lost his way.

Tom walked down the final steps and onto the floor. "He is not the only man on earth who can waltz, you know."

"I never said he was."

"Nor is he the only man who can waltz with you."

Now this perhaps she did believe. She visibly exhaled and shifted a little on her feet, sending her skirt into a crescendo of sparkles and shimmer.

He held out his arms. "Dance with me, Emma. Here on this great floor on this night that will ever end."

"I didn't know you waltzed."

"There are many things about me you do not know," he said, as she raised her arms to him. "Just as I suppose there are corridors and passageways I have not yet found in you. We are each as large as a palace, are we not? An endless series of doors to be opened as the years proceed."

It was a grand speech. Quite unlike him, and she was not sure if this was just another of his jokes, a way to jolly her out of this strange sadness. But it didn't really matter, and she let her left hand alight on his shoulder as he took her right in his. As he pulled her closer and began, without music, to waltz.

What would Konstantin have said, if he were now standing before them, watching? Probably that Tom knew the steps, but not the dance. His movements were small, neat, and tentative, and she matched hers to his. He began to hum, which made it worse, for there was no correlation between his music and his pace and their knees clanked against each other as they stepped slowly through the shape of a box. If he'd had a sword it would have surely poked her. And then the edge of his foot came down on hers.

"I'm sorry," he said.

"It's all right."

He brought his cheek closer. It was soft and fair and not that much higher than her own and he was humming again. There is no magic in this, she thought, bending back to look up at the ceiling, at the empty balconies and abandoned theatrical sets. There is no mystery. It is just me and Tom in the center of an empty room, but he has cared enough to come in search of me and he is trying to make it better. Trying to make up for something I have lost, even if he doesn't understand what it was and has no idea how to recreate it. They danced another box and then he stopped.

"Are your eyes closed?" he asked.

"Of course," she said. But they were open.

Chapter Twenty-Four

A Train Outside of Danzig

June 24, 1889

7:50 AM

They were an hour past the Russian border and moving steadily through Germany when he opened the envelope. It contained, as promised, a letter of introduction from the Grand Duchess Ella Feodorovna, written on her official stationery and describing his talents in such flowery language that he had no doubt it would secure him a berth teaching in the best dance academy of Paris. He refolded it carefully and placed it back in its envelope, reflecting that it was a strange thing that a man's whole future could be written on a single piece of paper.

His bundle at his feet held a blue velvet pouch, the contents of which he had not yet explored. Slowly and tentatively, taking care not to disturb his fellow passengers who were crammed all around him, he pulled the silken string on top. Inside was a golden egg. Konstantin took one quick look, enough to register the shocking value of the gift, and then thrust it back into the pouch. The others in the compartment all appeared to be sleeping, but it would not do to attract their attention with an object of such obvious value. Like anyone who had ever lived in the Winter Palace, Konstantin had heard of the Fabrege eggs, but had never seen one up close and he had no idea why the Grand Duchess would have chosen to bestow such a treasure on him.

"Take this," she had said. "Something to help you start your new life in Paris." But he had expected a handful of coins or perhaps a small bank note, certainly nothing as grand as this. Something which shamed him just to look at it, an object that would probably mark him as a thief if anyone knew he had it in his possession. But still, when Tatiana joined him…the sale of a Fabrege egg could buy them an apartment, simple furnishings, food in the cupboard, shoes on their feet.

At the thought of her, he reached down to the other bundle resting at his feet, the one tied with heavy paper and string.

The paper was still damp and the form of the package was bent in the center, where the water from the chapel rainspout had pounded against it as he had made love to Tatiana. He remembered the painting inside, their first meal together and their final one too, at least for a while. He tugged at the edge of the package and the paper tore easily. Sliding the string and wrapping to the side, he slowly revealed what was left of the picture.

He could see the city around them. The café tables, the stray cat which rubbed against their legs, the streets, the shop windows, the dome of a church in the distance. The details remained quite clear around the periphery but in the center the picture was washed out. The paint had run away, the colors probably still visible among the cobblestones outside the Chapel of Mourning.

"Leave it," she had said. She had seen the water pouring down upon the package and she had known that their image must have fled. But yet he had not left it, and now he was glad, for looking at the painting, holding it carefully by the corners with his fingertips, a bit of fear ran across him, as light and fast as the feet of a mouse. He allowed his mind to sink, just for a second, into the possibility that she would not follow him. That this goodbye had always meant something different for her than for him, that his escape had been bought at a high price. Yes, even higher than the value of a Fabrege egg.

The light from the window flickered on the painting in his hands. He imagined what it would look like on his wall, how many times he would have to study it before the meaning of all that had happened in the last few days would at last fully emerge. The picture was, Konstantin thought, the perfect memento of their affair. St. Petersburg would always be there. It was dark-edged and clear and full of the small realities of a city, the sort which anchored and framed you, the details of everyday life. A chair, a church, a wine glass, a cat, the pink splash of a woman's dress. But there was a great emptiness in the center. The lovers once found there were gone.

The Docks of the Winter Palace

11:20 AM

"That poor composer," the Queen said. "I suppose he is never to have his ball."

Trevor and Queen stood on the deck of The Albert and Victoria, watching the dockworkers roll the trunks up the gangplank and on board. It was a strangely unceremonious departure. No one from the Imperial family had come down to the riverbank to see them off.

"This is a singularly difficult country in which to make plans," Trevor said. "Perhaps in the future when invitations go out from the palace they should read something along the line of 'There will be a grand ball on this evening as long as no one is assassinated or kidnapped.'"

Victoria gave a little snort which Trevor hoped indicated amusement and gazed up the green lawn toward the Winter Palace. "My granddaughter informs me that there is to be a baby."

Hard to say what sort of reaction was expected to this, so Trevor decided to go with the most conventional one possible. "My congratulations, Your Majesty."

"And thus Ella is irretrievably gone," the Queen continued, her eyes never leaving the Palace. "Nothing ties a woman to a man more definitively than giving birth to his child and once she has a Romanov baby, she will be here forever. From some decisions, there is no turning back." She sighed. "But at least Alix has come to her senses."

"Something to be grateful for," Trevor said, making note as one especially long and ungainly sack was rolled aboard, most likely containing the earthly remains of Cynthia Kirby. "A gun pointed toward a carriage which held her own sister must have done what three previous murders could not. Provided evidence beyond question that Russia is not a safe place in which to marry and raise a family."

The Queen pulled her gaze away from the Palace. "One would think so, but that wasn't what convinced her. Alix was far more deeply shocked by Ella's decision to turn her back on Lutheranism and convert to Orthodoxy. Apparently Nicky wished to mark their understanding with the gift of a diamond brooch, but she tells me that she has returned it and informed him she could never marry a man of a different faith."

"My congratulations, Your Majesty."

The irony of the repeated response was not lost on the Queen. Her mouth twisted into a grim smile as she turned toward an approaching servant. The same fellow who had served them dinner on their voyage over, Trevor recalled. He wondered where the crew of the yacht had been during their time in St. Petersburg. Living onboard most likely, awaiting word that Her Majesty's business was concluded and they would once again be required to spring into action. It was a strange life being in service to the Queen. Long stretches of inactivity, followed by bursts of extraordinary effort.

With no further comment, the Queen turned and processed down the steps, presumably to her cabins below, her manservant following smartly behind. A sharp blast of the ship's whistle indicated that departure was imminent, and within minutes of the sound, Rayley and Davy emerged up the same steps to join Trevor on deck.

"And so we are off," Rayley said, as the ship begin to pull from its berth.

"Where is Tom?" Trevor asked.

"Already in his bunk, Sir." Davy said. "I think he celebrated his last night in the Palace a little too much."

"And what of Emma?"

"Also below deck, consoling Alix," Rayley said. "Or perhaps it is the other way around. This country has a strange effect on people, does it not? Despite everything, I feel we have all fallen a bit under its spell."

"I have a question, Sirs," Davy said, as the yacht began moving toward the center of the Neva, the engines settling down into a low steady drone.

"We may not be able to answer, but by all means, give it a shot," said Trevor.

"Should our loyalty toward ideals be greater than our loyalty toward people?" Davy asked, cupping his hand to be heard above the wind and the engines.

This was a bit more philosophical than either Rayley or Trevor was prepared for, and for a minute they all simply stood, still facing the Winter Palace. The eternal Palace. It seemed it would take as long to leave it as it had to approach it.

"We discussed this very topic during one of our meetings," Trevor said. "One of the ones you missed. As I recall, we failed to come to any conclusion."

"You have obviously given the matter some thought," Rayley said. "What do you think?"

"I feel I've done the wrong thing, Sirs," Davy said, his voice cracking. "In fact I know I have. I've lied to you, Sirs, and I have to get it off my chest or the trip back will be a proper torment…"

"Hold on, son," Trevor said. "What are we talking about?"

"One of the lads in the Volya," Davy said. "Vlad. I saw him on the dock last night and I could have given chase and I…I didn't." He was green with agony, gripping the railing as if the seasickness which had plagued him during the first trip had already taken hold of him again. "Then I didn't tell you even after that was over, and this was as bad as a lie too, isn't it Sir?"

"Yes, you should have given chase or called for help or at the very least you should have told me the truth when you returned to the courtyard," Trevor said. His voice was neither scolding nor sympathetic, merely matter of fact. "But you didn't, and it's done. Orlov is dead and Krupin is arrested and they are the two who matter. As long as the sharks are caught, I can live with the fact that a minnow slips through the net now and then."

"We did a similar thing, you know," Rayley said, although it was unclear whether the comment was directed toward Trevor or Davy. "We might have announced that Filip Orlov was with the Volya, but we didn't, and neither did Prakov. We let everyone believe he died a martyr to the tsar."

"Things will likely go better for his widow that way," Trevor said. "Based on what Tom told us, that poor woman's position is precarious enough without us adding to her troubles."

"So at times the truth is overrated?" Rayley asked, with a sly smile. One rarely got such an admission out of Welles.

"I wouldn't say that," Trevor answered. "I'd rather say that sometimes the truth is complex."

But Davy was not totally convinced, so he continued to seek absolution. "Vlad swore the revolution was behind him,

Sirs. Said that his mother had already lost one son to violence and he was going to go home and eat chicken and potatoes before she lost another."

"Which may indeed have been the case" Trevor said. "A brush with death has a way of making a man crave chicken and potatoes."

"And even if it wasn't," Rayley added, "perhaps it was simply not this boy's fate to be captured."

"Fate?" Trevor said, stroking his mustache. They had at last sailed beyond the looming shadow of the Winter Palace and the sun struck them suddenly full in the face, causing them all to flinch and shield their eyes. "I say, Abrams, you're talking just like a Russian. There's no such thing as fate. It's just the word men give to decisions which have worked out badly."

"Fatalism is the national disease of Russia," Rayley said with a laugh, cupping both hands to his brow in an effort to stop the assault of the light. "Tom says the Grand Duchess Ella told him that and it seems most contagious indeed. And yet, Welles, you're the only one of us who never caught even the slightest sniffle. I wonder why."

Trevor turned his back on the sun, the palace, and Russia. "I fear I am too English," he said.

From high on the riverbank Vlad Ulyanov watched the royal yacht slip from view. The kidnapping had been a failure, but even failures served their purpose. Hangings were surprisingly good for recruitment, boys being what they were, and the ranks of the Volya would soon swell with new recruits. Young and impressionable revolutionaries seeking guidance from the more established members and now that the British had sailed and Gregor and Filip were out of the way…

His destiny was fully upon him. He would climb to heights that even Sasha had failed to reach.

It was the fashion of the Volya for the leaders to choose new names. The custom was partly to protect their families from retaliation should something go wrong in this long and dangerous struggle. But mostly it was to signal their rebirths, to announce to the world that their old lives meant nothing to them once they had aligned with the Marxist party. Names based on the physical features of Russia were especially popular, since they seemed to suggest that the men and their cause had organically sprung from the very land they loved. Mountains, prairies, oceans, rivers…

Perhaps he should name himself after the Neva, Vlad thought, and then almost immediately rejected the idea. He would not so honor a river that flowed within sight of the Winter Palace, but would rather choose something humbler, more distant, more reflective of the true nature of Russia. There was a river in Siberia - the Lena, and he tried the sound on for size.

Yes, he liked it. It was a good name, strong and simple and solid. He uttered it out loud, called the name up into the sky, shattering the silence of the river and causing the birds above him to startle. Over and over he shouted the words, like an Adam newly christened into a world newly born. For this was the start of everything, was it not?

And so he said his name once again: Vladimir Lenin.

What's Real?

I hope that City of Silence has inspired readers to learn more about this pivotal time in Russian history, i.e., the thirty years which marked the end of the imperial age and the rise of the Marxist Party. I knew very little about imperial Russia before I began my research – as I suspect is true of most Americans - but quickly fell under the spell of the endlessly fascinating and exasperating Romanov family.

The murders of the ballet dancers and the characters of Tatiana, Filip, and Konstantin were entirely fabricated. The fictional character of Cynthia Kirby was named in honor a friend of mine, a lovely woman with most excellent manners, who in no way deserves to be disposed of in such an inelegant manner.

In contrast, the tales of the royal families of both Russia and England were largely based on fact. Alix and Nicky truly met when Serge and Ella married, and carried on a long distance courtship to the dismay of both their families before ultimately marrying when she was twenty. The personalities and relationships within the Winter Palace are as close to accurate as I can imagine them, based on letters and diaries from the time.

My sins are mostly against the calendar. While Tchaikovsky did have a triumphant tour of Europe, he was not honored in St. Petersburg during that particular summer. Likewise, Vlad was not in St. Petersburg in June of 1889, nor was there an attack on any members of the tsar's family at that time, although the previous attempts on the tsar's life and the involvement of Vlad's brother Sasha are based on fact. For dramatic purposes, I also collapsed the time frame of the courtship between Alix and Nicky, implying that events which occurred months or years apart, actually all happened within a two week period.

One aspect of the story which I did not have to adapt for dramatic purposes was the Queen's reservations toward the men her granddaughters chose as husbands. Victoria did indeed dislike Russia, and used all of her influence in an effort to dissuade her granddaughters from marrying into the Romanov family. Many of the Queen's quotes are taken directly from her letters.

And as history shows us, her fears were well founded. Both Alix and Ella died horribly brutal deaths in 1917 at the dawn of the Bolshevik Revolution. Their murders and those of their families were decreed by none other than the single-minded leader of the Marxist party, Vladimir Lenin.

What's Next?

If you enjoyed City of Silence, look for the first two books in the City of Mystery series: City of Darkness, which takes place in London and explores in the infamous case of Jack the Ripper, and City of Light, which travels to Paris on the eve of the Exposition Universalle, the World's Fair which introduced the Eiffel Tower.

City of Bells, in which the Scotland Yard forensics team will travel to Calcutta to defend Gerry's first love from a charge of murder, is due in late summer, 2013. To be notified of when it is available, either "like" the City of Mystery page on Facebook or leave your email address at cityofmystery@gmail.com.

Made in the USA
Charleston, SC
06 February 2013